HEALING

Hearts

CW01498998

MT CASSEN

Copyright © 2024 by MT Cassen

All Rights Reserved

The content contained within this book may not be reproduced, duplicated or transmitted without direct written permission from the author or the publisher.

Under no circumstances will any blame or legal responsibility be held against the publisher, or author, for any damages, reparation, or monetary loss due to the information contained within this book, either directly or indirectly.

Legal Notice: This book is copyright protected. It is only for personal use. You cannot amend, distribute, sell, use, quote or paraphrase any part, or the content within this book, without the consent of the author or publisher.

Disclaimer Notice: This is a work of fiction. The names, characters, businesses, places, events and locales are either the products of the author's imagination or used in a fictional manner. Any resemblance to actual persons, dead or living, or actual businesses, companies, events or locales is entirely coincidental.

CONTENTS

MELODY IN HER HEART
HEALING HEARTS (BOOK ONE)

FIGHTING HER TOUCH
HEALING HEARTS (BOOK TWO)

PROTECTING HER HEART
HEALING HEARTS (BOOK THREE)

A dedication from Morgan Cassen to medical workers in all corners of our world:

Morgan is in awe of the work done by the frontline workers of the noblest profession. The recent events have only increased my appreciation of the difficulty and danger associated with your line of work. I would like to thank you from the bottom of my heart.

MELODY IN
HER
Heart
BOOK 1

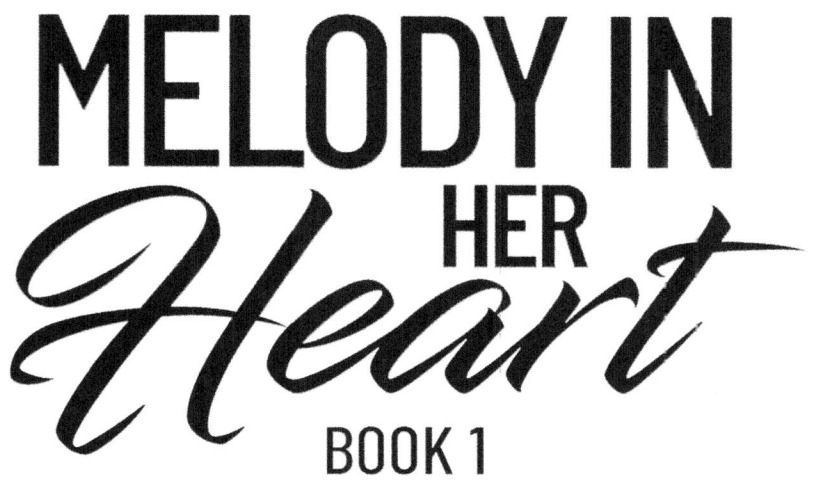

 HEALING HEARTS
A *Lesbian Medical Romance* Drama Series

MT CASSEN

CHAPTER ONE

Tabby

The scent of lavender drifted through the halls of the emergency room as Tabitha Brickly exited one of her patient's rooms. Lavender, for its calming effect. Tonight, it provided tranquility more than it did previous nights. She heaved a sigh, taking in the whiff that was briefly intermixed with the smell of coffee. As nurses, they all thrived on coffee—some more than others—and Tabby caught herself needing a massive caffeine kick at that very moment.

Tabby grabbed a carafe and poured herself half a cup. She only had fifteen minutes left, then she would be out of there. Sometimes, the minutes seemed to tick by, taking way too long to finalize the night. She checked her watch as she sunk into a chair at the nurses' station.

Tabby took a sip of coffee, then reached for her phone. After dialing her home phone, she waited as the line rang three times. Tabby tapped her foot along to the sound of each ring. *Answer the phone, someone.*

She was just about to hang up when someone picked up. "Hello?" Brittany, her eldest daughter, said.

"Hey, Britt. How are you doing? I didn't think anyone was home."

"Dad was playing his music so loud," her daughter replied, her voice a near-groan. "Are you coming home? We're starving!"

Tabby forced a smile. Her life was left to working, cooking, cleaning, and anything that wasn't a leisurely activity. Usually, she didn't let that bother her, but the starving comment struck her at that moment. After working twelve hours in the ER, all she wanted to do was crash, not think of what to have for supper. Still, as a wife and a mother, she knew it was impossible to stand her ground all the time. But this one time left her wanting to tell her family they should fix something themselves.

"I'll be home in half an hour. What sounds good? Pizza?" It was an easy thing to make—toss it in the oven, and you're done. The groan on the other end wasn't promising.

"We just had pizza," Brittany argued. "Remember?"

"I'll figure something out," Tabby said, stifling a yawn as she took a sip of her coffee.

"Tabby! Emergency coming in!" She looked up to see Hanna rushing past her. Tabby quickly stood up.

"I'll see you all in a bit," she said. "Gotta run."

"Bye, Mom," Brittany said, and Tabby disconnected the call.

As she hurried to the doors where the nurses had all gathered, Tabby knew it was less likely that she would be out of there in ten minutes. She couldn't think about that, as it would only be another disappointment to her two children. Brittany, who was thirteen, might be more apt to understand. But Callie—she was only nine. Seeing the disappointment in her younger daughter's eyes was always hard to swallow. It wasn't like they were home alone, though. Drew was there and able to manage just fine, but Tabby only hoped that he would step up to the plate and take over certain responsibilities, as their father should do.

The doors opened, and two EMTs came rushing in with one gurney. "Multiple vehicle accident," the one woman said. "There's more to come."

The few nurses there went to work as the gurneys came through the door one by one. Tabby went along with one of them, pushing a woman into one of the vacant rooms.

"Jane Doe," an EMT started. "Eighteen to twenty years old. Crushed legs in the crash as she was thrown from her vehicle and another vehicle landed on her lower extremities."

"Has she gained consciousness yet?" Tabby asked, leaning over her as she started to cut her clothes off. They waited for the ER doctor to take care of her case.

"For about ten minutes, a witness states. Lost a lot of blood."

"Thanks," Tabby said grimly as Dr. Maxwell entered the room.

"What do we have for IV access?" Dr. Maxwell said in a cool and professional voice.

The EMT replied, "We have two 18-gauge IVs running lactated ringers wide open."

"Someone had better call blood bank," Dr. Maxwell said. "We'll need four units of O-negative packed red cells, fresh frozen plasma, and platelets —STAT." He pulled a stethoscope from his lab coat and listened intently to the patient's chest. "Where's the radiology tech?"

One of the ER nurses replied, "He's rounding the corner with the mobile X-ray machine."

"Good," Dr. Maxwell said. "We'll need a head-to-toe bone series."

Behind Dr. Maxwell was a flurry of activity as nurses placed orders for labs, X-rays, and CT scans. Tabby ran the vitals as Dr. Maxwell conducted an exam and Sally, another nurse, worked on preparing the patient's legs to be checked. Once the patient was stabilized, she was ready to be wheeled off to her first CT scan.

Tabby hurried through the hallway with Sally at the other end of the gurney, and they pushed her into the radiology suite across from the emergency department. "I thought you were in the nursery tonight. I haven't seen you all night."

"We're having a slow night, and we heard there was an emergency coming in. Gotta go where you're needed."

"Absolutely. How are the other patients?" she asked. "Have you seen?"

"Two deceased that I know of," Sally said. She shook her head. "Life can be so unfair, don't you think?"

Tabby nodded. "It can be cruel. That's for sure."

They passed the radiology desk and entered the chilly room housing the CT scanner. The CT techs were already waiting for them and carefully transferred the patient to the scanner's movable table. Tabby leaned against the wall and stared down at her watch as Sally propped herself against the wall across from her.

"You're going to be getting out late, aren't you?" she asked.

Tabby sighed. "Can't be helped. It's the life of a nurse."

"Love it or leave it, and we all love it too much, so how could we leave it?" Sally smiled as she spoke the words.

Sally was right. Tabby loved working as a nurse. Even though she had gotten into the profession thinking it was a way to help her growing family, she had found that it was a way to serve the community and feel the difference she was making to the world. She never once regretted her decision.

While she worked in the emergency room part-time, her main focus was the cardiology ward. Going into the field, she had assumed she would thrive best with pediatrics. Quickly, she had learned that she couldn't stomach seeing a child in pain. It was even harder when it was one of her own, but she couldn't keep working in pediatrics when her heart ached for those kids. Cardiology seemed to be a good fit. When they needed fill-ins, she was there to help out. They appreciated that despite Tabby having a family, she still found time to lend a hand when they needed it. It didn't always please her family, but even they understood the importance she brought to Capmed. She just hoped they weren't upset with her that she had broken one more promise.

THE LIGHTS WERE ONLY LIT IN THE KITCHEN AS TABBY DREW closer to the driveway. She heaved a sigh and parked her car. She could picture Drew already asleep. The clock on the radio ran a few minutes late, but it was nearing nine o'clock, and that was two hours longer than she expected it to be.

"It's my job," Tabby rehearsed, heading up to the front door. "I couldn't just leave."

She didn't even know the purpose of rattling off her pleas for him to forgive her for missing the children's supper. It wasn't like it was anything new, and if he wanted to be crabby when she first saw him, then nothing she said would change that.

Tabby stepped into the foyer. The silence was the first thing that hit her. The glow remained from the kitchen and down the hallway. She dropped her purse and headed toward the light. When she rounded the corner, she saw Drew sitting at the kitchen table, his back to her.

"Are the kids in bed?" Tabby asked.

He looked over his shoulder, then shook his head and stood. "Hello to you, too," he huffed. "Do you know what time it is? Of course they're in bed. They have school tomorrow. You would have been angry if they weren't." He paused beside her. "Don't worry; I fed them a peanut butter sandwich. They're fine."

"Do you want something to eat? I can whip you up something in less than fifteen minutes." Tabby rushed over to the counter and started pulling things from the cupboard. She wasn't sure what she was going to cook, but she would make something work.

"Don't bother," he mumbled. "Not hungry."

He left the kitchen, leaving Tabby alone. She stared down at the pots and pans on the counter and immediately started putting them away. There was a knot in the pit of her stomach. It wasn't different from any other night. She spent many nights in the kitchen, alone, just eating by herself. Yet she always expected things to get better. But why?

Tabby opened the cupboard and pulled out a box of cereal. In two minutes, she would have dinner and pretend like she was having steak or some other fancy feast that someone else prepared for her. Drew's music started as she took her first bite.

Drew was a good father, where it mattered. He didn't abuse the children, he loved them, and he was around, mostly. That was mainly because he had nowhere else to be. Clients weren't exactly beating down his door, hoping he'd provide musical services for them. It wasn't surprising since Tabby rarely saw him out there trying to get gigs. I have to hone my skills, Tab. You're not a musician; you just wouldn't understand. If she had a nickel for every time he gave her that line, she would surely be rich, and he wouldn't need to work. As it stood, she provided all the income anyway. And it was precisely why she stayed all the extra hours she could. Did she want to stay away from her daughters for that long? No!

These were their impressionable years, the years her children should look back and not have to say that things were messed up for them. Tabby hoped she wouldn't hear them one day say they regretted the time she spent away from them. She was doing this *for* them. That was the one line she had to tell herself repeatedly.

She took a bite of her cereal and cringed as Drew hit a shaky note. The note was clearly out of tune, and if she knew him well, she knew that any minute, he'd come storming into the kitchen, complaining that he needed some new strings.

She rolled her eyes at the sound of incoming footsteps. *Just like clockwork.*

"Stupid strings," Drew muttered. "I know I have some new ones in here somewhere." He pulled out a junk drawer and tossed it on the table, then started to leaf through it like he was a madman looking for some buried treasure.

"Are you sure they aren't in the room?" Tabby asked. "I feel like—"

"What are you yammering about?" he asked, turning to look at Tabby.

She dropped her eyes to the mess he had already made on the kitchen table. "Your guitar strings..." She looked up and met his gaze. "I feel like they're on the top of the dresser in the bedroom."

He huffed and turned away from her. "I would remember if they were," he said. "I haven't seen them in several days." He went back to rummaging, then flipped the drawer over, emptying the contents on the top of the kitchen table.

Tabby's eyes fell to the mess that had only gotten bigger. Drew mumbled something incoherent and stormed out of the kitchen, leaving the mess behind. Tabby shook her head and took another spoonful of her cereal. She wanted to ignore the mess, just like he had. It wasn't her style, though. After she finished her food, she washed her bowl and spoon and put them back in their correct places, then turned to the mess that Drew had left behind for her to clean up.

His footsteps sounded, coming back down the steps, but Tabby didn't stop. She soon had everything back in the drawer, which she put away before turning the light off and leaving the kitchen. When she hit the hallway, the music sounded again. She stopped in the living room.

"Find the strings?" she asked.

"Yeah," he mumbled, never looking up from his guitar. She would never say I told you so, because that wouldn't get her anywhere.

"All right then. I'm going to head on up to bed. Are you coming?"

"I've got too much work to do. Goodnight." Again, his eyes stayed on his music.

"Goodnight," she mumbled before leaving the living room and going up the stairs to peek in on the girls. Drew just sometimes didn't realize the way he cut across, especially when it came to being around Tabby. There were times when she thought hard about what it would mean to walk away from their marriage, but that was never an easy decision. For her, it came down to the girls. She didn't want to uproot their lives; it wasn't fair to them. But it also wasn't fair for her to stay if she wasn't happy.

She stopped at Callie's room and peeked her head inside to see her daughter sleeping soundly. Callie's light was on, next to her bed, and her glasses were still propped on her nose. Tabby entered the room and reached to take her glasses off.

"Mom?" Callie whispered groggily.

"Shh," Tabby replied, kneeling next to her. "I'm sorry I wasn't home."

"It's okay," she said. "You were taking care of people."

Tabby smiled, brushing her hand along Callie's forehead. "That's right, honey." She leaned in and kissed her forehead. "Go back to sleep."

"Goodnight, Mom," Callie whispered before rolling onto her side.

Tabby could see Callie being the daughter that would want to live with Tabby for the rest of her life. She was a momma's girl, and Tabby loved that about her sweet little girl, even if it wasn't realistic. She turned her lamp off and then left the room, giving her one last look before stepping into the hallway and closing the door behind her. It was a relief that Callie wasn't upset, as Tabby thought she would be. Now on to Brittany to see if she had to smooth things over with her.

She reached Brittany's room, noticing the door was ajar. She carefully pushed the door open and looked at the bed. Brittany had a book propped on her legs, with her book light attached. Tabby cleared her throat, and Brittany jerked to attention. Even in the dark room, Tabby noticed her daughter's cheeks turning red.

"Hey, Mom!" She closed her book and put it off to the side. "I was just about to go to bed."

"You should have been in bed nearly an hour ago." Tabby sat down on the chair that rested against Brittany's bed. Brittany gave a sheepish grin.

"I couldn't sleep knowing you were out there. I had to wait up." She batted her eyelashes, and Tabby smiled gently. Out of her two children, Brittany was the one with the big imagination. She was thirteen going on thirty and had a mind of her own. Thus far, it worked in her favor, so Tabby felt no need to discipline her for staying up past her bedtime. She was a straight A student and would get up in plenty of time to meet the bus, probably an hour before she needed to.

"Now that you see I'm here, you'd best get some rest for those pretty blue eyes of yours." Tabby kissed her forehead. "Sweet dreams."

"Night, Mom." Brittany turned off her book light, and Tabby walked over to the door.

"Goodnight." She gave her daughter one long look and then left her room.

Brittany was Tabby's world. When Tabby found out she was pregnant at seventeen, she feared that everyone would say she had to get rid of her. In an instant, the baby growing inside of her had become her life. Yet she had worried that she wouldn't be able to be the parent that she always wanted to be. Her parents were a great example for Tabby, and she wanted a family like that.

There was a time, though, during the first months of her pregnancy when she had considered raising Brittany alone. How different might her life if she had? Days like today when she struggled to have a simple conversation with Drew seriously made her wonder.

Her family and Drew had all pushed her into marriage. While she had wanted to get married before Brittany was born, Brittany had other ideas. She had come a month early into the world, derailing most of their plans. For years, they had the perfect family, until slowly, things started to fade. The honeymoon phase started to wane. Then came Callie. After she was born, their marriage got better. They had gotten married too young, and marriage counseling had been key in helping them learn how to compromise and grow in their love because they had lost sight of that somewhere along the way. But now things were only growing darker for them as a couple and a family.

Tabby stepped into the bedroom and looked over at the empty bed. There used to be a time when Drew would never want her to go to bed alone. She couldn't even remember the last time they made love. Her nights had become lonely. How much more of that could she take? Something needed to change, or there was no way this could last, kids or not.

CHAPTER TWO

Jenni

Traffic was a nightmare. Horns blaring at people going too slowly on the freeway, a crash that caused one off-ramp to shut down completely, and people just trying to get to their destination safely. Jennifer just wanted to get to her board meeting.

Her car inched up one more spot, then came to another complete halt. "Come on!" she yelled at her front window, staring at the line of traffic in front of her. Her day was already one fiasco after another. From waking up late to rushing to shower and get out the door, only allotting time for one cup of coffee, she had figured the day would be a bust. Then, as she had gotten into her car, her blouse had torn at the seam, and it was back in the house to find something else to wear.

When she got on the freeway, she had assumed it would be a smooth ride. She hadn't accounted for the traffic that would be out in full force. Jenni looked down at her clock radio. If she could barrel through traffic and not have to worry about stopping for even one second, she would only be five minutes late.

She groaned and tapped on the steering wheel. There wasn't any chance of that happening, so she just needed to try to calm down. A person whizzed out from around her, honking their horn as they zoomed by, and Jenni looked out at the traffic in front of her. "Why didn't I think of that?"

She quickly skirted out around the cars and pressed her foot on the gas, going ten over the speed limit. For the first time since getting on the freeway, she was able to get some momentum going. "Finally!" she muttered. As long as there was a break in traffic for her to pass other cars, she would be able to get off the ramp and make it to Capmed before they sent out the search dogs.

When a siren sounded, Jenni glanced in her rearview mirror, her eyes dropping as she clutched her steering wheel. Just one more thing to keep her from getting to her destination. She maneuvered her vehicle to the side of the road, fuming over the fact that she was the only one to be pulled over.

"License and registration," the officer said in greeting. She leaned over and whipped it out of her glove box, wanting to explain to him that it wasn't her idea to cut around everyone like that. She was only following the other driver's lead. She didn't think the officer would take too kindly to that, though. Jenni stared straight ahead, anxious for him to just give her a ticket and let her on her way.

Twenty minutes later, she turned into the parking lot of Capmed with a ticket and a hefty fine pinned to her visor. Such was her day. Maybe if she had time for more than one cup of coffee, she would have wound up with a better morning. Thus far, the day didn't seem to be on her side.

Jenni hurried from the car with her purse over her shoulder, which hit her as she jogged to the ER entrance. They couldn't start the board meeting without her, which was all the more reason to try to get there before too much time had been lost.

She stepped over a root that came up through the ground, and her ankle twisted, accompanied by a snapping sound. Jenni froze. "You have got to be kidding me." She reached down and pulled her shoe off, staring at the broken heel in front of her. Mark it up to one more rotten notch on her day. She could only be thankful for one thing, that she hadn't gone flying face-first to the ground. Don't even consider that, or it'll happen next.

Jenni reached down and pulled off her other shoe, then carried them both in one hand as she ran through the parking lot. It would beat the hobbling she would be forced to do if she kept only one heel to the ground. Who cared if she looked like a madwoman, running toward the hospital, bare feet kicking up dust along the way?

As she approached the curb along the parking lot, a woman with a young son and daughter in tow approached. The little girl giggled and pointed at Jenni's bare feet.

"Mommy, look," the girl said.

The mother nodded and smiled sympathetically at Jenni, understanding passing between them. Broken heels were something most women could relate to. Jenni waved at the little girl as the family of three walked away. Jenni paused, watching them as they located their car. Her heart ached, a pang of longing strong in her chest. She had always wanted to be a mother and had dreamed of it most of her life. But sometimes life didn't go as planned. Jenni doubted she could even conceive anymore, at her age.

She had hope once. She had a wife. And after months of trying, they were close to finally conceiving. But then she had lost everything in an instant...

Brushing the thought aside because it wouldn't get her anywhere, she turned, speed walking toward the ER entrance. As she passed through the sliding glass doors, another woman simultaneously came up to the door. They collided, making Jenni bounce back in shock. "Wow, guess I need glasses," Jenni said jokingly.

The woman turned and looked at her. "It was me. I wasn't paying any attention. Sorry," she mumbled.

Jenni took a moment to recover, caught off guard by the woman's dazzling blue eyes. Her blonde hair cascaded around her shoulders, and a barrette pulled back her bangs. Her hair was shiny, perhaps freshly highlighted. The woman had smiled when they made eye contact, but it didn't reach her eyes. If anything, Jenni thought she saw tears. Like maybe she had been crying the morning away and only just stopped. The woman's eyes were slightly red, and with her lack of makeup, they didn't go unnoticed. At least, not to Jenni. Her eyes were beautiful but distant, and her nose was small and slightly upturned. Her face lacked wrinkles, the kind that came with old age. She had a youthful impression about her, even though she looked like she was in her early thirties.

Jenni had the urge to reach out and hug her, to tell her everything would be okay. She knew what it was like to hurt, and she only wanted to help this beautiful woman with her pain.

The woman's lips curved into another forced smile, and Jenni caught herself returning the gesture. Jenni realized she had been staring heavily, the board meeting forgotten. She pushed her hair behind her ear and quickly looked away. Next to this woman, Jenni felt like an old hag, trying to imitate someone who still had life in her.

"No harm. I wasn't injured or anything." Jenni laughed, hoping she would see the woman smile again. Mission accomplished.

Jenni caught herself breathlessly, releasing another laugh. Calm down, Jenni. Your heart is racing, and you're liable to make a fool of yourself. Although Jenni was pretty sure she had already achieved that. All that gawking had to be making things a bit awkward.

"So, um, yeah.... I should get going," Jenni said.

"Yeah, me too." The woman's eyes dipped to Jenni's shoes, and she frowned.

"Long story," Jenni mumbled. "Such is my day. And with that note..." She started to push past her, and her eyes moved to the woman's left hand. There was a wedding band on her ring finger. It wasn't the least bit surprising, because the woman was magnetizing, but a pang of regret hit Jenni in the chest. She probably also had a house full of kids. She continued past her. "Nice to bump into you." She smirked. "Literally."

"Same," the woman said. As Jenni rushed past her and to the elevator, where the door was just closing, she felt the woman's eyes on her. Perhaps it was her imagination. Yet, when she turned around, she met the woman's gaze. Jenni smiled and waved, and the door closed. She wasn't wrong. The woman seemed distracted by her, though it was likely only because Jenni looked a chaotic mess. She shook her head and fell back against the wall of the elevator. The woman was dressed in scrubs, so she was obviously an employee there. But where? What department? She didn't recall any interactions with her before, and they surely wouldn't have gone unnoticed. She would have remembered that face and those eyes.

What unsettled Jenni the most, though, was how the woman sparked something in her that reminded her of the spark she originally had with her wife, Wendy. She missed Wendy and still found it hard to think of her.

23

She also missed companionship and someone to come home to. She filled her life with work because it distracted her from the loneliness and fading memories.

She heaved a sigh and shook her head. It was best to just forget about the strange woman. Longing for something she could never have—kids and a loving wife—would only create stress. She was too old to conceive, and moving on without Wendy would fill her with too much guilt. She needed to focus on work because there was a lot at stake.

The doors opened, and she straightened her outfit and headed straight for the boardroom. When she pushed through the door, the talking stopped, and they all turned to look at her. She scrunched her nose.

"Sorry I'm late. I've had a day that no one could have prepared for."

"Looks that way," Brian Chandler, the CEO, said. He was looking at her hand, which held her shoes. Jenni rolled her eyes and took her seat.

"We don't need to discuss that." There was a scattering of snickering around the table of men and women around her. "Now, what did I miss?"

She released a breath, relieved she was finally sitting there and didn't have to think about everything that had gone wrong this morning. Though she tried to stop herself, her mind drifted back to the beautiful woman she had met a few moments earlier. Wedding ring or not, it didn't keep her from wanting to know more about her. Why had she been so sad? If Jenni saw her again, she wanted to at least get to know her. They could be friends, couldn't they?

CHAPTER THREE

Tabby

The sound of the beeping from the monitor ticked in time to the seconds on the clock over Holly Hutchinson's bed as Tabby documented the numbers from her machine. When she left the hospital the night before, she hadn't known Holly's name, but during the night, the woman had woken up. She had easily remembered facts, such as name and age and how to reach her family. The accident, on the other hand, was a whole other story; she couldn't remember a thing about it. But as doctors liked to point out, that wasn't necessarily a bad thing when the patient's mental status was normal. Sometimes blocking out trauma could work in a patient's favor.

Holly shifted in the bed and made a noise. Tabby looked at her, asking, "Do you need anything? Water?"

Holly shook her head, then dropped her eyes to look down at her legs. Tabby slid her pen into the clipboard holder. It was her job to get Holly's mind on something else, anything else, other than what her body was going through. "My name is Tabby. I'll be the head nurse assigned to your case. It looks like you had a long night, but I'm glad to see you're up and moving."

Holly scoffed. "Moving, right. As I see it, I may never walk again."

"You don't know that. You'll be put through extensive therapy, and we're going to do everything we can to get movement back into your legs. Just think positively because none of us will think otherwise until we've exhausted all measures." Holly nodded, then winced and shifted in her bed. "Are you in pain?" Tabby asked.

"A little," she mumbled. Tabby pressed the button on her IV pump to administer a dose of pain medication.

"In a few minutes, you'll start to feel much better. If you need anything, be sure to press the button for a nurse. Just try to relax. We're going to do everything we can for you. Got that?"

Holly nodded, then closed her eyes. She needed rest. Tabby finished her paperwork and quietly left her room. As she headed to the front desk, she spotted Hanna sitting at the computer and waved, but her friend's eyes were looking elsewhere. Tabby turned and noticed that the woman from earlier was slowly walking to the front door, mostly distracted by her phone. Her shoes were no longer in her hands, so that was a good thing. Perhaps she had thrown them away. Tabby, though, would have probably found a way to get that broken heel fixed. Money didn't come easily, and the shoes were leopard print and looked to be real leather.

Tabby approached the desk, and Hanna turned her attention to her. "How's Holly doing?"

"I'd say a tad depressed. Think we'd better monitor that."

Hanna nodded. "When I was in her room this morning before you got here, I talked briefly to her. I got the same vibe, so good call." Hanna went on to punch something on the computer.

Tabby looked toward the door where Jenni stood, still on her phone.

"Who is that woman, by the way?" Tabby asked, pointing toward the door.

Hanna looked up. "Do you mean Jennifer Jennison?" She smirked. "Even her name gives you the vibes of 'rich and powerful,' right?"

Tabby chuckled. "I've never met the woman until today. I bumped into her when I was coming in. She wasn't paying attention. Or I wasn't. Either way, head-on collision."

"I'm not really surprised. Jenni is always in a rush."

"You seem to know her well, like you're on a first-name basis."

Hanna stood, shrugging. "Guess you could say we've been friendly through the years. It's not like we do anything outside of the hospital, but

I met her once, and now we're BFFs inside the hospital." She laughed. "I'm partly teasing. Anyway, mind if I go to lunch?"

Tabby shook her head and watched as Hanna left the ER. Jennifer Jennison was one of those women everyone knew was rich and powerful. It was no secret that she had put a lot of money into Capmed. Yet, it was more of a behind-the-scenes endeavor, which was why Tabby hadn't recognized her. It was rumored that others had seen Jenni in passing, but in all the five years that Jenni had invested money in the hospital, Tabby had never crossed paths with her. She wondered why she was seeing this woman twice in one day.

Tabby looked over at Jenni again, who was still completely engrossed with her phone. She rolled her neck with a sigh and a strand of hair slipped from her bun. There wasn't anything unusual about it, but a sudden urge flared in Tabby to cross the distance between them and tuck the hair back in place. She'd never paid attention to how attractive another woman was, but something about Jenni drew her in. She carried herself with ease, even when rushing, and she had kind, friendly eyes. But when they had bumped into each other earlier, she had sensed a bit of sadness behind Jenni's gaze—the same sadness inside Tabby.

As Tabby continued staring, she noticed how Jenni's hips curved beautifully in the skirt she wore. Jenni was pretty, but Tabby wasn't sure why she was noticing that so much. The desk phone at the nurses' station rang, startling her. She picked it up, watching Jenni saunter away. "This is Tabby Brickly. May I help you?"

"Mom?"

Callie's voice came on to the phone, and Tabby smiled and leaned back in her seat. "Hey, Callie, what's going on? Are you at school?"

"Yeah, but Jamie let me borrow her cell. You know she's my age, right? She's had a cell phone for two years. Don't you think—"

"Callie," Tabby stated sternly.

"Yes, Mom?"

"We've been through this before. Brittany only just got a phone, and if we were to get you one, that wouldn't look right. You know that."

"Times are a-changing, Mom," Callie argued.

Tabby covered her mouth, stifling a laugh at that archaic response coming from her nine-year-old daughter. Someone had clearly put that phrase into her head. As far as Tabby was concerned, she wasn't ready for her little girl to be growing up so fast. The longer she could keep Callie from wanting to have all the things her older sister had, the better.

"I'm sure you didn't borrow the phone just to rehash over how you're not getting a phone, at least for a few years. Or did you?"

"Right. Anyway, I was just checking to see if you were going to be home for supper tonight. You left early, so I'm hoping you are. I thought I would cook for everyone. It's chicken mar...mar...mar...ugh. I don't remember what Mrs. Davies called it, but it was sooo good yesterday when we made it in class."

Tabby snickered. "What happened to the highlight of your day being recess? You're now making meals? And was it chicken marsala?"

"That's it," she squealed.

Tabby smiled and shook her head. "Honey, that sounds amazing, but we'd have to stop by the grocery store. I doubt we have the ingredients."

"But, Mom," Callie whined.

"I'll tell you what," Tabby began. "I'll be home at six tonight. Let me make supper. Then this weekend you and I will go to the store, and you can buy all the ingredients you want. How does that sound?"

"Okay, I guess," Callie muttered. "I love you!"

"Love you, too. Have a great rest of your day at school. I'll see you when I get home." Tabby dropped the phone into the receiver and stared at it. Moments like that were when she knew that she would do anything to provide for her daughters.

When Tabby had first started working at Capmed, she was eighteen, a brand-new mom, and in need of a job that would help with tuition reimbursement. She had worked as a lab tech, monitoring the front desk and organizing files for the department. She had wanted a career that would give her family financial independence, and it had worked out. Plus, she was able to help save lives. It put her life in perspective when she came home at night and only had cereal for supper. If she weren't doing it all to help others and benefit her daughters' lives, it would be an easier choice to walk away from her career. She wanted to be home every night, mothering her kids, helping them with homework, and cooking supper for her family. It just wasn't realistic. So Capmed was where she was going to be, as long as it would help her provide for those she loved.

TABBY WALKED INTO JOANNA KINNER'S ROOM. HER PATIENT sat on the edge of the bed, her daughter right beside her, gripping her hand. "Well, are you all set to leave? How do you feel, Joanna?"

"Pretty good," she said. "Maybe a little nervous, but I'm anxious to be going home. It's been a few weeks since I've been able to walk into my own house. I feel ready, but does the doctor think I'm ready to go?"

Tabby smiled at her. "If the doctors were at all hesitant, you would be spending a few more days in that bed. Just enjoy it." She held out a packet of paperwork, and her daughter took it. "In there is a prescription for some medicine. If you have any chest pain, return to the hospital immediately. If you experience nausea, do the same. We're not leaving you out there unattended. You should follow up with your primary care physician in three to five days so they have your records. Do you have any questions for me?"

Joanna shook her head, still looking hesitant. She was eighty-nine years old, and from talking to her daughter, Sidney, Tabby knew she was worried that she would never get to go home to her three beloved cats. Tabby was relieved to see that they could keep their promise to get Joanna out of the hospital.

"How about you, Sidney? Any questions?"

Sidney looked up and met Tabby's gaze, then shook her head. "Thank you," she said, standing up and hugging Tabby, "for everything. We're glad you were here."

Tabby smiled warmly. "You're welcome. Your discharge is complete. Patient transport will wheel you out to the front. Let me lead the way." She walked ahead, leading them out of the hospital room and to the nurses' station, where Becca, another nurse, sat at the computer. "Becca, if you could, please sign Joanna out. They're good to go."

She reached out and squeezed Joanna's hand. "Don't hesitate to reach out to us for any reason. You're not in this alone. I'll see you guys around."

"Hopefully not too soon," Joanna replied, smiling.

Tabby nodded and turned away, heading back into the room to clean up in case a new patient needed a bed. When she finished, she left and headed toward the next patient she needed to check up on. She turned a corner and stopped. Jenni, in sleek black high heels, a tight-fitting skirt, blouse, and black jacket, was walking straight toward her. She hadn't noticed Tabby, since she was focused on her phone yet again.

Tabby swallowed as Jenni got close enough that she could smell her perfume. Jenni quickly sidestepped so they didn't have another collision, and Tabby cleared her throat. "Uh, you look like you're lost."

The woman looked up, eyes widening in recognition. A smile grew on her face. "Not lost. At least I have both my heels on today." She looked down at her feet.

Tabby nodded. "I noticed."

Jenni quirked an eyebrow. "Oh? You were looking at my feet?"

Tabby's cheeks burned. Why was she suddenly hit with embarrassment? She tried to look away, wondering if she should get back to work, but Jenni had a grin that just wouldn't quit, and Tabby found herself studying the woman's lips.

"It's not that I was looking," Tabby quickly responded. "I mean, I just happened to be looking down when you headed this way. That's all." It was a good save—hopefully, a believable one. Jenni nodded, and Tabby released a breath.

"We haven't been introduced. I'm Jenni Jennison."

Jenni gave her name with such confidence it made Tabby shrink inside. She was embarrassed to mutter her own last name. Yet, it was better than her maiden name, Char. "Tabitha, uh, Brickly," she said. "Or, I answer to Tabby, if you'd prefer."

The woman grinned. "Tabby it is." She held out her hand, and Tabby shook it. Jenni's grip was firm, warm, and inviting. Part of Tabby expected Jenni to go into details about finances and how she gave donations aplenty to Capmed, but instead, Jenni said, "I had a cat named Tabby when I was four years old."

Tabby was so embarrassed, she wanted to crawl under the desk. She wasn't sure how she was going to respond to something like that. Luckily, she didn't have to, since Jenni started laughing.

"I was wondering how you'd respond to that. Looking back, I realize that it wasn't quite the icebreaker I expected." She laughed loudly, and suddenly Tabby didn't mind. Jenni had an infectious laugh, and if that's what ended the awkwardness, then she would graciously accept it.

"Actually, I had a cat named Jenni," Tabby replied. Jenni stopped laughing, and her jaw dropped. Tabby shook her head. "Gotcha."

Jenni chortled, and for a few minutes in that hallway, everything that Tabby needed to accomplish before her day was over vanished. Jenni was captivating and gave her a sense of comfort she'd been lacking in her life for a long time. She was happy to linger in the hallway with Jenni just a few more minutes before the stress of work and life came flooding back in.

CHAPTER FOUR

Jenni

The sound of Tabby's laugh was like the sun coming out on a rainy day. When Jenni heard it, it made her want to smile. It brought her joy, and after the past couple of days she had had, she certainly could use that right about now.

"I have to get back to work," Tabby said. She waved, and Jenni nodded and moved past her.

Jenni turned to get one last glimpse, lingering around a corner, where she could quickly hide if Tabby noticed. Jenni watched as Tabby spoke to a patient waiting outside a room. Even from a distance, Jenni could see the kindness in Tabby's eyes and the respectful way she treated her patients. Of course a warmth like that would draw Jenni in.

A knot formed in the pit of her stomach. *What about Wendy?*

With a sigh, she left the area and continued down the hallway, heading straight for Dr. Charles Richards's office. She tapped on his door, then turned to look back to where she had left Tabby. She was busying herself at a computer, oblivious to Jenni watching her. She tapped again on the door.

"He's not in there."

Jenni looked to her right and smirked. "Apparently not, because he's right there in front of me." Jenni stepped away from the door. "Thought I would see if you were working today."

"Aren't I always?" he asked, opening his door. She followed him into his office. "Have a seat. I have a few minutes."

Jenni sunk into the chair facing his desk. Since she had started shelling donations into the hospital, she had become friends with Charles and his wife, Cecilia. He had become a confidant she could talk to when she was dealing with hospital matters, and it was nice to have someone there that she could work alongside when it seemed like everyone else looked down on her. A few people frowned upon the fact that she was part of the board of directors. She had become friendly with a couple of members of the board, but there was always that nagging thought that people didn't think she belonged there. Sometimes, she thought that was true. Her wife had always been the charismatic one with a strong influence. Jenni was there only by default.

"What's going on?" he asked. "You look like you have a heaviness weighing on your heart."

She smiled. "That sounds like something your wife puts in those romance novels she writes."

He laughed. "Maybe that's where I got it from." He leaned back in his chair and clasped his hands behind his head. "Still, it works in this situation. What's running around that mind of yours?"

Jenni sighed, desperate to let out all her thoughts. She wanted to be honest, but sometimes she worried that being completely honest wouldn't be appropriate. She was needed for her donations, but was never asked for her input on hospital matters. Her biggest fear was that she knew nothing about the medical community, so why try to pretend she did?

"Have you heard anything about what's going on with the hospital?" she asked.

Charles shrugged. "I know they're talking about expansions. It's a good thing, though. This place hasn't been renovated in over thirty years. I know that I, for one, will be happy to see this place improved."

"Well, it's more than that," Jenni said.

A knock on the door interrupted them. "Come in!" Charles hollered.

Jenni turned to see Tabby at the door. Tabby's eyes widened in surprise and confusion at seeing Jenni sitting across from Dr. Richards. "Hey, Tabby," Jenni greeted

"Hello," Tabby said, straightening her gaze from Jenni's. "Sorry to interrupt, Dr. Richards," she said.

"No worries, Tabitha."

"Ms. Rivers is complaining about chills and chest pain. She doesn't have a fever, but she asked if we could increase her meds. What do you think?"

He took the chart from Tabby and examined it. While they mused over it, Jenni looked over at Tabby. Her eyes never once swayed from looking at the chart, so Jenni's gaze went unnoticed.

"Yes, let's go ahead and add a transdermal nitroglycerin patch every six hours. Thanks, Tabitha."

"You're welcome, Doctor." Tabby nodded at Jenni. "Sorry again for the interruption." She quickly left the office, and Jenni looked toward the door as it closed.

"What do you know about her?" Jenni asked, turning back to Charles.

He tilted his head. "Well, not a whole lot. I try not to get too involved with the nurses who work in my ward. But I can say that I know she's married."

Jenni rolled her eyes. "The wedding ring told me that. Happily? To a man?"

Charles laughed and leaned back in his overstuffed chair. "What happened to *I'll never fall in love again*?"

"Who said anything about love?" Jenni crossed her legs. "I'm merely curious. I did just meet the woman, after all."

Charles nodded. "Married to a man. She has either one or two kids. That's the extent of my knowledge. She's a great nurse, but I doubt that was what you were thinking about when you were staring."

Jenni frowned, slightly abashed. Though she had to admit she found Tabby stunning, there was something beneath the surface she was drawn to. "Tabby seems like a warm, genuine person, and she's easy to talk to. I can tell she's a great nurse."

Jenni smiled. "But that brings us back to what I was saying earlier, as to what's happening here."

"Ahh, yes. Other than the expansions, of course. Do tell."

Jenni heaved a sigh, dreading what she was about to say. "They're cutting staffing funds. People are going to lose their jobs. They're doing a pretty hefty hack, too."

Charles's eyes narrowed. "Not my job, I hope."

"They aren't talking about doctor staffing—as of yet. They're saying they'll start with people who have been here the longest and work down the line."

He frowned. "How does that even make sense? We're going to lose our most seasoned employees?"

"They get paid the higher bucks, and they're trying to shave those off." She shrugged. "I don't agree with it, and a lot of people are going to lose their jobs over it. The economy is struggling right now. This is only going to make things tougher on everyone."

He shook his head. "And there's nothing that can be done?"

Jenni had considered that numerous times since getting the news the day before, but it seemed like an impossible feat to save all of the employees. She shrugged despondently. "I don't think there is."

"That's a bummer," Charles said. "It's going to put a burden on everyone, though, including the staff—heck, especially the doctors."

Jenni nodded. That was another thing to think about, but the board seemed adamant that was the only course of action. She hoped that it never came down to that, but if it did, then she would have to accept it.

"Enough negativity. How are Cecilia and your little rugrats?"

He smiled. "Ornerier than ever, and the kids are, too." He laughed and reached for a picture that was framed on his desk and holding it up. "The kids aren't so little, though. Not anymore." His eyes shone brightly, and Jenni smiled. "But they ask about Auntie Jenni often, so you might want to pay them a visit."

"I'll definitely have to make sure to do that," she said, still grinning.

There was once a time when Jenni thought she would be one of those doting parents who flashed pictures around when others inquired about her kids. That obviously hadn't worked out, but she didn't want people to see how much that bothered her. It was just the hand she had been dealt. There wasn't any reason to feel sad about it. Her years with Wendy, even though they hadn't had kids, were something she would never change. It was best to pretend nothing bothered her. She had grown used to doing that.

THE MICROWAVE DINGED, AND JENNI OPENED THE DOOR AND pulled her TV dinner out. She dropped it on the counter and grabbed her silverware, then carried everything to the kitchen table.

It was what her life had been reduced to over the years. When she first got out of college, she thought living a single life would be pure bliss, allowing her to do what she wanted and be who she wanted, and never have to apologize for it. That all changed when she met Wendy. It was an accident that had brought them together, a fender bender in a suburban neighborhood. Wendy was only two blocks from her home when she had swerved to keep from hitting a dog, and wound up hitting Jenni's car. At first, Jenni wasn't pleased. She was determined to read the riot act to the person who hadn't been paying attention and rammed into her. She hadn't seen the dog, but when she saw Wendy, nothing else mattered.

Wendy had sparked something deep and passionate inside her. Wendy was caring and a joy to be around, and her smile was infectious. She had a way of putting Jenni at ease, even after a stressful day. Three years later, they were married.

Jenni took her last bite of her TV dinner. It wouldn't last all night, but she would grab something to snack on before she headed off to bed. This was her life and routine. Why change that now?

She got up, tossed the container into the trash, and went to the living room, where a photo album sat on a coffee table. Jenni sat down on the couch and grabbed the album. She flipped it open to her wedding pictures.

It was the happiest day of their lives. Wendy was the most beautiful bride that had ever walked down the aisle. With her dark auburn hair and green eyes, she captivated everyone, but especially Jenni. She couldn't imagine her life without Wendy and the warmth she brought to everyone who knew her. Their dreams stemmed from getting married and starting a family. It was a struggle, though, spending so much time finding ways to get the baby they wanted. They had been hopeful when they tried in vitro fertilization, using the sperm from one of Wendy's coworkers. That had turned into another bust, leaving them more devastated than ever.

They had started the adoption process when the unthinkable happened. Wendy was T-boned coming home from work one night at her waitressing gig and died on impact. It was a drunk driver—a kid only eighteen years old. In the blink of an eye, two lives ended that night. The problem was that Jenni didn't know if she could ever start living, or loving, again. It felt like a betrayal of her true love.

She closed the album and put it back down on the coffee table. She could always hear Wendy's words in her head. If anything ever happens to me, I need you to promise me something. Promise me you'll move on. I don't want to be in Heaven knowing that you're not living, and I will haunt you. So, promise me.

Back then, Jenni always thought that when she had made that promise, she would never actually need to keep it. Wendy would never know.

Jenni was forty when Wendy took her last breath. It had taken a long time, but things had slowly started to improve. Now, at forty-five, she wanted to try to keep that promise to her. So, when she first saw Tabby, she was taken aback. A spark she thought died with Wendy had suddenly been reignited. Tabby was the first woman Jenni had met, other than Wendy, whom she felt this instant connection with.

Jenni brushed the tears from her eyes and leaned back in her seat. Was it time for her to finally move on and let Wendy go? The only thing was, she wanted it to be with someone who would reciprocate those feelings with her. Her feelings for Tabby were doomed, since Tabby was married. Jenni looked down at the cover of the photo album. A beaming picture of both Wendy and Jenni on the cover stared back at her. "I know you want me to be happy, Wendy. I'm trying, baby."

She stood up from the couch and headed to her bedroom. It wasn't easy spending nights alone, but maybe one day she'd fulfill her promise to Wendy and find a new love. If only she could allow herself to move on.

CHAPTER FIVE

Tabby

C allie shifted in bed as Tabby leaned over her, tucking her in nice and tight. "How's that?" Tabby asked.

"Perfect." Callie shifted her gaze to her light, then back to Tabby. "Mom?"

"Yes, Peaches?" Tabby asked.

Callie's grin widened. "You haven't called me that since I was in kindergarten."

Tabby laughed. "If memory serves me, that's when you said you were too old to have a nickname. Since we're alone, I didn't think you'd mind."

Callie quickly shook her head. "Mom? Tonight was good. You know, you being home and making supper. Like we were a real family."

Tabby sat down on the edge of her daughter's bed. "Well, we are a real family."

Callie giggled. "I know, but it has been a while. I liked it. I'm sure Brittany did, too."

"Well, I'll tell you something." Tabby leaned in, her breath warm as she caressed her daughter's cheek and rested her lips on her ear. "I did, too."

Callie giggled and held out her arms so they could embrace. It was moments like these, tucking her daughter into bed and having these sweet conversations with her, that Tabby treasured.

"Now, you get some sleep, little one." Tabby stood up from her bed. "We'll go shopping this weekend, and you can make your dish for the whole family."

Callie clapped her hands and beamed. "Love you!"

"Love you too, Peaches. Sweet dreams." She looked over at her as Callie shifted in bed and turned, her back facing the door. Tabby turned off her light and left her room. As she stepped into the hallway, she heard the faint sound of Drew's guitar coming from downstairs. She heaved a sigh and moved to Brittany's room. She tapped on the door before opening it. Brittany was in her bed, pulling her earbuds from her ears as Tabby entered.

"Hey, Mom."

"Hey, sweetheart. Are you going to get ready for bed?"

Brittany groaned. "I'm thirteen and surely don't need the same bedtime as my younger sister."

Tabby chuckled. "Well, it is Friday night, so I suppose you have a point there. What are you listening to?"

Brittany arched an eyebrow. "Grunge. You wouldn't understand it."

Tabby let out another laugh. "You're probably right." Kids nowadays were a lot different from when Tabby was a kid. It didn't even seem like that long ago. Some days she felt like she had to grow up so fast at seventeen that she had lost her youth in the process. It was hard to fathom that she had been only four years older than Brittany was when she bore her first child.

"Did you like what we had for dinner?" Tabby asked.

Brittany's eyes shone as she nodded. "It was good. Even better that you were there to enjoy it with us."

That was the consensus for all three of them. "I'm glad I was here, too." Tabby walked over to Brittany and kissed her forehead. "I know you're nearly an adult," she teased, "but don't stay up too late."

Brittany smiled as Tabby walked away. "Night, Mom."

"Goodnight." Tabby blew her a kiss and left the room. The music still played downstairs, and Tabby hesitated at her own bedroom. She wanted to just slip into her room, fall asleep, and not have to face her husband. With a sigh, she headed for his music room.

Drew had been quiet at dinner. While she and the kids had chatted about school, he had seemed to be in his own little world. Tabby wondered what was on his mind that had kept him so quiet. As she drew closer to the music room, the guitar playing got louder, then stopped when she stepped into Drew's sanctuary. He had his head down as he wrote something down. Tabby was hesitant to interrupt him, and after watching him for some time, he started to play again.

She remembered vividly the first time she saw him playing. She was sixteen years old, and she had thought it was the coolest thing. She had never thought she would one day wind up meeting him, hooking up with him on that winter night, and ultimately finding herself in a position to get married. She had thought it was love at first sight. And in many ways, she had walked down the aisle, to the altar, feeling that way, too. But looking back, it was more the thrill of Drew being a bad boy. Her parents had disapproved of him from the get-go, but Tabby had wanted to prove them wrong and prove to herself that she could have an amazing family of her own.

Drew stopped strumming and went back to writing something on his music sheet. "If you're going just to stare..." he started.

"I didn't want to interrupt," she said.

He looked up. "Too late for that."

His snarky response would have normally sent her running out of the room, but if she couldn't have a civil conversation with him, then maybe they were going about this all the wrong way.

"You were quiet at dinner," she said.

He sighed and looked away, shaking his head. "What do you want me to say, Tab?" he asked, turning back to face her. "Do you want me to praise you for making it to one dinner? Is that it? Do you realize these kids are your responsibility, too? And yet, you stay out all hours of the night and expect me to be Mr. Mom. Well, you made it home for one dinner. Bravo." He clapped, and Tabby stared at him, frustration coursing through her veins. She willed the tears not to fall. It wouldn't help anything if she started crying. It would only egg him on and add to her torment.

"It's not like I'm out carousing the neighborhood like a stray cat. I'm working. I'm trying to give this family the life they expect. I'm bringing home the money, Drew. I don't see your hobby paying the bills."

His eyes darted up to hers, and his jaw hung slightly. "Nice." He shook his head. "I can't believe you just said that to me. You used to love that I played music. But now you think my job is just a hobby?"

"Drew," Tabby started. "I didn't mean it the way it came out. I understand your passion, and I want you to follow that passion and go wherever it leads you. Unfortunately, it hasn't led you to paying gigs. That's a problem, so it makes me strive to get in more hours of work. Otherwise, we're looking at losing electricity and water. Is that what you want for your kids?"

A groan came from him, and he shot her another look. "You know it isn't. I love those kids, and I love you. You know that."

Tabby nodded, swallowing the lump in her throat. It'd been a while since he said those words to her. Yet she hadn't been able to say them to him, either. So, it wasn't like it was one-sided. She wanted to believe it was love that kept her from leaving, but lately, she wasn't so sure.

"It's getting late. The kids are in bed, and maybe we should just go to bed, too."

He shook his head and looked down at his music. "I have work to do. It might just be a hobby to you, but I'm working to make it more. If you were home more often, you would know this. I'll head up later," he grumbled.

"All right," Tabby said despondently.

She left his music room and went up the stairs, her heart breaking with each step she took. Giving him space seemed to be something she had to do every night. The more space she gave him, the bigger the wedge between them. It was too much to believe they could fix it.

As she lay in bed, attempting to get some sleep, the sound of Drew's guitar continued to filter through the vents. If she could hear it, she was confident her kids could, too. The only saving grace was that they were heavy sleepers and hopefully already dead to the world.

Time seemed to tick slowly by, but what could Tabby do to change his mind if Drew didn't want to come upstairs? She tossed and turned, hoping to fall asleep, because she needed some rest, and Drew did, too. Yet he remained downstairs, just strumming on his guitar. At one point, he even started playing his harmonica. That's when Tabby grabbed his pillow and pushed it down on her face, hoping it would muffle the music. No such luck. She placed the pillow down and sat up.

"Two thirty?" she mumbled, floored that Drew was trying to prove a point that kept him going into the morning. What respect did that provide her children? None, in Tabby's opinion.

If Drew was trying to prove a point, he had done it. He wanted to turn his hobby into a full-time gig. She got that, but this wasn't changing anything. She tossed the covers back and slipped out of bed, trying to salvage at least some sleep by telling Drew to stop.

The music stopped. Tabby hesitated at the door, then heard footsteps coming up the stairs. She hurried back to the bed and got back under the covers. A moment later, the door opened.

"You're still awake," Drew mumbled.

Tabby sat up in bed. "I didn't think you were ever going to come to bed."

He went over to a chair and grabbed his lounge pants and T-shirt. He looked over at her and shrugged. "Needed a break."

"From me?" Tabby asked.

He heaved a sigh. "Tab, I'm tired of arguing all the time. So, yeah, from you. From us. From marriage. From life."

"Wow," Tabby muttered, tossing the covers back aggressively.

"Where are you going?" he asked as she reached the door.

Tabby slowly turned to face him. "You're not the only one who needs a break. I'm trying to hold on to this marriage, and you're trying to push me away, saying you need a break? How do you think that makes me feel? I'll tell you how, like my feelings are worth nothing."

He snorted, making Tabby step backward. If he didn't want to appreciate that she was trying, then maybe she could do nothing to fix this.

"I don't see you trying." He looked up and met her gaze. "If you were, then you would make sure to be home every night to fix us supper. You would change your hours to accommodate your family. But you're not."

"It's not that simple, Drew." She looked away from him, then moved farther out the door. "But you'll never get it, right? I need some air." She turned and hurried down the stairs. The moment she stepped outside, she slammed the door behind her. Tears were brimming on the edge of her eyes, and she flicked them off. *Don't cry, Tabby. It's what he wants.*

What was it that she wanted, though? If only she could figure that out herself, then maybe she wouldn't be stuck in a marriage that was failing right in front of her. She turned and looked up at the window that peered into their bedroom, seeing Drew's shadow. The moment she locked eyes with him, he shut the window curtain. That was the story of their love. It was slowly fading away.

TABBY ENTERED THE MARKET WITH HER DAUGHTERS AND looked over at Callie. "The grocery store is all yours. I'll grab the cart, and you put in what you need."

"I can't believe you're letting a nine-year-old feed us," Brittany muttered. "What if we get sick? What if we die?"

Tabby ruffled her daughter's hair. "Don't be so dramatic." She leaned against her ear. "I'll be there along the way—no worries."

The look on Brittany's face still indicated she was worrying, but she nodded as Tabby grabbed the cart, and they followed Callie through the store. One by one, Callie tossed items into the cart, and Tabby's mind went back to the previous night. The arguments with Drew weren't the worst they had ever had, but still, it was tough to just be okay with it. After twelve years of marriage, she wanted to do what she could to get through the rough patches, but it was getting harder to maneuver through them.

Callie reached an aisle and peered through the rows of bottles. Tabby jerked herself out of her reverie and looked at her. "What are you doing?"

"The recipe says Marsala wine. I've never shopped for wine before. Do you know where it is?" She looked up, hopeful.

Tabby grabbed the recipe from her and looked down at it, then at Callie in amusement. "It can be left out. Let me rephrase that. In this case, it will be left out."

"Mom," she groaned. "I want everything to be perfect."

"And it will be." Tabby raised an eyebrow. "But we're not putting wine in this recipe. Got it?" Her tone was stern, and she bit down on her lip—no need in taking out her frustration with her kids. "I promise you," she said, brushing her hand under Callie's chin, "it will still taste amazing."

Callie groaned again, but nodded. Tabby handed the list back to her and sighed, shaking her head. At least she was coherent enough to have prevented that from going into the cart. She turned and pushed the cart into another cart next to a woman looking at the shelves.

"Sorry about that," Tabby said.

The woman turned, and Tabby's eyes widened when she realized who it was. "Hello there," Jenni said.

"Hi. Didn't see you there." Tabby turned to her two children, who had suddenly grown shy. She wrapped an arm around her two daughters. "This is my daughter Brittany," Tabby said, motioning her hand over Brittany's head. "And this is my daughter Callie."

Jenni nodded. "Pleasure to meet you both."

"And this is Jenni. She has business dealings with Capmed." She cringed. Was that even an accurate way to describe Jenni's relationship with the hospital? She looked at her two children, who simply nodded and cowered behind her. She smiled. "They're more of the introverted type."

Jenni smiled wider. "I know the feeling. I am, too."

She spoke directly to both Tabby's children, and Tabby relaxed when she saw both girls smile. "Callie is making dinner tonight for all of us. It'll be her first time preparing the whole meal."

"Oh? Nice," Jenni replied. "How old are you, Callie?"

Tabby opened her mouth to respond for Callie, but Callie seemed more at ease. "Nine. I'll be ten in thirty-four days."

Tabby chuckled. "Not that she's counting or anything."

Jenni grinned. "That's a big endeavor for someone so young." That made Callie smile even wider. "And how old are you?" she asked, looking over at Brittany.

"Thirteen," Brittany quickly answered.

"Ahh, to be a teenager again."

Brittany nodded, perking up.

"How old are you?" Callie blurted out.

Tabby wanted to duck into a corner as she placed her hand over Callie's mouth. "Kids say the darndest things," she said sheepishly.

Jenni laughed loudly, then knelt closer to Callie. "Forty-five. I know, super old. Don't tell anyone."

Tabby appreciated that Jenni spoke to her kids as if they were on the same level rather than treating them as immature children. It was nice to see another adult acting that way. And it impressed her that Jenni hadn't flinched when Callie had asked how old she was.

She remembered days when she, the kids, and Drew ran errands together. Their daughters were a lot younger, but they had actually spent and enjoyed time as a family, laughing and exploring the world. Now, she didn't know who Drew was anymore.

Jenni was so different. While Drew always seemed to be looking through her, Jenni gave Tabby her full attention, smiling and speaking kindly. What a contrast to Drew's snarky responses and awful attitude.

She imagined how being with Jenni would make her so much happier.

She bit her lip and looked at her feet. Jenni was making her think all kinds of strange thoughts. She'd never considered being with another woman, but there was something about Jenni...

"Um, we should get going," Tabby said, trying to maintain her composure, though her heart was beating a mile a minute because of Jenni's proximity. "It was good to see you."

"You too, Tabby. Nice to meet you, Brittany and Callie." As Jenni passed, she touched Tabby's shoulder and gave it a soft squeeze, which sent a jolt through Tabby.

As Jenni went to another aisle, Brittany and Callie grinned, no longer the shy individuals they were five minutes ago.

Tabby tried to calm her racing heart as Callie continued to grab things for her dish, and they paid and left the store. As the three loaded the groceries into the trunk of their car, Tabby's phone dinged from a text message.

"Finish up, girls," she said, grabbing her phone and looking down at Drew's message.

I need some space tonight. I won't be home until late. Don't wait up.

Tabby typed back furiously, *What? Your daughter is making supper. You're going to miss that?*

Don't get all high and mighty with me. It's not like you haven't missed plenty of meals.

None that our daughter was making.

Differences...differences...make an excuse for me.

Incredulous, Tabby pocketed her phone. She couldn't believe she was about to make an excuse for Drew for whatever he felt was more important than Callie's dinner. She pocketed her phone. If he didn't want to be there, he didn't want to be there.

"Is something wrong, Mom?" Brittany asked when they had all loaded into the vehicle.

Tabby forced a smile and looked in the rearview mirror. She couldn't stand seeing the smile fade from either of her daughter's faces, but especially Callie's. She watched Callie in the backseat, wondering what Drew had deemed to be more important than sharing in his daughter's meal.

"Unfortunately, your father has somewhere he needs to be tonight."

Callie turned and caught her gaze in the mirror. "He's not going to be there for my meal?"

Tabby shook her head. Damn you, Drew. "He has a sick friend he's looking after tonight. He says he's really sorry he won't be able to be there, but we'll keep some leftovers for him."

That brought a smile to Callie's face, and Tabby turned back to the front to pull out of the parking spot. She looked over and saw Brittany staring at her intently. Tabby forced a smile of her own, hoping her daughter bought it, then continued her route to the house. Even if it was to protect Drew, lying was better than seeing the disappointment on Callie's face.

When they got to the house, the three of them worked to unload the groceries. When Callie stepped away to grab more bags, Brittany reached out for Tabby's arm, halting her. "Are you lying?" she asked. "About Dad helping out a friend, I mean?"

"We don't need to get into this now," Tabby replied, turning to look at her elder daughter.

"Mom, I'm not a kid. I know that you and Dad have been experiencing some difficult times." Tabby opened her mouth, but Brittany continued. "Do you know that most of my friends have divorced parents?"

Tabby's voice softened. "No, honey, I did not know that."

"They're thriving just fine." She shrugged. "Most of them, anyway." She turned to leave the kitchen to help Callie with the rest of the bags. Tabby stood there, shocked by Brittany's precociousness. If her kids were aware of their issues, then she and Drew weren't fooling anyone, but this was one more thing she would need to discuss with her husband. They shouldn't bring their children into their mess unless they were ready to make some big changes. Letting their daughters down was the last straw, in Tabby's mind. It was time to have a talk with Drew.

CHAPTER SIX

Jenni

Jenni's head pounded as she rounded the corner. She fell back against a wall and started to massage her temples. *Just an hour,* she silently pleaded. *That's all you need to give me to get out of the hospital and home. Then I can rest all night. Please, pain, just an hour.*

She had been working for five hours, and she found herself plagued by a migraine that threatened to make her throw up. The lights in the hospital didn't help any, and the fact that she had left her medicine at home was just the cherry on top.

"Are you okay?"

She opened her eyes to see Tabby running up to her. Tabby reached for her arm, but Jenni straightened up and tried to force a smile. "Uh, yeah, I'm fine," she lied, gritting her teeth.

"You look like you're ready to pass out," Tabby said. "Come on."

Jenni leaned against her, and Tabby helped her into an empty room. "I'm fine," Jenni said again, even as Tabby helped her onto a bed.

"And I stand by the fact that you look anything but fine. Your color is completely faded from your cheeks."

Without warning, Tabby brushed her fingers against Jenni's cheeks in concern, and Jenni fought to not reach toward the soothing touch. If she wasn't already flushed, she'd be burning from the feel of Tabby's hand.

Tabby frowned and then felt Jenni's forehead. Jenni always felt a tad warm when she got migraines. They tended to affect her whole body.

"I just have a migraine. No biggie."

"Have you taken anything for it? If you have, it's not working." Tabby knelt in front of her, looking concerned. Tabby was a nurse; it was her job to be concerned. Yet Jenni couldn't shake the resulting warmth that bubbled inside her.

"I left my meds at home. I only have an hour left here, and then I'm headed out. It's not a problem."

"It doesn't look like it," Tabby said. "Wait here." She hurried out of the room and was only gone less than a minute before she returned with a cup of pills and bottled water. "Take this."

"Stealing drugs from the hospital? Someone could report you." Jenni joked weakly, quickly downing the pills. "I feel better already," she teased.

"At least you've got a sense of humor," Tabby replied. "This is a hospital. It makes no sense for people in pain not to get the relief they deserve. That's what meds are for. But don't worry, I didn't steal anything. These are from my private stash. It's the least I can do for my patient. And that's what you are right now—my patient."

"Oh, great," Jenni mock groaned. "I know what they charge here. My bill will be astronomical." She shook her head in jest and immediately regretted it as pain radiated through her whole body.

"We'll just say it's pro bono," Tabby replied. "Hopefully the meds will kick in soon, though. But seeing that this is a hospital, it makes me question why you didn't seek out help before you almost passed out in the hallway."

"I didn't want to bother anyone," Jenni quietly replied, glancing up at Tabby. She wasn't used to someone caring for her. For years, she'd been toughing everything out on her own. Now, Tabby was here showing her compassion and trying to help her feel better. Her heart fluttered.

"You donate money to this hospital, Jenni. You're not bothering anyone. Especially me." Tabby averted her gaze, looking a bit shy from such a bold statement.

She made a valid point, but Jenni had never thought of her assistance to Capmed as something that needed to be reciprocated. She didn't give the money because she wanted praise. She did it because she knew Wendy would want something good to come about from her death.

"So," Jenni started, trying to switch the topic from her migraine and on to anything else. "Did Callie end up making that dinner last Saturday? Your kids are adorable, by the way."

That brought a smile to Tabby's lips. "Thank you, and yes. I have to admit, she's not a bad chef. Might even be better than her mother." Tabby laughed. "She was happy to be cooking. I stayed in the kitchen, but..." She frowned suddenly. "Why are we talking about this?"

"Because when I don't think about my stupid migraine, I feel better," Jenni pointed out.

"Well, may I ask just one thing, and then we can drop it?" Tabby asked.

"If you must," Jenni sighed.

"How long have you gotten migraines, and have you ever had them observed?"

Jenni arched an eyebrow in mock disdain. "You just asked two things." She laughed and said, "I would say it's been going on twenty-five years, and I have had numerous doctors and specialists take a look, and they all say the same thing. I just need to deal with it." She shrugged. "So that's what I do. Deal with it. Now, back to Callie and her meal. What'd she cook?"

Tabby looked like she didn't want to drop the subject, but replied, "Chicken marsala. Without the Marsala." She grinned. "Callie was confused about why she couldn't have the wine in her dish. But it tasted good, nonetheless."

Jenni laughed, immediately forgetting her headache. "I was wondering why you were in the alcohol section. Both your daughters seem like sweet girls, by the way."

"They're the best," Tabby said. Her eyes darkened, and Jenni wanted to delve more into the topic of her family. She opened her mouth, but the door flew open, breaking into their conversation.

"Oh. Sorry," the nurse said, backing from the door.

"It's all right, Hanna." Tabby got up from the chair and looked over at Jennie. "Just finishing up here."

"Yeah, thanks so much, Tabby." Jenni jumped off the bed and scurried out of the room past Hanna and a patient. She didn't want Tabby to get into trouble. She somehow felt better, but that was more from just talking to Tabby rather than from the meds she had just taken. There was something soothing about being around Tabby, and she was left even more curious about her.

JENNI WALKED INTO THE CLUB AND LOOKED AROUND. SHE WAS glad she no longer had a migraine and equated that to the fact that she had had a great conversation with Tabby and that she had gotten plenty of rest after. She spotted her best friend, Kim, engrossed in a conversation with a man who stood at a table. As she drew closer, she caught how strongly Kim was flirting with the guy. It was subtle to other people, but to someone who knew Kim so well, it was so obvious that it should have slapped the guy in the forehead.

He, however, seemed unaware. While he rattled off the specials, Kim batted her eyes in time with every drink from the list. Jenni rolled her eyes as she reached the table. Either he was clueless or just plain uninterested.

"The peach mango smoothie with a shot of tequila sounds heavenly," Kim cooed. "I'll take that. Unless you would suggest something else?"

"No, that's a fine choice, ma'am. Coming right up." He looked over at Jenni as she grabbed the seat across from Kim. "What can I get you, ma'am?"

"I'll take a beer, light. Thanks." He nodded and walked away. Jenni turned to her friend, whom she hadn't seen in nearly a year. "You realize there are two problems with him, right?"

"He's a total babe and has a killer a...abs." She smirked. "What's the problem with that?"

Jenni shook her head. "He's no older than twenty-one, and he's probably gay."

"I'd be able to tell if he was gay," Kim protested. "My gaydar hasn't gone off once. As for the age, he's legal. It's clearly not something that would keep us from hooking up in the bathroom, or the alley, or on top of the stove in the kitchen. I'm not picky." She winked, and Jenni shook her head, unable to keep from smiling.

"I've missed you."

"I've missed you more, Jenni. Gosh. It's been way too long. How've you been? Tell me everything. I feel like way too much time has passed, and I'm dying to hear about everything."

Before Jenni could open her mouth, the waiter came back with their drinks. Kim looked in his direction. "My friend here and I have a bet going on, Coolio. Care to help us decipher the winner?"

"I'll do whatever I can, ma'am," he responded.

Kim tossed a look over to Jenni, and Jenni laughed silently. She didn't know what Kim was trying to prove, but whatever it was, it was sure to be entertaining.

"It's a two-parter," she continued. "How old are you, and are you gay or straight?"

Jenni covered her face and shook her head. Kim hadn't changed at all. They were best friends from first grade and had been inseparable until college. Then Kim decided to move to California, which had worried Jenni. What if their friendship couldn't withstand the distance? She was glad to find that wasn't an issue as they continued to keep in contact with one another. Even though they didn't see each other often, they still talked frequently. But Kim was, by far, the bold one out of the two of them. Jenni would have never had the courage to ask the waiter such personal questions.

Coolio just smirked as he leaned onto the table. "Which one is betting I'm gay?" he asked, shifting his eyes from one to the other. Jenni pointed to Kim while Kim pointed in her direction. Jenni felt her face turning every shade of red, and she was ready to crawl under the table. Coolio just laughed.

"I'm twenty-two, and I am indeed gay. Does that settle it?" He winked and then left the table. Jenni watched Kim's eyes linger longer than necessary on Coolio's butt as he continued to walk away.

"Damn," she huffed, looking over to Jenni. "My gaydar was way off on that one."

Jenni took a sip of her beer. "Maybe next time you'll trust me. Besides, with a name like Coolio....Come on." She shook her head in jest and continued to drink her beer.

Kim laughed and shrugged. "Oh well. He's nice to look at, anyway."

Jenni smirked and looked around the room. Her eyes stopped just two tables from theirs. Sitting there were Tabby and some other women from the hospital. She quickly looked away.

"We should get something to eat. I'm famished." She kept her eyes focused on the menu, oblivious to the fact that Kim was scrutinizing her.

"Did you see something over there?" Kim asked. "You're all pale, like you saw a ghost or something." Jenni looked up as Kim looked over to Tabby's table.

"Stop it!" Jenni hissed, reaching out to grab her friend's hand. Kim looked back at her, eyebrows raised.

"Who's over there? Now your cheeks are all red." She leaned over the table, her eyes locked on Jenni's, firing off questions. "What's going on? Did you find someone? You look like you're ready to bolt. Is it someone at that table?"

She turned to look again, but Jenni grabbed Kim's hand. When Kim looked back, her jaw dropped. "It is. Who is it? The pretty redhead over there? The blonde with dazzling blue eyes?"

Jenni tilted her head. "We're not that close to them. How can you see their eye color?"

Kim shrugged. "Looks blue from over here. I could go and get a closer look." She started to get up, but Jenni kicked her under the table, and she laughed and fell back into her seat. "Come on, Jenni. You're withholding info from me. Who are you attracted to? I haven't seen this look on you in over five years."

Jenni rolled her eyes and looked down at her menu. "You're reading it all wrong," she lied.

"I think not," Kim replied. "A couple of them are headed this way. Is it either of them?"

Jenni looked up and stared straight at Tabby as she headed toward their table. Jenni pushed her hair behind her ear, hoping she didn't look awkward. "Hey, Hanna. Tabby." She put a smile on her lips but made sure to direct it toward Tabby especially.

"Thought that was you over here," Tabby said. She cast a look over at

Kim, but Jenni didn't introduce her, and Kim didn't say anything. She quickly turned away. "Enjoy the rest of your night."

"Bye, Jenni," Hanna called out, then grabbed Tabby's hand and pulled her away from the table, heading in the direction of the dance floor.

Jenni caught herself looking at the floor as Hanna, Tabby, and a few of the other nurses danced. Kim cleared her throat, making Jenni look back in her direction.

"So was it the woman who was making googly eyes all over you?" Kim asked.

"What? She was not. For starters, she's married with two children."

Kim laughed. "You clearly knew which one I was referring to." She looked back down at the menu as Jenni sat there, nervously shifting in her seat. "Curly fries or crinkle?"

"I don't care," Jenni mumbled, closing her menu and pushing it away. She wasn't ready to eat and just wanted to pretend that interaction hadn't happened. She looked out on the dance floor again. No one was paying her any mind. Kim had definitely been mistaken when she said that Tabby was making eyes at her. Jenni shook her head. Why get caught up in some fantasy?

"Wanna talk about it?" Kim asked.

"Nothing to talk about," Jenni remarked. "Are you ready to order? You're only in town one night, and the last thing I want to discuss is how foolish I am."

"I hear you. We can always discuss that later," Kim replied jokingly.

"Yeah, yeah," Jenni said. She just wanted to forget that Kim had ever said anything and try to move past the evening. There wasn't anything between Jenni and Tabby, and the lack of eye contact from Tabby was proof. Logic and reason always differed from where Jenni's mind tended to stray, though, and as Tabby danced, Jenni's eyes remained glued to Tabby, imagining what it would be like to be dancing with her, and hoping that one day she would get the chance.

CHAPTER SEVEN

Tabby

A s much as Tabby was enjoying the night out with her work pals, she couldn't stop thinking about the girls. She and Drew really hadn't gotten anywhere, despite their attempt to talk after he had stayed out until three in the morning the previous Saturday. He had said he needed space, and Callie had seemed to forgive him, so Tabby decided it was best to ease up and accept it. But it was also the main reason she had decided to make her own escape from the house, if only temporarily. But now, she feared it was only hurting her daughters in the process.

"That was weird, didn't you think?" Hanna yelled over the music as they danced.

"Huh? What was weird?" She didn't want the women to think she was blowing them off by not being fully there with them. Since she had allowed them to whisk her off to the club, she would try to appreciate the time away. Yet, thoughts of Callie and Brittany wouldn't stop plaguing her mind.

"Jenni. I mean, we've talked in the past, but she's been around the hospital more often lately. And now, I'm seeing her at the club like it's a normal thing. It just seems strange, don't you think?"

Tabby looked over to the table, where Jenni was watching them dance.

She quickly looked away. She wondered if Jenni was on a date, but tried to shrug that thought away. It wasn't her concern if she was. "Maybe she wants to have more of a role in the hospital. As for being here, I'm sure she goes out every once in a while. Everyone needs a life."

"I guess, but when she first got involved with the hospital, she was closed off. I heard something about her spouse dying. Strange that we've never really been filled in on her story."

"Well, maybe she's ready to make some changes." Again, Tabby shrugged. It all sounded plausible, and though she craved to learn as much about Jenni as she could, she worried about getting too close, especially with the strange feelings Jenni had been stirring lately. Jenni kept glancing over at her, so Tabby kept looking away, but she really liked how Jenni looked tonight. She wasn't used to seeing her in a dress. It really showed off her legs.

She frowned at herself. She had to stop thinking about Jenni so much. She was worried about her girls.

She glanced at her watch. It was only nine o'clock. It would be way too early to run home. She could already hear the ragging her friends would give her. She continued to dance, looking over at Ginger and Sally. They were dancing as if a slow song was playing. Then again, why not? They were happily in love, even sharing a kiss while they danced. Tabby smiled at them. She couldn't remember the last time she and Drew had shared a kiss in public. They barely kissed in private.

"I think I'm going to have to go," she said, turning to Hanna.

"You can't be serious. The night is still early."

"But my daughters..." she started.

Hanna reached out and touched her arm. "Is everything okay? You seem to be a bit rattled lately. If you have to go, then you have to go, but I don't want you leaving because you're not having fun. We could go somewhere else."

"It's not that..." Tabby started to argue. She paused when she felt her phone vibrating. She pulled it out of her pocket and looked at Hanna. "I'll be right back." Tabby hurried off the dance floor to a quiet place. "Hello?"

"Mom?" Callie's voice came onto the other end of the line.

She sighed. For a moment, she thought it would be Drew telling her there was a problem at the house. Hearing her daughter's voice was a relief. "Hey, it's past your bedtime. You know that, right?"

"When are you coming home?" she asked.

Hearing the heartbreak in her daughter's voice made Tabby think about running out right there.

"I said I would be home late, and your father would be tucking you in," Tabby responded. "Where's Brittany?"

"She's on the phone with a friend. Dad's busy with his stupid guitar."

"Put him on the phone, please." Tabby could feel the blood curdling inside of her. She only wanted one night out with friends. She didn't think that was too much to ask when he had done the same. Or so she thought. She had never gotten a definitive response as to where he was that night. If he didn't respect her enough to offer up the truth, then why couldn't he at least give her some time to spend just doing her own thing? It was the least he could do.

"Yeah?" Drew's voice rang out.

"Drew? You promised me that I could hang with my friends tonight and that you would occupy the children so they didn't think about me not being there. What are you doing?"

"She wanted to talk to you. Is that a crime? We're fine. If you want to spend all night out, then go for it. I'll get her to bed. I'm not the one that called you. Remember that, dear, and don't pin this on me. Have a good time. I'm not saying you have to come home, by the way."

Tabby sighed. "Is Callie there?"

"Hello?" Callie answered the phone.

"Go get in bed, and I'll be home in a minute. I'll finish tucking you in when I get there."

"Okay. See you soon," she said before hanging up.

Tabby went back over to her friends and sighed. "I'm sorry, ladies, but I have to head out. Crisis at home."

"What?" Ginger and Sally asked in unison. They stopped dancing and turned to Tabby.

"It's what happens when you're a mom. I'm sorry. I had a blast, though. I'll see you all at work." She waved and then hurried out of the club. She fished her keys out of her pocket and didn't stop running until she reached her car.

The conversation with Drew had her bothered. If she couldn't rely on him taking care of the girls for a few hours, then what *could* she count on? She knew now she shouldn't have thought she'd be able to go out and have fun without any hitches.

She turned the key, and her car made a noise, then died. She tried again, but nothing happened. *This cannot be happening right now.* She tried one more time for good measure. Still, the car didn't start. She slumped forward and shook her head. Could anything else go wrong?

———

A LIGHT TAP SOUNDED ON TABBY'S WINDOW, MAKING HER SIT up. It was Jenni. She turned away and wiped the tears away that had escaped her eyes. She then rolled down her window and looked up at Jenni's concerned gaze.

"Are you all right?" Jenni asked.

There was nothing all right with how Tabby was feeling. She had so many thoughts running through her mind, but no words would come out. She finally looked up and gave a slight smile.

"Car won't start."

"I kind of figured that," Jenni said. "If you need a ride somewhere, I wouldn't mind taking you."

It was like an answer to an unasked prayer. "I don't think I could ask that of you. Are you even ready to go? It's still so early."

Jenni shrugged. "I'm good to go if you need to get out of here. You can call a tow truck for your vehicle."

"Are you sure?" Tabby pressed.

"Absolutely. I'm parked over there." She motioned toward the red Camaro that was only two aisles from hers. Tabby got out of her car, locked it, and followed Jenni. She looked back at the club's entrance to ensure that none of her coworkers had walked out. She didn't want this to get out and for people to talk. When they reached the car, the lights flashed, and Tabby opened the passenger door.

"Thank you for this," Tabby said, getting in.

Jenni got in from the driver's side and inserted her key into the ignition. "Don't mention it. It's the least I could do, especially since you put your nursing skills to good use when you gave me those pills." Jenni lightly touched Tabby's knee in gratitude. Warmth radiated up Tabby's leg, and she was sad when Jenni withdrew her hand.

Tabby looked out the window with a smile. "I graduated with top honors for how well I open medicine cabinets and find over-the-counter pills," she said sarcastically.

Jenni laughed. "It's the little things. What's your address?"

Tabby gave it, and Jenni put it into her GPS. As Jenni pulled out of the parking lot and headed to the house, silence filled the air. Tabby looked at the place on her knee that Jenni had touched. It was an awkward situation to be in, and the lack of conversation left her feeling even stranger.

It was Jenni who spoke first, breaking the silence. "I have a confession," she said.

"Oh yeah?" Tabby turned to look at her. Jenni nodded.

"I saw you were rushing out of the club, and I was curious, so I rushed out after you."

Tabby shook her head. "What about the person you left at the table? Was she your date?"

"Oh, no," Jenni said, laughing. "She's my BFF. We've been best friends for longer than you've been alive."

Tabby didn't know why she was relieved to hear that Jenni hadn't been on a date. She looked at Jenni, whose eyes had lit up when talking about her friend. Jenni said, "But she's only passing through. She lives in Cali, and I was going to see her for a few hours. That's all. I'll text her and tell her what happened."

Jenni made a turn, then continued. "It used to be that when we got together, it was like no time had passed. Tonight felt strange. Like maybe we were drifting apart or something."

"I don't know that BFFs can drift apart like that. I mean, maybe there's something you're both going through, but I feel a friendship like that is always worth salvaging. Don't you?"

Jenni's lips curved into a smile as they made eye contact. "I absolutely do. This is also why I know she'll forgive me for rushing out like that. I'll just say that I had a friend in need. Who can object to that?"

Tabby turned and looked back out the window. That was a good excuse, as far as excuses were concerned. Yet, as far as she knew, she couldn't classify Jenni as a friend. They didn't know one another all that well. Besides, Jenni was out of Tabby's reach when it came to stature and power.

"So, what about your BFF?" Jenni continued.

The question brought a crease between Tabby's eyes as she thought about that. If she was honest with herself, she had lost contact with all her friends once she had gotten married. Sure, she had made new friendships at the hospital when she started working there, but no one she would consider a best friend. She had always said that Drew was her best friend. Now, she laughed when she thought about that. They were more like roommates now—strangers, even.

"I guess I would say my husband," Tabby concluded, hating how pathetic that sounded. Her best friend couldn't be her husband when she was the one who had to rush home to ensure her children were okay because he was too busy being selfish.

"That's sweet," Jenni said. "Believe me, I understand that. In many ways, my wife and I..." Her words trailed off, and the two of them resumed sitting in awkward silence. Tabby turned to Jenni, wanting her to continue and talk about her wife. It was the first time she was getting a deep, introspective look at the woman next to her. Hanna had mentioned a deceased spouse, and now Tabby was intrigued.

"We're here," Jenni said, pulling up to the curb.

"Oh." Tabby turned and looked out the car window. Sure enough, her house stood in front of them. "Thank you again for getting me home. I appreciate it."

Jenni gave a soft smile. "No problem. I hope everything works out."

Tabby started to get out of the car and then hesitated. She had an urge to touch Jenni, and couldn't stop herself from lightly placing her hand on Jenni's, which was on the steering wheel. Jenni's eyes shot to hers. "I heard about your wife," Tabby said. "I can't imagine what you've been through."

Jenni looked surprised and nodded slightly, remaining silent as Tabby finally got out of the car. She ran up to the door, and at the front porch, she turned and waved to Jenni, who waved back before driving off. Tabby lingered a moment, touched by how quickly Jenni had come to her rescue.

Jenni always seemed to be doing that. She seemed to genuinely care about Tabby and her family, and that was touching. It was getting harder and harder not to think about Jenni, who was slowly working her way into Tabby's life.

Steadying herself, Tabby entered the house. At first, silence hit her, but then she heard Drew's guitar. She hurried up the stairs to Callie's room. She opened the door and tiptoed inside to see Callie lying in bed, sleeping soundly. She backed out of the room and shut the door behind her.

She then went to Brittany's room. Her elder daughter was asleep as well. She headed back into the hallway and heaved a sigh of relief before going back down the stairs and entering Drew's music room.

He looked up, surprised. "You're home? I wasn't expecting you until midnight or after."

Tabby slumped down on the couch and shook her head. "Are you kidding me? It sounded like you and Callie weren't getting along. She wanted me here."

"But she's in bed, isn't she?"

Tabby released a breath. "She is, but when I talked to you, you acted like I should be ashamed of myself. I needed *one* night out, away, to have some time for myself, and you acted like that was an issue. But then the other night you went out and did whatever you wanted. You still haven't told me where you were or what you were doing. Is that fair?"

"You're being dramatic," he said as he went back to strumming his guitar.

"Dramatic. Okay. Guess I'm just paranoid or too sentimental. Whatever." Tabby stood up and was walking away when the music stopped again.

"What do you want from me?"

Tabby spun on her heel and stared at him. "That's what you have to say? What do I want from you?" She shook her head. "I want us to have a marriage that counts. I want us to be able to tell each other anything. I want my best friend back."

Drew looked down at his guitar, silent. There was her answer. Tabby felt a tear slip down her cheek. She wiped it away and turned to him. "My car is broken down at the club. I'll need to get it towed somewhere."

"Something else to care of," he mumbled.

Tabby sighed. "I'll handle it." She left the music room and was going to head up the stairs when she hesitated and chose a different route. She went through the kitchen and stepped out onto the back porch. She sat down on the chair that looked out to their backyard. The tears wouldn't stop as she tried to move her thoughts from Drew to something more positive. Yet, no matter how hard she tried, she had difficulty remembering anything but the condescending look Drew gave her. She had nearly lost hope for any reconciliation and just needed the strength to get through it all.

CHAPTER EIGHT

Jenni

J enni looked at the clock on the wall. They had been in the room for an hour and all she could deduce was that there was a lot of bickering and arguing going on. She rubbed her temples and silently urged for one of two things to happen. Either get a major migraine that forced her out of there, or keep the migraine away because she didn't want to barf all over the boardroom table.

"Twenty people?" Dr. Gregory O'Shea asked. "That's a lot of employees. Nurses *and* receptionists? How are we going to handle the layoffs?"

"We'll figure it out. The others will have more hours, for sure," Brian, the CEO, spoke up. "But I know there are many employees who would love to have some extra income."

"It sounds like we're just shifting from one employee to the next," Judith Crosby, a nurse practitioner, spoke up, shaking her head. "How does that help Capmed?"

"In the end," Brian stated, "we'll have employees who make less money employed here, which would save the hospital money."

"That's a crock," Dr. Ivan Wesley spoke up. "As I see it here, we're laying off many nurses in the ER. What are we supposed to do without nurses, tell the patients that no one can take care of them? Do you see how that makes no sense whatsoever?"

"You're not looking at the big picture," Brian replied. "Once renovations are done, we can hire some of these people back. Or we can hire new candidates."

"Who start at the bottom of the barrel," Ivan replied. "Is that it?"

Jenni looked over at Charles. He hadn't once spoken at all during the meeting, but she was sure he had some ideas of his own running through that mind of his. He didn't want to risk losing cardiology nurses. He sat back and listened, observing it all. Much like Jenni was doing.

"And there's no other way?" Dr. Regina Masterson asked. "You can't figure any way to save these jobs? And you're saying *twenty* is really the starting point. By the end of it, who's to say how many people actually end up being terminated. Is that correct?"

Brian looked around the boardroom. You could have heard a pin drop. Jenni waited to see exactly what he would say. Her migraine was on the verge of emerging and she braced herself, reaching up to massage her temples once more.

"I have looked at many avenues. I assure you, the board did not decide this lightly."

"What about you, Jenni?" Jenni shifted her gaze to Ivan. "How do you feel about this? After all, your money goes to the hospital, and you're okay with terminating twenty of its senior staff?"

Jenni swallowed and cringed as her headache quickly rushed to her forehead. No, she wasn't okay with it, but what could she do about it? "I wish there were another way," she began. "I have thought about offering up more money, but I don't want to be tapped out, especially if we're looking at Capmed's expansion. I have concluded that my realm of knowledge doesn't go far when it comes to HR."

"And believe me," Pamela Hobson from the HR department spoke up. "If we could find any other option, we would take it."

There was some more grumbling around the table, and Jenni grabbed a small container, which contained two pills, from her pocket. She popped the pills in her mouth, then took a swig of water. She should have done that first thing in the morning, but who would have known how troublesome the meeting would have gotten?

"I vote we take a recess until next week," Brian stated. "At that time, we'll see if anyone can bring some ideas to this meeting that are worth listening to. Meeting adjourned." Jenni jumped up and left the room but waited outside for Charles so that she could discuss the meeting with him.

"What do you think?" she asked.

He shook his head and led the way to the elevator. "Twenty employees are no joke. More than half will be nurses. If I lose some of my staff, I don't know what I'll do. The cardiology department could be in danger of closing down. I don't see how this is beneficial. They need to realize that we'll lose business." He stepped into the elevator and pressed a button. "But I guess we'll see."

Jenni pressed the button for the main floor. "I think if we all put our heads together, we can figure out a way to salvage these jobs."

"I sure hope so." The doors opened, and he stepped out, but reached his hand back in to stop the elevator from going down. "Cecilia wanted me to invite you to dinner. When are you free?"

"Whenever." She smirked and jokingly corrected, "I mean, my social calendar is *super* busy. You'd better text me a list of dates and I'll get back to you."

He smiled. "Friday night?"

"What do you know? I'm free."

"Great! Come by at sixish and we'll see you then." He waved as the doors closed.

Jenni took the remaining two floors down to the cafeteria. She had gotten her pills in her, but she needed to do the same with food. She stepped into the cafeteria and headed to the seafood counter, grabbed her food and drink, then paid for it and exited through the patio doors to find a seat outside. She found a nice, secluded spot and started to eat.

Jenni didn't mind eating alone. It was something she had grown accustomed to, but as the surrounding tables filled up with friends, she caught herself watching each one and wondering what a difference it would be to have someone sit with her and provide some good company. She took a bite of her seafood salad and kept her eyes lowered to her plate, but she could only look at her food for so long before it made her feel even lonelier, not to mention pathetic. She took a sip of her water and looked up.

Tabby stepped out onto the patio, food in hand. There wasn't an empty table out there, so when Tabby looked in her direction, Jenni motioned for her to come over and join her.

"Are you following me?" Jenni teased.

Tabby's cheeks were bright red. She quickly shook her head. "I swear it's just a coincidence that we always seem to be running into one another. I can find another table to sit at, though."

"What? I was only teasing, Tabby. Sit down. Besides, I would rather have someone here than pretend it isn't awkward being the only person with no one sitting with them. You're doing me a favor."

"In that case," Tabby said, sitting down, "I agree with you. It's awkward eating alone."

Jenni smiled and took a bite of her salad. "I'm glad we ran into one another, though."

"You are?" Tabby asked. "Maybe you're the one who's following me."

Jenni opened her mouth and Tabby laughed. Jenni snapped her mouth shut, glad to see that Tabby was teasing her back.

"Anyway, were you able to get your car fixed?"

"Ahh, yes. I was, thank you. And thanks again for taking me home. It was really nice of you."

Jenni shook her head. "Right place, right time."

"But your friend..." Tabby's voice waned, and Jenni laughed.

"We're still friends. No need to worry about that."

Undoubtedly, Kim had been confused by the sudden way Jenni had left the club, but she had called her BFF later that night and explained the issue, and Kim had accepted it. They would get together before another year could come between them, and she was glad she was able to get Tabby safely home. Deep down Jenni wondered why Tabby had so quickly fled to her house after touching her hand the way she did. Jenni hadn't known how to react when Tabby had offered so much empathy for her wife. It only made her feelings for Tabby deepen.

"What are you eating?" Tabby asked, pointing. "That seaweed sort of thingy."

Jenni snapped out of her thoughts, taking another bite. "It's not so bad. You should try it sometime. Wendy introduced me to this type of food. Never thought I'd ever choose it over a burger and fries." She shrugged. "She surprised me, though, and I've been eating it ever since."

"Wendy?" Tabby asked.

It hit Jenni that she had said Wendy's name for the first time. "My wife," she explained. "The one who passed. She was the health nut in the relationship."

"How did she pass?" Tabby asked softly.

"Drunk driver." Jenni looked down at her salad.

"You don't have to talk about it if you don't want to. I shouldn't have pried."

Jenni looked up. Just having someone interested enough in hearing about Wendy made her feel good. She never used to want to talk about her or bring her up in conversation, but it wasn't because she didn't like talking about her. She knew talking about her in the past tense would mean Wendy was definitely gone.

"She was always trying to get me to work out—something I frowned upon. Then she introduced me to seafood, and it suddenly became something that I craved. Who would have thought? This is a shrimp and tuna salad with a bit of broccoli. Do you want to try it?"

Tabby made a face, then shook her head. "Thanks, but I'll stick to my burger and fries."

Jenni snickered and continued eating. "Tell me about your husband. What's his name? What does he do?"

Tabby dropped her gaze to her plate of food and Jenni worried she had made a grave mistake in asking. "Drew," Tabby finally replied. "He's a musician. Or trying to be. The fact is, he doesn't get many gigs. He has one coming up at a family-friendly venue, but that's only because a friend of a friend got it for him." She smiled, but it was clearly forced. Her eyes were so dim that they startled Jenni.

"Is he good?" Jenni asked.

"Define *good*. I mean, I think he's good. He used to be great. I think over the years he lost confidence, so that hasn't helped his self-esteem when it comes to his playing. He's good enough to get people to listen, but that doesn't necessarily mean he should do it as his full-time job. Does that make any sense?"

"Makes perfect sense. Just because you're good at something doesn't mean you shouldn't do something else to bring home the bucks."

"Yes, and lately…"

When Tabby didn't finish her thought, Jenni touched her hand. "What is it?"

She thought Tabby might brush the sudden touch away, but she didn't. Jenni's pulse quickened.

"Lately," Tabby continued, "I don't know what's happening in our marriage. He says he loves our girls, but he's not pulling his weight. Paying the bills is put on my shoulders because he's always 'trying' to get more gigs. And he's always so angry and bitter. We barely talk, and when we do, it always ends in a fight." Her eyes became misty, and she looked away. "To be honest, I'm a bit lost. I'm not happy and not sure we're still in love. But it's scary to think about ending things."

She wiped her eyes and forced a smile. "Sorry for venting."

Jenni squeezed her hand. "Don't apologize. I'm always here to listen."

The two women gazed at each other and something unspoken passed between them. While it thrilled Jenni, Tabby shifted and looked down, pulling her hand from Jenni's.

Jenni wanted to dig deeper and see why Tabby had pulled away. Still, for now, she was just glad to have Tabby finally open up to her.

JENNI TOOK A SIP OF HER WINE AND PUT IT DOWN ON THE coaster. She sat back in her seat and tried to see if she could hear Charles or Cecilia talking to their kids as they tucked them into bed. There was nothing but silence. She guessed that was a good thing, since she felt awkward trying to eavesdrop on their family time. It'd only been fifteen minutes since they took the kids upstairs, temporarily leaving her alone in the living room.

She checked her watch. It was still early, or she would have said her goodbyes and headed home. But going home to an empty house seemed less appealing than it did most nights, so she didn't bolt out of Charles's home. She leaned forward and picked up her glass once more to take a drink. As she did, she spotted a flyer on the coffee table and picked it up. Drew Brickly, Guitar Soloist. A can't-miss concert! She scanned her eyes over the flyer, and when she heard footsteps on the stairs, she dropped it onto the table and took another drink.

"Wifey is finishing getting them to bed," Charles said, coming into the living room to take a seat. Jenni looked up and smiled, then glanced down at the flier.

"What's that?" she asked nonchalantly, pointing to the flier.

He grabbed it and smirked. "Tabitha," he said, then looked up and met her gaze. "She's the one that you found quite appealing, right?"

Jenni looked away from him. "You said that, not me." She took a sip.

He chuckled. "Right. Anyway, her husband is performing at this show tomorrow night. It's family friendly, so she asked if we wanted to come."

"Are you going to?" Jenni asked, looking up.

He dropped the paper to the table and shrugged. "We talked about it, but we're not sure. You should go. She was asking a bunch of people around the hospital."

"I don't know," Jenni replied. "You don't think that'd be odd? I mean, I don't really know him or anything. I barely know her."

"Nah, it's open to the public." He shrugged. "You should consider it."

Jenni already *had* considered it, and she was worried that if she showed up, Tabby would think she was stalking her. But she couldn't say that, not in front of Charles.

"We'll see," she said, leaving it at that. Cecilia came down the stairs and heaved a sigh as she entered the living room.

"Tonight was exhausting. Probably because they didn't want to go to bed while their Auntie Jenni was here."

Jenni smiled. "Your kids are so precious."

She was glad to have Cecilia there so that she didn't have to talk about Tabby's husband's band, or Tabby, for that matter. She did find herself curious about the band. Tabby said her husband was good. If she did go, that would be a reasonable excuse, right?

Still, it wouldn't be a good idea. It was best just to forget it. No need to put herself in an awkward situation, especially if she ran into Tabby at the concert. She definitely shouldn't go.

But even as she tried to convince herself, she knew her heart was set on going. She was too curious to see what kind of a man and musician Tabby's husband was, and she liked the idea of "bumping" into Tabby there.

"I think she's zoned out, dear," Cecilia said, breaking Jenni from her thoughts.

"What?" she asked, turning to face Charles's wife.

Cecilia laughed. "I was just being nosy, but you looked like you were lost in your own mountain of thoughts. Or just didn't want to answer my question."

"Most likely both," Charles chuckled. "Can I get you ladies some coffee?"

Jenni nodded. She had been drinking wine most of the night, and if she planned on leaving any time soon, she needed to do something to get the wine out of her system.

He left the living room and went to prepare some coffee, and Jenni glanced over at Cecilia. "So, you were saying?"

Cecilia had a sweet smile on her lips. That was one thing that drew her to the Richards household. Even though Charles was a top cardiologist in the Chicago area, if not the entire Midwest, he and his wife were down-to-earth people. She felt welcome being around them.

"I was just inquiring if there was any lady that had caught your attention recently." Cecilia tilted her head. "Of course, you don't need to answer. I'm just curious. You deserve someone who will make you happy."

"I don't mind, Cecilia. I guess it would be nice to have this conversation with a woman who wouldn't judge me. There is someone..." Jenni's words trailed off. Tabby was married, so it was ridiculous to even think of pursuing her, yet she also couldn't ignore what Tabby had shared with her about feeling lost and unhappy in her marriage. Did that leave an opportunity for Jenni to fill the void? "While Charles isn't here, do you mind if I let this out?"

"Of course not. Please continue."

"As you know, it's been five years since Wendy passed away. In my heart, I know that's enough time for me to move on. Part of me feels ready, but there's still something nagging inside of me. What if I open myself up to love someone and ultimately get my heart broken? And there's the question about age. I'm substantially older than this woman, so should that determine whether I go for it?"

And the fact that she's married should probably come into play, right? She bit her tongue.

"It does seem like this woman has been occupying your thoughts. I can see it in your eyes; you like her." Jenni blushed and looked down as Cecilia continued. "I think it's great. I mean, I have seen you struggling with your wife's death, and to think that you feel you might be ready to open yourself up is truly a step in the right direction. As for the possibility of your heart getting broken, you can't worry about that. If you feel this woman is worth it, then you should absolutely put your heart out there."

"And the age thing?"

"What's a few years' age difference?" Cecilia asked.

"More like fifteen," Jenni said, then grabbed her glass and downed the last of her wine.

"What's fifteen years? I say you have to do what your heart is telling you to do. Don't listen to your head, because it screws you up."

It *was* what Jenni wanted to do, but she also wasn't trying to be a homewrecker. Of course, the decision was ultimately Tabby's, but maybe it was time Jenni made her interests clearer. Did she and Tabby have a chance at love?

"There's one more thing," Jenni began. "She's married."

Cecilia's eyebrows shot up and she opened her mouth to respond, when Charles returned.

He held up the tray of coffee. "Coffee is served."

Jenni released a breath. Hopefully, Charles hadn't heard their conversation and she could keep this minute detail to herself. What Cecilia said did make sense. It was something Jenni had always strived to do: keep her heart open and follow where it led her. She never planned to confess her feelings to a married woman, but she also never planned on falling for Tabby. Now it was just about figuring out the right place and time to tell her.

———

THE CROWD WAS PACKED, AS OVER TWO HUNDRED PEOPLE stood outside waiting for the concert to start. It was in a field near a bar and grill, where you could go inside for shelter if it rained. Jenni looked up at the sky, which had already grown quite dark, and she wasn't so sure she wouldn't be forced to run inside with the rest of the concertgoers.

Jenni stood in the back, mainly out of the way so she could hopefully go unseen. A crack of thunder sounded, and Jenni looked up at the sky again, bracing herself for the downpour that the weatherman had called for. "Just hold off until his set is over," she pleaded to the sky.

She wasn't sure why she was there, other than she wanted to get a feel for the man who had said I do to Tabby. She had the pleasure of meeting their kids and knew they were great, so she hoped to find a man up on the stage who didn't deserve the love of Tabby. It would make her feel better about having feelings for a married woman if Drew wasn't a good guy. Another crack of thunder sounded, and she shivered, not sure she would get the chance to see Drew perform.

"You did decide to come." Jenni whirled around and saw Charles, his wife, and their two kids.

"Auntie Jenni," his daughter Lesa squealed, throwing her arms around her.

"Hey, there. Glad to see you all again," she said, looking at Charles and Cecilia.

"Good to see you," Cecilia replied, pulling Jenni into a hug. "There's a large crowd," she said, parting from the embrace.

"The concert is rain or shine," Charles said. "Hopefully it won't pour until the performance is over." Jenni nodded and turned to the stage.

"Daddy, let's go up here," Noah, Charles's son, insisted, grabbing his father's hand and pulling him closer to the stage.

"Are you coming?" Charles asked, peering over his shoulder.

Jenni smiled and shook her head. "I'm good back here. Might have to cut out early. I'll see you all later." She waved and was grateful they didn't argue. The last thing she wanted was for Tabby to find out she was there. That would bring up too many questions she didn't want to answer. Although, there were a lot of people there, so it wasn't like she couldn't just go with the "I just wanted to enjoy a concert" story.

The music started, and a man came onto the stage. The crowd cheered, so Jenni joined in. "Hello, ladies and gentlemen. My name is Drew Brickly. Thank you for coming out to my first show after a long hiatus. It's good to be back."

As Drew performed, the audience continued to cheer for him. Jenni scanned her eyes around the crowd until she spotted Tabby and her two kids. They were all clapping, but Jenni saw how Tabby's happiness didn't quite shine through her smile and didn't reach her eyes.

I just want to see Tabby happy. The way she smiles around me and how she looks now are like night and day. Am I wrong for thinking we might have a future together? Jenni took a few minutes to get into the music, and she realized how good Drew truly was. She had initially shown up to find evidence that she had every right to go after a married woman, but as the band played, things slowly shifted. She just relaxed and clapped to the music along with the rest of the crowd.

She didn't see anyone from the hospital other than Charles and his family, and it was nice to be unnoticed while she stood in the back. The sound of thunder cracked and a few raindrops fell, but no one left.

As she watched Tabby and her two girls, she felt a twinge of regret for all of her thoughts about Tabby and Drew splitting up. That would be hard on their girls, and even if Tabby wasn't happy, she probably didn't want a divorce. What had Jenni been thinking by coming here?

Just one more song. One more song and she would leave and forget this silly notion about going after Tabby. When the song ended, the crowd jumped up and cheered for Drew.

"Thank you! Thank you! You're all wonderful, sticking out the rain with me and the band. Let me introduce everyone. On keyboards you have Joel Hathaway." The crowd cheered, and he went through the rest of the members, then turned back to the crowd. "As I mentioned at the start, I'm Drew Brickly, and I wouldn't be here if it wasn't for three amazing people in my life. I'd like to bring them up on the stage right now. Baby, come on up here."

Jenni, along with everyone else, looked toward where he pointed. Sure enough, he was pointing at Tabby and the two kids. They walked up on stage, and Drew turned to Tabby. "I haven't always been the best husband to you," he said. "But after tonight, I promise you that I'm going to change all that. I love you." He pulled Tabby into his arms and kissed her.

Jenni's jaw dropped. In that one moment, Jenni had gotten all her answers. She shouldn't confess her feelings. She didn't want to put Tabby in a stressful situation. It was better to remain friends and colleagues only. Jenni turned and walked away.

CHAPTER NINE

Tabby

A s the kiss ended, Tabby looked up at Drew. He gave her a huge smile, and the crowd cheered wildly. Tabby turned to the audience and squinted through the rain. Was that Jenni walking away from the crowd? She shook her head. She was probably just imagining it.

"This is my beautiful wife, Tabby," Drew continued. "And these are our beautiful children, Brittany and Callie." The crowd continued to cheer, and the rain fell around them even harder. "I'll tell you what, folks. You've all been so great, I'm going to perform one more song. Darling..." He motioned to the stage exit and Tabby, Brittany, and Callie headed off the stage. As Tabby descended the steps, she spotted Charles and his family.

"Thank you for coming!" she said.

He nodded. "Your husband has an amazing talent."

She smiled, not sure how to respond. She had no credit to take when it came to Drew's talent. She went back to the spot where they had stood before Drew had awkwardly called them on stage. She had been completely blindsided. She had to go up there and be the doting wife, or how would that look? The rain continued but Drew didn't let that stop them. They were under a canopy that was waterproof and kept the instruments safe. He did seem to be in his element, and it reminded her greatly of how he performed when they first got together.

It was emotional, even. She wiped a tear from her eye. The last song he played, titled *You Lift Me*, he had written for her when they had first started dating. A tear slid down her cheek and Brittany wrapped her arm around Tabby's waist. She looked down and Brittany gave her a soft smile. She kissed the top of her head, grateful for her daughter's support. The song ended, and the crowd applauded. She joined in, even cheering Drew as he walked off the stage.

People put their umbrellas up, shielding themselves from the rain, and Tabby did the same. She looked around, waiting to find Drew. After a moment, she spotted him off to the side. He was talking to a blonde woman who was dressed in very little clothing. She was leaning into him, trying to stay out of the rain.

Tabby stayed back until the woman walked away and left Drew alone. "Let's say goodbye to your dad," Tabby said. "I need to get you girls home to bed."

Callie groaned. "Do you?"

Tabby arched an eyebrow. "You know the deal. I said you needed to get home right after the show. That's why we drove separately." Both girls nodded, and they walked over to where Drew stood talking to the band. "We're gonna head out. I know you have autographs to sign or something."

Drew grabbed a towel and dried his hair as they stood under a canopy tent. "All right, babe," he said. He wrapped his arm around her waist and pulled her to him—possibly something that he was doing for show. He kissed her hard, with all eyes on them. Tabby played along since avoiding the kiss would have looked bad in front of the crowd.

"I'll try not to be too late. Don't miss me." He winked at Tabby, who gave a weak smile. How could they pretend like everything was all right? She wasn't the type to forgive and forget.

The three of them turned and left through a back alley to get to their car. When they reached the car and were inside, Callie spoke up. "Dad is great, right?"

Tabby looked over her shoulder to her daughter, who was in the back-seat. "Your dad is one of the best," she said. When she turned back around, she noticed that Brittany's brows were furrowed. Tabby reached across the seat to touch her daughter's hand. Drew's sudden change was confusing for her, so it must be even more confusing for their thirteen-year-old.

She pulled out of the spot and headed home. If Drew was sincere, that was one thing, but how could she trust any honesty coming from him? There had been too much deceit in their marriage to think that he was suddenly going to turn a corner. She didn't buy it.

When they pulled up to their house, Callie was sound asleep in the backseat. "Callie?" Tabby whispered, shaking her lightly.

Callie groaned, then turned and opened her eyes. "Are we there yet?" she mumbled, stretching out and sitting up in her booster seat.

"Yep. We're here. Brittany is already upstairs getting washed up for bed." She helped Callie out of the car, and they went inside and headed upstairs.

"Mom?" Callie asked.

"Yes?"

"When Dad gets home will you ask him to come upstairs and tuck me in?" She turned to look at Tabby as they reached Callie's bedroom. Tabby nodded and Callie pushed open her door.

"I'll be in in a minute to check on you." Thunder cracked from outside, shaking the whole house. Callie's eyes bugged out. "And read you a story for bed. There's nothing to fear, Peaches."

"Except fear itself," Callie replied.

"That's right." She pulled Callie into her arms, holding her tightly. "Now, go get cleaned up, and I'll be in soon."

Callie went in to grab her things as Tabby walked to Brittany's room. She knocked, then opened the door. Brittany sat on the edge of her bed, her head down as she clutched a stuffed teddy bear in her arms. For a moment, she looked like a toddler again, and Tabby's heart melted. Tabby walked in and sat in the seat next to her. When Brittany looked up, she was crying.

"What's wrong, sweet girl?" Tabby asked, brushing a couple of tears from her eyes.

"Tonight was like it used to be. Like I remembered it. But..." Her words trailed off. Tabby pulled her into her arms.

"It's going to be okay. I promise you. We're all going to be okay," Tabby said, stroking Brittany's hair.

As Tabby continued to soothe her daughter, she feared that was one promise she wouldn't be able to keep. She didn't want her children pulled into this, but that was exactly what was bound to happen.

"Shhhh," Tabby whispered. "Everything is going to be just fine."

THE LIGHT FLICKED ON IN THEIR BEDROOM. TABBY OPENED her eyes and turned to the door as Drew wandered into the room. He stumbled over to the bed and leaned on her. Immediately, she smelled Coke and Jack Daniels on his breath.

"What time is it?" she whispered, looking over to the clock. "Three o'clock?" She reached up to push him off of her. "Where have you been?"

"Baby, I need you," he said. "Shhhhhhh." He grabbed Tabby's wrist and pulled her to him, kissing her hard on the lips.

"No," she groaned, pushing him off her. "Talk to me." She pushed him back.

"Talk to you? I don't want to talk. I want to have sex. Don't deprive your husband." He straddled her as he pushed her down on the bed and tried to kiss her again. He grabbed her T-shirt and tugged on it.

"I said no!" She pressed her fists hard against his chest, pushing him until he fell off the bed.

"Are you kidding me?" he yelled, stumbling to his feet.

"You're drunk," she said, scooting off the bed. "How'd you get home?"

"Cab." He shrugged. "I'll get my car tomorrow. What's the big deal? We're *married*. And with the way I introduced you tonight, I assumed I'd have you like putty in my hands."

Tabby's jaw dropped. Putty in his hands? Who did he think he was messing with? She wasn't about to have sex with him because he was portraying himself as a caring husband.

"What was that? Trying to get good points with your boys? Trying to get people to think you're a great guy? Well, you might have fooled them, but you sure as hell didn't fool me. You got that?"

She hurried toward the door, but he beat her to it, blocking Tabby from leaving. "What are you going to do? Force me to have sex with you? You might be going through some changes, changes that I don't even understand, but you would never force me into doing something I didn't want to do. This isn't working and you know it."

Drew's eyes dropped down to the floor, and for a brief moment, Tabby saw sorrow in his gaze. When he looked up, his drunken eyes had softened, and he stepped aside. "I'm sorry," he mumbled.

She nodded and was reaching for the door handle when he spoke again. "They hired me on to do two more weeks of shows. Adults only. It'll be at a different venue this time—a club. We'll have some more money coming in. I guess I got carried away with the celebration."

Tabby hesitated and looked over at him. What bothered her the most was that she knew the man Drew was, and that man was not the same person standing before her now. She wanted to be happy for him. Deep down, she was, but her heart was shattered in so many ways that it was hard to hold on to.

"Congratulations, Drew," she quietly replied before walking out and going down the hall to the spare room. She escaped inside and closed the door behind her, then fell to her knees, her head down. There wasn't a way of getting past this. It was time to make some serious decisions, and that meant saying goodbye to the way her life had been the past twelve years.

CHAPTER TEN

Jenni

Jenni was eating lunch at the hospital. She took a bite of her burger and looked over the budget that she had spread out on the table. She stared at the money going out, comparing it to what came in. If she could swing a bit more funding, then maybe they would drop the horrible idea of firing people. It would be a struggle, but it was possibly worth it. She sipped on her Diet Coke as she stared at the numbers.

"What are you staring at so intensely?"

She looked up and saw Hanna standing there, leaning over to see the paperwork. "Nothing!" Jenni said, flipping the papers over. It was important to her that no one got wind of what was going on until they finalized the details.

"Clearly looks important," Hanna replied, laughing. "Mind if I sit here? I hate sitting by myself."

"Nope. Have at it." Jenni straightened the pile in front of her and pushed it to the side, making some more room. "Don't you usually eat with Tabby or one of the other nurses?" Jenni asked. She cringed when she mentioned Tabby's name, as she didn't want anyone to suspect that she was interested in her.

"Usually. But Sally and Ginger are off today and Tabby had lunch plans with her husband." She shrugged. "They're having a pretty important talk, I assume."

"Oh? How so?" Jenni asked, hoping she sounded nonchalant.

Hanna took a bite of her salad, then shrugged. "I don't know. I don't want to talk smack about her marriage or anything, especially since she's not here to defend it, or him. It's just, I sometimes get the feeling she wishes she had said 'I don't' at the aisle." She shrugged. "But, hey. Some marriages just aren't made to last. Divorce is a popular alternative, or so I hear."

Jenni frowned. She needed to know more. Tabby had told her about her unhappiness, but was she really considering divorce? "They have two kids, right?" Hanna arched an eyebrow. "I ran into them at the grocery store," Jenni explained hastily.

"Yeah," Hanna said, continuing to furrow her eyebrows. "Anyway, just because you have a child doesn't mean it's still all rainbows and kittens. This stays between us, okay?" Jenni nodded, drawn by Hanna's every word. "I've caught Tabby crying in the storage closet. She shrugs it off, but I've worked here long enough to see women who are abused, and sometimes I wonder if maybe Tabby is one of those women."

"Abused? Physically?"

"I couldn't say that," Hanna quickly replied. "It wouldn't be fair to go there without having physical proof. But sometimes emotional abuse is even worse—at least, in my opinion. And I could be totally wrong." She dug into her salad as Jenni watched her. "I really shouldn't have said anything. It's not my place, so please don't tell anyone I said this."

Jenni shook her head. "You don't have to worry about me. I won't say anything."

The two sat silently for a few minutes, each lost in their own thoughts. Jenni's mind was all over the place. Maybe everything Drew said at the concert was just for appearances, so that people would think he was a saint —a man who loved his wife and kids and would never harm them, whether physically or emotionally. She popped a fry into her mouth. It was already one of those days when she felt she needed a greasy burger and fries, and now, she realized she needed it even more.

"You've been here a lot lately," Hanna said, changing the subject. "Are you attached to the hospital food that much?"

Jenni smirked and nodded. "Yep. You caught me." She thought about the financial budget that still lay on the table. "I was just thinking that investing money in this place should mean I invest in the employees, too. That's all." She tilted her head. "How many years have you worked here, Hanna? And what's your number one reason you love your job?"

"Twenty-one years. Can you believe it? Sometimes it feels like no time has passed. Other days it feels like I'm living in a never-ending loop." Hanna snickered. "But I do love my job. I would say getting to meet new people is one of my favorite things about it. Are you interviewing staff for the news?" She laughed, taking a bite of her salad.

Jenni listened to the crunch of Hanna's chewing, searching for a reason. "No, but twenty-one years is no joke."

Even though Jenni didn't know yet who was getting terminated first, she knew it was likely that Hanna would be at the top of the list. They were starting with the most senior staff, and Hanna fit right in that bracket.

She dropped her eyes and stared at her food, her stomach dropping. She couldn't eat another bite. It was impossible having to let go of the people that she had gotten to know, even the ones she was newly getting to know. For whoever did get fired, it was going to be a blow to their families.

"I wouldn't do anything else," Hanna admitted quietly. "Capmed has become my life."

She smiled wider as she talked about her job, which bothered Jenni even more. Everyone was getting blindsided. Why couldn't they do this some other way? "I hate to eat and run, but I have to head out," Jenni said, grabbing her tray and snatching up her papers.

"All right. See ya." Hanna waved and Jenni hurried off, dropping her garbage into the trash. She rushed out of the cafeteria and headed straight for Brian's office. His secretary wasn't there. Good. Brian's door was shut, and she pounded on it. She heard a muffled response and opened the door.

Brian looked up. "Jenni! This is a surprise." He started to get up, but she held out her hand.

"Stay seated. This won't take long." She stepped into his office and pleaded her case. "I know that you think going behind everyone's back to terminate employees is the best route, but what if there was another option?"

"Like what?"

"Bring everyone together, sort of like an assembly. Talk to them. Get their insight. You brought the doctors here, but *they* aren't the ones who'll have to worry about losing their job. Prepare these people."

Brian sighed and looked down at his computer, shaking his head. "I know that you're thinking with your heart, and I have always valued your opinion, which is why we invite you to all the board meetings, but I don't want people freaking out. If I tell them that we're terminating employees, those who are safe will start to get nervous. They'll go out and look for other jobs and we don't want to have a mass exit. Do you understand that?"

"Yes," Jenni admitted. "But I also know that I have been in a similar position. I worked at a company that made layoffs. I was blindsided and lost my job. I bounced back, but some of these people might have families and have to support those families. I just think it would be important for them to have notice so that they can be prepared and maybe look for some other options."

"There will be severance packages," Brian stated. "We're not terminating anyone who isn't going to have compensation while they're trying to get back on their feet."

Jenni frowned. "But is that enough?"

He groaned. "Jenni, it probably would never be enough. That's something that we'll have to accept. I will say this, though. I'm doing everything I can to save some of these jobs. That's why we haven't carried this decision out yet. There are a few things that we're looking into. So don't fret."

She nodded, feeling a bit reassured by his words, and walked to the door. "Thank you for your time." She turned away and started to leave.

"Jenni?" She turned around, waiting for Brian to speak. "At the next board meeting, I'll be passing out a list of people we have to let go. You'll be one of the first to know. If you decide then to prepare someone from that list, or multiple someones, then I won't stop you. Just so you know."

She smiled. "Thank you." She turned away and closed the door behind her. Jenni reached her fingers up and massaged her temples, her migraine slowly working its way back into her head. It was the stress. She knew that, but hopefully soon she would have the knowledge she needed to move forward.

CHAPTER ELEVEN

Tabby

Tabby stared at Drew from across the table as he noisily crunched on his food and then wiped his mouth, barely removing the mayonnaise that was on his lower lip. She looked down at her half-eaten chicken, now cold. It was nearly time to get back to work, and as things stood, she wasn't confident they'd gotten anywhere with their talk.

"So, are you going to support me in my gigs?" Drew asked.

Tabby looked up and stared at him, ready to toss her napkin on her plate and storm out of there. Had he even spent the hour listening to her, or had everything gone in one ear and out the other?

"What?" he asked, chomping down on his sandwich.

"Counseling. Are you for it or against it?"

He smirked. "Do I even need to answer that?"

Her jaw clenched. If Drew wasn't willing to put in the effort, then why should she? It would be one-sided and fail miserably. She was trying here, but Drew didn't seem the least bit interested. She pushed her plate to the edge of the table.

"Are you finished, ma'am?" the waitress asked, approaching them.

She looked up and nodded, then looked across at Drew, waiting for the waitress to leave. "We've done counseling before, and it worked."

"Mostly," he said. "Guess it didn't stick if we have to do it again."

"Not because of my choice," she hissed, glaring at him. "Please tell me you don't see this as all my problem. We don't communicate anymore. I'm trying to fix this."

"We stopped communicating because you stopped coming home at night," he said. "That's not my problem."

"You're right. I was working, and for that, I apologize." She fought the urge to roll her eyes, then heaved a sigh. Arguing with him would only cause more turmoil, and Tabby had decided that working things out for their kids was something she was prepared to do. If she got even an inkling that he was ready for the same, she'd feel a lot better. "If you don't think counseling is something you're willing to put your heart into, then okay. We can separate right now."

His jaw dropped at those words, and Tabby continued to stare him down. His eyes softened a bit, and for just a little while, he looked like the man she had fallen in love with. She felt the tears burning at the back of her eyes and looked away from him. She didn't want to cry, not there, not in front of him, but she was struggling. She lifted a hand to her face and flicked the tears away.

"Don't cry, Tabby Bear," Drew whispered.

She turned back to him, her breath hitching. The last time he had called her that pet name was the night they had conceived Callie. It burned in her memory because it had been so long ago. She opened her mouth, but bit back her words. He reached out and touched her hand.

"I do love you. You know that, right?"

"I think so," she replied softly. She nodded and looked down at his hand as he intertwined their fingers. "And I love you, which is why I want us to get help."

"If it will make you feel better, then we'll do it." His eyes were actually showing concern, and she wanted to believe his every word.

"Thank you Drew." As the words left her, his phone started ringing. He grabbed it from the table and slid his finger across the screen to answer it. "I have to take this. Put the meal on the card." Then he was gone.

Tabby was too shocked to comprehend what had just happened. They were, for once, having a sweet moment. Then suddenly, it was gone, all because of a phone call? He couldn't call the person back? She grabbed some cash from her purse and tossed it down on the table. She didn't have time to wait for the waitress to bring her card back anyway. As it stood, she was already going to be late getting back from lunch. Luckily, the hospital was within walking distance, and she had good shoes on.

She got up from the table, her mind still on the abrupt way Drew left. She walked out of the restaurant and was headed back to the hospital when she paused and reached in her purse, rifling for her phone. She turned to go back to the restaurant when she saw Drew standing against the building, just hidden in an alley. When she drew closer, she could hear whispering. He looked up, and when his eyes met hers, he turned and walked away.

Tabby stared after him. He had definitely seen her. Who was he talking to and why the secrecy? Tabby frowned as she entered the restaurant, walking back to her table and spotting her phone. She grabbed it, relieved, but as soon as she did, her thoughts returned to Drew. *Maybe you're being paranoid. Maybe he didn't see you.*

As Tabby left the restaurant, she looked up and down the alley to see if Drew was still around. When she was certain he had disappeared, she hurried back to the hospital. Worrying about it now wasn't beneficial to anyone, least of all her. She had work to do. Still, it nagged at her, nearly making her crazy as she clocked back in.

She left the breakroom utterly confused, when then the worst-case scenario struck her. What if everything Drew had said to her was a lie, and he was only trying to appease her? What if the person on the other end of the line was a woman that Drew didn't want Tabby to find out about? Tears slowly started down her cheeks as she got in the elevator and pushed for her floor.

You don't even know. Why worry about something that might not even be true? So much disappointment had plagued her over the years that the only plausible excuses seemed to be the right ones. The doors opened, and she stepped off the elevator, her tears no closer to stopping. As she rounded the corner, she spotted Jenni. Their eyes met and Tabby quickly escaped into the storage room. No way was she going to get caught bawling in front of Jenni.

She leaned against the wall, covering her face in her palms.

"Tabby? May I come in?" Jenni's voice sounded through the door, followed by two knocks.

Tabby cleared her throat and desperately looked around for her escape, or at least something to wipe her eyes with. The knocks came again. She groaned and fell back against the wall. There was no use. She had been caught.

Tabby opened the door and Jenni's brows furrowed. "Are you okay?" she asked.

The look on Jenni's face was so concerned and so caring. It was such a contrast to Drew's constant indifference toward her, how he looked through her and was sweet one second only to flip personalities the next. She missed feeling cared for and loved. She missed having a stable relationship.

She flung herself into Jenni's arms, not caring how it looked. Jenni had been such a source of warmth ever since they had met, and the way she felt drawn to her was always in the back of her mind. For a moment, she just wanted to give in. She wanted Jenni to hug her, soothe her, and tell her that everything was okay. That all the conflicted feelings Tabby felt about her attraction to Jenni and her failing marriage would somehow make sense.

Without hesitating, Jenni returned the hug, wrapping her soft arms around Tabby and pulling her into a comforting embrace. "Tell me what's wrong," Jenni said with such tenderness that more tears flooded out of Tabby.

Tabby had reached her breaking point.

JENNI LISTENED INTENTLY AS TABBY SPILLED EVERYTHING. From the way her marriage had been slowly crumbling over the years, to the moment she had seen Drew hurrying away from her in that alley. Jenni didn't interrupt, and Tabby was relieved to finally get it all off her chest. She looked up and sighed.

"I didn't mean to blubber that whole story out to you," she said, wiping the tear from her eye. "It just needed to come out, and I guess I didn't realize how much I had to tell someone. I'm sorry, for your sake, that that person was you."

Jenni shook her head. "Give me a minute." She left the closet and Tabby stared awkwardly at the door. Had she scared her off? A moment later, Jenni returned with a box of Kleenex.

"Thank you," Tabby sniffed.

"You don't have to apologize. Not to me. You needed to let this out and I'm glad I was here. I'm sorry that you're going through this," she said, frowning, "but I don't regret you telling me all that." There was a slight pause, and she looked at Tabby. "So he was your best friend, huh?"

Tabby huffed. "Well, he was, at one point. I guess I never wanted to admit that things had gotten so rough, especially not to someone I was just getting to know." Tabby looked down at the floor, suddenly feeling vulnerable. "You must think I'm a real nutcase."

They met each other's eyes, and Jenni quickly shook her head. "I don't. Not at all."

Tabby wanted to believe that, but after spilling her life story to this woman, she worried that she would be seen as less of a woman in front of her. But Jenni seemed to have a kind and honest demeanor, and Tabby let her fears slip away.

"Drew thinks that I should just be his happy wife and support him when he goes out to all these music gigs, but someone has to stay home with the girls. These gigs are at a club, so what does he expect me to do with Callie and Brittany? I *will* support him, by being where our daughters need me. At home." Tabby wiped her eyes and shook her head. "I just never dreamed my marriage would come to this."

"Are your parents around?" Jenni quietly asked, taking a seat on the floor next to Tabby.

"My dad had a heart attack a few years back. We sent him into a nursing home because my mom couldn't take care of him anymore. He died a couple of months later. My mother moved to Florida for her job and she'll probably retire there. We used to be really close. Then I married Drew and, well, things sort of changed."

"She doesn't come around to see her grandchildren?" Jenni asked.

"They FaceTime. But, no, not a whole lot. She just doesn't see eye to eye with Drew on most things. Sadly, I'm now really seeing that, too."

Jenni nodded. "Seems like you have a burden on your shoulders and don't really have the support system to handle it. So, trust me, I don't mind listening."

Tabby smiled. "Thank you." She looked at her watch and groaned. "And now I'm going to get fired because I was supposed to be back thirty minutes ago."

"I'll handle that," Jenni said, standing to her feet.

Tabby frowned. "What? No. I can take care of it."

Jenni tilted her head. There was a sincerity in her look that made Tabby bite back her argument. "You can't go out there feeling the way you're feeling. Pull yourself together. Put your chin up." She smiled as she pressed her thumb to Tabby's chin and lifted it, and smiled.

Tabby lifted her gaze to meet Jenni's. Despite feeling torn about the possibility that Drew was having an affair, she smiled. Tabby felt compelled to do what Jenni said, because as it stood, Jenni was the only one who seemed supportive of Tabby.

"You got this," Jenni said.

Tabby reached out and touched Jenni's arm before she could leave. Jenni looked over her shoulder and Tabby released a breath. "Please don't tell anyone about this. I mean, my mental breakdown and my marriage problems. I try to hide it, you know?"

Jenni nodded, but as she turned, Tabby reached out for her arm again. "I was going to ask, were you at the concert the other day? I thought I saw you, but when I went searching for you after, you were gone."

Jenni looked away, then shook her head. "Must've been my doppelganger. I had better get back to work myself. I've got you, though." Then she spun on her heel and left the closet.

Tabby leaned back against the wall and stared up at the ceiling. That was strange. She was almost positive she had seen Jenni, but that didn't matter. What mattered now was pulling herself together. She couldn't fathom what Jenni would tell her superiors, but she trusted her. And though she suspected things about Drew, she didn't have any proof. And there was still the possibility that it was all in her mind. Either way, she wanted to get to the bottom of it, once and for all.

CHAPTER TWELVE

Jenni

T he conversation with Tabby wouldn't leave her. She didn't know why Tabby felt the need to stick it out with her husband, and surely her daughters would be better off without a toxic marriage playing through their lives.

Still, she could only stand on the sidelines and watch it play out in front of her. It saddened her, but she didn't know what else she could do about it. Still, that didn't stop her from walking into the club that Drew was performing at that Saturday night. She would only stay an hour, tops. At least, that's what she told herself.

As she stood in the back, leaning against a table, a beer in hand, Drew came onto the stage, the band playing behind him. She sipped on her beer and tried not to sway to the music. He was talented, but she was there to be a spy, not enjoy herself. What she was spying for, exactly, she wasn't sure. She just had the feeling she needed to get to know Drew a little bit more to have a real understanding of who the guy was.

"Let me hear you all sing," he yelled out. Jenni looked around. Everyone there seemed to know the song and was singing it right along with him. She then looked back to the stage and really took the time to study Drew. He seemed charismatic and down to earth, and the crowd seemed to love him. She caught herself clapping in time to the music. As the song died, she stopped clapping and shook her head. It was stupid to get too caught up in it. She felt like she was just making a fool out of herself by being there.

She listened to a few more songs, after which the band took a break. She turned around to leave. If she was only going to fall under his spell—more like ruse—then she didn't want any part of it. All marriages had bad spurts, and maybe Tabby and Drew were only going through one of those. If she wanted to help, she needed to give them the respect their marriage deserved.

Before she could leave, though, she spotted Charles and Cecilia. His eyes lit up as he saw her. "Hey there. I didn't know you were going to come back out to another concert. Cool scene, isn't it?"

Jenni forced a smile. It was a scene that was too young for her liking, but then again, Charles was only a few years younger than her. Maybe she had somehow gotten too old. "Just came by for a drink. I didn't even know he was performing." She turned to Charles and Cecilia. "Where are the kiddos?"

"With the babysitter." He wrapped his arm around his wife. "Out on a date with this beautiful woman. It isn't often that I get to hang out, and we enjoyed the concert the other day, so I thought we would take advantage of one of his gigs. He's a great musician, and there's nothing like showing support for Tabitha." He took a sip of his beer. "Do you want to have a seat and join us?"

"No, but thank you. I was just about to head out." She started to move away from them.

"Nonsense," he said. "It's early. At least have another drink." He got up from his seat. "I'll go get you one. What do you want?"

"You don't have to do that," Jenni argued, "but thanks. I'll go grab my beer." She turned from the table and went to the bar. One more beer and then she'd be out of there.

"What can I get ya?" the man behind the bar asked.

"I'll take a beer—anything you have on tap." Jenni sat down on the stool and waited.

"This seat taken?" She turned to see Drew, of all people, grabbing the stool next to her. He had a smirk on his lips, and she shook her head, then quickly looked away from him. There was a gleam in his eyes the moment she met his gaze. He continued. "It's a beautiful night to stay in, don't you think?" He placed his order, and she frowned, turning to him.

"Meaning?"

"It's starting to storm out there. Reminds me of the last time I performed, at an outdoor venue. I'd definitely say this is a better fit. Wouldn't you?" He took a sip of his beer and their eyes met again. He winked as Jenni grabbed her glass and downed more of the beer than she should have in one gulp.

"Have a good night," Jenni muttered.

He reached out and touched her arm. It was a soft touch that sent the hair on Jenni's arm standing. "Don't rush off. The concert is only in intermission. It will be back for another hour, then maybe after that we can get to know one another better." He winked at her, and she stared back in shock. "Come on. You're sexy, and I saw you watching me from afar. I'm game if you are."

Jenni looked down at his ring finger. His ring wasn't there, but she saw the faint tan line. She looked up and slowly pulled her arm back. "I don't think my girlfriend would like that too much."

He shrugged. "Bring her along. We'll make beautiful music together."

Jenni looked at her drink, considering tossing it straight into his face, then met his sneaky grin. He was a player, and Jenni wondered if Tabby realized that. If he was hitting on her, then chances were that he had hit on several other women along the way. Tabby deserved better than that.

"Not interested," she replied.

He looked surprised, then quickly composed himself. "Babe, that's not usually the response. Are you sure you know what you're saying? Perhaps you're lost in my dazzling smile." He reached out for her wrist, clamping down with his grip. She tugged her arm back, but his grip got tighter.

Jenni latched down on her lower lip, glaring at him as he kept his hand strongly wrapped around her wrist. "Listen here. When a woman says no, she means no. Got that? Let go of my wrist before I knee you where it hurts most." He released her wrist, and she stepped back from him. "Have a great night." She yanked her hand away, spun on her heel, and hurried to leave.

"Jenni," Charles called out. She had forgotten about Charles and

Cecilia. She forced a smile as she glanced in his direction. "Aren't you going to get that drink?"

"Already had it. But I'm starting to get a migraine, so I'm just going to head home. You both enjoy the rest of your date. I'll see you around." She escaped before they could ask any more questions.

She was only a few feet from the door when she heard her name. "Jenni? Is that you?" Jenni jerked her attention to another table, where Hanna and a man sat. Hanna jumped up. "I didn't expect to see you here."

Jenni gave a slight grin and turned to look up at the stage as Drew rejoined the band and started to strum some notes on his guitar. "Just came in for a drink," she lied.

Hanna nodded. "Oh. That's Tabby's husband." Hanna pointed to the stage.

Jenni's jaw dropped. "Oh wow, really? What a coincidence!" Her head started pounding, and she really felt that migraine coming on. "Small world, huh?" She backed up toward the door. "I had best be going. Not feeling the greatest."

"Oh? Take care!" Hanna said, waving and turning back to the guy she was with—probably her husband, Jenni assumed.

Jenni left the club with a sick feeling in her stomach. It was possible that Hanna would tell Tabby she saw her there. She just hoped that Hanna would forget the short encounter and be too engrossed in the man she was with. Otherwise, Jenni was liable to have plenty of explaining to do.

CHAPTER THIRTEEN

Tabby

The sound of light music played over the speakers as Tabby sat at the desk and stared at the computer absentmindedly. She grabbed a pen and started tapping, lightly going along with the music, but then dropped it and rubbed her eyes. If the afternoon was going to continue dragging on this long, she couldn't fathom being stuck there for one more minute. The good thing was that the ER didn't have enough sick patients to occupy the three nurses on duty. The bad thing was that it meant sitting and staring at the computer, hoping for a trauma patient to come in, which wasn't great.

She groaned and stood up from the computer, turning to find Hanna coming out of the supply closet with an armload of supplies tucked in her arms. Tabby hurried over to help, wheeling a cart over and grabbing some items before they fell to the floor.

Hanna snickered. "It's pretty slow when two of the three nurses have to stretch to find things to do. But Sally has it all under control. What are we needed for, eh?"

"Supplies, supplies, and more supplies," Tabby chuckled.

"A nurse's job is never done," Hanna joked as they entered a vacant room.

The quietness of the room settled over them as Tabby and Hanna restocked the supplies. As her mind wandered, Tabby thought of the way Jenni had held her and comforted her at her lowest moment. Though none of her problems were fixed, being with Jenni like that made the weight on her shoulders feel lighter. She smiled softly to herself.

After fifteen minutes of going room to room, Hanna looked over at Tabby. "Did you see Jenni today or something?"

"No, why?"

"Because you're smiling."

Tabby froze. *Strange. How did Hanna know I was smiling because of Jenni?*

Before she could get into it, Hanna switched topics. "Oh, I went and saw Drew last night."

Tabby hesitated, then slid her eyes to Hanna. "Oh yeah? How was it?" she asked nonchalantly.

"Good. He's super talented. I know I've mentioned I thought so before, but he really seems to be in his element when he's performing. And the crowd adores him."

"Yeah, they usually do," Tabby muttered, reaching to the back of the drawer to pull some instruments forward.

"What was that?" Hanna asked.

"Oh, nothing. Glad you enjoyed it."

"Matt and I both did," she said. She looked up and met Tabby's glance. "I know you're a very private person, Tabby, but are things okay at home?"

Tabby quickly looked down at the drawer she was working on. "I don't know what you're getting at. You're pretty private as well. I think it was a few years before I even knew Matt existed." Tabby chuckled to make light of Hanna's question.

Hanna didn't laugh back, so Tabby sighed. "Things can be complicated, but you know that. Marriage isn't for the faint-hearted."

"That is very true. I just want to make sure you know that you have someone here you can chat with if you want. That's all." She gave Tabby a heartwarming smile, which Tabby appreciated, but bringing her home life into the hospital was something Tabby felt she had to steer clear of. Besides, now that she had Jenni to talk to, she didn't have to worry about not having a friend she could confide in.

"What brought this on, anyway? Did you think I was hiding something about my marriage?"

"Well, I sort of expected to see you at Drew's performance last night. When I didn't, I wondered if maybe something was going on at home. There's nothing to be ashamed of, and I'm sorry for assuming. As you said, marriage is tough. Lord knows Matt and I have had our share of issues. We've worked through them, but we also never had kids. We haven't had to share our love and time with a family. It's only the two of us."

"I appreciate your concern, but since we do have kids, someone has to stay home with them. There's nothing more to it than that. Thanks for voicing your concern. No worries, though."

Tabby closed the drawer she had been working on for way too long, and Hanna said, "You're welcome. And if you ever need to talk…"

"I'll know where to turn. Got it. Thank you." They left the room and moved to the last room in the hallway that needed restocking.

"Oh, you know who I saw at the performance?" Hanna asked.

"Who?" Tabby asked, pushing the cart into the room.

"Jenni. I was surprised to see her. She said that she just happened to be at the club. What a coincidence, right?"

Tabby stared down at the cart of supplies that were left to be loaded into the room. It was more than just a coincidence. She had confided in Jenni about Drew and mentioned the club and his upcoming performances. She knew he was going to be there. What was she doing? Spying?

"Tabby?" Hanna asked, breaking into the silence.

"Sure, it's a coincidence, but I'm sure bigger coincidences have happened. That's all she said? That she just happened to be at the club?"

"Yep. I just bumped into her for a few seconds."

"Was she alone?" Tabby inquired.

"I didn't see her with anyone, but as I mentioned, it had happened so fast," Hanna responded, continuing to stock the room.

Tabby wasn't sure how to feel. She didn't want to jump to conclusions, but it was odd that Jenni had gone to see Drew right after she had told Jenni about her suspicions. Jenni had been so kind, but she didn't ask Jenni to help, only listen. It felt like Jenni was overstepping an unspoken boundary by going to check up on Drew behind her back—if that's what she did.

As they worked, Tabby got a call. "It's the hospital," she said.

"Maybe it's an emergency," Hanna replied, dropping her items back into the cart.

"Hello," Tabby answered.

"It's Bianca at the front desk. Jennifer Jennison is here to see you. Are you free?"

"Sure," Tabby replied. "I'll be right there." She pocketed her phone and looked at Heather. "I have a visitor. I'll catch up with you after."

"No problem. I'm almost done anyway."

Tabby quickly left the room and walked down the hallway to meet Jenni. This was good timing, as Tabby wanted to talk to her. She didn't appreciate Jenni going to stalk her husband. What was that going to prove, anyway?

Bianca was waiting on a patient when Tabby reached the desk, and Jenni was leaning against the counter. When Tabby walked around the corner, Jenni looked up and met her eyes, stepping away from the desk.

"We need to talk," Jenni stated.

"You're right. We do," Tabby responded. She grabbed Jenni's arm and pulled her behind her toward the nearest closet. Once inside, she locked the door and turned to stare at Jenni. "I know you went to see Drew perform the other night and it can't be a coincidence. I didn't ask for your help with him."

Jenni's jaw dropped. "I know you didn't ask for my help, but what about your husband? Don't you want to know the truth?"

"You can't go out stalking my husband. What made you think that it would be a good idea?"

"I wanted to protect you."

Tabby laughed. "Protect me? I don't need your protection. And to find out from Hanna because she saw you there? Luckily, she thinks you just happened to be there, but you and I both know that's not true. This is not okay, Jenni. You should have just minded your own business."

"You deserve better than Drew," Jenni insisted.

Tabby threw up her arms. "That's not for you to say. I shouldn't have trusted you. You betrayed my trust by going to spy on him. What point are you trying to make?" Tabby turned and stepped away, frustrated.

"I know that when I have a friend who's hurting, I try to fix it. Blame me for that—for caring too much. I guess I'm a monster for trying to do the right thing."

Tabby turned on her heel and stared at her. "But it got you nowhere, did it? Brava." Tabby clapped. "It just doesn't make sense that you thought this was the only route you could take."

Jenni stepped closer to her. "It made me see the jerk you're married to."

Tabby snorted. "What did he do? Throw a guitar pick out to a beautiful woman, or wink at her? I know what musician life means. Drew is a musician, and that's how he drew me in. A guitar pick and an eyewink. It's not exactly something he's going to change. I get it, and that's what I signed up for. He comes home to me, and that's what matters."

"You don't really know who your husband is, Tabby. You think he's this guy who's just gotten distant at home and doesn't see how hard-working you are. And barely acknowledges you when he is home. You see him as someone who doesn't listen, but deep down you'll accept that because he's your husband and the father of your children. But what I saw..."

Jenni shook her head, and Tabby frowned. "I saw a man who goes to a club and is grateful you're not there because then he can flirt with all the women he wants behind your back and you'll have no idea. I'm here telling you the truth. Whether you want to listen to me or not, that's totally fine, but he's a cheat, Tabby. Until you realize that, you're liable to screw up your life even further."

"What are you talking about?" Tabby asked, clenching her jaw.

"I'm talking about your husband, the one that you said doesn't understand what you go through. The one you said doesn't see you and puts on a front for others. You deserve more than what he's willing to offer. Because last night, if he had started chatting up the wrong woman, he would have been hooking up in the back alley or something. He tried it with me. And then he offered me a threesome with him and my 'girlfriend.'"

Tabby's jaw dropped. "*What*?"

"I lied and told him my girlfriend wouldn't appreciate it if I hooked up with him, and he said to bring her along."

Tabby laughed and shook her head. "He was clearly joking. Drew might be a jerk, and I know I expressed doubts about his faithfulness, but he's not a cheater. I would know if he was cheating on me." Her stomach churned. Even as she said it, Tabby had a hard time believing her own words.

"That's what you think," Jenni huffed. "I'm just telling you what I saw. He was going to have sex with me if I gave him the green light."

"Stop saying that!" Tabby said.

Jenni moved closer, trying to comfort Tabby with a soft touch on her shoulder, but Tabby jerked away. The way Jenni's eyes stared deeply into her soul sent chills up Tabby's spine. Jenni tried to touch her again, and this time she didn't pull away. Jenni drew her closer, until their bodies were mere inches apart. Jenni continued to close the distance between them until her lips pressed against Tabby's. Tabby's head spun as the kiss continued and she gave in to her desire of wanting to feel emotionally and physically connected with someone. At that moment, nothing else mattered except the feeling of Jenni's body so close to her own.

As Jenni's tongue slid across hers, Tabby realized what she was doing and pulled back. "Why did you...?" Tabby gasped, pushing Jenni away and turning.

"Tabby..." Jenni whispered. Tabby moved quickly to the door. She wanted to get out of there.

"Ugh!" Jenni groaned suddenly.

Tabby turned to find Jenni clutching her head and kneeling on the ground. No matter how much Tabby wanted to leave, she only had one option. Something was wrong with Jenni, and she needed her help.

CHAPTER FOURTEEN

Jenni

J enni looked at Tabby as Tabby nervously bit on her fingernails. The kiss from moments ago was still racing through her mind, but she knew that Tabby had to be thinking about it even harder. Still, Tabby wouldn't look in her direction, and now they were stuck in a hospital room.

"I'm fine. It's just a migraine. Nothing I haven't been through before. There's no reason for me to be in this hospital bed."

Tabby shook her head. "You said that you've gotten them for years. You were brought down to your knees in pain. Wouldn't you feel better getting this checked out?"

"All the doctors have done what they could do. I've seen plenty."

"I would just feel better if we knew," Tabby murmured.

"Don't you have to get back to work?" Jenni asked.

"I'm on break. Now, just be quiet and wait for Dr. Wesley to get here." Tabby leaned back against the counter and dropped her eyes to the floor.

Jenni leaned back in bed and stared up at the ceiling. This wouldn't have happened if she hadn't felt the urge to immediately rush to Tabby and give her the news about Drew. What did she think that would accomplish? Did she think Tabby would fall into her arms and thank her for stalking him, then give her a passionate kiss? Well, the kiss had happened, but now things were abruptly changing between them.

A knock sounded on the door, and Jenni perked up. "Yes?" she called out.

Dr. Wesley opened the door and walked inside. "Hello, Jenni," he greeted. He looked over at Tabby, surprised. "Tabby? I didn't know you were in here."

"I was with her when she collapsed."

He nodded slowly. "I didn't collapse," Jenni blurted out.

From the corner of her eye, she saw Tabby roll her eyes, then focused her attention on Dr. Wesley as he spoke. "Well, let's hear what's going on. So, you have migraines? For how long?"

"Twenty years or so," Jenni said under her breath.

He looked up, arching an eyebrow. "And this is the first time you're having them checked out? Are they getting worse?"

"No, it's not her first time, but the doctors haven't been able to fix this, and the migraines are clearly getting worse," Tabby interrupted. "She was literally on her knees."

Jenni shifted her gaze to Tabby. Why was she suddenly so invested in how Jenni fared? She glanced back at Dr. Wesley.

"Tabby isn't wrong. The migraines have slowly been getting worse. I've taken ibuprofen, but it doesn't always do the trick. I've seen doctors, but they say there really isn't anything they can do for me." She shrugged. "So I just try to deal with them. Sometimes they're pretty debilitating, but I doubt anything will change, and I wouldn't be in this hospital bed if it weren't for Tabby here." She grimaced when Tabby shot her a look. "If you'd like to send me on my way, that's fine. I have a board meeting to get to."

"Well, before you rush off, I'd like to ask you a few more questions, if that's all right."

Jenni nodded, seething that she was there, and just wanting to bolt. "I'll answer whatever questions you have."

"When's the last time you saw a doctor?" he asked.

She shrugged. "For the migraines? Probably five years."

Dr. Wesley wrote that down, then looked up. "Right now, how's the pain? On a scale from one to ten."

"Fifteen? Maybe twenty," she teased.

He smirked. "I'll just write 'off the charts.'"

"Good idea," Jenni replied, glancing over to Tabby, who had gone back to chewing on her nails. The concern that Tabby appeared to have for her left Jenni on edge, with that one question hovering over her. Why?

"Have you taken any meds today for it?" he asked.

"No. I sometimes attempt to get through the pain without meds. I know it sounds silly, but it's how I try to manage."

Dr. Wesley looked at Tabby. "Will you go get her something from the cabinet?"

"Right away." Tabby hurried away and Jenni followed her with her eyes. Dr. Wesley cleared his throat as the door shut behind Tabby, drawing Jenni's eyes back to him.

"Tabby is a great nurse, but an even better friend."

"I can see that," Jenni responded.

Dr. Wesley eyed Jenni for a few moments. "Have you met Dr. Antonia Samson in the neurological department?" he asked.

"I don't think so," Jenni slowly replied.

"Well, she's fairly new to Capmed, but I have gotten to know her over the past two months, and she comes very highly recommended in the neurological field. She was telling me about this research study that she's part of. They are working on a new drug for migraines, and if you qualify, all costs are paid for by the research study. They're only taking a few candidates, and I could recommend you. It's fast-moving, though, so you would have to let me know right away."

The door opened and Tabby came back in with the pills and water. "Thanks," Jenni said, grabbing them from her. She quickly downed the pills, drinking a third of the water. "What kind of effects would I possibly see?" she asked Dr. Wesley.

He shrugged. "For that, you might want to confer with her. You know that all drugs have possible side effects. Sometimes you have to weigh the good with the bad."

"What's going on?" Tabby asked, looking between Dr. Wesley and Jenni.

Jenni saw Tabby's concern, but turned back to Dr. Wesley and said, "I would like to meet with her." She ignored Tabby's question because it wasn't her choice whether Jenni participated in the study, and she didn't want anyone to find a reason to convince her not to do the study. "Thank you."

"My pleasure. You'll hear from us no later than tomorrow. I'm sure she'll want to get you in right away. But in the meantime, I would suggest continuing self-medicating when you need it. You can't expect to feel well enough not to need the pills fully. They can be your crutch until you're able to have your appointment."

"Thanks again, Dr. Wesley."

He smiled. "Take care, Jenni. If you need anything, don't hesitate to reach out to me." He shook her hand, then looked over at Tabby.

Tabby's brows furrowed, which Jenni tried to ignore. Jenni swung her legs over the hospital bed and followed after Dr. Wesley. Tabby was only a couple of steps behind, but hurried up beside her, nearly bumping into her.

"What was that about?" Tabby asked. "Are you going to see another doctor?"

Jenni stopped walking and turned to her. "There's this specialist who Dr. Wesley thinks might be able to get me into a research study—a new drug or something for migraines. I'm having him set up an appointment."

Tabby frowned. "I don't know. I mean, if it's new, it's hard telling what the side effects could be, and I think it could be worse off for you."

Jenni sighed. "I understand your concern on the matter but it's my decision and my decision alone. If I think this could help me, then it might be worth it. I've been struggling with this for twenty years and I don't want to struggle for twenty more. Can you respect that?" Tabby nodded without hesitation. "Good."

Before Jenni could leave to get to her board meeting, Tabby spoke up. "I think we should talk about what happened before your migraine came on."

Jenni shrugged. "You were leaving the storage closet. That's how I recall it."

Tabby shook her head. "You know what I mean. What happened before that?" She fidgeted from one foot to the other and Jenni dropped her gaze.

"We don't have to talk about it. Emotions were running high. We can just acknowledge it happened and just leave it at that. I really have to get to my meeting."

"If that's how you feel," Tabby quietly replied.

It wasn't, but it was the easiest way she could get out of there without having to dive into the whole conversation again, especially hashing over the fact that Drew had flirted with her and that Tabby didn't want to believe it.

"It's for the best," Jenni replied. "I'll see you around."

She spun on her heel and hurried to the elevator. It *was* all for the best, even though, in that discouraging moment, her heart slowly broke into two. She had finally opened herself up to moving on from missing Wendy only to lose the one person who had pushed her there.

By the time Jenni reached the conference room, most of the attendees were already there. She sat down in one of the few empty chairs. Less than a minute later, Brian walked into the room. He looked around and sat down at the end of the table and indicated the folders that were placed in front of each seat. Jenni opened hers to see a blueprint of the hospital's beginning plans. She looked it over and continued to the next page.

It was a single two-paged sheet—*Terminated Employees*, it read. She flipped it over to the other side, scanning the names that were on the list. Her eyes landed on Tabitha Brickly, and she froze. Hanna was listed too, as were several other people she had gotten to know over the years she had worked with the hospital. She looked up. Brian was speaking to one of the advisory board members. She cast another look over the list, her eyes shifting back to Tabby's name. This wasn't happening. She had to do something to change their minds. Tabby needed her job, and Jenni wasn't going to sit back and watch the hospital tear that away from her.

Brian cleared his throat, and all eyes went to him. "I have called you all here so we can go over the list of staff members that we'll be letting go first."

Jenni raised her hand, and he looked straight at her. "Yes?"

"Why these people? What's the reasoning behind it? I see several people listed on this list who are considered the best employees Capmed has. What's going on?"

Brian looked around the table until focusing his attention on her. "I'll be explaining much of this during the meeting. If you have any questions beyond that, you're free to speak with me after the meeting is adjourned. Okay?"

Jenni nodded and sat up straight in her chair, the headache still moving through her head. The pills would hopefully kick in soon, but then again, her stress was causing enough pain to keep the migraine going despite the medication.

Brian continued speaking, but only about finances and things that had already been discussed at prior meetings. Jenni kept her eyes down on her folder, itching to storm out of there, telling him that what they thought was the right way to go was, in fact, all wrong. Her throat grew dry halfway through his financial monologue. She did get up, but only to go over to the table and grab a glass of water. She went back to her seat and took a sip, letting the words flicker through her mind.

"Any questions on the financial aspect of this decision?" Brian asked the room.

Jenni looked up, relieved to see no one raising their hand. After all, they had already gone over countless times the finances that had led to this choice.

"Moving on," he said. "So, to answer some questions—why these employees? I can see disapproval on some faces over the termination list, and I want to start there. We feel that going with the ones who have worked here the longest will give us more financial gain. It is unfortunate that some of our best will be the ones hit, but that's just something we'll have to deal with. None of this is personal. In due time, I'm hoping that some of these employees will be able to be rehired. Of course, we won't know that until construction is nearly finished."

A hand went up, and Brian called out, "Yes, Charles?"

Jenni turned to face Charles, holding her breath.

"There are a few names on here that do cause me some concern. For starters, Tabitha." He hesitated, and Jenni released her breath. If anyone could get through to Brian, it was Charles.

Brian nodded in acknowledgment. "When we made these cuts, we didn't intend on cutting with our heart. We went solely by those who have years of service. That's all. Again, I fully believe that there will be a lot of unhappy doctors in the bunch. After all, they're losing strong nurses, but I know that we have trained all the nursing staff well, and they will be able to pick up where we're suffering from loss. Trust me on this. I've been doing this for almost thirty years, and I know what I'm doing. Let's move on."

Jenni's face, and her heart, fell. Brian was making these cuts without taking into consideration the lives it was going to hurt. She sat back, waiting for him to reach the end of his spiel, and hoping he would open up the floor for more questions. However, as the meeting died down, he didn't open the floor again.

"Folks, I have to get to another meeting. If you have further questions, you can filter them through my office. Have a great rest of your day, everyone."

Jenni jumped up and hurried over to him before he could leave. "I just have one question," she pleaded. He turned to look at her as everyone else filtered out of the room. "Do you think terminating the employees who have the most experience is good business? You're taking away staff that has built a connection with many patients. I don't see how that could be the right answer."

Brian sighed. "Jenni, I have always valued your opinion, but in this case, you have to stick to your own lane. This isn't your realm of business, and you need to leave the choices to the ones in charge. Our choices weren't made lightly. I know that while you and others might be frustrated, this decision isn't up for debate. Now, I need to go."

"How long before you start letting these people know they're out of a job?" she asked, wondering how long she had to change the current outcome.

He turned to face her. "Two weeks is when we're making the cuts." He didn't say anything more than that, just headed toward his office, while Jenni stared blankly at a couple of people who were still milling around the conference room.

She shook her head. That wasn't much time to work to change this unhappy fate. She knew one thing, though. There wasn't any way she could be around Tabby while this major secret was looming over her head. She also didn't want to be the one to spill the news to her. This would be something that would tear Tabby down even more. Jenni wasn't about to watch that, or even let it happen. If there was any way around it, she'd find it. But hiding it from Tabby was going to be tough.

CHAPTER FIFTEEN

Tabby

Tabby flipped to the nearest radio station, not caring about the music. She turned on her vacuum cleaner and ran it through the living room, unable to hear the music anyhow. The moment she started, her mind went to the kiss with Jenni two days earlier. *Stop thinking about it, Tabby. It's not doing you any good.* Yet, her heart and head had both replayed that memory over the past forty-eight hours.

Even though it laid heavy on her heart, she decided right away that she wasn't going to tell Drew about how Jenni had claimed he had flirted with her at the club. There were a couple of reasons why. One, she didn't want him angry that one of her friends had spied on him and to consider that maybe she was behind all of it. And two, there wasn't any proof that Jenni was telling the truth. She felt guilty for thinking Jenni would lie, though, and she wondered if she was simply in denial. The scenario she now weaved in her mind was that Jenni was secretly attracted to her and looking for a reason to come between her and Drew, but that was a crazy thought. Her marriage had already been on the rocks even before she had met Jenni.

She shifted her vacuum cleaner when she realized she had been running it over the same spot for the past fifteen minutes. She finished up in the living room and turned the vacuum off. Cleaning the house was something she found therapeutic, especially on her days off. She wasn't going to waste the day away by not doing any housework.

She grabbed the dust rag and ran it over the living room furniture. Soon, her thoughts went back to Jenni. Never had a kiss opened her up to so much excitement as it had when Jenni had kissed her. She had met Drew when she was a teenager, and he was the first—and only—guy she had ever kissed. It was overwhelming to think that her most erotic and delicious kiss came from Jenni.

Tabby stopped moving the rag mid-stroke and closed her eyes. The kiss came crashing back to her like it was the only thing keeping her alive. Jenni's tongue had stroked Tabby's in a way that had lit Tabby on fire. She shivered as her thoughts made her melt. She could practically feel the way her body would melt against Jenni's, and she had to snap her eyes open and catch her breath. If one kiss had Tabby feeling this way, what would a whole electrifying night do? You will never find out, Tabby thought firmly to herself.

She shook her head and moved to the hallway, dusting the table and light fixture that was in the foyer.

With every step she took, her thoughts leaned heavily toward the one woman she wanted to put out of her mind. Her phone rang from the living room, and Tabby was relieved to have something that could distract her from her memories of that moment in the closet. She rushed into the living room, turning the stereo off as she passed it. When she grabbed her phone, though, she spotted Britney's school's phone number. Her chest caved in.

"H...hello," she stammered.

"Is this Tabitha Brickly?" a man asked on the other end of the line.

"Yes, this is she."

"This is Adrian Parker, the principal at your daughter, Brittany's, school."

"Right, Principal Parker. How can I help you?" She attempted to make her voice sound stable and not torn up, but she couldn't think of any good reasons as to why Principal Parker would be calling.

"Your daughter was brought into my office. It appears she has gotten herself into a fight, and while I believe every story has two sides, we have a no-fighting policy. I would like to meet with you and your husband to discuss the matter."

Tabby nodded, her throat dry. She swallowed. "I will try to reach my husband, and we'll be right there. Thank you for calling. See you in a bit," she managed to get out.

Tabby hung up and sunk onto the couch. Brittany wasn't the type to get into altercations, and Tabby didn't want this to be the first of a string of disciplinary actions. As far as Brittany's school behavior went, she was always getting A's and was considered a stellar student. It bothered Tabby to think that maybe her daughter was headed on a rough path. The sooner they could change that, the better.

Drew's phone didn't ring, but went straight to voicemail. "Drew, it's me," Tabby said urgently. "Call me as soon as you get this. Brittany is in the principal's office, and we have to go speak with him. Please call me back ASAP."

When she disconnected the call, she wasted no time grabbing her keys and purse and hurrying out the door. Drew could meet up with her; she didn't have any time to lose. Brittany was in trouble, and Tabby was determined to get to the bottom of it.

———

BRITTANY KEPT HER EYES ON THE FLOOR AS TABBY LOOKED IN her direction. She had been there for fifteen minutes, and that was fifteen minutes too long. Drew still hadn't arrived, and she was anxious to get the meeting started. She checked her watch, then looked up at the principal.

"Let's get started. My husband must've gotten detained."

Where, though? She wasn't sure, but that wasn't what mattered, because she needed to focus her attention on her daughter.

"Are you sure?" the principal asked. "We can give him a few more minutes."

Tabby shook her head, and an unbidden thought came to her. If Jenni was somehow her spouse, *she* would be there. Tabby knew that in her heart. The more time she spent with Jenni, the more she saw how much Drew was failing as a father. If he wanted to fail *her*, then fine. But how could he fail their daughters?

Jenni would be there for a school meeting in a heartbeat. And Tabby had the feeling that marriage with her would be so much more fulfilling and wonderful.

Tabby clenched her fists. Drew hadn't once called her back. For all she knew, he was ignoring her pleas for him to come to the school. Either way, he wasn't there, and waiting a few more minutes wouldn't change that. "Let's begin," she said.

Principal Parker looked between Brittany and Tabby. "I'll make this short. I don't know what has gotten into Brittany, but this isn't like her. She was caught fighting during her lunch period and it took three teachers to break it up."

Tabby looked over at her daughter, who had a slightly smudged-looking bruise on her cheek. She looked back at Principal Parker, who continued. "As I mentioned, we have a no-fighting policy, and we make all children abide by that."

"Understood," Tabby replied. "I will ensure this never happens again. You have my word on that. And Brittany's. Isn't that right, Brittany?" Tabby gave her a stern look.

Brittany nodded, not looking up. She had been quiet the entire time, from Tabby's arrival to her conversation with the principal, and had barely made any eye contact.

Tabby looked back to Principal Parker. "I'm sorry for the trouble this has caused the school." She hesitated, then said, "May I ask who the other girl is?"

"Boy," he responded. "Richie Bates. I spoke to his parents an hour ago, and they have taken their son home."

Tabby's jaw dropped. "Brittany was fighting with a boy?" She turned to stare at her daughter, who finally looked up. There were tears in her eyes. Tabby wouldn't embarrass her by asking her to explain herself right there, but there were so many questions running through her mind.

"Who started it?"

Principal Parker turned to Brittany, and there was a long silence that ensued before he glanced back at Tabby. "Neither one was in the right, and because of it, both are facing suspension for one week." Tabby nodded, dazed. Suspension? This wasn't her daughter. She could have pictured Callie in a situation like this, but not Brittany.

The principal continued. "The teachers have put together her homework assignments for the next seven school days. If there are any questions regarding the assignments, she can email the teachers directly."

"All right. Thank you." Tabby took the papers that he offered her. "And again, please accept our apologies." Tabby nudged Brittany, who looked up and gazed at her principal.

"I'm sorry," Brittany said. "I didn't mean to cause any harm."

"Kids will be kids," Principal Parker stated. "But it's our job to ensure this doesn't happen again. You are better than this, Brittany. Remember that."

She nodded, then dropped her gaze again. Tabby stood up and shook his hand. "Thank you, Principal Parker."

"I'm sorry we had to meet under such circumstances, but thank you for coming in as quickly as you did. We look forward to you coming back to school, Brittany."

"Thank you, Principal Parker," she mumbled.

Tabby and Brittany left the office, and Brittany walked a few steps ahead of Tabby. Tabby stayed quiet until they reached the car. Once inside, though, she turned to her daughter.

"We are going to talk about this," Tabby said firmly.

Brittany rolled her eyes and looked out the window. Tabby reached out and touched her arm, but Brittany slowly pulled away. Brittany moved her hand to her eye, and it hurt Tabby when she saw her flicking away a couple of tears. Tabby turned and looked out the front of the window. She drove home, the silence as strong as ever as they moved through the streets of Chicago.

When she pulled into the driveway, she thought maybe Brittany would bolt out of the car, but to her surprise, her daughter walked slowly to the house, staying in step with Tabby. Once they were in the foyer, Brittany turned to her.

"Are you and Dad getting a divorce?" Brittany asked.

"What?" Tabby asked. "You are thirteen and you do not need to be worrying about things like this."

Brittany shook her head. "I'm thirteen and no longer a child, Mom. I deserve to know. I need to prepare myself, and I've heard you fighting. I've seen when you go to the spare room to sleep. My anxiety is going through the roof, Mom, and I need some answers. Otherwise..." Her words trailed off, and she looked away. Tabby spotted a few more tears. Tabby reached her hand up to her daughter's cheek and stroked it softly.

"Is that what the fight was about?" Tabby asked.

Brittany turned to look at her. "It was stupid. I was already having a rough day and was walking through the halls, practically in a daze. I got to the lunchroom and Richie came busting through. He bumped into me. What's stupid is I know it was an accident. He wasn't trying to knock me down or anything. But because my thoughts were all over the place and I was so angry, I pushed him. That seemed to startle him. He didn't deserve to get in trouble, too. He never hit me. I tripped and fell, causing this bruise." She touched her cheek. You should have seen him. He just was trying to defend himself—really."

She covered her eyes. "I should have talked to you before it got to be this bad."

Tabby pulled Brittany into her arms and hugged her tightly. "I'm sorry that you felt you had no choice but to push someone. Fighting is never the answer, but you *should* have talked to me. I would have been there to hear whatever you wanted to talk about."

When Brittany pulled back, more tears stained her cheeks. "I don't want you to think that you have to stay in this marriage because of us," Brittany whispered. "If you're not happy, then we have to be strong for you."

Tabby pulled Brittany back in her arms again and Tabby felt her own tears stinging the backs of her eyes. "We'll get through this together."

Brittany nodded. "Just be honest with me, Mom, please," Brittany pleaded, pulling back and looking up at Tabby. "Do you think about divorce?"

Tabby stared into her daughter's eyes, and her heart ached. She bit down on her lip, then nodded. "But I want you to know that we're not doing anything yet. And this isn't your battle. But I will be honest with you now. You can trust that."

"I love you, Mom," Brittany sniffed.

"I love you, too. Now, go up to your room and start on your homework because you have enough to last you awhile. Are you hungry?" Brittany nodded. "I'll bring you up a sandwich."

"Thanks, Mom." Brittany threw her arms around Tabby's waist, then went up the stairs. Tabby watched her go, waiting for the door to shut before she looked away. It was hurting her children, this dance between Drew and her. That was the one thing she didn't want to happen. But now, she was going to have to take a stand. Drew couldn't even be bothered to come to the meeting, which spoke volumes. There wasn't anything more important than making sure her children were taken care of. That was where Tabby's heart was, above all.

CHAPTER SIXTEEN

Jenni

Jenni stared at the names of the employees, as she had done for the past week. She was no closer to figuring out what she was going to do about making sure that Tabby didn't lose her job, along with others. Maybe she could somehow move everyone on the list to other hospital areas that needed help. But then the hospital would still be keeping the same amount of payroll, which would put it back at square one—needing to make staff cuts.

She leaned back in her kitchen chair and considered all the options, but nothing new came up. From only cutting half the staff to shifting the employees into other positions, every option she considered brought on a hundred reasons why it wouldn't work. Even making a pro and cons list wasn't working. She knew the cons far outweighed the pros in this situation. There was nothing positive, in her eyes, about these employees losing their jobs, no matter the money Capmed would save.

It isn't your problem to fix, Jenni. Yet she felt otherwise, because if she had more money to put into the hospital, then perhaps she could save these jobs. She scooted her chair back up to the table and looked the list over, thinking hard. If there was more money going into the hospital....That would truly solve so many things. But how? Where could that money come from?

It was true that Jenni didn't think she was the only one in the Chicago metro area who had money to filter into the hospital. Others were just as wealthy as her, if not more. If she could get more money coming in, the hospital wouldn't have to worry about the money going out.

Jenni sat up. It was an idea, and one that might work.

Jenni grabbed the list and folded it up, then slipped it into her pocket. She was doing this for all the nursing and administrative staff that were on the list. And if it didn't work, it was their jobs on the line. However, if it did, the hospital could have its renovations *and* keep its valued staff.

Jenni got in her car and headed to Capmed, ideas streaming through her mind. They could start with a benefit fundraiser, maybe even have a concert or two that would draw in money and donations. When she reached the hospital, she actually felt hopeful. This could actually work. Right now, it was the only idea out there that she couldn't see reasons for being shot down.

The first stop she made was the cardiology floor. If she got the doctors on board, then maybe they would be able to help her push her ideas with Brian and the rest of the board. Charles's door was open when she reached his office. She knocked, and he looked up and smiled.

"This is a pleasant surprise," he said.

"Well, I wanted to see your thoughts on an idea I have." He sat straight in his chair and tilted his head. "We want the nurses to keep their jobs, right?"

He nodded. "Can't disagree with that," he said. "But I have worked with Brian for years, and I know that he isn't one to give up easily once he makes up his mind. I don't really know what we can do about it. I guess writing up recommendations for the nurses might be the best bet. I know I'll do what I can to ensure that Tabitha gets a job shortly after getting her pink slip."

"What if there doesn't need to be any pink slips, though?"

Charles looked at her endearingly. "I'm not surprised you're going to try to change the outcome. You've always been one to do what's right. What do you have?"

Jenni started telling him the ideas she had about a benefit and fundraiser. He listened intently without interrupting. He nodded a few times and kept his attention focused on her, absorbing everything she was saying. When she was finished, he, too, looked hopeful.

"I don't hate the idea. It could actually work. It's just—getting Brian convinced. We could probably get free entertainment. Maybe even Tabby's husband would perform."

Jenni nodded, but deep down, she knew that would likely not happen. She didn't want Drew to be a part of it, and by now, she hoped that Tabby would agree.

"Are you going to take it to Brian?" Charles asked

"I am, but I want to have some support behind the proposal before I do. That way it's not just some frivolous idea that someone came up with."

"There's nothing frivolous about it. I like the idea. If you need me to put my statement out there, just let me know."

"Thank you."

There was a knock on the door, and Charles looked up. "Come in," he called out.

The door opened and Tabby entered. She immediately looked over to Jenni, and Jenni quickly stood up. The intensity of her stare was as real as if Tabby had lasered her gaze on her.

"Sorry to interrupt," Tabby said, turning from her. "Mr. Carlson is complaining of chest pain radiating up and down his left arm."

"I'll be right there," Charles said.

She nodded and then looked over to Jenni. Jenni nodded slightly, but without acknowledging it, Tabby turned and hurried out of the room. Charles stood up and chuckled as he moved toward the door.

"If I didn't know Tabby was married, I would say that there's some tension between you. Sexual tension—just so I'm being clear."

Jenni moved quickly to the door. "What? You're absolutely misreading things," she lied.

He shrugged. "Well, as I said, I know better. Anyway, let me know if you talk to Brian, and what he says."

"I will."

Charles headed for his patient's room, and Jenni looked around the halls of the floor, but Tabby was nowhere to be found. She shrugged it off and continued toward the elevator. As she pushed the button, her phone started to ring. She took it out of her handbag but didn't recognize the number.

"Hello?"

"Hello, is this Jennifer Jennison?"

"Yes? May I help you?"

"This is Bridgette from Dr. Antonia Samson's office." Jenni had been anticipating that call but had given up hope after the third day of waiting. "I am calling because I have you down on the list to be a part of the research study Dr. Samson is currently working on. She would like to get you in for an evaluation this afternoon. Are you free?"

"Um, yeah, I suppose so."

"Two o'clock?" Bridgette asked.

Jenni checked her watch. That was only an hour away. She was already at the hospital, so that part worked out, but deep down she worried that she would find the meeting to be a waste of her time and that she wouldn't be eligible for the study. But worrying would only give her reason to stress out even more. Stress brought on the migraines, so she needed to steer clear of that.

"I'll be there," she said.

"Great." Bridgette told her where Dr. Samson's office was located, then finished with, "We'll see you then." She hung up before Jenni could rethink her concerns. She had one more stop to make, and then she would focus on her appointment.

She took the elevator down to see Brian, hopeful that she was on her way to saving all of the jobs that were in jeopardy. She reached Brian's office and waved at his secretary, who sat at her desk.

"Hello, Jenni," she said.

"Hey, Phoebe. Is Brian free? I just have something really quick to run over with him. Won't take any more than two minutes."

"Yeah, he's free. Go on ahead."

Jenni smiled, heading for Brian's office. She knocked on the door and heard him mumble something, which she took as a "come in."

He looked up, his face falling at the sight of her. He shook his head. "Are you here to tell me how I'm doing my job all wrong? We've been through this, Jenni. There isn't any other way."

"But I think there is," Jenni pressed on.

He sat up and clutched his hands together. "Okay, I'm listening."

"I have donated a lot of money to Capmed. I think that if other people had the option, they would gladly pool their money into the hospital, too. I think you should hold a benefit concert and fundraiser. Get donations. It will help with the renovations, and you won't be forced to fire half your senior staff. It will work, Brian. I know it will."

He sighed. "And who's going to pay for this concert and fundraiser?"

"I will gladly offer some of my money to assist, and I think we can do it relatively inexpensively. People can volunteer, including the hospital staff. I've already talked to some of the doctors, and they think it's a great idea."

Brian raised his eyebrows. It was a lie, but not entirely. She was confident other doctors would jump on board if they knew they could do something to not lose their staff. "I know that you think it will be a waste of time, but I'm asking you to at least try."

He shook his head. "I don't know. It might be too little to do any real good for us."

"But we can try. That's all I'm saying," she urged.

After a moment, Brian sighed. "I'm not saying yes. I'm saying that I will consider it."

Jenni smiled. That was better than hearing a no. If he was willing to think about it, she could continue working on him to make sure he eventually agreed. There wasn't any reason not to give it a try. She was already eagerly planning everything out in her mind.

JENNI WRUNG HER HANDS ON HER LAP AS SHE WAITED FOR THE nurse to come back into the room. Two hours had passed, and she was nervously anticipating the results of her lab work. But she knew she would have to wait another day or two to receive that.

A knock sounded on the door, and she looked up. "Come on in."

Novalee came into the room. Her name was another that was on the list that Jenni had spent hours looking over. It was difficult to interact with all these people when Jenni secretly knew that their lives could be uprooted later.

"Here are the brochures that Dr. Samson wanted me to pass along to you. They go over the clinical trials, adverse reactions, expectations, frequently asked questions, et cetera. Once your lab work comes back, providing everything is within the levels that we need them to be, we'll call you and schedule your appointment for the next visit. Do you have any questions for me?"

Jenni shook her head, her hands shaking as she took the papers from the nurse. "Thank you." She looked down at the first brochure, on which there was a photo of two women who had bright smiles. That seemed uplifting, but it also meant they advertised well.

"You're free to go. Expect to hear from us in a couple of days. If you have any questions, the direct number is located on the back cover of each brochure. Have a great rest of your day."

"You too."

Jenni left the room feeling even more hopeful than she had when she had gone in. At least she was being considered as a valid candidate. And if she were accepted into the study, it could make her life better in the long run. Nothing could be wrong with that. Even if she experienced side effects, she was ensured that they were minimal, and only five percent of participants experienced those. Even the brochures stated the same. Why look for something wrong in something that was probably totally fine?

Jenni reached the lobby of the main floor and headed straight for the exit. Her thoughts were so focused on the fundraiser and research study that she didn't pay attention to the person on her left, heading in the same direction, until they collided with one another. She dropped her brochures and reached out to grab them at the same time that Tabby reached down.

"Sorry about that," Tabby said. "Wasn't paying attention."

"That makes two of us," Jenni replied, looking tentatively at Tabby.

Tabby looked down at the brochure in her hand, then quickly looked up. "You got into the clinical trial?"

"Working on it. I just finished the first appointment and had lab work done. We'll see how that goes." She took the brochure from Tabby's hand.

"I'm happy for you," Tabby replied. "I hope it all works out."

"Thank you," Jenni said warmly.

They walked outside the hospital together, heading toward the parking lot. "How've you been?" Tabby asked. "Have the migraines been staying away?"

"Pretty much," Jenni answered. "With any luck, they'll even be better going forward."

"Yes. It's good to stay positive about that," Tabby replied.

The conversation died as they stepped into the parking lot. "How've you been?" Jenni asked. As they reached an aisle in the lot, Tabby stopped and motioned to her vehicle.

"I've been doing all right," she said.

Jenni saw Tabby's eyes darken, but she wasn't in a position to ask about that, though she wanted to. She wanted to share conversations together, even though the kiss lingered in her mind.

"That's good," she finally said. She could ignore her desire to inquire further as long as Tabby didn't burst into tears in front of her. If she wanted to talk to Jenni, surely she knew that was an option.

"It was good catching up with you," Tabby said. No matter that the conversation had barely lasted a few minutes.

Jenni nodded and forced a smile. "Anytime you want to talk, you have my number." Tabby's mouth opened, and she quickly closed it and looked away, which disquieted Jenni. "All right then, you take care."

Before Tabby could utter a response, Jenni quickly walked away from her. Gaining distance was ideal at that moment. If she had to say one more minute, she would pull Tabby into her arms and plead with her to be honest and to tell her everything that had been going on with her over the past week.

As she walked away, Tabby grew farther and farther behind her, as did the idea of asking her those questions. No, it was better for her to let Tabby come to her if she so chose. Then Jenni would allow Tabby all the freedoms she needed to tell her everything. That's when Tabby would fully be able to share everything, and Jenni would be able to wrap her up in her arms and tell her that she was there for her. She would always be there for her.

CHAPTER SEVENTEEN

Tabby

T abby leaned in and hugged Callie. "Goodnight, sweetheart."

"Goodnight, Mom!" Tabby squeezed her arms around her and closed her eyes as she held her younger daughter. "See you in the morning."

"Not if I see you first," Callie said, a big smile on her lips.

Tabby was glad to see that Callie was not yet phased by her marriage problems. Tabby would only hope for Callie to stay young and innocent like that forever. She blew her a kiss from the door, then left her room.

Tabby had been glad her shift had ended early, so she could have dinner with the family and possibly have a heartfelt conversation with Drew. One problem had popped up, though. Drew had never come home for dinner. He must've assumed Tabby would make it home to take care of the kids, or maybe he was at the point where he didn't care about being a good father, which troubled Tabby.

Drew? Just wondering where you were. I thought you'd be home for supper. We really need to talk. It was the message she had left on his voicemail only an hour earlier when she had attempted to get through to him. The call hadn't even rung—just went straight to voicemail. It had been a common occurrence over the past week. She now wondered why she even bothered trying to talk with him when she knew he would disappoint her yet again.

Tabby knocked on Brittany's door. "It's open!" Brittany hollered.

She entered and looked around the spotless bedroom. Though Brittany had been suspended over the past week, she hadn't allowed herself to neglect her chores. If anything, she had made sure to keep up with the cleaning. Tabby was grateful for that.

Britney was a good girl and mature for her years. Tabby knew she could trust her older daughter to stay home alone when Drew wasn't there. And lately, that was often. She kept the neighbors on standby but allowed Brittany to stay home alone. Brittany hadn't let her down.

"Doing homework?" Tabby asked.

Brittany nodded and held up a book. "I have a book report due next month. Mr. Notting said that we should make sure to read the book twice through. I was just starting up the second read. She dropped the book and met Tabby's gaze.

"I'm so proud of you," Tabby said, sitting down on the edge of Tabby's bed.

Brittany scrunched up her nose. "Even though I caused a fight?"

Tabby nodded. "I know that you've been through a lot, and it's not right to punish you for things that even we adults don't understand. You will do the right things when you get back to school next week." Tabby leaned in and brushed a kiss against Brittany's forehead. When she pulled back, Brittany frowned.

"Dad missed dinner tonight."

"Well, yeah, but he's busy. He has another show tomorrow night and just wanted to rehearse with the band. That's all."

Brittany's answering smile didn't quite reach her eyes. "Love you, Mom."

"Love you, too." She squeezed her daughter's hand and got up from the bed. As she headed to the door, she cringed. She didn't like lying to either one of her daughters, but this was a time she knew that being honest would do more harm than good. She stopped and looked over her shoulder. "Let me know if you need anything before going to bed."

"I will. Night, Mom."

"Goodnight, sweetheart." Tabby spent a few more seconds just staring at her daughter before turning away and leaving the room. Once she returned to her bedroom, she looked over to her dresser. Two pictures sat on top, one of her and Drew's wedding day and the other of the family. She picked up that picture and stared at it. Her fingers ran over each of her daughter's faces, and it broke her heart that she had been put in this position of wondering. What if? What if one day the picture of four was minus one?

What if she really did divorce Drew? She wanted her girls to grow up in a stable home with lots of love, but raising them alone would be hard. Would Jenni stick around? She loved children, and there was a spark between them neither of them had fully addressed.

Tabby smiled to herself, letting her mind wander. She imagined waking up every day to Jenni's beautiful smile. They would be true partners and best friends, and she could see the four of them spending time as a family, going to events together and having fun. Jenni would never bail on her when times got tough. Tabby was confident of that.

Her smile faded, and she came back to reality. After the kiss, Jenni seemed to be fine with letting it go and moving on. She might not feel as strongly as Tabby did, and they weren't even in a relationship. How could Tabby be fantasizing about Jenni becoming her wife? It was a silly thought.

She put the picture down and pulled out her phone. Still no missed call from Drew. She pulled up his contact info and called him. It went to voicemail right away.

"Hey, Drew. Me again. Now I'm just worried. Where are you? I'm starting to think the worst. That you've gotten into a car wreck or something. Please give me a call. Perhaps you forgot to tell me you had plans, and if that's the case, so be it. But I'm going crazy here. *Call me.*"

She disconnected the call and looked over to the empty bed. She felt a tear break free from her eye and slowly trail down her cheek. She closed her eyes and brushed the tear away. He was fine, just ignoring her call. But the agony inside of her was pulling her into a deep, dark hole. Which would be worse? That Drew was ignoring her calls, or that something bad had actually happened? At least the latter wouldn't be intentional. That thought tugged at her heart. To wish for something like that was killing her inside, but where was he? And why wasn't he calling her back?

THE MOMENT THE LIGHT FLICKED ON IN THE BEDROOM, TABBY opened her eyes. She turned to watch Drew as he sauntered over to the bed. She had to scoot out of the way so he didn't fall onto her. "Hey, baby," he said, kissing the air in her direction.

"That's all you have to say?" Tabby asked. "I've tried calling you not once or twice, but three times. You had me scared to death. And you're drunk? Are you kidding me?"

She got off the bed and stood up, staring at him, until he slowly started to laugh. "What's crawled in your panties?" he asked.

Tabby walked over and shut the door, attempting to keep her children from hearing. She turned back to him. "Where were you?"

"Out," he said. "Some of the guys wanted to grab some drinks. That's all." He shrugged.

Tabby shook her head. "I'm not buying it. I called you at seven o'clock. It went straight to voicemail. I called you again at eight-thirty. Again, voicemail. Then I called you at one. So don't go giving me that. If you were out having drinks, you could have had the decency to at least call back. Give me a straight answer, Drew. I mean it. Where were you?"

He arched an eyebrow. "I was out," he said.

"Okay. With a woman? You reek of alcohol and women's perfume, so don't you dare try to lie to me. Are you cheating on me? Is that it?"

He pulled himself up and sat on the edge of the bed, his eyes downward, at the floor, all while Tabby stared at him from behind. His lack of response was enough for her to know that she was on to something. It was also clear that Jenni wasn't making anything up. Her husband was a flirt and now a cheat.

"I have my answer," she said. She stormed over to the closet, opening the door and pulling a bag out.

"Where are you going?" Drew asked. Before she could turn to him, he had come up behind her. Tabby smelt the fragrances even more strongly than before. It caught her breath, and she turned away from him.

"Anywhere but here. The kids are sound asleep, so I'll let them be, but I can't stay here with you."

"Baby, just listen," he pleaded, touching her shoulder. Tabby tensed up, her arm tightening from his touch. "It isn't what you're thinking. It's not like I'm having an affair." Tabby looked over her shoulder and his eyes softened. "I promise you." He brushed his hand against her cheek, and she tightened up again. "It's not an affair."

"That's what you keep saying. What is it then?" She turned to face him. "Be honest, Drew. I can't handle this, and you know what? Neither can your children. Brittany is already asking if we're going to get a divorce. What's going on?"

He dropped his gaze from her and turned to head back to the bed. He collapsed on it, and covered his eyes. Tabby watched his body shaking and didn't move to console him. She simply watched in agony, waiting for him to speak or do something. He sniffled and then sobbed.

"It happened once," he wailed. He looked up, tears streaking his cheeks. "I was weak and should have been stronger. I didn't mean for it to happen, but you and I have grown distant, and you haven't exactly been willing to give me what a man needs. I slipped. I shouldn't have and I'm sorry, but I'm not entirely to blame."

Tabby turned to her dresser drawers, tears already stinging her eyes. There, she had it. He had been unfaithful to her, but was what he said the whole story? She wasn't sure she bought it. She shook her head and started grabbing random items from her drawer, enough to keep her supplied for a couple of days.

"Where are you going?" he demanded again. She hesitated and turned to look at him.

"I told you. I'm going anywhere but here. You slept with another woman. I'm not going to let you walk all over me like that. I will call tomorrow to talk to the kids." With that, she hurried out of the room and to the bathroom, where she grabbed a few toiletries, and then was down the stairs and out the door. She reached her car, and that's when the floodgates opened and she couldn't hold back her tears. She looked up at the house and saw how dark it suddenly seemed. Drew hadn't come running after her, and she wasn't about to rush back inside and listen to more excuses.

She backed out of the driveway, headed in an unknown direction. The farther she drove from the house, the more confused she was. The only person she knew she could possibly stay with was Hanna, but that would mean she would have to get real and tell her everything about her failing marriage.

Thirty minutes later, though, she pulled up in front of Hanna's house. The house was completely dark, and there was only one vehicle in the driveway. It didn't look promising that she'd be able to get a hold of Hanna, but she had to try anyway.

She knocked on the door and waited. When no one opened the door, she knocked again. It was two o'clock in the morning. *She's probably* asleep, you idiot. But Tabby had pounded hard on the door, loud enough to have awoken the dead. She was certain of that. She headed back to her car and sat in the driveway for a moment. Hanna and her husband could have gone out and used Hanna's vehicle, leaving his at the house. But it was highly unlikely they would be away from the house that late. They were in their mid-forties, after all. Tabby couldn't fathom them being out at this time.

She backed out of the driveway and began driving aimlessly, not knowing where she was going to wind up. The few hotels she passed had No vacancy signs out. Tabby turned into a parking lot and sat there, the darkness overwhelming her. If she waited much longer, she'd be sitting with the sunrise.

Tabby grabbed her phone and pulled up Jenni's number, her movements slow and hesitant. She didn't want to wake her up, but Jenni had said to call if she needed to talk. This seemed as good a time as any to give her a call. It's the dead of night. Think again, Tabby. Still, she pressed the Call button.

Jenni answered after three rings. "Hello?" Her voice was hoarse, and it was clear she had been sound asleep.

"I know it's late," Tabby said in a rush, "and I probably just woke you up. For that, I'm deeply sorry. But I need someone to talk to."

"Tabby? Where are you?"

Tabby broke down into tears, the weight of everything she had been holding slowly crumbling down on her, and her heart shattered. Drew didn't deserve her tears. On the other hand, her children were the ones who would pay the price, and Tabby feared that things were going to come crashing down all over them.

CHAPTER EIGHTEEN

Jenni

J enni handed Tabby a hot cup of coffee, and Tabby looked up. "Thank you."

"You're welcome." Jenni took a sip of her own and sat down across from her. She had been surprised to get a call from Tabby, but she hadn't hesitated in directing her to her house. She had heard the tears in her voice and had just wanted to help her out. Now, all she could do was watch her and be there to lend a listening ear.

Tabby sighed as she took a drink. "Sometimes I wonder what I did to deserve the way Drew feels he can treat me. But I never wanted to believe that he was capable of cheating on me." She huffed. "I don't know why I found that so ridiculous. After all, he wanted to force me to have sex with him the other day. Of course he would be capable of this."

Jenni just listened, waiting for Tabby to share whatever she wanted to share. Tabby shook her head. "I should have believed you when you tried telling me that he was flirting with you and wanted to hook up."

"Tabby, I don't find it odd that you didn't want to believe that. He's your husband. You want to believe the best in him. I understand. And I'm sorry that you had to deal with this tonight."

Tabby took another sip and stared down at her cup. Jenni watched her appear almost childlike.

"I'm the one who's sorry," Tabby said. Jenni, looked up, surprised. "I came to the house so late tonight. I just abused your friendship."

"Tabby, don't be silly. You were out driving around in the middle of the night, and you needed to be somewhere safe and warm. I'm just happy I could accommodate. You can stay as long as you need."

Tabby smiled and held up the coffee. "Just one night should suffice." She sniffled, then added, "Maybe two."

Jenni smiled. She would allow her to stay there until she was ready to leave. She was sure Tabby would need to get home to her children, but Jenni wouldn't turn her away.

"And thanks for the coffee. I really needed it." Tabby took another sip, and Jenni nodded.

Jenni leaned back in her chair and let the quiet seep into her kitchen. Tabby hadn't even changed out of her pajamas. It was clear she had rushed out of there in a hurry. Jenni didn't blame her. When Tabby had spilled the news to Jenni, her voice had broken, just as Jenni believed Tabby's heart had broken at that moment. Even though they didn't have a picture-perfect marriage, it was still a marriage. And with children involved, it was bound to be a rougher road.

"I look like an absolute mess," Tabby mumbled.

"You're not a mess," Jenni protested. Don't say that."

Tabby lifted her gaze, along with the corners of her lips. "Let's talk about something else," Tabby replied. "Have you heard anything about the clinical trial?"

"Actually, I just got a call this afternoon. I'm supposed to go to an appointment on Monday, which is when we'll get started."

"That's good news." Tabby's eyes lit up. For the first time, she didn't look like she was thinking about the husband she had left back at the house. "I'm hopeful it can really work."

"Me too." While that was good news, Jenni still believed that Tabby, along with many others, were on the verge of losing their jobs. A board meeting was set up for the following Wednesday, and she hoped that she would be able to convince everyone to move forward with her ideas for saving the jobs. She'd be pretty surprised if the stress from that didn't give her a migraine.

She looked to Tabby, who was back to surveying her coffee. There were so many ways she had considered telling Tabby about the expansion project that could eliminate her job, but she always changed her mind. What Tabby didn't know wouldn't hurt her. And Tabby had so much on her mind already. She didn't need one more thing to worry about. Hiding this information was her way of protecting Tabby. Keep telling yourself that. It doesn't make it true.

"I'm mentally and physically exhausted," Tabby murmured.

"You should try to get some rest. I'll show you where the guestroom is."

"You're right," Tabby replied. They left the two mugs on the kitchen table and headed down a hallway to a room, where Jenni had already put Tabby's single bag.

"The restroom is right down the hallway on the right. My bedroom is upstairs—the first room on the left—if you need anything. And there are extra blankets in the cabinet right there." She turned back to Tabby. "Can you think of anything else?"

Tabby shook her head. "Thank you."

"Have a good night," Jenni said. As she turned, Tabby reached out and touched her arm, startling Jenni.

"Jenni?" Tabby began.

Jenni looked at her, and her heart hitched, right along with her breath. Seeing the affection on Tabby's face made Jenni want to melt. She tilted her head.

"I can't thank you enough for this. I really appreciate it."

"You don't need to thank me," Jenni said, her tone going up a notch as she concentrated on the heat that came from Tabby's touch. "I'm happy to do it."

"I could never repay you, though. But I can do this." She moved close, kissing Jenni and sending a wave of shock coursing through her as Tabby snaked her hand up Jenni's shirt.

Jenni wanted to go further. It was every fantasy that she had imagined being played out, but she breathlessly pushed Tabby away.

"We can't," she argued. "Not like this."

Tabby looked away. "Great. Now you're going to reject me."

"Tabby," Jenni pleaded. "I'm not rejecting you. I would give anything for us to go on kissing and ultimately wind up in bed together. I am *very* attracted to you. You have to know that. When I kissed you the other day, it wasn't by accident. You have to believe that."

"They why stop?" Tabby asked.

Jenni let out a breath. Her dreams were laid out right in front of her, but doing the right thing wasn't always the easy thing to do. "Why? Because if we do this, you're no better than Drew, and you and I both know that you *are* better than him. Talk to him. If you dissolve your marriage, then that's a different story. But I'm not rejecting you. I'm stopping us before you can regret any decision you make tonight."

"I know—you're right," Tabby whispered.

Jenni backed out of the spare room. "I'll see you in the morning, and we'll talk." She turned away and headed upstairs. The farther she got away from Tabby, the better. Otherwise, she would succumb to her needs and forget everything she had just very reasonably explained to Tabby. But she needed that release and didn't know how much longer she could wait for it.

JENNI TOOK HER TIME IN THE BATH THE NEXT MORNING. SHE hadn't been able to get much sleep last night because every time she closed her eyes, her thoughts went to Tabby. Or, more importantly, Tabby under the bedsheets in the spare room. The images wouldn't leave her mind. With a twenty-minute bath behind her, she was prepared to go downstairs and see Tabby. At least, she was mentally prepared. She wasn't so sure about her heart and desires, which craved the woman she had so abruptly turned away.

When she went downstairs, her one hope was that Tabby would still be sound asleep. No such luck, as she entered the kitchen and spotted her at the stove. Jenni cleared her throat and waited for Tabby to turn around and look at her.

"Good morning," Jenni said cheerily.

Tabby smiled at Jenni, something she hadn't been able to do the night before when they were chatting. "Morning. Give me three minutes and breakfast will be served." She turned back to the stove.

"You didn't need to do that. I could have whipped us up something."

Tabby laughed and shook her head. "I'm used to it. As a mother and wife, cooking comes second nature." She continued working on their breakfast as Jenni took her seat at the kitchen table.

"Did you sleep all right?" Jenni asked, trying to make small talk.

"Well, I'd be lying if I said I slept like a baby. Maybe a newborn baby that wakes up every fifteen minutes crying." Her words seemed upbeat, but Jenni could only imagine the pain that was laced through them.

"I'm sorry," Jenni said.

Tabby shrugged. "It's nothing you should be apologizing for. I'm the one who called you in the middle of the night, needing a place to stay. I'm the one who should be apologizing to you. For many reasons, in fact." She looked over her shoulder and met Jenni's gaze. "I'm sorry for the abrupt kiss that I pushed on you last night. That wasn't called for, and you were right. I wouldn't have been any better than Drew."

Jenni sighed. "Don't apologize for that. Like I said, if I weren't working hard to be strong, I definitely would have kept it going."

Tabby smiled. "It was just bad timing. Ain't that the truth."

She turned around and busied herself, filling two plates with eggs, sausage, bacon, and hash browns. Jenni was mesmerized as Tabby grabbed things from cupboards like she had been in Jenni's kitchen her whole life. Tabby put a plate down in front of Jenni and looked at her.

"Orange juice? Milk? Or coffee?" she asked.

"Whatever you're having," Jenni said. Tabby turned and grabbed two glasses, then filled them both with orange juice.

Jenni scrunched her forehead as Tabby pushed her glass toward her. "I have to ask," Jenni started. "How do you know your way around this kitchen so well?"

"Well, as I said, when you're waking up every fifteen minutes, you can get a lot accomplished. That includes touring the kitchen to learn where everything is so I would know when I made breakfast this morning. Eat up before it gets cold."

Jenni looked down at her food. It was more than she was used to eating every morning, since she would typically reach for cereal or oatmeal. "Looks delicious," Jenni said, digging into the eggs. She nodded, wiping her mouth. "This was unexpected, but very good. Thank you."

"It was the least I could do," Tabby said.

The conversation died down as they both ate silently. Fifteen minutes in, as Jenni chewed on a strip of bacon, Tabby spoke. "I called the girls this morning."

"Oh yeah? How'd they take the fact that you left in the middle of the night?"

"Well, turns out Drew didn't tell them that. He just said that I had to go into work this morning." Jenni opened her mouth, and Tabby nodded. "Yeah, I was surprised, too. Then again, if he had told them the truth, that I ran off in the middle of the night, he would have had to mention how he had a part in it. I'm guessing he doesn't want the girls to know that he's sleeping around. Not so surprising."

"Yeah, I suppose so," Jenni replied, finishing off her bacon.

"He has a show tonight and I'll need to watch the girls, so I'll head on home so I can be with them. I'll probably leave here about six or so."

"Whatever you want," Jenni softly whispered. She stared down at her breakfast and felt Tabby's eyes on her. She looked up, and sure enough, their gazes met.

"Do you think I'm foolish?"

"I don't think you're foolish, Tabby. You have to be home for your girls. That's only common sense. I just hope you don't let Drew walk all over you. You deserve much better than that, so promise me that you'll speak to him only when you know what you're going to say."

Tabby let out a breath. "I'm not sure I'll ever fully know what to say to him, but I can tell you this." She hesitated, staring down at her plate of food while Jenni waited for her to respond. Tabby's eyes darkened in those few minutes that she struggled to find the words. When Jenni saw a tear slip down her cheek, she got up and went over to wrap her arm around Tabby's shoulder. "My marriage is over," Tabby said, her voice breaking.

Those four words were spoken as if a weight had been lifted off her shoulders. Tabby spoke them again, then covered her eyes and started to sob. Jenni never left her side, keeping her arm tightly wrapped around her. It was going to be all right. Jenni would do anything to make sure Tabby believed that.

CHAPTER NINETEEN

Tabby

T abby sat on the couch, just staring at the fireplace, the logs burning slowly, the light flickering and lighting up the living room with a soft glow. She wiped away a few tears that had been falling periodically, as memories of her marriage kept trailing through her mind. When the front door slammed shut fifteen minutes past midnight, she jerked to attention and turned to watch Drew walk around the corner.

"Hey," he said.

"Hi." Tabby sat up straighter and kept her eyes fixated on his. "How was your show?"

"Good. Long." He sat down in the chair across from her. "It's dark in here." He stood and went to one of the lamps, turning it on. "That's better." He resumed his seat and looked her way, but she quickly looked away from him. Her eyes were red, and her cheeks were splotchy. "Or not," he muttered.

She shrugged. "It is what it is." She was relieved to see he wasn't drunk, stumbling around the living room with slurred speech and blurred vision. It might help them have a decent conversation, one she had practiced numerous times through the night. "What we have going on here isn't a marriage. It hasn't been a marriage for a long time. And if you're willing to be honest, you'll admit that you know this."

"Babe," he started. Tabby tilted her head and locked eyes with his. "Tabby. We can get things back to where they were."

Tabby sighed and fell back against the couch. There were so many times she would have given anything to hear him say those words, but now she was just tired, and she didn't have any fight left inside of her. What she felt with Jenni was so much more than what remained between her and Drew. They could try to fix their marriage, but Tabby didn't believe Drew would really commit to change. And her heart was already with someone else. Someone who would treat her with the kindness and respect she deserved, making each day more magical and fulfilling than the last.

"You want counseling? Then fine. We'll do it."

"We've been there, done that. Don't you see? We've been constantly jumping through hoops, trying to save our marriage, and I'm tired, Drew. I'm tired of not knowing when we'll fight next or if we'll get through the turmoil. It's not working, and I don't know that I want to fight for it anymore."

"So, what are you saying? You want a divorce?"

Divorce was too final of a word. "I think the kids are going to need an adjustment period. We'll start with a separation. Then once the kids are settled in and understand what's going on, we'll move toward divorce."

Tabby dropped her eyes. Just saying the word left her drained. In her parents' relationship, divorce was a dirty word. Tabby believed she would always do anything to make her marriage work. But it wasn't just up to her, and if Drew wasn't always going to give a thousand percent, then why should she be the only one?

"What are the next steps then?"

"I think it only makes sense that the kids and I stay in the house and you go to a hotel. It will be easier to transition the kids if they don't have to leave the only home they know. Agreed?"

"Makes sense," he mumbled. "Guess we'll start that tonight then." He stood up from his chair.

"It's after midnight, Drew. You'll have to pack, so you might as well stay here tonight. Tomorrow, we can let the kids know what's going on."

When Drew glanced at Tabby, his eyes seemed to be looking right through her. It startled her as she stood up from the couch.

"It's best to just get it over with. I'll leave and go to a hotel and then come here tomorrow to get some clothes. Why delay the inevitable?"

"I don't hate you, Drew. We just grew away from each other. You're the father of my children, and I'll always love you. You don't have to make this awkward between us."

He shook his head. "You're kicking me to the curb, Tab. It is what is. That's what you say, right? No need to second-guess your thoughts."

Tabby frowned. That wasn't what she was doing. She wasn't second-guessing herself. She knew she was following her heart and doing what was right.

"I'm not kicking you to the curb, Drew."

"Yes, you are," he snapped.

Tabby looked away from him, fearful that she would start crying and show him the emotions she had been feeling all night.

"I make one mistake. I sleep with one woman and you're like 'off with your head.' Makes me wonder if there's more to it."

"Drew! It's not about sleeping with one woman. It's about the whole marriage. It's about finding that we're growing away from one another, instead of further in love. I'm sorry if you don't understand that, but I'm not trying to be unreasonable."

"Fine! If that's what you think." He turned away from her, and she slowly followed him to the door. She was going to watch him drive away and that was going to be it. At least, that was the way it was looking.

"Drew," she whispered.

He turned back to her, and before she could step back, he wrapped his arms around her and hugged her. "I'm sorry."

Tabby keenly felt those words as he slowly began to weep. Maybe she was all wrong. Maybe he was a changed man and counseling would help them through it.

Instead of telling him this, she held onto him and said, "Thank you for your apology." He slowly pulled back from the embrace. "I don't hate you," she reiterated.

He nodded, turning away and walking out the door. In that moment of silence as she watched him get in the car and then drive away, Jenni's words echoed in her mind. Don't let Drew walk all over you. Would changing her mind and trying counseling again be something that would give Drew his way? No matter what, she had to take a stand, and letting him drive away was the only thing to do.

THE CAFETERIA WAS BUSY WITH PATIENTS' FAMILIES MILLING about and staff on their lunch break as Tabby took a sip of her coffee. She glanced down at her watch and sighed. Her lunch was going by way too quickly. She only had ten minutes before she had to get back to work, but she would soak up every last drop of those ten minutes. She took another sip and then put down her cup and closed her eyes. Just four more hours of work. Then she could leave and get the girls from school. Surely the afternoon would fly by.

"Is this seat vacant?" She opened her eyes and looked up as Jenni approached the table.

"Oh. Sure." Tabby sat up and waited for Jenni to take a seat. It'd been nearly a week since Tabby had spent the night at Jenni's, and it had been the longest week of her life. "How are you doing?" she asked.

"Good. It's been a few days since I started the treatment for the migraines."

"Oh, that's right. You were starting that Monday, right? How'd it go? Experienced any side effects yet?"

She shrugged. "I've been a tad tired, but overall, I'm doing well. They said that it can take a few weeks before I finally see it working toward migraines, but I feel that so far, so good. I haven't had a migraine this week, so that's good."

Tabby nodded. "Happy to hear that." She looked down at her empty tray and then at her watch. Time was ticking by, and she only had six minutes left of her break—not nearly enough time for everything Tabby needed to say to Jenni.

Tabby finally took a breath and looked up. "I want to apologize. I did mean to call you and let you know what was going on. I've just been so emotionally drained and physically tired. So, I'm sorry. I want to talk about us. I just need a little time to wrap my head around everything."

Emotionally draining was an understatement. She couldn't get the memory of telling her girls about the divorce out of her mind.

"Your father and I are separating," Tabby had said earlier that week as Drew and she sat across from the girls Sunday morning. To her surprise, Brittany had stayed strong for Callie, wrapping her arms around her sister and waiting for Callie to start crying. But the tears never came. Callie was stronger than Tabby knew.

"Will we see Dad?" she had asked.

Together, both Drew and Tabby had assured them that they would get equal time together, which both Callie and Brittany seemed glad to hear.

That had been such a hard conversation, but it was out of the way now.

Tabby stood from the cafeteria table, checking her watch. "My lunch is over," she told Jenni, "but just know that everything is going to be okay. Drew is staying at a hotel and the kids know that we're separating. From there, I guess we'll just take it one step at a time. I appreciate your willingness to give me a shoulder to lean on. It means everything to me."

"Anytime, Tabby. You know where to find me." Her genuine smile was something that made Tabby feel even warmer inside.

"I have to go. I'm so happy your migraines are getting better." She touched Jenni's shoulder. "Please give me a little time and be patient." She waved and then hurried from the table, dropping her tray into the trash can.

Tabby went back to the cardiology floor and went straight to the desk, looking through the files of her next patient. It was the job that would help her take care of the kids, just as it always did. She would do her part in making sure neither Callie nor Brittany ever looked at their father negatively, but she was going to be the strong woman she needed to be. It wasn't going to be easy, but she could do it.

CHAPTER TWENTY

Jenni

J enni leaned forward and looked at the plans in front of her. It would be hard work, but if done correctly, the board wouldn't have to do any of it. She would be more than happy to pick up their slack, and with the staff's help, it would surely be a fundraiser that no one would forget.

She took a sip of her water, then flipped through the pages of various donors that had already come in. She was pleased with the funds she had secured so far. With the way things stood, she wouldn't have been surprised if that was all they needed to ensure that all nurses and administrative staff would remain employed.

Her phone rang and she looked at the caller ID, surprised to see Tabby's name flashing on the screen. She was giving her time and space, but it was difficult to be apart.

"Hello?"

"Hey, Jenni. I was just thinking about you." The hairs stood on the back of Jenni's neck. "I mean, not thinking about you, but thinking about everything. You know, all that's been happening and stuff."

"Oh. Sure." Jenni released a breath. Her heart started racing and she had to calm herself down. Clearly, her mind was in a different space than Tabby's. "How are you doing?"

"Okay, I guess. Just sent the kids off to be with their dad tonight and was sitting here thinking about, well, you know."

Jenni didn't know. She was already confused, and the conversation was only getting stranger by the second. She didn't respond, hoping Tabby would see that she was making no sense.

"I'd like to talk, if you have time. Are you available to come over tonight?"

"Oh. Uh, yeah, I'm not really doing anything." She glanced over to the pile of work that Tabby couldn't know anything about. "I'll head over now."

"I'll see you in a bit." Tabby disconnected the call and Jenni got up from the table and looked down at her worn-out T-shirt and faded jeans. That wasn't going to cut it. She hurried up the stairs to her bedroom, where she rifled through her clothes. She tried on not one or two, not even three, but four different variations of outfits. Then she finally settled on a loose sweatshirt and jeans. It didn't look like she was trying too hard. It would look like she had grabbed the first thing she saw in her closet and thrown it on.

Satisfied, she left her room, steeling her resolve. She couldn't go into Tabby's home thinking that anything would happen between them. She had to be strong. Until the marriage was dissolved, nothing could happen.

With Tabby's text, her purse, and her car keys in hand, Jenni was out the door ten minutes later. She put Tabby's address into her GPS and drove twenty minutes to Tabby's home. She pulled into the driveway, noticing the porch light was on. Tabby's house looked cozy from the outside, and Jenni wasn't nervous walking up the trail that led to the front door. When she knocked, it didn't take long for Tabby to answer the door.

Jenni's eyes couldn't do anything but wander down Tabby's front. She wore a tank top and tight jeans. It was far from the scrubs she was used to seeing Tabby wear, and it made Jenni groan internally. Her breasts were tight against her tank top, and Jenni instantly wondered how those breasts would taste. She had to bite back those thoughts and remind herself she wasn't going there.

"Would you care for a drink? Wine? Water? Wine?" Tabby laughed. "Whatever you want. I think Drew even has a few beers, if that's more your style."

"I appreciate the offer, but the drugs they have me on don't let me have alcohol. Not that that needs to stop you or anything. By all means, if you want to drink, go ahead. I'll just have some water."

"Water for two, then. I wouldn't drink in front of you. Don't be silly." Tabby motioned toward another room that was connected to the foyer. "Have a seat and I'll be right there."

Jenni walked into the living room and looked around. The fireplace was already lit. On the mantle was a string of pictures. Her eyes went to the family portrait. They looked happy. Brittany looked to be ten years old, so the photo must have been taken a few years ago, but the whole family appeared to be smiling.

"Here you go," Tabby said, interrupting her thoughts. Jenni grabbed the water from her. "You saw the picture, huh?"

"You all look so happy," Jenni pointed out.

Tabby took a sip of her water and looked at the picture. "I would say we were happy, to an extent." She smiled. "It's hard to know what to do with the pictures, though. I keep them up for now because the kids are living here. But eventually..." Her words trailed off, and she shrugged. "They'll have to come down or go into the girls' rooms."

Jenni quirked up an eyebrow. "So, you're thinking this is really over?"

"Most likely, yes. We've already had a long talk with the girls and they were surprisingly accepting of the situation."

Jenni sipped her water, processing those words. Though she had feelings for Tabby, she ultimately wanted Tabby to do what she thought was best. If that meant trying to work things out, she would have to accept that. That was the power of change. People could change their minds at any given moment, and Jenni didn't want to get her hopes up on just a possibility.

"You know," Jenni began, "marriage is always hard work. There's little that can be disputed with that. If it's worth fighting for, then by all means, you should fight for it. If you wake up every morning thinking about your husband and the love you have for him, then you should surely keep that love intact."

Tabby's eyes shifted toward the fire. Jenni wished she could read her mind. What was she thinking? Did her words resonate with Tabby at all?

"What if you start to feel that maybe love doesn't have to be a part of your marital union? You have two kids that you share. You can equally love them but live in the same house and just find ways to cohabitate together," said Tabby.

"So, you're saying you would be all right if Drew went out and lived his life, and you lived yours, but you stayed together just for the children?" Tabby looked down, and Jenni waited for her response, but it never came. "Tabby, that isn't any way to live. I'd like to believe you're smart enough to realize that."

Tabby looked up, shooting a glare in Jenni's direction. "What else is there to do if we did stay together? It feels like it's over, but Drew keeps making these comments to suggest we have other options other than divorce. And my parents always taught me to do everything I can to fight for marriage."

"At the expense of your happiness?" Jenni argued. "Why should you put your happiness on the back burner, just because you want to save a marriage? Do you love him still? Can you honestly look at me and tell me that you are in love with your husband?"

Tabby tilted her head and slowly shook her head. "I care for him and probably always will, but to say I'm in love with him..." She shook her head harder. "It's tough to utter those words."

Jenni saw the agony in Tabby's eyes. She didn't want to make Tabby feel worse about her situation. She had come here because Tabby needed someone to talk to, a shoulder to cry on, a heart-to-heart, and that was what Jenni had to give her.

"I know I don't talk much about Wendy," Jenni began. "But she was destined to be the one I would grow old with. We were so similar that it was sometimes hard to imagine we were two different people and walked through two different paths. Wendy immediately had my heart from the moment that we met. A chance encounter that never should have happened suddenly turned my life around. I saw that I had meaning in my life once again. Never in my wildest thoughts would I have ever dreamt that she would disappear from my life so suddenly. One minute she's here and the next she's gone, and I think about her every day. It wasn't until I bumped into a certain nurse that I believed I could ever move on."

Tabby's cheeks turned bright pink as Jenni continued.

"There you were. When I saw you, I didn't know if you were gay, straight, or bi. I just knew that you were the first person who made me feel something inside. And when I got to know you, I started to feel these emotions that I thought had died right along with Wendy. It saddened me to learn you were married, but as I grew to know you and saw the way you were being mistreated in your marriage, all that mattered was showing you the love and kindness that you deserve out of life."

"Wow," Tabby said breathlessly.

"I'm not trying to tell you all this thinking that it will change the outcome. I think you truly need to do what you think you need to when it comes to Drew and how you want things to work between you two. For me, I think you need to respect yourself when you make your decision. But you're the one who needs to make it."

Jenni stood up from her seat, and Tabby quickly followed suit. "Where are you going?"

"I don't think I can stay here. The temptation is too much, being around you."

She started to move toward the foyer, when Tabby reached out and grabbed her hand, startling Jenni. "Don't go. Please. I know what I need, and I need you. I know you said to wait until everything is finalized, but....You may think it's foolish, but I *do* need you."

Jenni's heart slowly rattled in her chest as she studied Tabby. Foolish or not, with Tabby showing Jenni her desires, Jenni couldn't turn from it. She didn't want to. She moved in closer, following the lines of Tabby's fingers and clutching her hand in hers. She breathlessly kissed Tabby, her moan echoing through the living room, her tongue slowly wrapping around Tabby's. She pulled back, giving Tabby time to rethink what she had said. When Tabby only gazed back fiercely at her, Jenni grabbed her face between her palms and pulled her closer, kissing her harder.

With one push, she had Tabby seated on the couch, and she straddled her legs around the woman of her desires. Their tongues quickly collided, and she slowly snaked a hand up Tabby's tank top, breaking from the kiss only to toss the tank off to the side. They didn't know where the night would lead them, but Jenni knew she was looking forward to exploring every curve that would get her there.

WITH ONE ARM WRAPPED AROUND TABBY, JENNI PULLED HER closer and kissed her hard, her tongue smoothly sliding along Tabby's. They had moved their sexual endeavors to Tabby's bedroom, something that felt so intimate and so right. There were moments when Jenni thought she should stop and see if they wanted to continue in the spare room, but Tabby seemed to be completely engrossed in it. If Tabby wasn't pulling back, then Jenni wouldn't either.

Jenni pulled herself up and shifted her body on top of Tabby. She broke from the kiss to gaze at Tabby and saw that her eyes were sparkling. Jenni ran her hands over Tabby's bare breasts, and she moved in and pressed her lips between Tabby's cleavage.

Tabby giggled, then shifted her body beneath Jenni. "You have no idea how much I needed this," she whimpered. Jenni shifted both palms and slowly started to knead Tabby's breasts between her hands, leaning forward to kiss Tabby with a passion that was finally realized.

"Me too," Jenni whispered, moving her tongue in to claim another moan from Tabby. She had lost count of how many times Tabby had moaned. It was something that sent electric shivers up and down Jenni's spine.

"You're breathtaking," Jenni whispered, slipping her tongue in and out of Tabby's mouth, filling with heat at the sound of Tabby's groans, which lit her insides on fire. Her body was tight and petite, to be expected with the age gap that trailed between them, but Jenni didn't allow age to be a factor in their electrifying night together. It just felt like everything had finally come together, and knowing that Tabby was starting to realize her worth made Jenni even more invested in being with her.

Tabby broke from the kiss. "This has given me so much to think about. It's opened my eyes to the world in so many ways. And I feel like I'm ready to have some breathing room to figure out what I'm going to do."

"Which is what, exactly?" Jenni asked.

"Well, for one, sit down and talk to Drew. Before he left, he said he was actually open to doing some marriage counseling, and if he truly is, then maybe I need to get some insight into that."

Jenni's jaw dropped at this turn of events, and she rolled off Tabby and stood. "You're telling me this while we're having sex?"

Tabby stood too, tears in her eyes. "I'm sorry for being this way. I'm just scared, and I don't know what to do. Everything is so confusing. Do I owe it to my family to cover all of my options? I needed this tonight, but I also need to take into consideration what's best for everyone. I can't be selfish."

Jenni nodded. "You're right. You have your children to consider, and apparently, you have Drew to consider. But I don't like feeling used. When you kiss me, you need to be one hundred percent certain that it's me you want. My emotions are involved in this, too." She turned and stormed out of the room, anger slowly turning into disappointment. When she reached the living room and started to get dressed, she heard Tabby's footsteps.

"Don't rush off like this," Tabby pleaded.

By now, Jenni's eyes were clouded with tears. "I don't know that we have anything to talk about. At least not yet. Clearly, tonight meant more to me than it meant to you."

"That's not true," Tabby started, reaching out and touching Jenni's arm. "It meant the world to me, but I have to be realistic here. Should I just throw away a marriage that's lasted nearly thirteen years?"

"When that man has been sleeping with probably every single woman in town, then I would say you don't owe anything to him."

"He said it was just one woman," Tabby argued.

Jenni covered her eyes and shook her head. "Tabby, I've been around the block a few times. Surely you can't be that naïve." Tabby looked down, abashed. "But until you figure all that out, there's nothing I can do here. The call is up to you."

With that, she turned and walked away, leaving the house. She hesitated once she reached her car, thinking that if she went back now, she could pull Tabby into her arms and plead with her to choose her. But it wasn't going to play out like that. This was one decision she couldn't make for Tabby, no matter how much it was breaking her heart.

CHAPTER TWENTY-ONE

Tabby

Seeing how upset Jenni had been when she left the house had made Tabby pause. She had never had a night with someone who made her body so aflame, and it was exhilarating to think about the two of them continuing where they'd left off. Yet she owed it to herself and her kids to fully understand where her marriage was going. If divorce was the outcome, then having this transition period was necessary.

Three days had passed since that night, and Tabby had been able to avoid Jenni and her own erotic thoughts because, for some reason, she hadn't seen her at the hospital at all. At least that was a relief, as it gave her some breathing room to think about her marriage.

On that third day, she entered the breakroom and caught a group of employees all gathered at one table. They were looking over a paper and whispering to one another. Tabby went over to the vending machine and was browsing the selections when she heard one of the women gasp. She turned around and looked toward the table. "What's so exciting?" she asked.

It was Greta, who worked down in the pharmacy, who was the first one to speak. "Have you heard about the renovations that will be starting at the end of this week?"

Tabby shrugged. "I've heard a little about it. I haven't been paying much attention when it comes to what's been going on around here. Why?"

Myra, who worked in ICU, looked over at Tabby. "Well, a list has been leaked." She looked around the table. "We don't want to get anyone in trouble, so we're just going say someone showed it to someone, who then showed it to someone else, who then showed it to someone else." She shrugged. "You get the picture. Anyway, this list shows that some hospital staff are on the brink of losing their jobs."

Tabby's eyes widened. "Who's on it?"

Myra grimaced. "I'm on it, as are Hanna and Greta." She shook her head. "Looks like they're getting rid of the people who have the most seniority."

Tabby frowned. "Give me that." She skimmed through the first page, then moved on to the next page. There her name was. Shocked, Tabby said, "Wow. Guess it doesn't pay to work your butt off anymore." She put the paper down. "Whose brilliant idea was this?"

Greta replied, "No idea. But it looks like the board members have all signed off on it." She turned it over to the last page and held it up. Tabby looked over the names, and right at the bottom of the list was Jenni's signature. She grabbed the list back and stared at the name, shaking her head. It wasn't possible. She had spent enough time with Jenni that if this were going on, Jenni would have told her. Did the intimacy between them account for nothing? "This was signed two weeks ago," Tabby muttered.

"Yep," Myra said.

"Guess I should be glad that I'm a newbie," a man said, slumping down in his chair. "But that means I'll be losing all my friends that I've made."

"Wait a minute," Tabby started. "We're not going to go down without a fight, right?"

"Tabby," Greta began. "We're not even supposed to be seeing this list."

"Well, we *have* seen this list. And I don't know about you, but I'm going to talk to someone about it. We can't just sit back and wait for them to give us our termination. That's not happening—no way, no how." She shook her head vehemently, but everyone else looked concerned. "If I have to fight this myself, then I will, but where's the Capmed fight that you all used to once have?"

Some staff stammered some excuses, and Tabby turned from the group, the list still in her hand. "Where are you going?" Greta asked.

When Tabby turned back to face them, Greta had gotten up from the table, looking serious. Greta continued, "I got this list secretly and I would prefer to make sure no one is aware who this came from. So you have to let me know where you're going."

Tabby tossed the list back to the table and Greta quickly snatched it up, clutching it to her chest like it was the last thing giving her life. "I will keep you out of it, I swear. But I have a family that needs me to support them, and I can't just wait for Capmed to give me my walking papers. I have to at least try to get some answers. If I do it alone, then so be it."

She turned and headed out of the breakroom, the door swinging behind her. She reached the elevator and entered, pushing the button for the main floor. She looked up as the doors were about to close and saw the rest of the group headed her way, including the three people who weren't at risk of losing their jobs.

"If you're doing it, then we're all doing it. We're in this together," Myra said softly. "We've got your back."

Together, they reached the main floor and walked down the hallway that led to Brian's office. Tabby led the way, and they approached his assistant's desk. The assistant's eyes widened when she saw the group. "May I help you?" she asked.

Tabby looked at the assistant's name tag. "Hello, Phoebe. We're here to see Brian," she stated firmly. "And we're not leaving until he sees us, so you might want to let him know that."

The woman's eyes narrowed in on the group and she nodded as she dialed Brian's office. She turned her back, so they could only hear the muffled sounds of her voice. "They said," she started, her voice raising an octave—to the point where Tabby nearly caught word of what she was telling Brian—but then lowering to a whisper. "I'll let them know," she finished.

She swiveled her chair around to look at them. Tabby braced herself, convinced she would have to do some complaining if Phoebe attempted to turn them away. "You can head down the hallway. He'll see you." Tabby turned and looked at the rest of the staff, who were right at her heels. They all nodded with eagerness and resolve.

"Thank you," Tabby replied. They turned and headed toward Brian's office. Tabby had a million things she wanted to say to Brian, most of which started and ended with, How could you treat us like that?

"Come in," Brian called as she initiated the knock on his door. When they walked inside, he looked up, his eyes glancing over each one of them. He scooted back from his computer and locked eyes with Tabby. "I hear you wanted to see me."

Tabby looked over her left shoulder, then her right. No one spoke up, so it was all up to her. She turned back around and nodded. "Brian, we like to believe you think we work hard at our jobs. The ones who stand before you strive to make sure we do what is asked, before it's asked. We kick butt."

She bit her lip and shifted her stance from one foot to the other. "But it's come to our attention that the hospital that we all put in the work to help thrive is looking to let many of the senior staff go. And we're here to demand answers."

He arched an eyebrow. "I assume you've seen a list or something."

"Something like that. And we know that all of the board is behind this. What we don't understand is, why? Are our blood, sweat, and tears not enough?"

For emphasis, she leaned forward and pounded on his desk with her fists. His eyes went down to her fists, and he looked up, raising his eyebrows sternly. Tabby slowly pulled back. "Sorry. We just demand some answers."

Brian cleared his throat, then looked at the staff standing before him. Tabby waited for him to look at her again. "If memory serves me, not all of you are on the list." He looked over at the guy who stood directly behind Tabby, on her right. "Brett, you've been here how long?"

"A year, sir," he said.

Brian nodded. "That's right. You're not on this list. What sort of reasoning do you have to be here?"

"I'm standing up for the ones being terminated. I have made friends here and I can't picture this hospital without them."

"I've learned in my position that it doesn't pay to make friends."

Brian's eyes landed back on Tabby. "With that being said, the list isn't finalized. And it shouldn't have been leaked."

"Are you saying we're all not getting terminated?" Tabby asked.

"I'm saying that we haven't made the final cuts. We're still working on it. We still have some things to iron out. Rest assured that once we make those cuts, we'll better understand where we are. Understood?"

Tabby frowned. It wasn't quite the resolution she was looking for, but she nodded. "We all are pleased with the jobs we do here. You shouldn't let finances rule over everything."

He responded with a frown of his own. "I'll consider that. Now, if you'll please leave; I have some work I need to get done."

With nothing resolved, the group left his office. Before they parted, they all agreed to keep silent about the list so that other staff wouldn't be alarmed. In a place like Capmed though, Tabby fully expected the entire hospital to know about the cuts by the end of the day.

Tabby reached the elevator to go to the cardiology floor just as her phone rang. She glanced at the caller ID and saw Jenni's name flashing on the screen. She had probably gotten word that the list had leaked and was working to do damage control. Tabby wasn't going to allow her to beg for Tabby's forgiveness.

Tabby stepped off the elevator with a voicemail message. She considered automatically deleting it, but ultimately settled on listening to what Jenni had to say about the staff cuts. She was surprised that Jenni didn't bring up the cuts at all.

"Hey, Tabby, it's me. I was hoping we could catch up later. There are some things I need to discuss with you that have been weighing on my mind. Give me a call. I look forward to hearing from you."

Her tone was so sweet and clean, which confused Tabby as she slipped her phone into her pocket. It was only a ploy to get what she wanted, and Tabby wasn't falling for it, even if Jenni was the one person Tabby wanted to talk to. She was possibly losing her job, and Jenni was the only one who could console her and tell her why, but Tabby wasn't going to reach out— not if it meant falling for Jenni's ploy.

CHAPTER TWENTY-TWO

Jenni

Brian stood at the front of the conference room as Jenni looked over her notes. She had everything written down, ready to plead her case, and anticipated that everyone would willingly agree with all of her points. She needed to make sure she didn't leave any stone left unturned.

"Thank you all for meeting here at the hotel," Brian started. "They've started construction at the hospital, and I just thought this way, we wouldn't be in their way when they're working on the boardroom. I've spoken to Lesa Niel, who owns this hotel, and she's agreed that we can have access to their conference room going forward. There's a lot to go over, so let's not wait a single minute. I know that Jenni has a lot to discuss, so I want to give the floor to her. Jenni..."

Jenni stood up, dipping her head in acknowledgment. "Thank you, Brian."

She looked around the table at the rest of the people who were present, including the doctors, who would state their cases. "Thank you all for being here. So, I have been working on getting donors who are more than willing to provide financial assistance to Capmed." She held up the list and rifled through the pages she already had. "I know that it's only a start, but I'm prepared to fight every step of the way. Saving these jobs is what I'm passionate about."

She dropped the list to the table. "I have given this a lot of thought. I've spoken to D.M.J. Country Club, and they are willing to offer a place for us to have a fundraiser and charity drive."

A hand shot up, and she pointed to Charles. "Yes?"

"What type of things were you thinking for the fundraiser?" he asked. "Food? Auctions? You said charity drive? What does that all include?"

"Glad you asked, Charles. There would be a dinner. I have one of the donors listed here, who is willing to cater the fundraiser. For the auctions, I was thinking we could involve the whole city. We can have items donated to charities. It will get all of Chicago involved, and what's even better is if the staff knew that their jobs were in jeopardy, they would probably be willing to help out in any way they could. This will be something that will require little work for everyone, as I'll be putting in a lot, if not most, of the work. But this is what I love to do."

Jenni scanned the room and saw several board members nodding their agreement on the matter. "There's some work to do to iron out all the details, but I think we're nearly there. If you're all on board, then I will go full force and get this started."

She stopped her gaze on Brian, unable to read his facial expression. After a moment, he simply nodded. "You have put a lot of work into this matter; I can see that."

"I'm passionate about this because I've been in a position in which I was going to be terminated and no one was there to help. I want to be their voice."

"You should have been in my office yesterday, then," Brian snickered.

"I'm not following," Jenni said.

"A group of employees stopped by my office yesterday. Turns out the list of potential terminations was leaked, and the staff wasn't going down without fighting first."

Jenni considered those words. *Who were the pages leaked to?* She tried to push that thought from her mind and from her conscience. "I see," she finally answered. "Well, I would have been their voice, no doubt." She turned her gaze to the rest of the staff. "So, is everyone on board?"

"Let's take a vote," Brian said. "All those in favor, raise your hand." Slowly, everyone's hand went up, including Brian's.

Jenni beamed and nodded, relieved that they had gotten somewhere and eager to put things in motion. "Great! Now, we just need to come up with a date."

They worked on finalizing those details, and as the meeting came to a close, Jenni realized that she had singlehandedly made things work out. None of the doctors had to voice their concerns, and it was something that brought her a sense of pride. The meeting didn't go over an hour, and when they adjourned for the night, Jenni thought about the logistics of several ideas she wanted to carry out.

As she left the room, she spotted Charles coming over to her. "Well done, indeed."

She shrugged. "It was nothing."

"I wouldn't say that. This was all you. Kudos. You should be very proud."

She nodded, just satisfied that it had worked out in her favor. "But I wonder who leaked the list," Jenni pointed out. "And I wonder who saw it."

She mostly wondered if Tabby had gotten her eyes on it. If she had, she wanted to get to her and make sure she knew that the danger of Tabby losing her job had subsided. She had tried calling her the previous day to meet with her and tell her about the whole fiasco. But Tabby had never called back. She was worried that Tabby thought she was out of a job.

"You're looking at him," Charles replied, chuckling.

Jenni's jaw dropped. "You? But why? Didn't you think that would cause an uproar within the nursing staff?"

"That's exactly why I did it. I wanted to give them the fury to want to fight for themselves. It wasn't fair that they were being left in the dark, and I wanted to light a fire under them. It looks like it worked."

Jenni bit the corner of her lip. It did, but without any repercussions? She wasn't so sure.

"Gotta run. Cecilia almost has dinner ready. Talk to you later." He waved and then hurried away from her.

Jenni slowly walked toward the lobby, thinking about what Charles had said. Here she had done everything to keep the news from Tabby, but

Charles had made sure the whole hospital would know. Now what? If Tabby had seen it already, would Jenni be able to convince her that she had kept the list from her to protect her?

As she reached the door, she dug into her pocket for her phone, then groaned. She had left it in the conference room. She turned to cross the lobby again and abruptly ran into a man. He hesitated and looked at her, tilting his head as if he recognized her. Jenni quickly looked away. He may not have recognized her, but she recognized him right away. "Excuse me," she mumbled.

"No problem, dear," he said. He winked at her and then proceeded toward the front desk, where a blonde stood. When he approached her, he kissed her with a slow and passionate hunger—making Jenni's jaw drop—then proceeded to the elevator.

Jenni attempted to shake that image from her brain. Drew and a blonde were headed up to a room, certainly to do the obvious, in Jenni's mind. She shivered as the nasty thoughts plagued her mind. While Tabby was taking care of his children, he was still off having sex with other women. For once, Jenni didn't care about the outcome. She wasn't going to sit back and let what Tabby didn't know hurt her even more.

———

Jenni stepped up to Tabby's front door. She paused, just staring at it. She was busting in to disrupt Tabby's life yet again when Tabby could still be having dinner with her kids. She hesitated, then turned to leave.

The image of Drew and the blonde popped back into her mind. They had been making out as the elevator doors were closing. The woman looked to be no older than eighteen. Tabby deserved to know her husband was out there still treating her so disrespectfully. She turned back to the door and knocked.

A few moments later, the door flew open. It wasn't Tabby, but Callie. "I know you," Callie said.

Jenni smiled. "Callie, right?"

Callie nodded, then called out, "Mom? Your friend's here."

It didn't take long for Tabby to round the corner. "Hey, Tabby," Jenni said in greeting.

"Callie, run on upstairs and shower. I'll be up in a bit to tuck you in."

Callie turned to Jenni. "Bye!"

Jenni waved back as Callie went up the stairs, and Tabby turned to her.

"What are you doing here?" Tabby asked. "You should go."

Jenni cowered a little as Tabby tried to push past her to get to the door. "Why? There are some things you need to know. This won't take long."

Tabby huffed. "There's nothing you can say to me that will surprise me. I saw the list, Jenni. What I don't know is why you didn't feel the need to tell me."

"I was trying..." Jenni started, but Tabby held up her hand and cut her off.

"I don't need to know. You signed off on it, which meant you were all for it. Well, that's nice to know. You don't care whose job is at stake. Brava, Jenni. You clearly fooled me."

Jenni frowned. "I wasn't for it. I didn't sign off on anything."

"Oh really? You're going to lie to me?" Tabby stormed past her and went into the living room. A short time later, she returned with a paper and pointed to the bottom of it. "That's your signature, right?"

Jenni took it from her and stared down at her signature. She looked up and nodded. "That's my signature, but I didn't sign this."

"So someone forged it. Bet Brian would love to hear you say that." Tabby shook her head, and the disappointment on her face made Jenni's heart ache.

"I'm not saying someone forged it. I'm saying that they took my signature from another form and transposed it onto the paper."

"That sounds like a lot of work, don't you think?" Tabby asked.

"Yeah, but it's the truth," Jenni said.

Tabby looked away from her and shrugged. "I don't know what to believe anymore."

"Well, this isn't entirely what I came here to discuss with you," Jenni started. "Perhaps you'll choose not to believe me about this, too."

Tabby shifted her gaze, her eyes softening slightly. "What?"

"I had a board meeting at the hotel on the corner of Fifth tonight, where I saw Drew. He wasn't alone."

Tabby's eyes narrowed in on her. "He was with another woman? They were doing something?"

Jenni nodded. "They were making out. I wanted you to know."

Tabby nodded. "Thanks." She walked to the door and opened it for Jenni. Jenni slowly moved to meet her at the door, not wanting to leave on such a low note.

"Tabby," Jenni began.

Tabby looked up, tears in her eyes. "I don't want to talk about it. Not tonight. And frankly..." Her words trailed off, and she looked away from Jenni.

"You'd rather not talk about it with me. Understood. And I'm sorry," Jenni mumbled. Without another word, she turned away and went to her car. If she looked over her shoulder, she wouldn't be able to leave. She could only imagine the pain coursing through Tabby's veins, and seeing that fixated on her face would have torn Jenni up inside. Tabby needed time to heal, and when she was ready to do that, Jenni would be there for her.

CHAPTER TWENTY-THREE

Tabby

T abby tapped her finger on the desk, staring blankly at the computer monitor. She leaned back in her chair and tried to focus on the words on the screen, but it was no use. After two days of trying not to think about Jenni, she found that her situation with her was the only thing she could think about.

She screwed up! Plain and simple. Get over her. But that was impossible. She was already losing complete control of her life, and with Drew off having sex with whomever he wanted and the kids spending more time with friends, she was left only with her thoughts, which all revolved around Jenni. What if she was being honest with her about having no recollection of signing that document? What if Tabby had pushed her away for no apparent reason?

More like plenty of reason. She didn't tell you that you were on the verge of losing your job. She knew and decided to leave you out of that.

While she didn't trust Jenni regarding matters pertaining to Capmed, Tabby did believe her about Drew. She had no reason to believe Jenni had made that up, especially since Jenni didn't know what hotel Drew was staying in. Her so-called husband was clearly not done messing around with other women.

The front desk phone rang, and she reached over and grabbed it. "Cardiology. This is Tabby."

"Thank goodness you answered." Hanna's rushed voice came on the phone. "I'm the only one here and the ER has been swamped. Any chance you can help a woman out?"

Tabby looked around the dead hallway. Working in the ER would be something that could clear her mind of Jenni; it was precisely what she needed. "Give me five minutes to let them know. I'll be right there."

"You're a blessing, Tabby. See you soon."

Tabby dropped the phone into the cradle and went to find the nursing manager. Three minutes later, she was heading down the elevator and straight to the ER. When the doors opened, she spotted the waiting room and sighed with relief. It was just the thing she needed. She picked up the pace, hurrying toward the front desk.

Hanna came out of a room and let out a relieved breath. "Thank heavens you're here. I've gotten some people into a room but haven't fully triaged them. The charts are there. If you could grab some and do the triage, that'd be great."

"I'm on it," Tabby replied. She grabbed the first file folder and walked over to a room. When she opened the door, she saw a young girl sitting on the bed. She was clutching her arm, and a woman knelt beside her.

"Hi, there. My name is Tabby, and I'll be one of the nurses taking care of you. What happened here?" She grabbed a stool and wheeled it over to the bed, glad to finally be able to clear her mind of all her problems.

For the next hour, Hanna and Tabby worked simultaneously on assisting patients. It gradually became a well-oiled machine, and they kept it going. Tabby grabbed another folder and looked at the room number. She headed down the hallway, spotting Hanna as she rounded the corner. Hanna no longer looked stressed, and she was smiling again.

"Couldn't have done this without you, Tabby."

Tabby nodded. She always felt a sense of belonging when it came to Capmed. It was something she would surely miss if she did find herself terminated. She knocked on the next door. A voice sounded on the other end, which she took as an invitation to enter.

"Hello, I'm Tabby and I'll be your..." Her voice dropped when she saw Jenni sitting on the bed. "Jenni!" Tabby exclaimed. "I didn't notice it was you."

She looked at the chart, and sure enough, Jenni's name was in bold lettering. She felt foolish for having missed that small detail. "Is everything all right?" She sat down on the stool and let out a small, embarrassed laugh. "Well, of course everything isn't all right. You're here."

She opened the folder and looked at the main reason Jenni was there. She frowned, her brows furrowed. "The drugs aren't working?" she asked. "Looks like you've been throwing up for twenty-four hours and your migraine is at a twelve on a scale of ten."

Jenni looked down at the floor. "I'm feeling much better," she said in a small voice. "I shouldn't bother you. Just thought Hanna would be my nurse."

"Sorry to disappoint you," Tabby muttered.

"It's me disappointing you—that you have to be stuck taking care of me. Maybe I should have gone to another hospital."

Her eyes darted to Tabby's, but then she winced and fell back against her pillow. Tabby stared at her. It appeared that even sitting up for two minutes was too long for Jenni. "Lean back," Tabby ordered.

Jenni rolled her eyes and reclined in a more comfortable position. Tabby helped her lie back, positioning a pillow behind her head. "Thank you," Jenni said.

With the way Jenni was looking at her, Tabby felt weak herself. She turned away and moved back to her stool, then slowly sat down. "So, twenty-four hours, huh?"

"Give or take," Jenni replied. She closed her eyes and Tabby looked down at the file.

"The medicine was working," Tabby said.

"It probably still is, but I've been busy and haven't been able to take it regularly." She shrugged. "Gotta do what you gotta do."

"At the expense of your health?" Tabby asked, arching an eyebrow. Jenni opened her eyes and looked over to where Tabby sat. "Doesn't seem smart, if you ask me."

Jenni sighed. "I didn't miss the drugs on purpose. I've just been busy and ultimately just forgot. They warned me that this could happen if I missed two consecutive doses. They weren't wrong." She sat up, then clutched her head and slowly lay back down. "I just need some anti-nausea pills and then I promise I won't be missing any more of my medication."

"I would advise you not to," Tabby replied. She stood to get the thermometer and took Jenni's temperature. "One hundred point three." She tilted her head. "You have a fever, you're visibly shaking, and you're as pale as a sheet."

"Must be a wonderful sight," Jenni said. Her sarcasm wasn't very effective since the pain in her head was so strong, she had to speak in a whisper.

"I'm not saying that to be cruel. Just pointing out the obvious. Maybe you have more than just a reaction to not taking the medicine."

Jenni shook her head, then grimaced. "I would say it's just a reaction. I know my body is putting up a fight because I haven't been kind to it. That's all."

"All right then," Tabby softly stated. She grabbed the BP cuff and put her stethoscope in her ears. As she pumped the cuff up, she spotted Jenni watching her.

"Tabby," Jenni whispered.

"Shhhh," Tabby ordered. "I have to concentrate." She looked back down at what she was doing, but Jenni's eyes didn't sway from her, though Jenni didn't attempt to interrupt her again.

"BP is a little high," Tabby said. "Does it usually run high?" Jenni shook her head as Tabby documented the information. "Could be part of it, as well." She walked over to the door, then looked over her shoulder at Jenni. "I'll grab a doctor. They'll be in with you soon."

Before Tabby could leave, Jenni spoke up. "Are we going to talk about it?" she asked.

Tabby sighed. "I'm not sure we have anything to say to each other."

"I don't think that's true," Jenni quietly replied. "I know that I have a ton I want to say."

Tabby shrugged. "Just concentrate on getting better. The doc will be right in with you."

She left the room and closed the door before falling back against it. She didn't like seeing Jenni in pain, but dwelling over what she couldn't change wasn't going to do anything. She needed distance.

She dropped the file into the bin attached to the door and stood there for a moment, wondering if she should go back in to tell Jenni that all was going to be well. Instead, she headed back to the front desk for the next patient. She didn't know if all would be okay, but she knew that she had taken steps to ensure she was in a better position.

Tabby slipped her phone back into her pocket as she left the breakroom and headed to the elevator. As she rounded the corner, she spotted two employees by the bulletin board. She hesitated before she proceeded to the elevator. "What's going on?" she asked.

A woman turned to Tabby. She had only seen her around a few times, but she knew she worked in the basement, where the archived medical records were.

"They just put up a sign-up sheet for the upcoming fundraiser." Noticing Tabby's frown, the woman continued, "You know, the fundraiser?"

Tabby looked confused. "I haven't heard about it, but I have been pretty busy." Life and work had been hard to balance, especially with her marriage in shambles and her trying not to think about losing her income. "What is it?"

The other woman, a newer employee, at least according to the tag on her name badge, said, "They're having a fundraiser to save the staff. Look."

Tabby looked at the sign. "Save the Staff—catchy name."

The younger woman laughed. "Either way, I'm excited to help out in any way I can. I might not be one of the ones in jeopardy, but you just never know when you might need help."

Tabby nodded and looked at the signatures that were already present. Jenni's name was the first on the list, and her contact information was listed. "Jennifer Jennison is in charge?" she asked.

"Appears that way," the older woman, named Hazel, responded. "She not only donates money, but pitches in when needed."

"Looks like it," Tabby said. She picked up the pen attached to the list and signed her name on one of the few spots left. The fundraiser might be part of the reason Jenni was too busy to remember to take her medicine. It wasn't an excuse to ignore her health, but it was a sign that Jenni wasn't on board when it came to letting the employees go. The two women left, and Tabby pulled her phone from her pocket.

She hadn't heard from Jenni since she had assisted her in the ER two days earlier, and she had considered texting her to see how she felt, but had always stopped herself. If she reached out, that would mean that she was ready to forgive Jenni completely. She hadn't been ready, but she knew now that she was wrong in the way she had been treating Jenni.

She dialed her number, but it went straight to voicemail. "You've reached Jenni. Leave me a message and I'll call you back. Have a blessed day."

"Hey, Jenni. It's me. I know you're probably going to be surprised to hear from me, and I don't blame you. If the positions were reversed, I would be, too. Anyway, I was hoping we could talk. I saw the volunteer sign—or, at least, one of them. And..."

She paused, then continued. "Well, we'll discuss it when we can see each other. I work for another two hours and then I have a small errand I have to take care of. The kids are staying at friends' houses tonight, so I have the whole night free. If you have some time, maybe we can chat. Maybe I can swing by your place. Let me know. I'll be waiting for your call. Goodbye, Jenni. Oh, and I hope you're feeling much better." She hung up and got on the elevator to return to the cardiology floor.

It was a busy night, so Tabby found herself lost in work and not thinking about what she would say to Jenni. After her shift, she changed into everyday clothes and left with her purse in hand. She was hopeful that she'd be able to talk to Jenni, except Jenni hadn't called her back, and that made her feel strange. Maybe Jenni wasn't going to easily forgive her because Tabby hadn't believed her about the staff cuts.

Tabby drove with purpose, to make the one stop she knew she had to make that night—the hotel where Drew was staying. With the kids away from the house, she would use that time to have a real conversation with Drew; she was ready to make that happen.

She approached the front desk, determined to get to his room, tell him why she was there, then leave. The quicker she could get through it, the easier the departure would be.

"May I help you?" a young petite blonde asked.

"I need the room number of Drew Brickly," she replied, confidence oozing from her tone.

The woman looked down at her computer and nodded. Without hesitation, she swiveled in her chair and grabbed a room key, then handed it over to her.

Tabby frowned. "I'll just knock." She pushed the key away, and the woman frowned.

"The way it works is you go in and..." Her words trailed off, and she lowered her voice. "Make yourself comfortable."

Tabby's jaw fell open. Without questioning the receptionist, she grabbed the key from the woman's hand and looked down at the number. "Thank you," she mumbled.

Tabby didn't waste any time getting on the elevator and taking it two floors up. Make herself comfortable? Was that what the staff was used to saying? She tapped her foot nervously, in tune with the music that played over the speaker in the elevator. When the doors opened, she walked to Drew's room. She stood, looking at the room key before taking a deep breath to steel herself.

Tabby swiped the key and opened the door. The first thing she was struck with was the darkness of the room. Perhaps Drew wasn't in. She moved in farther and heard the sound of running water. He was there. She hesitated, fearful of what she would discover in the bathroom. Or worse, in the shower.

A woman moaned, followed by the sound of something hard hitting up against a wall. Tabby shook her head and moved forward. "Drew!" the woman cried. That sound set something off inside of Tabby. She wanted to see Drew and the woman face to face.

Tabby threw the door back, and the woman—a brunette—along with Drew, abruptly stopped and turned to face her. The woman's eyes were round, her mouth wide open.

"Tabby!" Drew exclaimed.

Tabby shook her head. "There's not a single word you could say to me that would make this okay. And everything I want to say to you would make me look *very* unladylike. You don't deserve for me to even speak to you. You'll be hearing from my lawyer."

She spun on her heel and didn't shed a single tear. She ignored Drew, who was calling out for her. She was done with him, and there wasn't anything that her soon-to-be ex-husband could say to change that.

When she got to her car, she collapsed against the back of the seat, a feeling of relief washing over her. She was grateful that she was getting out of a dangerous situation—dangerous to her heart, anyway. Her phone rang, and she grabbed it before it could go to voicemail. Jenni's name flashed like bold letters, beckoning her to where she needed to be.

"Hello?"

"I'm sorry I'm just now calling you. My phone battery was dead, and I just got your message."

"I need to see you. Are you free?" Tabby asked.

"Come on over," Jenni said. Tabby put the car in drive and headed the short distance to Jenni's, knowing full well that when she saw her there would be no stopping the way her body and heart would react. She was finally right where she was supposed to be and hopeful that Jenni felt the same way.

CHAPTER TWENTY-FOUR

Jenni

Jenni paced in front of her bedroom mirror, then turned back to her reflection. She untucked her shirt from her jeans and tilted her head. "My goodness, Jenni, you're acting like a lovestruck teenager." She groaned and grabbed a hair tie, then pulled her hair into a loose ponytail. At least now she didn't appear like she cared how she looked.

Tabby rang the doorbell, and she jumped. She had wondered why Tabby had suddenly changed her mind. Was it just because she saw the posters calling for volunteers? She hadn't considered that might be the thing that would make Tabby reach out. At least the posters showed Tabby that Jenni was trying to help Capmed's staff, not get them fired.

Jenni left her room and hurried down the stairs, only slowing when she was close to the door. She had already mentally prepared herself that nothing was going to happen, but it didn't mean she couldn't look cute while Tabby was gently letting her down.

She opened the door to see Tabby turned away, looking out at the street. Her eyes darted to Jenni's. "Hey," Tabby said softly.

"Hey."

Tabby moved in closer, and for the first time in a while, she smiled. It was ever-so-slight, but it was there. It brought renewed hope to Jenni's mind.

"How are you feeling?" Tabby asked.

"Much better. I took my medicine, as planned, and I'm no longer nauseous." Jenni leaned against the door opening, realizing Tabby was still standing on her porch. "Silly me. Come inside." She stepped back, opening the door wider for Tabby to come into the foyer.

When Jenni closed the door and turned back around, Tabby swooped in for a kiss. Her hands softly but firmly grasped Jenni's face, knocking the wind out of Jenni. "Tabby," Jenni breathlessly gasped.

Tabby pulled back, her eyes now steady on Jenni's lips. "I couldn't wait to do that. I'm sorry, Jenni. I'm sorry I didn't believe you about the hospital. I'm sorry that I turned my back on you. The truth is that from the moment I got to know you, I started falling for you. It was scary, but also one of the best feelings in the world. Knowing that I was married caused me shame, but I don't regret these feelings I have. What I do regret is looking for a reason to push you away."

She shook her head. "No more. Now I'm only looking for a reason to stay in your arms. I hope that you can accept my apology."

"I already have," Jenni said, wrapping her arms around Tabby and pulling her into a passionate and lingering kiss. "I already have," she whispered again before her lips crashed back onto Tabby's and their tongues collided wildly. She grabbed onto the base of Tabby's shirt and pulled her as they maneuvered back to the stairs.

As they walked up, their mouths still glued to each other, Jenni stumbled, which brought them both to a fit of giggles. They ran up the stairs, not stopping until they reached Jenni's bedroom. Tabby grabbed for the tie to Jenni's ponytail and quickly tugged on it, releasing Jenni's hair around her shoulders. Tabby pushed Jenni toward the bed, and together, they fell onto her pillowtop mattress and started pulling at each other's clothes until they were all shed and lying in a heap.

"I've been falling for you from the moment I first saw you," Jenni whispered between kisses. "That very moment." Her tongue swooped in, claiming a moan from Tabby.

Jenni reached up and slowly started to tweak Tabby's nipples between her fingers, eliciting some of the most pleasurable sounds Jenni had ever heard. Tabby maneuvered her body until she straddled Jenni, leaving Jenni breathless and gasping for air. She tossed her head back, groaning and just letting Tabby pleasure her as she wished.

Was she dreaming? It almost felt like she was, and she didn't want anything to wake her up. With her eyes closed, she allowed Tabby's soft lips to do as they pleased.

She grabbed handfuls of Tabby's hair between her fingers and didn't shift her body beneath her. She was getting everything she desired and more. There wasn't any fear that Tabby would rush out on her and go back to her husband. There weren't any thoughts that Tabby wasn't right where she wanted to be. There were only the two of them, and it felt so good.

JENNI PULLED HERSELF UP AND LOOKED AT TABBY, WHO HAD A content smile on her lips. "Did that just happen?" Jenni asked.

Tabby nodded, grinning from ear to ear. "Not once, but twice. Give me a minute and I'll be ready for a third round." Tabby brushed her lips against Jenni's, still smiling. "Who knew love could feel so amazing?"

Jenni laughed. "Who knew how much I would love hearing you call it love." She kissed Tabby harder and brushed her hand over Tabby's face. "Who knew how much I was truly falling for you over the time I was getting to know you?"

"I think I hoped." Tabby smiled. She sighed happily and fell back, the covers dipping lower to reveal her right breast. Jenni looked down at the perky nipple and she groaned, biting back the desire to move back in and claim another taste. Who knew a new love could be so exciting?

"What I didn't know," Tabby began, like she read Jenni's thoughts, "was that I would come here and immediately jump in bed with you. I didn't know a conversation I needed to have with Drew would end with me catching him and his mistress together in the shower."

Jenni sat up, her jaw dropping. "You what?" Jenni asked.

Tabby nodded. "I went to the hotel he's staying in. When I asked for his room number, the receptionist simply handed over a key and told me to just go on in. Who's to say how many trysts he's had since we've been separated, or even before? But I can tell you this—no more. I'm done. I'm not going to find myself in a situation like that ever again." Tabby shivered, her eyes moving over to the bedroom window with a faraway look. "He played me like a fiddle repeatedly, and I allowed him to do that. How stupid could I be?"

"Don't say that," Jenni murmured. "You're not a fool. He's a jerk, and he never deserved you. But something good came out of your union. Two good things, in fact. You have two beautiful children together. They know the light you are in their lives. So, don't worry about your husband."

"Soon to be ex-husband," Tabby asserted.

"Have you started the paperwork?" Jenni asked, hope lifting her voice.

"I called my lawyer on my way to you, and she's drawing up divorce papers as we speak. Well, it's kind of late, so probably tomorrow." She laughed. Her whole face lit up, and Jenni couldn't remember seeing Tabby look so happy. Even after the first night they had sex, she seemed to be struggling. This was a good sign, Jenni believed.

"I'm truly happy for you," Jenni said, kissing Tabby, then pulling back and moving down to take her nipple into her mouth. She sighed with pleasure, releasing it from her lips to look up at Tabby. "It was just waiting for me."

Tabby laughed. "Couldn't help yourself, right?"

Jenni smiled deviously. "Not hardly." She kissed Tabby's shoulder, overwhelmingly in love with the way she felt around Tabby. Every look sent shivers of desire through her, and Jenni was ready to shout from a rooftop how much she cared for her.

"So did you sign up to volunteer for the fundraiser?" Jenni asked, changing the subject.

"What do you think?" Tabby asked, arching an eyebrow.

"I would hope yes, because it wouldn't be the same without you." Jenni brushed a kiss on Tabby's forehead before pulling back. "I'm famished. Aren't you?"

"Sex does make a person need food," Tabby replied in jest. "Let's eat."

They both left the room, neither concerned with putting clothes back on. The night had started in a way that sent pleasurable shivers down Jenni's spine, and they were both looking for a more intense and erotic night than they'd ever spent together.

Jenni grabbed two glasses, a carton of milk, and a pie out of the refrigerator and started setting up the table. When she sat, she saw that Tabby was no longer smiling, but biting her lip nervously.

"What's wrong?" Jenni asked.

"Do you think you'll be able to save our jobs?" Tabby asked.

Jenni nodded and looked at her lover reassuringly. "Honestly, I believe that with the donors we've already gotten, everyone's job is safe."

Please grab the life-affirming epilogue by scanning or clicking the
QR code below:
[Or Type or Click here: https://BookHip.com/LJDAWWT]

Happy Reading,
Morgan
P.S: Thanks, www.kindlepreneur.com, for the QR code generator,
and www.booklinker.com for the universal links.

FIGHTING HER *Touch*

BOOK 2

HEALING HEARTS
A *Lesbian Medical Romance* Drama Series

MT CASSEN

A dedication from Morgan Cassen to medical workers in all corners of our world:

Morgan is in awe of the work done by the frontline workers of the noblest profession. The recent events have only increased my appreciation of the difficulty and danger associated with your line of work. I would like to thank you from the bottom of my heart.

CHAPTER ONE

Liz

The breakroom smelled of burnt popcorn as Elizabeth Fletcher stepped inside. She chewed her lower lip, the weight of the world pressing on her shoulders. A few people were sprinkled throughout the breakroom. One woman sat along the windowsill, her phone in hand as she looked up and nodded her greeting. Liz gave a slight wave, but the woman had already looked back down. A man sat in the corner, eating something that looked like cereal, or perhaps oatmeal, his eyes locked on a woman who was halfway across the room. She seemed oblivious to his gaze, or maybe she was playing it cool.

Liz quickly looked away. The last thing she wanted was for him to catch her staring, and she was probably too tired for decent conversation. Her eyes darted to the microwave as another woman who looked to be in her mid- to late forties took the popcorn out of the microwave and opened it up, dumping the contents into a bowl. Her eyes caught Liz's, and she grinned.

"Breakfast of champions, right here," she said. "Want some?"

Liz smiled and held up a granola bar. "Thanks, though." She walked over to an empty chair and collapsed into it, careful not to make too much of a disruption as she tore back the wrapper. Liz released a sigh and took a small bite out of the bar.

Three weeks into the job at Capmed, and still, she wasn't all that comfortable. She kept her eyes drawn to the top of the table, hoping that if she did happen to look up, no one would be staring. Just fifteen minutes; she could handle fifteen minutes of waiting out clock-in time. She was already positive that the day would be a busy one. That was one thing about her nursing gig; she never had to worry about downtime. If she wasn't rushing around trying to learn the ropes from a fellow nurse, she was being pulled in a thousand different directions to help out where needed. Every day, she returned home with aching feet, an aching back, and a throbbing headache. What if she wasn't cut out to be a nurse?

Give this shot. Transport this patient here. Don't do that. No, do that. File these records. She was exhausted just thinking about it.

In all honesty, she was glad she chose to go to nursing school, but she somehow thought this path would have more flexibility. *Give yourself time, Liz. Geesh. You're less than a month in.* She was a little naive but liked to call it optimism.

"This seat taken?"

She looked up. The woman with the burnt popcorn stood propped against her chair. Liz shook her head, scared even to fathom turning the woman away. She looked like she could throttle a person if they even dared to disagree with her.

"Thanks!" The woman slid down onto the chair and popped a handful of popcorn into her mouth. "I'm exhausted."

Liz frowned. "The day hasn't even started."

The woman laughed. "For you, maybe. For me, though, I've been here ten hours and eleven minutes." She glanced at her watch. "Correction! Twelve minutes."

She released a yawn before she scarfed down some more popcorn. "Last night, the ER was swamped. I saw ten patients the first hour." She released another yawn. "Don't worry, though. Took care of them all before you got here." She smirked and turned back to her popcorn.

Liz nodded politely and looked away. Her gaze returned to the woman on the windowsill. She was wearing a lab coat, so she was probably a doctor. Something about her was alluring. She looked older than Liz and pretty, but it was something else drawing Liz in. The way she carried herself. And her eyes...

After a moment, the woman glanced up, and Liz quickly looked away, her cheeks warming. Why had she been staring? Must have been the exhaustion. Liz shoved the last of her granola bar into her mouth.

"You're new around here, right?"

Liz turned her attention back to the woman sitting across from her. "Newish," Liz stuttered, then coughed, her granola bar going down the wrong pipe.

The woman jumped up and went around to pound on Liz's back. "Are you okay?" she asked.

Liz coughed, attempting to catch her breath, then held up her hand. "I'm fine," she exclaimed, clearing her throat, and looked up at the woman. "Yeah, I'm good. Thanks."

She coughed again to clear her throat, then nodded. "As I was saying—new, as in I've been here three weeks. Pulmonology floor."

"Snoozefest!" the woman said, making a fake yawn, then smirked. "Just teasing. Someone's got to do it, right?" She then quirked up an eyebrow. "Silly me, I sometimes get off on these tangents. I haven't even introduced myself. Name's Hanna."

She stuck out her hand for Liz to shake. Hanna had this infectious smile that made Liz want to respond in kind. "I've been here going on twenty-one years. So, you being here three weeks, that's definitely new." She laughed loudly, which brought a smirk to Liz's lips.

Twenty-one years *was* a long time, considering Liz was only twenty-three. "Elizabeth!" she responded, then looked down at her name badge. She wanted to crawl under the table and hide. "Obviously."

Hanna giggled, then held up her badge, which hung down at her waist. "Don't want people to find my name easily." She winked.

"You'll find there isn't a very rapid turnover here. Hey, Rob," she called out to the man who was checking out a nurse several tables away. He quickly glanced over and arched an eyebrow. "How long have you worked here?"

"Too long," he muttered.

Hanna tilted her head. "Serious answers only, please."

"Who said I wasn't serious?" He then smirked and slid his eyes to Liz's. "Ten years."

"See," Hanna replied. "He started when he was ten."

Rob rolled his eyes, but the woman he had been eyeing laughed, which made Rob grin and turn back to her. "That was pretty funny, huh?" he asked, a sly smirk attached to his lips.

Hanna shook her head. "Let's just call him the hospital flirt."

"I have a boyfriend," Liz quickly pointed out.

Hanna tossed her head back and howled. "I'll tell ya, honey. That has never stopped him before."

Hanna turned to the woman who was now engrossed in a conversation with Rob. "That's Sally. She's been here over twelve years, so once you're here, you're here for life. She works in the ER part-time and the cardiology department the rest of her time." She tossed a look to Liz. "And in case you were wondering, yes, Sally is fully aware that Rob is crushing on her. Which is fine, because frankly," she held her hand up to her mouth, so no one else could hear her, "she feels the same."

Liz smiled. In those fifteen minutes, she had suddenly gotten the whole landscape of the hospital with one quick swoop. Already three weeks in and this was the first time she felt comfortable.

She couldn't help but glance back at the woman on the windowsill. "Who is that?" she asked Hanna.

Hanna turned her head to look. "Oh, that's Marisa. But be careful with her. She can be a bit—"

Liz shot to her feet, just noticing the time. "Shoot! Sorry. I have to clock in, but it was nice meeting you."

"Same to you, Liz. Sure I'll see ya around." She waved and went back to her popcorn. Liz couldn't hide her smile as she tossed away her wrapper and clocked in for her shift, for once expecting that her day would run just as smoothly.

———

To Liz's dismay, while the moments before her shift were the best fifteen minutes of her three weeks at the hospital, things slowly derailed from there.

"Are you a nurse?" a woman asked, rushing up to her just five minutes after she clocked in.

"Um, yeah, I mean yes..." Liz held out her badge, which she had moved to her waist. She turned from the elevator, which was only seconds away from opening. "Do you need something?"

Sure, it was a hospital, and everyone needed help of some kind, but Liz wasn't supposed to nab patients out of the waiting room. Some protocols needed to be followed, and Liz had been reminded of that repeatedly throughout training.

"My kid," the woman said. "She has a nasty bump. She fell. I need someone to take a look at her."

"Did you sign her in?" Liz asked, looking over at the front desk where three other people were waiting to be checked in. This wasn't even her floor. She was headed two floors up. She turned back to the woman. "If you have her signed in, then they'll—"

"They'll be with her. I've heard that story, ma'am. But we've been waiting for thirty minutes now, and she's not looking well."

Liz sighed and forced a smile. "Have a seat, and I'll see what I can find out."

The woman groaned but walked over to where her daughter was. Her daughter was slumped forward, her hands hanging limply. Liz frowned. She was right. The girl didn't look great.

She walked behind the counter where a disheveled-looking woman was plowing away on her keyboard. Her fingers were angrily typing, her eyes focused on what she was doing.

"Excuse me," Liz whispered. When the woman didn't even acknowledge her, Liz cleared her throat. "I hate to interrupt," she said louder and more forcefully.

The woman cast a glance toward Liz. "Yeah?"

"Could you tell me when you think the woman and her daughter over there will be helped?" Liz fidgeted from one foot to the other, ready for the woman to blast her.

The woman opened her mouth, then snapped her mouth shut before opening it again. "What's her name?"

Liz nervously bit at her lower lip. That would have been a helpful question to ask. At the moment, she hadn't even considered asking something so simple as *What's your name?* before putting herself out there like that.

The front desk clerk rolled her eyes over the intake clipboards. "Have at it." She then turned back to her computer and continued typing before calling the next woman forward.

Liz heaved a sigh and glanced at her watch. She was already fifteen minutes late getting up to her floor, and she could imagine the indecent words she would be spewed out by for not getting to her shift on time.

She rifled through the stack of charts. *Nosebleed, no. Dog bite, no. Car accident, no. No. No. No.* Finally, she pulled out a chart that was for a fall. And the girl's age was thirteen. This had to be it, but it was way at the bottom of the line.

"So, do they go in order?" Liz asked, turning to the woman's back.

"No. not in strict order. The triage nurse evaluates them and ranks the patients in terms of how serious their condition is. The order patients are seen in is the triage nurse's prerogative."

"I see," Liz said.

The woman released a breath, then nodded. "Patients always get impatient in the emergency room. It's par for the course." She swiveled back to face her computer.

Liz reluctantly went back to the woman and her daughter.

"They just have a few more patients to go, and they'll be right with her." Yes, it was a lie, but she didn't know what else to say. She wanted to avoid any further confrontation.

"A few more patients?" the woman asked. "Look around. This waiting room is full of patients. Who says they're more urgent than my daughter?"

"Mom? I feel like I'm going to get sick," the girl said, reaching out for her mother's hand.

Liz felt helpless as she looked around Capmed. She spotted Hanna and hurried over to her as the latter began to grab a chart from the top of the pile.

"Hanna, wait!" Liz hissed, reaching for her hand.

"What are you doing here? You're on the wrong floor, aren't you?"

Liz didn't have time to explain the whole situation as she looked at the woman. "Right place, right time. Or wrong place, wrong time," Liz groaned. "I don't know, but I need your help."

"I'm a little busy right now," Hanna laughed. "I get off in less than two hours. Hit me up then."

"You don't understand," Liz spoke, her voice pleading for Hanna's attention. "That woman and her daughter over there. The daughter is about to get sick, and she's had a nasty fall, and she needs to be seen."

"You're new here," Hanna stated. "The ER is a tough place to be. It's always overflowing beyond capacity. The waiting room may look busy, but it's a lot busier back there." She motioned to the hall where the doctors were working. Liz looked over to the girl, who lay against her mom's shoulder, her face flushed, then turned back to Hanna.

"Isn't there something that can be done? Maybe give her a bucket that she can throw up in or something. She doesn't look well."

Hanna scrunched up her nose and looked over to her, then glanced back at Liz. "Let me check on her."

Liz smiled and looked over at the woman and her daughter, then back to Hanna. "Thank you!"

From the corner of her eye, she saw the woman at the front desk shake her head, her face etched like stone.

Liz stepped back from the desk and hurried to the elevator. As the doors closed her in, she fell back against the wall and tried to control her breathing. Liz could already imagine the repercussions that would come from doing something that others would surely feel was quite trivial.

When the elevator doors opened, three people turned to gawk at her. "We were wondering where you were," Vicky, the lead nurse, said. "I hope you have a good answer."

Liz wasn't confident that anything she could say would get her out of this mess. Especially when she had already disobeyed their biggest rule: Follow protocol or expect to be reprimanded. She just hoped that it wouldn't be at the expense of her job.

CHAPTER TWO

Marisa

T he hallway was empty. Employees were stashed in rooms working on patients or patients were all stuck in the waiting room waiting to be seen. Marisa pushed through the breakroom door, expecting it to also be empty. It was halfway between lunch and supper. Typically, that meant her break gave her time to reflect on her day instead of being forced to talk to someone when she would rather...not. *Lab Weekly*, a blog published every Monday, was already calling out her name. Instead, she entered the room to find a woman trying to demolish the vending machine.

Marisa smiled. It was the same woman she had seen earlier in the breakroom near the start of the day. The one who had looked away from her bashfully. Marisa's gaze trailed down the young woman's body. Her scrubs were loose, but they didn't hide the woman's nice figure.

"Come on, you stupid thing, just give it to me." The woman slammed her fists against the machine, a look of distress coursing all over the lines of her cheekbones. Marisa checked the name on the woman's badge. *Elizabeth.*

"What'd that machine ever do to you?" Marisa asked just as Elizabeth forced her elbow into the machine. She looked at Marisa, her eyes wide, before collecting herself.

"For starters, not giving me my chocolate. Which I desperately need." She punched her fist against the spot that held her chocolate bar in place, then groaned. "Looks like maybe I'm just not supposed to have it. The universe has a funny sense of humor."

She pushed on the coin return. "And I guess I'm not supposed to get my money back, either. Go figure. About covers my day," she grumbled, dropping into the nearest chair.

Marisa walked over and punched the side of her fist into the machine. Immediately, the bar was released. She reached down to grab it, then tossed it over to Elizabeth's table.

Elizabeth grabbed the bar and stared at it before releasing a soft laugh. Marisa's heart skipped a few beats. That laugh was much better than the anger on her face a few moments ago. And her smile was stunning. But why so much frustration over a chocolate bar? She was sure there was more to it than that.

"Thanks," Elizabeth grumbled.

Marisa shrugged. "It's all in the wrist. I've had to release plenty in my day." She turned back to the vending machine, considering its plethora of options, then slipped her money back into her pocket and went to an empty table. "First day?" she asked, sitting down and crossing her legs, propping them up in a chair.

Elizabeth chomped down on the bar and turned to look at her. She snickered and shook her head, taking another bite into her mouth. "Might be easier if it were." She pulled out her phone and started scrolling.

Marisa did the same, figuring the woman might need some time alone. She pulled up *Lab Weekly* and skimmed through it to find her article.

Might be easier if it were. Those words played on a continuous loop through Marisa's mind. She finally looked up, ignoring the article. "Long day?"

"Might be my last day," Elizabeth mumbled, setting her phone down and pulling a crumpled-up paper from her pocket. After tossing it on the table, she rested her head in her hands.

Marisa got up from her chair and went over to pick it up, despite barely knowing this woman. She had a weakness for beautiful women and this one also intrigued her. "Dear Elizabeth Fletcher," she started, "please

183

report to conference room B tomorrow before your shift. We have some things to discuss with you and expect your prompt arrival."

She laughed, tossing the paper back onto the center of the table. "I wouldn't worry too much about it. We've all received letters similar to this in our employment."

Elizabeth looked up at her. Her eyes were narrowed into a thin line, her eyebrow was quirked up, and her lips were curved into a frown. Marisa lingered on those full lips for a moment too long. They were soft pink and looked completely natural, just how Marisa preferred.

Marisa shrugged. "I'm telling you. This letter alone doesn't scream termination. Take it from someone who's been around."

Without being asked, she took the seat across from Elizabeth. "Besides, they're having you finish out your day, right? That alone is promising. Also, they said, and I quote, 'before your shift.'" Its meaning seemed obvious to her, but Elizabeth's eyes continued to darken. "Why would they put that phrasing if they were planning on terminating you? It's spelled out right there. Don't you think?"

"I don't know." Elizabeth grabbed the letter, reading over it intently. Marisa knew it was most likely the thousandth time Elizabeth was reading those words. Why force herself to read them again?

"You're at an unfair disadvantage," Marisa stated. "I know your name, but you don't know mine. Marisa Cavanaugh. I'm the laboratory manager." She forced her hand out to Elizabeth. "It's a shame we're meeting when you're looking so upset."

She quirked her lips into a smile, but Elizabeth didn't respond. "I don't know you, Elizabeth, but I'd say you might be a worrier. Maybe just a little bit?" A worrier—or slightly immature. After all, she did look to be much younger than Marisa.

Elizabeth set the letter down, her expression even more tense. "I guess I've been told I am. But I've never been fired a day in my life. I was hoping that wouldn't change when I started this nursing venture."

Marisa raised her brows, making her smile wider. "Then have faith because you don't know why they're calling you to the conference room. I really wouldn't worry about it. Not to mention, what could you have possibly done that you think deems termination?"

Elizabeth sighed as Marisa waited for the explanation. Elizabeth proceeded to tell her the story of how an incident in the emergency room had led to her being late for her shift. Marisa simply listened, no longer interested in the article that was still on her phone. When Elizabeth was done, she seemed less tense.

Marisa nodded. "I can see you're still worried about it," she started. "The good news is, though, your eyes have softened considerably since I entered the room."

Elizabeth laughed, her cheeks turning into a rosy hue. *That's better.* Marisa nodded, forcing herself not to stare at Elizabeth's lips and imagine what they might taste like. She wanted to see Elizabeth smile, not fret over something she had no control over. That wasn't going to help anyone, least of all Elizabeth.

"I think you're worrying over nothing. Everything you just told me doesn't sound like something they would fire someone over. How long have you worked here?"

"Three weeks." Elizabeth covered her face and shook her head. "If I'm fired after three weeks, I'll never be able to live that down." She dropped her hands and turned her gaze to Marisa. She clearly cared what others thought about her, but it wasn't good to hold that much anxiety over what anyone else might think.

"Just try to relax and enjoy the rest of the day. By this time tomorrow, you'll probably be laughing about the fact that you were so worried."

Those words brought a bigger smile to Elizabeth's face, which Marisa enjoyed seeing, but deep down, Marisa had some worries about the matter. Capmed was usually an easy place to work unless the higher-ups felt compelled to make an example of someone. Marisa just hoped she wasn't giving Elizabeth some false sense of security. Or else she was liable to push the woman deeper into the emotional hole she seemed to be in.

Even more worrisome was Marisa's strong attraction to this woman. Their age gap was too big to pursue anything, so hopefully they wouldn't see much of each other. She didn't need any relationship drama right now.

Still, Elizabeth was cute.

After finishing her candy bar, Elizabeth stood and dusted her hands. "Well, I should get back. It was nice meeting you."

"You, too."

Elizabeth paused a moment, then bit her lower lip and turned back to Marisa. "You can call me Liz."

Marisa nodded, fighting the butterflies in her stomach. Was she imagining it, or was Liz being a little flirty? "Bye, Liz," she said, waving, as Liz scurried out of the breakroom.

This isn't going to end well.

MARISA STEPPED OUTSIDE TO THE WAITING BREEZE AND TOOK in a deep breath. Freedom. She always loved the smell of that. While Marisa loved her job as a laboratory manager, she sometimes felt like the world was passing her by. Maybe that was because there were times when Marisa had to stand back and wonder if she had rushed into things in life.

Marisa's life hadn't always panned out the way she had intended. After high school, she had anticipated seeing the world, maybe going to France, Italy, the Virgin Islands, or a million other places to explore. But life quickly derailed when her parents were killed in a house fire while she was away visiting her grandparents.

She realized then that life had a way of changing you. Marisa needed a way to take care of herself and threw herself into her studies. She graduated with honors and did her internship at the hospital. Right away, she was hired and never looked back. Now, at the age of forty-two, she wondered if there was more to life than hard work.

"Marisa! Wait up!"

She turned on her heel just before reaching the parking lot. Samantha came running up to her. "Thought that was you. You were on a mission to get out of here."

Marisa snickered. "Don't you ever feel that way?"

Samantha shrugged. "Remember, when I go home, I'm going home to a house full of people. My grandmother, mom, dad, pregnant sister, and her two-year-old. So, no, not really." She laughed and looked around the front of the hospital before turning her gaze back to Marisa. "I'm probably delaying you from getting on home. To your empty house and all."

Samantha tilted her head. "Don't you ever feel it's lonely?"

Marisa scrunched up her nose in thought, then shrugged. "Maybe, but honestly, when you just said how hectic your house is, it wore me out." Marisa smiled, which made Samantha laugh.

"Besides, tonight will not be one of those lonely nights." She laughed. "I have a bottle of wine calling out my name and a night of Netflix on my agenda."

Marisa stared at Samantha, wondering if there was a real reason she had stopped her. They were friends, or at least friendly, at the hospital, and had only hung out a few times outside of work. Samantha was twenty-one, and all their similarities ended with working in the same department.

Samantha worked at the front desk of the lab. She had started at the age of eighteen, right out of high school, and seemed more mature than most people who had held the job. Marisa supposed she had to grow up pretty fast after seeing her older sister managing a baby as a single parent, with another one on the way.

They walked together out of the hospital and into the parking lot. Samantha lingered by Marisa's side, a little too close. "Hey, I was thinking—"

"Hi," a familiar voice said; Marisa turned to see who it was. Her heart fluttered when she saw Liz approaching.

Marisa waved. "Remember what I said, Liz. I'm sure tomorrow you'll see you were worrying for nothing."

Liz smiled, the widest Marisa had seen since their encounter earlier in the day. "Thank you! Your pep talk helped. I do feel a little better. Well, I have to go, but have a good night." She waved and hurried off to the parking lot.

Liz's ponytail swished in the wind as she jogged toward her car. She was on a mission to get out of there as well.

Samantha cleared her throat, making Marisa turn back to her. Samantha's mood had grown stormy and her words were clipped. "Who was that woman?"

It was a quick change of subject, one that caught Marisa off guard. "Oh, just a nurse who works here. I met her today, and she got a letter from the hospital stating they wanted to meet with her."

"Interesting," Samantha replied. "Getting terminated?"

"She thinks so, but doubtful. I mean, what she's being called in for is so trivial." She started to explain before frowning. "How'd the conversation get to this?" She laughed loudly.

Samantha directed her eyes away from Marisa's, then shrugged. "You looked interested or something."

"I what?" Marisa squealed. "You were reading that all wrong," she argued.

Marisa cast a look over to the parking lot, where her eyes landed on Liz getting into her car. "It's absurd, really. For many reasons. The main one being, what is she, twelve?" She laughed. "No way—no. How am I going to rob that cradle?"

Samantha scrunched up her face. "She's older than me, I'd say."

Marisa laughed. "Well, okay, but we're not talking about you and me in that fashion. We're talking about you thinking you saw something when there's clearly nothing." She quickly shook her head, knowing she was trying to convince herself more than she was Samantha. "Besides, I think the whole hospital knows the toll that Shana took on me. I'm not going to go there again."

"Guess I misread the look, then."

"Glad that's out of the way," Marisa replied. "I should get home."

"Uh, wait," Samantha said. "What if I join you tonight?" She looked away, fidgeting with her bracelet. "Or we can go out. I'm happy to give you some company."

Marisa fished her keys from her purse. "Thanks, but I'll be okay."

"Are you sure?" Samantha grabbed her arm, stepping so close that Marisa could feel the heat radiating off her skin. "I promise I won't argue about what Netflix show we watch. I'll even supply the wine."

Marisa stepped away, pulling free of Samantha's grip. "That's sweet, but I really just want to relax alone tonight. Maybe some other time."

Samantha looked ready to say more but closed her mouth and turned away with a weak nod.

She must really not want to go home tonight. But I'm not up for company. "I'll see you tomorrow," Marisa said.

"Bye," Samantha replied, rushing off.

Marisa felt a little guilty about rejecting Samantha's offer to hang out, but she preferred a quiet evening focused on what she wanted to watch on Netflix and the kind of wine she was rearing to drink.

She reached her car, her mind on Shana and how similar they had been to each other. They both had to work through college in pursuit of their dreams. Sixteen years. That was how many years they had known each other before they decided to try their hand at a relationship.

And for four years, that relationship was good. It was one of the best things Marisa thought she had done in life. Then one day, it was gone. Shana decided her happily ever after wasn't with Marisa, and Marisa was left confused and brokenhearted. Not even a year apart could erase the years they had spent together, and Marisa wasn't really interested in starting up a new relationship. But when she did decide to find someone to be with, she wasn't going to look at someone she had to help mature. She didn't have time for that.

CHAPTER THREE

Liz

Liz looked at her reflection. If she could just crawl back into bed, she knew her aching muscles would be happier. Instead, she was dressed up in a black dress two inches above the knee, a slit that came up the side of her right leg, and heels that matched. She reached across the dresser and grabbed her beaded necklace. Her boyfriend, Chad, had gotten the necklace for her on their first anniversary. Since she was going out with him, it was only fitting that she would wear it. It added to the ensemble, but her heart still crashed hard against her chest.

Liz's thoughts turned to the hospital, and she felt this knot welling up in the pit of her stomach. Her chest tightened, and her head swirled with thoughts of what she was going to say to her supervisor. She couldn't recall the last time she was ever in trouble, but it would have been way back into her elementary school days. Even then, nothing would compare to the angst she would feel in that conference room the following day.

Don't think about it, Liz. Just go out tonight and enjoy yourself.

Way easier said than done. One last look at her reflection, and she was ready to leave her house. On the way to the restaurant, her thoughts played in the back of her mind. Why couldn't they have talked to her right then and there? If she were going to be fired, then at least she would have already known. Instead, she was forced to think about it and wonder how much she would need to plead with them for one more chance. It wasn't going to be an easy night to get through.

Liz turned into the restaurant's parking lot. The lot was already packed, and she had to grab one of the last spots in the back of the lot. It felt like it took her hours to get to the front of the restaurant. But finally, a man opened the door for her, greeting her with a smile.

"Welcome to Enrico's Italian Bistrot."

She forced a smile and nodded. "Thank you." The music played louder as she stepped into the dining area and looked around to find Chad.

"May I help you?" a woman asked, approaching the podium.

"I'm meeting someone here. There's a reservation for Hawthorne."

"Chad?" she asked, looking up.

Liz nodded and then was escorted to the very back of the restaurant. Chad always did like seating areas that were secluded. She wasn't the least bit surprised by his attempt to make them as withdrawn as they could have possibly been. Chad was already sitting at the table and looked up when she approached. He grinned and then stood to his feet.

"Thank you," she said, glancing at the hostess before she walked away.

Chad grabbed Liz's hand and pulled her to him, brushing his lips along hers. "Good evening," he whispered.

Liz gave a weak smile, withdrawing from the kiss. "Good evening."

He waited for her to take a seat. One thing that could always be said about Chad was that he was a perfect gentleman. He did things by the book, making sure that Liz felt like chivalry wasn't dead. She felt good about that, despite other things that nagged at her inner soul.

"I've taken the liberty to order our appetizer and white wine," he started.

"Oh. Okay. I didn't realize I was late." She glanced at her watch. "I'm sorry."

"You're not; you're right on time. I just wanted to get the evening going. I thought it would be nice to have the order started. I've already checked out the menu, so go ahead and see what you think you're going to have."

He clasped his hands together and waited as Liz looked up at him. She was sometimes annoyed by his eagerness to move everything forward and not take a moment to smell the roses. That was his niche, and to love him was to accept it. She smiled and closed the menu, pushing it away from her.

"I'm ready."

"That's my girl," he said. He looked up and motioned for the waitress to come over and take their order. As they waited, Liz nibbled on her lower lip. She couldn't wait to tell Chad about her impending reprimand. She hoped that he would make her feel better about the matter. After all, he was the CEO of his own company and was responsible for seventy-five employees. If anyone knew how to handle the situation, it would be him.

The waitress came to their table and they both placed their order. Liz waited until she was gone before she glanced at him. "You are not going to believe my day," she began. She just hoped she didn't get all choked up as she was telling him about everything that had happened.

"Can't compare to mine," he replied, groaning. "First of all, Stacy and Matt are having an interoffice affair, despite me saying that it's completely unprofessional, but Vicky caught them, and there was a whole lot of drama. And Curtis is threatening to go to another company if he doesn't get a raise." Chad heaved a sigh. "I shouldn't warrant behavior like that with a raise, but I do hate the thought of him switching to another job. I mean, you know that any one of my competitors probably would snatch him up so that they could have our inside secrets."

As Chad continued—running through the whole lineup of employees, it seemed—Liz took a sip of her wine. In typical fashion, she didn't stop him. She felt it wouldn't do any good if she attempted to interrupt him or interject her thoughts into the matter. She just sipped on her wine and patiently waited for her turn.

When he released an exasperated breath, he shook his head. "Tonight is about us, though. I don't know about you, but I would prefer to keep work out of it. What do you say?" He reached across and grabbed Liz's hand, tracing his fingers over her digits. She frowned. Just when she thought she would get someone to lend an ear, too, he turned her away. She nodded as he wished. There was no point in making a fuss.

Just fifteen minutes later, the waitress brought out their food, and they left the work talk behind them.

Sadly, that also meant giving them very little to talk about as they ate their osso buco. "I talked to Mom this morning," he said.

Liz looked up and nodded. "Oh yeah? How's she doing?"

"Good. No complaints." The conversation died at the end of that.

Liz tapped her foot and stared down at her food. Was that their relationship? Lack of conversation was easily the biggest demise she could see coming between them. She knew finances were something that would break up couples, but they didn't have to worry about that, since Chad owned a multi-million-dollar financial corporation. If anything came between them due to money issues, it would be because Chad felt she didn't need to work.

I can take care of you, Liz. Wedding band or not, you don't have to worry about money.

What he didn't take into consideration was her ambition to be able to support herself. And that would always trump Chad being the overprotective man in her life. As they came to the end of their meal, she looked up to see that Chad had his eyes zoned in on her. She blushed and quickly looked down. Maybe that was one reason she was able to see their relationship as continually blossoming. Chad still did have ways of making her blush. But then, that could also be because of her insecurities when she was around him.

"You're staring," she said, lifting her gaze to his.

He smirked. "Because I just happen to have the most beautiful woman in the restaurant. How could I not stare?"

Liz smiled. It was words like that that seemed to brighten her spirits, and that was one characteristic of Chad's that she loved most. "You have no idea how much I needed to hear that," she started, "especially today. It was such a long, tiring day and—"

"No work, remember?" he cut in. "Baby, I will tell you how beautiful you are forever and ever." He winked at her.

"I appreciate that, but work today..." She stopped there, shaking her head. "I need to talk to you about it. I need some advice."

"Later." He reached for her hand. "Tonight, it's just the two of us at this moment. Dance with me."

Liz was reluctant at first. Every time she began to mention the hospital, he quickly shifted to another subject. If it was an oversight on his part, then that was one thing, but over time, it slowly started to look intentional.

"Just dance with me." His voice softened, and he continued to hold her hand. His eyes brightened, pleading.

She stood to her feet, even though there were moments when she wanted to go back to the table and start all over again. He pulled her into his arms as a slow song played. "They're playing our song," he whispered.

Liz listened to the smooth instrumental that played over the speakers. She didn't know they had a song, and she didn't recognize this one. Yet, she went with it. The song slowly pulled the thoughts of the hospital out of her mind, so it was doing the trick. She had longed for the moment when she could go five minutes without worrying about the following morning.

When the song ended, she looked into his eyes.

"I did need that."

He pulled her close and kissed her.

"Let's go back to the table and have some dessert."

Liz touched her stomach. "I don't think I could possibly eat another thing. I'm stuffed."

"Nonsense," he argued. "You have to have dessert." He flagged down the waitress despite Liz's repeated refusals. She wasn't hungry, and if she even attempted to squeeze dessert in, she was positive it wouldn't go well.

"Chad, I don't think I could," she pleaded. He didn't pay attention and ordered two pieces of chocolate cake. When the waitress left the table, she leaned back in her chair and didn't say another word. If making a scene was her only option, then it was best to avoid it altogether.

When the waitress came back, she placed a piece of cake in front of each of them. "Bon appétit," she said just before leaving.

As Liz picked up her fork and stared at the cake, her stomach did flip-flops. "Dig in," Chad ordered.

Liz forced a smile, then slid her fork into the cake. She had just cut off a chunk and was about to eat it when she spotted something shiny slipped inside of the cake's middle. "What the..." She dug her finger into the cake and pulled out a diamond ring. She stared at it, then turned her attention to him.

Chad was already on his knee in front of her. "Elizabeth Fletcher, when we met five years ago, I thought you were just a woman our parents thought I should get to know. I never imagined that I would fall hopelessly, madly in love with you. Yet, you have become everything to me. As I am kneeling in front of you, with all eyes on us, I know that I will be the luckiest man alive. That is, if you say yes. Liz, will you marry me?"

Liz's jaw dropped, her throat going instantly dry. She quickly took a sip of the bland wine that remained in front of her. "Chad..."

"I love you, Elizabeth Fletcher. Make me the happiest man alive."

Liz looked around the restaurant, and her jaw dropped again when she saw her parents standing less than ten feet away from them. Right beside them was Chad's mother. Right behind her, his sister. They had this all planned down to the very moment she would say yes. How could she say no and disappoint all of them? She did have feelings for Chad, she had just never thought about marriage. But marriage was the next step, right? It would make everyone happy.

Liz turned back to him. "Yes, I'll marry you, Chad."

Her hands shook as he placed the ring on her finger. What else could she possibly have said with all eyes on her? She had to say yes, but the minute that word left her, her stomach clenched. What had she just gotten herself into?

THE DIAMOND THAT SAT ON LIZ'S RING FINGER STILL FELT strange. Liz touched it, sliding it around her finger over and over again. Next to her, Chad released a snore, and she looked over at him to see if he would be shaken from his sleep. He rolled onto his side and turned, his back toward her as Liz pulled her knees up to her chest and looked down at the ring. In the dark of the night, she could still see the shimmering crystals of the diamond. If she had to choose the perfect diamond, this would be it. Though it was more lavish than she would have preferred, it caught her breath every time she looked down at it.

Chad made a noise, and Liz checked on him once more. He was still sound asleep, his light snoring proving just that. Liz tossed the covers back and slid out of bed. It was no surprise that they ended up in bed together to end the night. It was what happily engaged couples would do, right?

No shame in that. She sunk into the chair across from the bed and stared at the ring. The light of the moon shone through her bedroom window.

When Liz's mom first told her about Chad, she was adamant that she didn't need to be set up with anyone and could easily find her match. As she headed into college, she looked forward to exploring men in the most natural of ways, expecting that she would date around. After all, it was the college experience, and according to her friends, a must to get through every exam. *You'll want this time to hook up and not have anything too serious.* It was everything, they said to her. But her mother had different ideas. It didn't help that her father seemed to agree.

When she met Chad, she forgot that her mother had anything to do with the setup. Their chemistry was off the charts, and he was the epitome of what she wanted. He was tall, tanned, handsome, and had a personality that even surpassed his looks. He was charming, genuine, and funny. He also had a very endearing smile. She always knew that she would make it through four years of college, and then they would talk about life ambitions and where they were headed. He was older by four years, so he was always waiting for her to get out of school.

Chad always dreamed of having his life mapped out for him and owning his own company by the age of twenty-five. He exceeded those expectations by making it at twenty-three, and it developed into the big conglomerate it became known as. Yet, work took a toll on him, and Liz quickly realized that it might be the most important thing in his life, especially when he disregarded her hopes, dreams, and desires. But it always came back to love. In her heart, she knew she did love Chad, and she always would. Putting the ring on her finger was something that made sense. But how was it possible for something to feel right yet so wrong simultaneously?

Liz touched the diamond and heaved a sigh. She got up from her bed and went over to the jewelry box. Chad was still sleeping, to her knowledge, and she dropped the ring into the top of her box. She couldn't continue to wear it without knowing if it really belonged on her finger.

"Baby?"

Liz froze as she closed her jewelry box. She turned to find him shifting in the bed. He pulled himself up and scanned the room until their eyes locked. A small smile grazed his lips.

"Get that beautiful body over here," he quietly said.

Liz walked over to the bed and slid in next to him, her body brushing against his. "What were you doing out of this bed?" He had a teasing grin that played on his lips as his hand brushed over her shoulder.

"Had to go to the restroom, then realized my jewelry box was open. I'm back here now." She moved in, touching her lips to his. It sounded like a plausible explanation. The way he kissed her proved he even believed it. As she moved into him, his hand reaching around for the nape of her neck, worry settled back inside of her. What if taking the ring was the biggest mistake of her life?

CHAPTER FOUR

Liz

Did time always tick by so slowly? Liz checked her watch for what felt like the fiftieth time; only thirty seconds had passed. She leaned back in the chair and crossed her legs, exasperated by the anxiety that was building inside of her.

She had gotten to the hospital an hour before her shift. That was on her. She knew that no one would be there, not even the chief medical officer. After all, he didn't need to fear the worst, that he would be unemployed by the end of a conversation. Liz checked her watch again and shook her head. Another ten seconds passed. Time was moving at a snail's pace, and she couldn't stand the thought of waiting another minute.

However, it wasn't just a minute Liz needed to wait. By her calculations, she had at least fifteen minutes left to think of the responses she would lay out to her superiors. *I know I was late to work, but I'm sorry.* Or, *I thought helping the patient was the best option. I apologize.* Finally ending with, *I need this job. I'm about to get married.* She mentally groaned. She wasn't going to say that last part. She couldn't even wear the ring; no one would be the wiser.

Liz was relieved that Chad hadn't noticed she wasn't wearing the ring. While she was pleasantly surprised, it did concern her. Wouldn't he have wanted to note the ring that he had placed on her finger just ten hours earlier?

The door opened, startling Liz. "Ms. Fletcher?"

She looked up to see Brian Chandler, the director of nursing, standing there. He held a generous smile on his lips, which pained her even more. He was going to be happy helping her out the door. To him, she was only a number. Liz swallowed the lump in her throat and stood up, following him back into the conference room.

"We didn't mean to leave you out here so long. Have a seat."

"That's all right," Liz said. *I was just practicing what I wanted to say and now feel like I might barf. But don't worry about me.* She sat down in a seat that faced not only him but Brenda.

"Hello, Elizabeth," she said. Brenda was Liz's supervisor on the pulmonology floor. The woman who had given her the opportunity to work at Capmed straight out of her clinicals. Elizabeth nodded to her. Of course she would be there. After all, Liz was being fired for not being to work on time. Brenda had a huge stake in losing an employee. Perhaps she would even be the one giving her the pink slip. Liz started to wring her hands even more, nerves seeping inside of her.

"One more will be joining us soon. He's just running a little late," Brian started, grabbing the seat next to Brenda.

Who else could be coming? Liz couldn't fathom who needed to be there. Wasn't it hard enough for two people to ridicule her? And now she was going to be faced with a third?

"We can get started. I know we haven't formally been introduced to one another," Brian continued. "I try to get out there and meet all the staff, but unfortunately, time just doesn't allow that. I leave it up to the individual managers to mold the employees into what Capmed is today and will continue to be. And we all take that job seriously. If we feel someone needs to be shifted through the hospital or permanently removed, then we have to take those actions and put them into motion."

The blood drained from Liz's face. She slumped back into the seat, then quickly sat up straighter. She couldn't look like a slouch right now. She had to take this news and try to rework it in her favor. She wasn't a quitter, and if that meant groveling, then groveling was what they would get.

"May I quickly say something?" she asked, her heart rapidly beating in her chest.

Brian's eyebrows narrowed, and he nodded. "Of course."

"I know that I shouldn't have been late. I know that I should have gotten someone else to help out in the ER and firmly insisted that I had to get to my department. However, when I saw the pain in that girl's eyes, I couldn't ignore it. That is my mistake, and I am deeply sorry."

Brian glanced over at Brenda, and he frowned. Brenda's eyes shot up in surprise, but that didn't stop Liz from going on.

"If there's anything I can do to change the outcome of this meeting, I will gladly do it. If you want to put me on probation, then so be it. I will take some time off and—"

"Let me stop you right there," Brian said, putting out his hand toward Liz.

She chomped back the words she was going to say, frustrated that he wasn't allowing her to plead her case. It was over and done. She had to take it and hope that they would be willing to give her a recommendation. That sounded like a laugh, though.

The back door opened to the conference room, and Liz followed the man who entered with her eyes as he grabbed a seat on the other side of Brenda. "My apologies I wasn't here sooner," he started. "Did I miss anything?"

Brian coughed, clearing his throat. "Not much, really." He turned his full attention to Liz. "I don't want you to continue because I think you might have the wrong idea about this meeting today. This is Frank Kinner. He's the supervisor of the ER. We're not terminating you, Elizabeth. We're asking you if we can shift you from the pulmonology department to the emergency department."

Liz's jaw dropped. "What?"

Brenda nodded. "As an organization, we know that the best thing to do for our new employees is for them to take up roles they are best suited for. We're wondering whether the ER would be a better fit for you than the pulmonology ward."

"I don't understand. I thought I was being..." Her words trailed off, and she sighed. "But I was late."

"And for a good reason," Brian said. "The girl whom you brought attention to had a concussion and needed to be monitored. Your quick actions might have prevented an adverse outcome."

Liz didn't know what to say. "I'm just surprised."

He smirked. "I can see that, but we all feel that the ER would benefit an employee who has such compassion as you have shown."

"So, what do you say?" Frank asked. "Will you join our team?"

Liz's jaw fell open. When her gaze went to Brenda, she beamed like a proud mother bear. "There's a waiting list of staff that would like to transfer to the ER. This is truly a great honor they are offering you here. We hate to see you go, but we couldn't possibly stand in your way."

Liz didn't know if she wanted to burst into tears or laughter. Either way, though, she couldn't believe how hard she had been on herself, and now she had options. She could take it or leave it, but it was up to her.

LIZ STOOD OUTSIDE THE CAFETERIA, PACING BACK AND FORTH, waiting for Hanna to appear. They had decided to meet up for lunch, but as time passed, Liz feared that her lunch would be over before Hanna even got there. Then, she spotted her turn the corner, and their eyes met.

Liz rushed up to Hanna. "Sorry I'm late," Hanna groaned. "Another hectic day in the ER."

"And I'm looking forward to that," Liz said.

Hanna turned to her, cocking up one eyebrow. "Meaning?"

"That's what they wanted to discuss with me at the meeting this morning. It turns out they're not firing me. Instead, they offered me a position in the ER. I'm going to be working with you. I start tomorrow."

Hanna squealed and tossed her arms around Liz's neck. "You have no idea how thrilled I am. Not just for you, but for me." She giggled, parting from the embrace and turning back to the cafeteria line, quickly moving forward to the next spot in line. "It's exhausting, most times. I can't even lie about that, but it does bring enjoyment knowing that you're healing these people who are in bad shape."

She held out a tray, which Liz grabbed. "Are you stoked?"

"Of course," Liz replied. "I mean, I thought I was getting fired. But I got to meet with Frank, and he seems like a good guy."

"Frank is the best. I've been in three different departments thus far, and I've had four, no, five, different supervisors in the ER. I would say Frank is my favorite. I'll take the fried chicken and noodles," she said, stepping up to the woman at the food line.

Liz skimmed her eyes over the choices for the day and settled on the bacon cheeseburger and fries. They both went to the cashier and paid, then found a table.

"It's great news, though. I knew they weren't going to fire you." Hanna smirked as she dug into her potatoes.

"I wish I had been as confident as you were. It would have saved a lot of hassle and worry." Liz took a big bite of her sandwich. She looked past Hanna and saw Marisa coming from the cafeteria line and heading over to a table. Marisa raised her hand and waved, causing Liz to respond with the same.

Hanna looked over at Marisa, then back to Liz. "You know Marisa?" she asked.

"Met for a bit yesterday in the breakroom. I told her how I was most likely getting the boot." Liz snickered, taking another bite of her sandwich.

"Well, you might want to get to know her," Hanna stated. "Won't find a better confidante than her. She's a good person. We went to college together, then did our externships here. The rest is history, but I would advise that you seek her out whenever you need to."

"Is that so?" Liz asked, taking a drink of her bottled water while Hanna continued.

"In the ER, there are plenty of times when lab tests get fucked up. If you're friends with Marisa, she'll have your back. Just hunt her down, and she'll be there for you."

Liz frowned. "So, what I hear you say is, you use her?"

Hanna laughed through a bite of her chicken. "That sounds so demeaning when you say it like that. I'm just saying Marisa is a good one, and you'll want to keep her happy, so don't irritate her."

Liz shook her head and looked over to Marisa as she chatted with a man at a table on the other side of the cafeteria. She thought about the way Marisa had patiently listened to her the other day when she was rambling about her work troubles. The entire time, Marisa had given Liz her full attention. Then she had talked Liz through her anxiety until she felt better.

She peeled her eyes away from Marisa, her stomach warming. "Marisa doesn't strike me as someone who gets irritated. At least not in the ten minutes I spoke with her."

Hanna's smile widened. "You're right. I'm just kidding, but just remember that you can typically count on her."

"Good to know," Liz softly replied, continuing to eat her lunch as time quickly progressed.

Halfway into lunch, Hanna's phone beeped, and she looked down at it and shook her head. "And my lunch is over. Gotta run. Emergency. Enjoy your lunch today, because tomorrow things will never be the same." She winked, then grabbed her lunch, which had barely been touched, and hurried from the table.

Liz went back to her food and kept her eyes down, lost in thought.

"This seat taken?"

She looked up to find Marisa's mesmerizing, caring eyes gazing down at her. She wore her normal lab coat, but Liz became too aware of how it hugged Marisa's waist, accentuating her hips. Marisa's hair was done in a messy bun, a few strands trailing the nape of her neck. Liz had the sudden urge to reach up and sweep the hairs away and run her thumb along Marisa's jawline.

Liz quickly shook her head, pulling her tray closer to her, giving Marisa more room. She avoided eye contact. What was wrong with her? She shouldn't be thinking such thoughts about Marisa or any woman. She was with Chad—engaged to him. She picked at her food, trying to calm her insides. She was probably just lonely and so exhausted her mind was doing silly things.

"So?" Marisa said, her light, cheerful voice making Liz's heart flutter.

"So...?"

Marisa rolled her eyes, then laughed. "The meeting this morning. How'd it go?"

A light, tingling sensation filled Liz's chest. She hadn't expected Marisa to recall their conversation from the previous day, let alone care enough to inquire about it. But, as Marisa stared at her wide-eyed, waiting to hear all about it, Liz knew Hanna's words were true. For the first time in a long time, Liz felt seen. Heard. Chad hated to talk about work and get into "heavy" topics, but Marisa seemed to genuinely care and want to offer support.

Liz wanted nothing more than to get to know Marisa. Talk with her. Be near her warmth. But she was still engaged to Chad and needed to remember that. She only wanted Marisa to be a friend. Nothing more. She just needed to keep her crazy thoughts in check.

CHAPTER FIVE

Marisa

As Marisa sat down and Liz started telling her about her earlier meeting, Marisa waited for Liz to take a breath. She smiled and shook her head as that break eventually came. "I believe I told you that you weren't going to get fired. Didn't I?"

Liz nodded. "So, this is the I-told-you-so speech?"

"Nah." Marisa laughed. "I won't go that far. But I'm happy for you. Sounds like a great opportunity."

"Yeah, and they said that I would have some say in helping to implement an easier check-in process."

Liz suddenly frowned, staring down at her food.

"Then why the long face?" Marisa asked.

Liz shrugged, her eyes still downward. She picked up a fry, then dropped it, then picked it up again, then dropped it. Marisa wasn't a mind reader, but she could tell there was definitely something bothering her.

"Saw you over here with Hanna," Marisa started. Still, Liz didn't seem to look up, so Marisa tried again. "Hanna is one of the good ones. We went to college together and became instant friends."

"She said the same," Liz mumbled.

"That doesn't have anything to do with the concern I see spread all over your face, does it?"

Liz looked up, arching an eyebrow in response. "Why would Hanna have anything to do with my concerns?"

"I don't know. Maybe the fact that Hanna works in the ER and you're clearly friends with her, so you might be feeling that you're coming in and taking over her turf." Marisa took a sip of her soda and shrugged. "Just a thought."

"Well, I am friendly with Hanna. We hardly know each other, though." Liz touched her fry again, then scrunched up her forehead before dropping it. She had been playing with her food for nearly five minutes, not bothering to eat.

Finally, Liz cocked an eyebrow, then sighed. "You're rather perceptive, I would say." She finally picked up the fry and put it into her mouth, then pushed her tray to the side. "I'm just getting to know her, and I don't want to ruin that by getting in the way too much."

Marisa took a drink, not completely convinced that was the reason for Liz's concern. Something else seemed to be on her mind, but she didn't want to pry. "I'll give you some advice. You don't have to worry about Hanna in that respect. She doesn't get caught up in gossip or drama. If I know her, and I'm sure I do, she's just thankful to have more help in the ER."

Marisa shook her head. "She'll know you aren't trying to come in and take over. I can tell she respects you. That's a good thing. Don't go worrying about something that probably won't happen. Besides, look at this morning. You were convinced you were on the chopping block, and yet, look at you now." She smiled, hoping that would relieve some of the stress that was running through Liz's mind.

Liz returned the smile and it lit up her whole face. Marisa's breath caught. Even with minimal makeup and a messy ponytail, Liz was stunning. Her lips glistened from a light dusting of ChapStick, and she thought of leaning across the table to taste it.

Marisa looked away, forcing her mind to focus on their conversation and not get lost thinking inappropriate thoughts at work. "But I don't envy you. The ER is no joke. Good luck with that one." She sipped her soda and watched Liz's wide eyes soften.

"That concerns me a bit," Liz replied. "Just a tiny bit." She held up her fingers, pinching her thumb and index finger, and Marisa nodded.

"But congratulations. I'm sure you'll do amazing. You seem to be the type of person who really cares. That's the most attractive quality in a woman." Her jaw dropped as she instantly realized the mistake she made. "I mean, in a nurse. Not attractive, but a good quality. Not that you're not..." She let her words fade so she didn't keep rambling.

A lovely shade of pink spread across Liz's cheeks as she stared at Marisa for a moment, lips parted. Then she shoved a forkful of food into her mouth, chewing while avoiding eye contact. "Right. And I do care. But that's also an issue when I care too much. I take others' feelings into account more than my own."

Marisa released a breath, happy they had moved on from her Freudian slip. She hated when that happened, especially when she was desperately trying to convince herself she wasn't attracted to Liz. She couldn't be. Liz was *way* too young. They could be friends, but that was all. Yet, when Liz stared at her with those deep hazel eyes, it flubbed up Marisa's mind. Her eyes drew Marisa in, confusing her in ways that no other woman had done in the past year.

Marisa stood, grabbing her soda. The longer she stayed, the more prone she'd be to slipups. "If you need anything, labs or whatever, just let me know. I have to run."

"See ya," Liz said, barely looking in her direction as Marisa scurried off.

Marisa wasn't feeling like her normal self today. One more second around Liz and she might not have been able to pull herself away. Getting lost in those eyes was making her forget everything she promised herself. She escaped into the elevator and waited for the doors to close before falling back against the wall. *She's too young for you, Marisa. You aren't ready for a relationship, anyhow.* If she could repeat that mantra—really drill it into her head— then she might be able to make it.

Liz didn't look any older than twenty-four. That was an eighteen-year difference, which meant Marisa would carry the weight of teaching Liz too much about relationships. Dating someone so young was absurd. When she was ready to start dating again, she would need someone with more life experience. Someone emotionally mature. She didn't yet know Liz well enough, but all women her age weren't emotionally ready for solid, long-term relationships. She had learned that the hard way. Never again.

The elevator opened, and she stepped onto the diagnostic floor and headed to the lab department. Samantha sat at the front desk, her legs propped up, and she had an apple in one hand and a book in the other. She pulled her legs down and swiveled to look at Marisa.

"Didn't mean to interrupt," Marisa mumbled.

"You're back early from lunch. Cafeteria must've been dead." Samantha closed her book and took a bite of her apple as Marisa grabbed the empty chair next to her desk.

"Something like that. What are you reading?"

Samantha grabbed her book and held it up. Marisa smirked when she read the title. "What's so funny?" Samantha pouted, tossing her book to the side.

"Harry Potter? That surprises me. I thought you'd be more about romance." Marisa shrugged. "Not to say there's anything wrong with Harry Potter or anything. Frankly, never read it, but it's surely popular."

"It's my younger cousin's. She let me borrow it over the weekend. Not bad, but I'm sure not everyone's cup of tea, either." Samantha looked down at her computer screen, a slight frown etched on her face. "But, speaking of romance," she started.

Marisa tilted her head and stared at her. She couldn't wait to hear what she had to say. Two lines had formed at the edges of Samantha's hairline, and her nose was scrunched up. Her dark eyes shifted back and forth, from Marisa to the lobby door and back. "There's this guy I'm seeing."

Marisa nodded, leaning back in her chair and crossing her legs as she waited patiently for Samantha to continue. Marisa liked giving advice, and if it didn't involve her own love life, she was all in. Besides, there were moments when Marisa felt like the mother hen to the young employees. It gave her a sense of purpose, and she was all for helping whenever she could.

"And I like him," Samantha continued, "but I'm starting to have feelings for a coworker. Feelings that I don't quite know how to handle. I've never felt like this before. It's all sorts of confusing and really unexpected, considering who it is." She lifted her eyes timidly to gauge Marisa's reaction.

How juicy! Marisa wasn't normally one for gossip, but she really needed the distraction today. "Is it Alan? I see you two chatting a lot and I know he's single."

"No, not Alan. This person is—"

"Wait. Dr. Harris? Even I'll admit that he's a nice-looking man."

Samantha smirked. "No, not Dr. Harris," she said softly. After chewing her lower lip for a moment, she locked eyes with Marisa and inhaled sharply, opening her mouth.

Before Samantha could continue, the door to the lab opened, halting the conversation. They both turned to look at the woman who walked in.

"The name is Beth Yancy. I have a one o'clock appointment. I know I'm early."

"That's all right," Marisa said, standing up from her chair. "Samantha will get you all checked in, and I'll be out for you in a minute."

She grabbed the order from the woman and took it to the backroom. Samantha's words had her on the edge of her seat, and the last thing she wanted was to leave without getting the full details, but work came first. She would have to remember to ask Samantha more about it later because not knowing who the mystery man who had captured Samantha's interest was would drive her crazy. At least she would have some distraction from what she was feeling for Liz. Anything to keep from thinking about those hazel eyes.

MARISA STEPPED OUT FROM THE BACK, RELIEVED THAT SHE finally had a lull in the afternoon. It was going to be short-lived, as she was the only laboratory manager on the schedule and their next appointment was in ten minutes, but it was long enough to hear more of Samantha's story.

"Sorry we haven't been able to talk," Marisa said, approaching her from behind.

"That's okay. It happens." Samantha swiveled in her seat to face her. "I'm wondering if maybe it's too much to lay out on you, though. I don't want you to think I'm getting overly dramatic or anything—just something I need to get off my chest. I'm not trying to be one of those teenagers who are all drama llama. You know what I mean?"

Marisa tilted her head and laughed. "Not exactly. Never heard that phrase before, but you don't have to worry. I don't think of you that way. You've always proven yourself to be much more mature for your age."

"Really?"

Marisa nodded.

Samantha's shoulders relaxed. "I'm really glad you think so. It makes our age difference seem less, right?"

Marisa took the seat next to her. "Well, we're friends. You know I'll always be here for you. Don't ever fear you're giving me too much. I've been around teens and tweens, so I can assure you whatever you have to say won't come across as overly dramatic."

If the drama ever got too much, she wasn't ever afraid to take a step back and tell someone that they needed to lay it on someone else. With Samantha, though, she had this overwhelming feeling that Samantha needed Marisa's help. She wasn't about to turn her away.

Things were harder for Samantha since she felt forced to continue living at home with her parents as she worked to save up money and move out. Marisa knew Samantha had dreams of going to college but wasn't presently in the position to make that happen. She had an unusual living arrangement, having multiple generations under one roof, but it eased their financial burden. Marisa admired that their family was so close.

"What's going on?" Marisa leaned back in her chair, watching Samantha.

"Um, well, about this coworker, I can't shake my feelings. They've been getting stronger the past couple of months, and I feel like if I don't say something, I'm going to implode."

"And you don't have any feelings for your boyfriend?" Marisa asked, urging the conversation forward.

"Well, he's not really a boyfriend. Just a guy I see every once in a while. Nothing too big to share there, but no. I don't have these feelings for him."

"Well, I can tell you that you'll ultimately hurt him in the process if you're not honest," Marisa replied. "So, for one thing, you need to make sure you're clear with him on what your intentions are. As for the other guy, you have to tell him, too."

"You see..." Samantha started.

The door opened and Marisa turned to face their next patient. "Have a seat, and we'll be right with you." Marisa grabbed Samantha's hand and pulled her into the backroom. "She can wait a few minutes. She's early anyhow. We can talk easier back here."

"Right," Samantha whispered. She shifted from one foot to the next, and Marisa saw the uneasiness in her eyes, even apprehension. She reached out and touched her arm.

"You look nervous. Is this coworker someone you shouldn't see? Like a guy who's much older than you? Or maybe someone much younger? Or a guy your parents wouldn't approve of? Whatever the case, I think you need to have a serious conversation with your mom and dad. They are your parents, and you should honor and respect them—most of all, love them—but they can't dictate your whole life. Remember that."

Exasperation showed on Samantha's face as she shook her head. "It's not that. It's just—"

"Hey, Marisa?"

Marisa turned to see Liz stepping into the room where they were. "Liz! What's going on? Everything all right?" Marisa stepped away from Samantha and toward Liz.

Liz looked down at the paper in her hand, then back up to Marisa. "I just was looking for you. I have an urgent blood draw from the pulmonology department. Dr. Barr asked me to get a rush on it. I see you're busy and all, but can I at least drop it off to you? If you could come to the floor at your earliest convenience and get the patient taken care of, that'd be great."

Marisa turned to Samantha, who shot Liz an angry glare and then walked toward the door. "I'll let the patient know that we'll be a few minutes late." Then she stormed off.

Wonder what that was about?

Marisa turned back to Liz. "Let Dr. Barr know that I'll grab my supplies and be right up."

"Thank you so much!" Liz gave a smile, then turned on her heel and left the backroom. Marisa walked out behind her and toward Samantha, who was typing something on her computer.

"Sorry for the interruption," Marisa whispered so the patient wouldn't hear her. "We can quickly finish our conversation if you'd like. I feel like you were just about to tell me anyway."

Samantha looked up and shook her head, her voice tense. "It's all right. Nothing to say, really. We'll discuss it later." She went back to her work as Marisa went to get the supplies for Liz's patient. She hesitated at the door and tossed a look over her shoulder. They would have to have that talk soon, and she would do everything she could to help Samantha out.

CHAPTER SIX

Liz

The minute Liz started working in the emergency room, she felt things improving with her employment at the hospital. She felt like she suddenly had a purpose, which was more than she could say when she first started working at Capmed. She had now worked at the hospital for over a month and was finally finding her own pace.

She grabbed the chart from the pile, sighing as she looked at the pile. She still had so many ideas of how they could triage the patients, but there was scarce time to figure out how to do it. In due time, she would see if they could make it a priority.

"Donovan?" she called out, stepping to the corner of the desk. A woman approached Liz with her young son. Liz smiled at the woman, then looked down at her child. "My name is Liz, and I'll be taking care of you today. Follow me."

The boy hovered next to his mother, his small hand in hers as they followed after Liz. Liz stopped at the scale and motioned for him to get on.

He was unsteady getting onto the scale. His mom had to hold his hand and whisper a few words of encouragement. Within seconds, the digital readout on the scale flashed his weight.

"Very good. Go ahead and go into that room right there, and I'll be right with you." Liz smiled at the mom, then stayed in the hallway and read through the previous history from that appointment. *Bloody nose. Bruising for unknown reasons.* Now add instability. While Liz wasn't a doctor, she didn't like the symptoms already.

She entered the room and shut the door behind her, addressing the mother. "Now, tell me, what brings you in here today?" While Donovan was only six years old, Liz didn't feel he would be able to reiterate his need to be in the emergency room on that Friday afternoon.

"We went to see our family doctor last week," his mother started. "He was experiencing a low fever, and he had a few bloody noses that we found odd. They just came on so suddenly. Then we found some bruises on his legs. We thought he just fell. Boys fall after all, and he goes to kindergarten all day. So we didn't think much of it. But the bruises didn't seem to want to go away. Our doctor ordered X-rays of his legs and they didn't show any fractures. But today we saw this." She pulled back his shirt, revealing his elbow, where there was a bruise the size of a quarter.

She shrugged. "He says he doesn't recall falling, and we have some concerns. Or, at least I do, that maybe something is going on at his school." She sighed. "There's no way of proving it, though." She then felt his forehead and nodded. "But now he has a fever. It's running just over a hundred."

Liz grabbed the thermometer and took the boy's temperature from his forehead. "One hundred point three," Liz said, quickly documenting that.

"And he says he's nauseous."

Liz looked down at her folder and wrote that down, then looked back up. "How long have you noticed the fever?"

"Just today. The bruise, this morning."

Liz grabbed hold of his wrist to take his pulse, which was rapid, going faster than she would have liked. She wondered if it had something to do with him having to sit for a while waiting to be seen. She documented the pulse and knelt in front of him. "Do you feel sick right now?" she asked.

He nodded. "Sore."

"Where are you sore, bud?"

He touched his head, then his knees.

"Stomach hurts," he said. He scrunched up his nose and rubbed his stomach.

"We'll get you taken care of." She ruffled his hair and stood up. "I'm going to grab the doctor, and he'll be right in with you."

"Thank you, ma'am," his mother replied. "I'm Victoria, by the way."

Liz smiled and turned to her. "Call me, Liz. Won't be too long." She left the room and logged onto the computer. There was one thing that did concern her, and it was the possibility of him being abused. However, it didn't account for his fever and the pain in his head and knees. More serious conditions had to be considered: idiopathic thrombocytopenic purpura, and even leukemia.

When she spotted Dr. Wesley, she walked over to him. "My patient in room three?" he asked.

"Yeah, it's a child."

He looked over the chart and nodded.

"I was the doctor that examined him last time. It's a shame he's back." He slid the pen behind his ear and shook his head.

"So, the mother says she has a concern that maybe his school is abusing him. Because of the bruising and stuff." Liz nibbled on her lip. "But how can you be sure that it's not the family? Like, maybe the family is just pointing fingers."

He nodded. "It can be a concern, for sure. I'll have a thorough talk with her. If I have concerns, I'll ask the social worker to come by."

"Dr. Wesley?" Victoria asked when they were nearing the end of his examination. "I was hoping you and I could speak alone for a moment?"

Liz shot a look to Dr. Wesley as he nodded.

"Donovan? Would you like to go with me and get a Jell-O?" Liz asked, turning to him.

His eyes lit up, and he eagerly nodded. Liz lifted him down from the bed, and they walked out of the room hand in hand. Liz escorted him to the nurses' station, where there wasn't anyone around. "What's your favorite flavor?" she asked, lifting him onto the counter and moving around to the refrigerator.

"Cherry?"

Donovan nodded, and she pulled one out of the fridge.

"You're in luck. It's the last one." She grabbed a spoon, then opened it for him. He took a bite, and his smile widened. He grew silent, focused on his eating. Liz leaned against the counter and just watched him. Looking at him, you wouldn't be able to tell he wasn't feeling well, other than the fact that his skin looked so pale.

She reached up and pressed her hand to his forehead, and he rolled his eyes. "Mommy does that all the time."

She laughed. "Well, I'm sure your mommy is just worried. It's what mommies do."

"Do you have any kids?" he asked, still eating from his Jell-O cup.

"No, I don't. But I know from experience with my own mommy. I might be much older than you, but mommies never stop worrying about their children."

"When I'm a daddy, I'll be the same." He proudly looked up at her, and she smiled brightly.

"I'm sure you will." She ruffled her fingers through his hair and frowned at the heat that radiated off him. "How are you feeling now?" she asked.

He nodded. "Better. This was really good." He took the last bite from his cup, and she took the empty cup and spoon from him.

"I'm pretty tired," he said.

Liz nodded in concern as she led him back to the ER room. "You are? All the time?" she asked.

He nodded, then looked down at his hands. "I don't like to say that because that makes Mommy sad, too."

"I understand that, bud. But you have to tell when you're feeling not like yourself. If you're feeling blah, then you need to let your mommy know everything. And you need to let your doctor know everything."

"And you," he said. "I need to tell you."

She smiled and nodded. "Now you've got it."

"I like you." His eyes went wider.

"I'll tell you a secret," Liz whispered. "I like you, too."

He giggled, and she was surprised when he pulled her into a hug. Liz allowed the hug to linger. While they embraced, Dr. Wesley walked out of the room and motioned for her to bring him back inside.

"Looks like they're ready for us," Liz said. As they entered, she fought the urge to cry. What was it about this situation that tore at her strings more than anything else? The fact that he was a child, no doubt, but something else was pressing on her, causing her to want to break down.

Dr. Wesley helped Donovan back onto the bed and then took a seat on the stool in the room. "Donovan, stick out your tongue for me, please."

Donovan did that, and Dr. Wesley pushed his chair up to the bed.

"Say ahhh…" Donovan obliged as Dr. Wesley looked down his throat. He nodded, then scooted back from him. "I'm a little worried about the bruising. As for the bloody noses, the air has been dry, so I'm prescribing some nose drops. This could all be part of a viral infection. I recommend plenty of fluids and lots of rest. Most importantly, you'll need to follow up with your family doctor in a day or two. But if you're not able to, you're welcome to bring him back here again. Do you have any questions for me?"

Victoria shook her head, and her eyes were bright red as if she'd been crying. Liz's heart tore at that sight; she couldn't fathom the pain a parent would have knowing their child wasn't feeling well.

"All right. Don't hesitate to come back or give us a call if you need anything."

Liz knelt in front of Donovan. "You are a special little man. Don't ever forget that."

Donovan nodded, then wrapped his arms around her again before pulling away. He had perked up a little, and even managed a faint smile.

She ruffled his hair with her hand, then stepped back as she left the room with Dr. Wesley. Dr. Wesley glanced in her direction as they stopped outside the door, and she shook her head.

"I can see the emotions swirling inside of you," he said. "Are you okay?"

She shrugged, then swallowed the lump in her throat. "Do you just think it's some virus that needs to run its course?"

He looked away from her, and she kept her eyes straight on him until he looked back at her and shrugged. "I think so, based on his signs and symptoms. His throat was a tad irritated. He's nauseous. He has a fever. If there are more concerns, we can get our social worker to reach out to the family. Was there something in particular you had in mind?"

"I was worried about leukemia," Liz muttered. She slipped her hands into her pockets and sighed. "My brother had leukemia as a child. But, if memory serves me, that's diagnosed by a blood test, and I don't see anywhere where one was ordered."

"It's possible," Dr. Wesley responded. "That's why I urged them to follow up with their family doctor or come back here if things persist."

"I don't understand." Her voice went up a couple of notches. "I don't mean to suggest that you're not doing everything you should. I know you're the doctor and all, but I don't see why you wouldn't do that first thing and rule it out."

Dr. Wesley crossed his arms. "Emergency medicine is a constant challenge. We don't want to miss serious conditions but we don't have the time and resources to work every patient up as thoroughly as we'd like. On top of that, we have to play a delicate balancing act in which we take responsibility for the patients' welfare without interfering with the relationship they have with their family physicians."

"Okay. I get it."

Liz looked away from him, tears threatening to fall. She was worried for Donovan. This was just one thing that was pulling her back to her past, reminding her of the heartache that her family had endured for nearly three years. She glanced back at the little boy through the doorway, fearing for his future.

"Excuse me." She fled before she finally broke down. She couldn't let Dr. Wesley or Donovan see her like that.

Hanna was passing by and noticed Liz's distraught state. "Liz? What's wrong?" she asked, rushing up to her.

"Sorry. I have to take a break," Liz said, pushing past Hanna to the elevator. She jammed her finger against the button. When the doors opened, she saw that someone was already inside.

"Liz!" Marisa exclaimed just before Liz rushed inside and collapsed against the wall of the elevator.

Marisa reached up and pressed the emergency stop button. Liz wanted to collapse in tears somewhere dark and quiet where no one would see her, but knowing Marisa was here was comforting. And now no one would bother them. "Thank you," she said softly.

"What's wrong?" Marisa pulled her into her arms, and Liz couldn't hold back anymore. As she rested her head against Marisa's shoulder, a flood of tears fell down her cheeks. She cried for her brother, who had succumbed to his illness, and she cried for Donovan, whose future might be uncertain. She just hoped that Donovan and his family wouldn't have to experience the same pain she had.

Through all of the painful memories clouding Liz's thoughts, Marisa was there—a soft, reassuring embrace Liz hadn't realized she'd been so long without.

LIZ PULLED HER ENGAGEMENT RING OUT OF HER JEWELRY BOX and slipped it back on her finger. Since she was headed out on a date with Chad, she had to make an effort to show him that she wanted this engagement to work.

She heaved a sigh as she looked at herself in the mirror. The problem was, she wasn't in the mood to go out to a concert or take a romantic stroll along a pier, which were the two things Chad had on tonight's agenda. After spending the morning crying at the hospital, she was ready to put on her lounge pants and crawl into bed.

Her phone rang, and she looked down at the number. She didn't recognize the number on the screen, but it was a Chicago area code, so she answered. "Hello?"

"Liz? It's Marisa."

Her heart sped up, butterflies entering her stomach. "Um, hi. How'd you get my number?" Liz sat down on the edge of her bed.

"I, well, I just, I'm sorry if this isn't okay. I asked Hanna, and she gave it to me."

She didn't know why Marisa wanted her number, let alone why she was calling on a Friday night, but she couldn't deny how happy she was hearing Marisa's voice. "I see," she slowly replied, her voice slightly husky.

"Is that okay? I mean, I don't want to bother you or anything, but after we saw each other today in the elevator, I just wanted to make sure you were okay."

Liz exhaled and smiled. Marisa was so thoughtful and caring. Liz still had Donovan and her brother heavy on her mind, so she appreciated that Marisa was checking up on her.

She closed her eyes, remembering the warmth of Marisa's embrace in the elevator. Marisa hadn't told her to stop or that she was silly for crying —something Chad often did. She had only held Liz and let her get her emotions out. She had been a blubbering mess, but Marisa didn't once judge her while she was crying. She had just needed to fall apart at that moment, and Marisa had been there to catch her. Since Marisa was an older woman, Liz had felt comforted and assured that everything would be okay. Liz didn't know if that was actually true, but in that moment, it felt true.

Once she had stopped crying, the urge to stay wrapped in Marisa's embrace was so strong that she had lingered a few extra moments.

"Liz? You still there?"

"Yeah."

"I don't mind that Hanna gave you my number. It's nice that you called. I'm sorry I was a mess earlier."

"Don't even worry about that. I can assure you that I've had moments like that at work. Many times I feel like falling to pieces. And it takes a special person to be a nurse, so you never have to shy away from me, Liz. I was just concerned about you. That's all."

A tear escaped Liz's eye, and she flicked it away. "That means a lot to me. Thank you." From someone she didn't know all that well, it meant even more.

Her doorbell rang, signaling that Chad had arrived. "I'm doing well. Well, maybe just okay. I'm holding out hope that Donovan only has a virus and that he'll feel better soon. Coworkers like you will help me to be stronger the next time I have to face a patient who might not get such good news."

Chad rang the doorbell again, and Liz stood up from her bed. "I'm sorry, but I have to go. I really can't thank you enough for calling. I mean that. I appreciate it so much."

Marisa was quiet a moment, then said, "Anytime. We'll talk later."

Liz disconnected the call, staring at Marisa's lingering number on the screen. She already missed hearing her voice. For a split second, she thought of telling Chad she was sick and calling Marisa back so they could talk more. But that was silly. Marisa was just a coworker and she didn't want to bug her. Marisa had already done enough.

After taking a moment to compose herself, she went to the front door to greet Chad.

"Gosh, babe," he said after she opened the door. "Didn't think you were going to answer. You trying to leave me out here in the cold?" He grabbed her hand and pulled her to him, planting a kiss on her lips.

The phone call was still on her mind. If Marisa cared about how she was doing, it would only seem right that her fiancé would share the same thoughts. He wasn't always receptive to her, but now might be a good time to open up. They were engaged, after all. She should be talking to him about the things that worried her. He should be her number one supporter.

"Been an emotional day," she said as she pulled back from the kiss. "So, I was hoping it would be all right if we just stayed in tonight. I'm not feeling like going out and having a good time. Maybe we could talk about my work? I have so much on my mind lately."

He frowned. "Are you serious? I'm dressed up and everything. And you are, too, for that matter. Don't be silly. We'll go out and have a good time." He grabbed her hand and pulled her closer. "I'll make sure you have the time of your life and don't have to think about your crummy day."

He tried to kiss her, but Liz pressed her hand against his chest, pressing him back. "Today, I saw a sick child. And it brought up thoughts of Jeremy when he was ill. So, I'm not in the mood."

He scrunched up his face, his eyes going darker. "I'm sorry about that, but there's nothing you can do, right? I know it was hard, but that's in the past. That doesn't mean you have to stop your life."

Liz's jaw dropped, and she looked away from him. "My brother died from leukemia," she said. She glanced up at him, and he simply nodded. "Just hit me hard today. That's all."

"I don't want you to think I'm a jerk. I know that's rough, and I'm sorry you had to deal with that. You're going to run into a lot of sick kids at your job. Maybe this is too stressful for you. I told you it might be, didn't I?"

Liz crossed her arms. "It's not too stressful. Just because I'm concerned about a patient doesn't mean I can't handle my work. Just because I have empathy for what the family is going through doesn't mean this isn't the perfect job for me. I love being a nurse. And I have such great coworkers."

He brushed the back of his hand against Liz's cheek, and she pulled back. "You have a kind heart. There's no denying that. That's why I'll be grateful when we're married and this will all be behind you."

"What do you mean by that?" she asked, stepping back and putting space between them.

"Well, when we're married, you'll give up this thought of working. You'll realize that I can support you. You'll just stay home and have babies."

Liz snickered and stepped around him to gain more distance. She knew that he thought she needed to—or perhaps, wanted her to—rely on his money, but telling her to stay at home and pop out babies took it too far. While she wanted children and planned on having as many as God wanted to bless her with, that didn't mean she was ever going to be willing to give up her passion for nursing.

"You know that I chose nursing so I could help people. I've told you that numerous times." She stared at him hard until he nodded. "So, why do you think that once we're married, I'll just decide to give that up?"

"Just trying to help you out, babe. Are you mad at me?"

She made a fist. Was he that oblivious? The look of confusion that played through his eyes said that he just didn't understand. "I don't think I can go out tonight. I'm sorry. I'm not feeling well." She turned and kept her eyes directed elsewhere.

"I didn't mean to upset you. If you want to continue working after we're married we'll talk about that. But I never..." His words broke off as Liz turned back to him. "I didn't mean to assume that you would want to give up the job. I just thought you were doing this job to make ends meet. The stress isn't worth it, is it?"

"Doing your passion and what you're meant to do is always worth it." She looked past him as a tear started to creep down her cheek. "Tonight just isn't a good night."

She pushed past him to the door. As she opened it, she felt glad she hadn't given in to Chad. She tried to walk in without him, but he followed her, shutting the door softly and turning her to face him.

He brushed a finger under her chin, lifting her head to look at him.

"I'm sorry. If you want to work, then you can work. I'm not trying to keep that from you. It's just that you seem so stressed today."

"I'm stressed today," she said. He brushed his thumb along a tear on her cheek. "And I was trying to talk to you about that. But feeling stressed doesn't mean I want to give up my passion."

He nodded and moved in to meet her lips. She stood there, stuck between urging him to leave and allowing the kiss to continue. He agitated her and she didn't understand why he didn't listen to her or respect her desires, especially now that they were engaged. If he kept pushing her to give up her job, it could break them. Was this really the person she should spend the rest of her life with?

But as the kiss deepened, her body responded. She craved comfort at that moment. The day had been so stressful in more ways than one. Not only was the past coming back to haunt her, but feelings for Marisa that she was afraid to explore were stirring in her chest. Ultimately, she relaxed into Chad's embrace, giving her thoughts permission to wander to the one person always on her mind lately.

As he pressed her against the door, she wrapped her arms around his neck, imagining the shapely curves of an older woman surrounding her body with warmth and comfort. A woman who made her heart dance, who listened to her when she needed support. A woman she wished were beside her at that moment more than anyone else.

CHAPTER SEVEN

Marisa

Marisa stepped into the cafeteria and headed straight for the shortest line. While the day had started slowly, it had quickly hit a turn for the worse, and she didn't think she would ever get away to get something to eat. As she stood in the pizza line, she looked over to a table, where she spotted Liz and Hanna eating. Before she could look away, Liz caught her staring. She waved, thoughts of holding Liz drifting through her mind.

Pulling Liz close in the elevator had been a reflex, her heart driving her actions. Liz had needed her at that moment and being able to offer her support—and being wanted—was what Marisa craved. Holding Liz had sent a spark of contentment through her and stirred something deep inside she thought had died with her last relationship.

The woman behind the counter cleared her throat, and Marisa's eyes shot back to the line. She was next. "Sorry," she mumbled. "Pepperoni and sausage, please."

The woman threw her pizza together and put it in the oven as she called over the next customer. Marisa casually looked back over to the table, where Liz now sat alone. She was leaning back, relaxing, sipping on her water, her eyes diverted from where Marisa stood.

"Ma'am," the woman behind the counter spoke. Marisa turned back to find her pizza was ready.

"Oh. That was fast. Thanks."

She grabbed it, pulled a bottle of water from the refrigerator, then paid at the cashier. She hesitated as she watched Liz scroll through her phone, avoiding eye contact. Should she go eat lunch with Liz? Her heart wanted to, but her mind was trying to be reasonable and tell her to stop getting involved. Liz was too young for her. Then Liz looked back up and smiled, her cheeks blushing.

It's just lunch. Nothing more.

Without any more hesitation, she strode to the table. "Hey, Liz."

Liz tucked a stray hair behind her ear. "Hi."

It had been a week since they had last talked, and while Marisa had considered reaching out to her, she pulled back, not wanting to come on too strong. She was still trying to control her feelings, but the more she talked to Liz, the harder it became. Letting herself fall wouldn't end well. Not only was she uncertain if she was ready to date again, but the age gap was too great and she didn't want to jeopardize Liz's job with a workplace romance. If her feelings started to show, others would notice. After all, the hospital knew where she stood when it came to being a lesbian. So far, Liz still didn't know and she wasn't ready for her to suspect anything.

"Do you want to sit down?" Liz asked.

"I don't want to interrupt if you and Hanna are having lunch together."

"We were but aren't anymore. She had to go back to the ER because Sally's getting ready to leave for the day. So, have a seat."

"Okay." Marisa sat down and opened her water. Her eyes skimmed Liz's loose ponytail and her rounded cheekbones. She had a light application of mascara on and her mouth was curved up in a soft smile. But her eyes looked tired and sunken. The stress of work was still getting to her. Marisa resisted the urge to reach out and take Liz's hand.

"How've you been? I've been thinking of you."

Liz tilted her head, and Marisa tried to cover up her fumble. "I mean, I've been thinking of your patient. Your situation. Not you."

"Gee, that means a lot. Thanks." Liz smirked and took a bite of her sandwich.

Marisa looked down at her pizza. Why was she acting like a nervous teenager around this girl? She was a grown woman and shouldn't find anything awkward about the situation. Sure, Liz was attractive, but she'd been around many beautiful women at the hospital. She had never gotten flustered like this.

"You know what I mean," Marisa mumbled, taking a bite of her pizza. She needed something in her mouth to prevent herself from saying something that would make the situation more awkward.

"I'm teasing. I know what you mean. But, yeah, I'm doing okay. No news is good news, right? At least, that's the motto I'll stand by. I haven't seen the little boy in the ER, so that's good."

"Well, that's something positive to take out of it." Marisa wiped her mouth with her napkin and took a drink. "Anything new otherwise?"

"Not really. But I'm tired of talking about me. What about you? Anything new with you?"

Marisa shrugged and then laughed. "We lead such interesting lives."

After not having had a conversation over the week, one would think there would be something to talk about. Maybe it was the attraction that made Marisa tongue-tied. She was doubtful about that, though. She looked down at her food, then continued with what little she had to go on.

"I'll keep your patient in my prayers," Marisa said. Was that lame? It felt lame. Yet it got a big smile from Liz, causing Marisa's chest to flutter.

"That's really nice. Thank you, and I'm sure both he and his mother would appreciate that."

Marisa nodded, taking a bite of her pizza and catching Liz watching her from the corner of her eye. She put her slice down and wiped her mouth, suddenly feeling self-conscious.

"Do you always do this?" Liz asked.

"Do what?" Marisa arched an eyebrow, thoroughly confused.

"Just have a way of making someone feel like they're being heard?"

Liz's cheeks went red, and she took another bite of her sandwich, but Marisa couldn't turn her gaze away. Not now, when it seemed like they were having a moment. *Am I ready for us to have a moment?*

Liz looked up and smiled. "It feels nice. When I started, I was told if I ever needed anything, you were the one I should go to."

Marisa was taken aback, and she dropped her slice of pizza. "You were told that?"

Liz nodded. "Hanna."

Marisa pondered this, surprised that was the one thing that Liz was told right off the bat.

Liz continued, "So, I know that you must be dependable. I can see that for a fact now."

Marisa knew her cheeks were showing her embarrassment as they quickly warmed up from Liz's words. "Since we're making observations, I'll tell you this: you have a very caring heart."

"You think so?" Liz looked up, locking eyes with Marisa. Marisa could tell by the way Liz was staring that not too many people had told her that. It was a shame because, in her opinion, it couldn't go unnoticed.

"I know so. You're showing so much concern and dedication after only meeting this boy once. I can see it on your face that you're concerned for his well-being. I can assure you that you should never lose that because the worst thing that could happen is to find yourself bitter. I'll tell you, Liz. Nursing isn't for the weak. And if you let it get to you, you will wind up living a rough life, and you don't want that."

Marisa scanned the cafeteria and almost let out a laugh as she caught sight of one of the tables. "See that person over there?"

Liz turned to where Marisa was gazing. "That's Edith, and she's surely ready for retirement. For some reason, she's holding out, though. That is who you don't want to turn out to be. She comes into work dreading it. She's lost sight of why it was important to work here. So, Liz..."

Liz turned back to look at Marisa, and Marisa smiled, hoping she would get Liz to do the same. Shortly after that, the corners of Liz's mouth lifted. "Promise me you won't be Edith. Seeing death can take a toll on someone, so I need you to promise me."

Liz laughed. "I will do my best not to be an Edith."

"Then you'll do just fine." She took a bite of her pizza, wiping her hands on her napkin and enjoying the soft chortle in Liz's tone when she laughed.

"I definitely needed that laugh," Liz replied.

"Then my work here is done." Marisa smirked, finishing off her pizza. Maybe friendship was what Marisa needed from Liz. Just because the chemistry she felt with her seemed to be surpassing everything she had felt from any other woman over the past year didn't mean she was ready to act on it. Or even should act on it. Just getting to know Liz was enough, wherever that might lead.

———

"Squeeze your hand for me," Marisa said as she pressed to find the patient's vein. As lab manager, drawing blood wasn't part of her job description, but she enjoyed having patient contact from time to time and always made an effort to maintain her phlebotomy skills.

"Nice and slow. There you go." She grabbed the needle and inserted it, then filled up the tubes of blood. "Very good. Almost done."

She pulled the tourniquet off, removed the needle, and covered the puncture site with a cotton ball. "You're good to go. I'll send your wife in."

"Thank you!"

She turned from the patient and left with her cart. Out in the hallway, she saw his wife leaning back against the wall. "You're free to go in, Mrs. Jacobs."

"Thank you!"

She went into the room, and Marisa continued down toward the elevator. She had just rounded the corner when Liz almost collided with her from the other way.

"Sorry about that," Liz said.

Before Marisa could continue to the elevator to get back to the lab, Liz stopped next to her. "Here to draw a patient?" she asked. Then she laughed and rolled her eyes. "Pretty stupid question. Of course you're here to draw a patient. You have the lab cart, and you're in the ER."

Marisa chuckled. "No problem, but yep. Just got done. How late are you here 'til?"

"Two!" Liz made a face, then laughed. "You?"

"I'm leaving in an hour. It's been a long and hectic day."

"That it has." Liz continued to move past her. "I'll leave you to get to the elevator. Have a great rest of your night!"

"I will. You, too!" Marisa pressed forward to the elevator, but Hanna headed over to her before she could get to the door.

"Hey," Marisa greeted.

It'd been three days since Liz had mentioned what Hanna had said about being able to rely on Marisa. She considered mentioning it to Hanna, but it didn't quite feel like something she had to bring up. If Hanna felt that way, it was nice, but it'd be awkward to bring it up and make it a big deal. But was it that obvious that Marisa just liked being needed by others? Giving advice?

"So, when should we have those lab results?" Hanna asked.

"I'll put it in when I get upstairs. I leave in an hour, but when the third shift comes in, they should be able to handle getting the results back to you. I'll put a rush on it. Is he spending the night?"

"Yeah, I think we're going to have to get him into a room. Won't be what he wants to hear, but it's probably for the best."

Marisa nodded. "Noted. I'll let them know." She was reaching to press the button to go up when Hanna reached out and stopped her with her hand.

"So, there's something I kind of want to say, and I don't know how to say it. But I'm just going to come out and say it. So, if it gets really weird, pardon me for that."

Marisa gawked, then laughed. "Just come out and say it because it can't be any weirder than what you just said."

Hanna smirked. "Well, that's easier said than done."

Hanna leaned against the elevator and sighed. "Okay, here's the gist. I don't know, and I'm probably reading the signs all wrong, so tell me if you want me to shut up."

"Gladly," Marisa teased. They had known each other long enough to easily be able to tell one another how they felt. That made hearing this conversation different for Marisa. Hanna seemed apprehensive and on edge as she spoke her concern.

"So, Marisa, you know I think you're a great person, and we've known each other for a long time. In this hospital, by far, you're my best friend."

"Yes, I would say twenty-five years is a long time of knowing a person. But you're freaking me out here a bit."

"Sorry, I'll try to get to the point. You're a good friend, and I care about you. I want you to be happy. I know that things with Shana went south for you and you've taken steps to get through that. So, I'm only saying something because I don't want you to get hurt by any means."

"Hanna, just come out with it because you're confusing me right now."

"Okay. Are you attracted to Liz?"

Marisa stared at her, waiting for Hanna to continue.

"Like sexually attracted, I mean."

Marisa swallowed and tried to maintain her composure. "You've got to be kidding me right now. You wanted to talk about *this*? This has to be a joke. Is there a camera hidden or something?"

She looked around, but when she caught Hanna's gaze, Hanna rolled her eyes. "No? Then there has to be a reason you would ask such a ludicrous question."

"Marisa, it's not all that ludicrous. I see you with her, like you're lurking around or something."

"So, I'm a stalker?" Marisa's jaw dropped, and she looked away from Hanna.

"I didn't mean like that," Hanna quickly replied. "I just think that maybe now you're ready to really open yourself up to love again and wondered if, when you looked at Liz, you got those sorts of feelings. Maybe it's lust, or it's—"

"Stop right there!" Marisa held up her hand. "You realize that she's like twenty-four, right?" Marisa asked.

"Twenty-three," Hanna corrected.

Marisa released a breathless laugh. "Okay, I stand corrected. Even younger. That makes a nineteen-year difference in our ages. Nineteen years, so even if something happened, which I don't want it to, that would be a huge age gap. And certainly, you wouldn't go that route either. So, you're crazy if you think that I would even have any of those feelings for her."

"You can be attracted to who you want to be attracted to," Hanna quietly replied. "Doesn't mean you'd act on them. I just think that it looks like you might be headed in that direction."

"Well, you're wrong," Marisa replied, shaking her head. Despite her outward assertion, inside, she was a mess. Her heart was pounding and her legs felt shaky. If Hanna was picking up on her attraction to Liz, that meant she had already gotten in too deep. "I don't feel anything but a friendship for her, okay? That's all. I would never go there. Ever."

Hanna clapped her hands together. "I'm just glad to hear you say that. Because I care about you both. I don't want you to get caught up in some foolish chase that would only end badly for you. Liz has a boyfriend, and no one wants to see you get your heart crushed, especially me."

As Marisa processed those words, she felt unsteady. Liz had a boyfriend. She was certain that in the times they had talked, that had never come up in the conversation. Not that Liz owed it to her. Still, Marisa would have assumed at some point he would have been mentioned.

"Well, you had the signs wrong. So, you can rest assured that I'm not sexually attracted to Liz or anyone else for that matter. Feel better?"

Hanna nodded and stepped back from her.

"I really should be getting back to the lab and getting these vials processed. But good talk." She reached up and pressed the button.

"I made it awkward, didn't I?" Hanna asked.

Marisa was still reeling when the door opened. She shook her head, trying to relax her body. "Hey, we've known each other long enough that if you can't make a conversation awkward, then there must be a problem. You're just looking out for us. No one can argue with that. but we're good."

She moved into the elevator and turned to face Hanna. "Have a good night." She let the doors close.

As she took the elevator to her floor, she felt like her gut had been punched and kicked. *Liz had a boyfriend.* She couldn't shake the thought. If she had been on the fence about her true feelings for Liz, everything was crystal clear now. Her feelings ran deep. But now she knew that she needed to pull back, way back, before the tension turned into more than either of them could handle. It was really the best option for her sanity, and going after a straight woman in a relationship was simply wrong.

Marisa returned to the back room and sat down in a waiting chair. Hanna's words had hit her harder than she wanted to admit. Things were going to have to be held in a strictly professional manner, and that was all there was to it. From that point forward, Marisa wasn't going to allow the attraction to get to her.

She just didn't know how hard it would be.

CHAPTER EIGHT

Liz

Liz took a sip of water and sighed as she collapsed into a chair. It was one of the most hectic nights she had faced at the ER since switching departments, and she had faced some pretty hectic times at work. She took another sip of water. She had made a promise she would only leave the ER for a few minutes to relax, then be ready to get back out there. She hoped that Hanna could manage alone, but she had to take a few minutes off her feet. She also needed to clear her head. Everything in her personal life, with Marisa, and with work was overwhelming her and making her mind cloudy. She had made a few dumb mistakes at work today and she couldn't let things like that happen again.

Her phone rang, interrupting her moment of silence, and she groaned. Her first thought was that the ER would say that the two minutes she had was enough. When she grabbed it, though, she saw Chad's number.

Even though she was gripped with thoughts of not answering the call, she hadn't spoken to him in over three days, and that was some record. She had to face him sooner or later.

"Hello?"

"Hey, babe. I wasn't sure you'd answer. Since you're at work, I mean."

"Busy night, so might not be able to talk for too long. But I might have a couple of minutes."

"Alright, then. I'll make it fast. I just wanted to let you know that I have to head to France on the red-eye tonight."

"France? For how long?"

A call beeped in, and she looked at the phone to see Hanna's name. She groaned. She had to take a few more seconds to figure out what was going on.

"A week, maybe two, a month max."

Her mouth hung open. "A month?"

"Max," he replied.

Another beep from Hanna. "All right, well, I have to go. I'm sorry. I'll call you when I get off."

"You get off at one, right? I'll already be at the airport. We might miss each other altogether." His voice already seemed so far away and distant.

"Then, if I can't get through, we'll have to talk when you land. But I have to go." She didn't wait for him to respond before she cut him off and picked up Hanna's call. "Hello?"

"Liz, it's Donovan. He's here in the ER."

"I'm on my way."

Liz disconnected the call and jumped up from her seat. She would have to worry later about Chad and process her shock at him leaving so abruptly. She tossed her bottled water and hurried out of the breakroom. When she got into the elevator, she thought of Donovan and quickly pressed the button, her tears aching to flow.

"You don't know what's going on," she mumbled to herself. Still, it was ten o'clock at night, and it wasn't the time to normally see a child at the ER unless it was a true emergency. She had no choice but to fear the worst.

Liz jumped out of the elevator when the doors opened. She ran over to where Hanna stood at the desk, pacing back and forth. She caught Liz's look and stopped pacing for a moment.

"He just got here," Hanna started. "He's in bed two."

"Thank you!"

Liz hurried down the hall, slowing her pace only when she reached the room. She entered and spotted Victoria next to his bedside, her hand tightly grasped onto his.

"Hey, what's going on, bud?"

"I don't feel good," he said. He leaned up and then fell back down, touching his head.

"He's complaining of feeling dizzy, and his nosebleeds seem worse than they were before. Plus, he had a fever at the house."

Liz grabbed the thermometer. "Let me see." She held it to his forehead and took the temperature. "One hundred and three," she said. "Are you cold?"

He nodded, pulling himself up onto the pillow but looking weak and pale as he lost his balance and fell back.

"I'm going to go grab you a blanket."

Liz left the room and grabbed some cool washcloths. When she went back to the room, she spotted his mother standing over him, mumbling something. It broke her heart, and she looked away so her emotions wouldn't quickly take root.

"Here you go. You should start warming up soon." She laid it over him, and he pulled it up to his chin. "When did this start?"

Victoria sniffled, and Liz reached out and touched her hand. "Look at me," Liz whispered. "Everything is going to be all right."

Victoria nodded. "Things were getting better. I was relieved because he didn't seem to be having any more fevers and the pain seemed to be easing up. So, it looked promising. Then this morning, he woke up with a fever, and I tried everything to get it down, but to no avail. I would have brought him in sooner, but he was doing better."

Liz reached out and touched her arm. "This is not your fault. Dr. Wesley is here, so I'll grab him and have him come in. Just remember you have done nothing wrong."

Victoria nodded, but there wasn't any convincing her. Liz saw that etched on her face. She was uneasy and fidgeting, cautiously looking over at her son, and nervously biting on her nails. When she looked back and met Liz's stare, she gave a weak smile.

"I just have to have faith, right?"

Liz nodded. A moment later, she turned and left to grab the doctor. They had to take drastic measures; she was certain Dr. Wesley would realize that, too. As Liz entered the information into the computer system, she kept looking over to the patient room that Dr. Wesley hadn't yet exited. It would have been rude to interrupt him, but she was beginning to think he would never escape from the other patient.

When it felt like he would never get out there, he finally stepped out of the room. He looked at the patient's chart in his hand and documented something, then tossed the file into the folder. When he looked over, she walked over to him and handed him the chart.

He sighed and looked up. "I'll order a lab workup. Have them put a rush on it. Come with me."

He turned and knocked on Donovan's room. His mother replied, but it was muffled. Dr. Wesley entered the room, followed by Liz. "Hello. Sorry to see you both here again. I'm going to order some lab work. We'll have the results back tonight. You're going to be just fine, buddy." He patted his hand on Donovan's knee, and Liz shook her head.

Once they were back in the hallway, she heaved a noisy sigh. "Why'd you say that?" she asked.

"Say what?" He turned to look at her, confusion etched on his brow.

"That he'll be fine. You don't know that."

"Because childhood leukemia has a cure rate approaching ninety percent. There's every reason to be optimistic about his complete recovery."

Liz shook her head as they moved to the nurses' station. She tossed her pad of paper down on a desk and turned to him. "Maybe I'm not cut out for this, then."

"One tricky patient, and you're going to just give up like that?" He looked away from her. "Never saw you as a quitter, Elizabeth."

"I'm not a quitter."

When he looked back at her, he smirked.

"Then prove it. These are the patients who made you get your degree. To help them through whatever ails them. Cases aren't always cut and dry, but they're always worth it. Don't give up on this little guy. I'm not."

He handed over the order with Donovan's lab work. "Tell them the sooner, the better."

Liz nodded and picked up the phone to dial the extension for the lab. After three long rings, a message came on.

"Thank you for calling the clinical laboratory. Our attendants are currently busy. If you need immediate assistance, press two to page the manager on call."

Liz dropped the phone on the receiver and hurried toward the front desk. Sophie, who was seated there, looked over in her direction. "If anyone asks, I had to run to the lab. There was no answer."

"Okay."

Sophie turned back to her next patient as Liz got on the elevator. She took the ride up to the lab department; it seemed to take longer than usual. She tapped on the side of the elevator, staring at the numbers as they slowly went up. By the time the elevator opened, she was ready to bust out of there. The floor was pitch black, except for a single row of lights that outlined both sides of the hallway.

"Creepy," Liz mumbled. She had never been up there after hours, and she would be all right if she never had to be up there again. It was too horror movie for her. She reached the lab and grabbed for the door. It was locked.

Liz frowned. She knew that using the lab after-hours was only for emergency use, but this was an emergency. Liz walked up and down the windows that looked out to the hallway. She peered through them, hoping to find someone in there. As she went back to the glass door, she spotted a note tacked onto it. *For immediate service, call the manager on call at 1-888-550-2525.*

Liz grabbed her phone from her pocket and dialed the number. It immediately went to a recording. "You've reached the lab department. Sorry, we've missed you. Leave your message, and we'll call you back."

"Uh, yeah, this is Elizabeth Fletcher, and I'm calling you because I have labs that need to be drawn for Dr. Ivan Wesley. This is an urgent matter, and I would appreciate you calling me back ASAP." She rattled off her number and then hung up.

As she waited there, not wanting to go back downstairs only to tell Dr. Wesley that she didn't know when the labs were going to be drawn. Liz tried the number again, and this time, the call clicked past the message. "You are caller number ten, and we'll be with you in a moment."

Liz frowned. It didn't make sense. Where was this call even going to? She hung up, not interested in sticking around to see if someone really would answer her after nine other people got through the line. She pulled up her contact list, and her eyes landed on Marisa's number. It wasn't right to rely on her to come through in a pinch, especially so late. *But Hanna did say that she was someone I could rely on.*

Liz hated to abuse the friendship she was building with Marisa, but she wouldn't be asking if it wasn't urgent. Who knew when someone would finally get back to her? It had to be done. Besides, it was possible that Marisa wouldn't even answer the phone.

She hit the button to call Marisa and held her breath, waiting for her to answer.

"Hello?" she answered after the second ring; Liz released her breath.

"Hey, did I wake you up? I'm sorry if I did."

"It's all right. What's going on?"

"It's Donovan. He's here at the ER, and Dr. Wesley wants labs to be done ASAP, and I can't find anyone to run the labs. I left a message with the manager on call, but I'm not sure how soon they'll call me back."

"Enter the lab orders in the computer and draw the appropriate tubes. I'll be there soon," she said.

"Are you sure? I wouldn't call and bother you, but..."

"Liz, it's fine. He needs labs done, and I'm only ten minutes from the hospital. I'll be there as soon as I can get dressed. No worries. See you in a bit."

Before Liz could voice her appreciation, Marisa hung up. It wasn't an ideal situation to have to plead with her to come to the hospital, but Liz was grateful that she at least had that backup. Now, she just had to figure out how she could express how much it meant to her.

———

ONE OF THE SENIOR ER NURSES WAS KIND ENOUGH TO HELP Liz draw blood from Donovan. She lined up three pediatric tubes, each with a different color: red, blue, and purple. When the tubes were filled, Liz affixed stickers with Donovan's name, medical record number, and a bar code corresponding to the test ordered. She placed the tubes in clear plastic bags and brought them to the lab where Marisa was waiting for her.

Marisa greeted her and said, "The results will be ready in less than an hour."

Liz started to walk away but stopped. She reached out and touched Marisa's arm.

"Thank you."

Marisa looked over her shoulder and shrugged. "It's my job, Liz. No worries."

Then she was gone. Liz heaved a sigh. "God, please. He's so young. Don't take him like—"

"Elizabeth?"

She turned and looked over her shoulder at Dr. Wesley, who said, "We need to get Donovan upstairs to a room. It's going to be a long night."

"Sure thing."

Liz walked back to Donovan's room and entered. Victoria had her son cradled in her arms, his eyes droopy. "We're going to get Donovan settled into a room for the night," she said gently.

Victoria's eyes went to her. "I don't want to leave him," she said.

Liz quickly shook her head. "You don't have to leave him. They'll set you up on a cot in his room. Just gather your things and make sure you don't leave anything behind. His labs are already running and you should hear some results within the hour. I'm going to go get him set up on the children's ward."

"Thank you," his mother said.

Liz nodded and forced a smile. The prayer she was about to utter moments ago remained heavy on her mind. She had to wait to complete that, though. Liz went to the nurses' station and called up to the fourth floor.

"This is Nadine. How may I help you?"

"Hey, Nadine, it's Liz down in the ER. I have an admission for you. His name is Donovan Prescott. Birthdate is April 12, 2015. Dr. Wesley wants him in for observation overnight while we're waiting on some results. Truthfully, he could use the rest."

"All right, I'll grab a couple of the girls to get a room around. Give us fifteen minutes before you bring him up."

"Sounds good. Thank you." Liz dropped the phone into the cradle and pressed her face into the palms of her hands. She was exhausted and, if given a chance, she would burst into tears.

"Liz?"

Liz looked up into Hanna's worried face. "You okay?"

"Not really." Liz shook her head. "Donovan is sick. I'm worried about him, Hanna. Really worried. It brings back memories of my brother all over again. How can I face that child when—"

"Shhhh." Hanna grabbed Liz's hands. "You can't think that way. I know that you're struggling. You haven't faced patients like that before, but I can assure you that if you lose faith, they'll lose faith."

"I know, but..."

"There are no buts." Hanna knelt in front of her. "Look at me."

When Liz turned her head, Hanna saw the concern etched all over her friend's face. "You've got this. Donovan will fight whatever battle he has to fight, but he's going to get through it. You got that?"

"He's going to get through it," Liz mumbled. She needed to keep saying those words. He was going to get through it because Liz would help him in whatever capacity she could.

She stood up from the chair, and Hanna joined her, wrapping her arms around her. "Thank you, Hanna."

"It's my pleasure, but eventually, you would have gotten there." She laughed, parting from the hug. "Go in there and put a smile on your face. His mother needs that."

Those were truer words than Liz could have thought herself. If she was showing despair, Victoria would quickly think the situation was worser than she needed to. She left Hanna's side and went back to the room. When she entered, Donovan's eyes were closed.

Victoria said quietly, "Donovan is the kind of kid to be so energetic. Even when he's sick, he doesn't show it. He never shows it. I know something is wrong because this isn't my little boy."

Liz wrapped her arm around Victoria. "He's in good hands, and the staff here is going to make sure that we can do everything we can for both you and him. That's why you're here, right?"

Victoria looked up and nodded. "I just never thought my child would have to go through such pain. It hurts my soul, you know?"

Liz simply nodded. "The children's ward will have a bed for him in just a few minutes. Let him sleep."

Liz reached her hand out and squeezed Victoria's. Victoria looked like she wanted to fall into a heap on the floor. Liz needed to be a rock for

Donovan's mother. If she needed sleep, she wanted her to get some rest. If she needed someone to talk to, then she wanted to be that someone. This was going to be just as tough on Victoria as it was on her son.

They waited there a few minutes longer while Donovan rested in his hospital bed. When it was time, Liz looked at Victoria. "Let's go."

Liz opened the door and pushed it back against the stopper, then pushed Donovan's bed out of the room and to the elevator. She pressed the button to go up. Victoria leaned against the wall as they waited for the elevator to reach them. Finally, it did, and they loaded the bed inside.

"How long will he have to be here?" Victoria asked. "I should call my parents to let them know and see if they can get me a change of clothes. Plus, Donovan needs some stuffed animals. He needs comfort from his home." She sniffled and reached her hand up to cover her face.

Liz wasn't sure of the answer to that question, as it would all depend on the results of the lab tests. She didn't want to give false hope or give an estimate that was way off. She reached out and touched Victoria's arm as Victoria uncovered her face. Her eyes were red again.

"I'm not sure," she admitted. "We'll get the results back and then go from there."

Victoria nodded, seemingly satisfied with that answer, even if the tears were fresh on her cheeks. The door opened, and they stepped off the elevator.

"Donovan Prescott?" a woman asked, stepping out from behind her desk. Another nurse stood to the side.

Liz nodded, her work finished for the time being. She stood back and waited for them to get Donovan and his mother settled into the hospital room.

Liz waited until the nurses left his room before she went inside. Donovan had woken up and looked over to her, his smile widening. It was like he didn't even know what road he was about to head down, which was a good thing; the less he had to worry about, the better.

"I won't keep you both. I just wanted to make sure you didn't need anything before I head back to work."

Victoria stood up from her chair. "Thank you for everything."

"No need for thanks. You both take care. I'll check on you when I get a chance."

"Thanks again." Victoria hugged her, and Liz closed her eyes. Again, the tears were on the verge of falling. She bit back the lump in her throat and pulled from the hug.

"Anytime. I'll see you around. Rest well, bud."

She ruffled Donovan's hair, then was out the door. She hurried to the elevator and got on before falling back against the elevator wall, the door slowly closing her in. Liz waited for a breath before pressing the button to head back downstairs to the ER. But, as it started to go down, she quickly diverted its direction by pushing for the floor of the lab.

When she reached the floor, the doors opened. Liz cautiously moved toward the lab and opened the door. It was dark, other than a soft glow coming from the back room. She knocked on the door before barging in so that she wouldn't surprise Marisa. But Marisa wasn't there.

"Marisa?" Liz called out.

Marisa exited a small room, frowning at a piece of paper in her hand. She looked up, her face a mixture of angst and confusion. "Liz, everything is going to be fine. You'll see."

Liz covered her face as the tears flowed down. Marisa pulled her into her arms and just held her. It was what Liz needed at that moment, as she processed the news that her fears had been realized. Donovan was about to be rushed into the same life her brother had. And there was little she could do for him.

CHAPTER NINE

Marisa

L iz took another sip of her coffee as Marisa intently watched her. She wasn't certain how long they had been sitting in the breakroom. They had found themselves there after Marisa had finished telling her that Donovan's white blood cells were so elevated that it sealed their worst thoughts.

Liz wasn't in any position to continue working her shift after that. She had a strong connection with Donovan, especially with the way things had ended with her brother. So, Marisa just needed to be there for her and let her be. Liz took another sip of her coffee, then brushed a tear away from her eye. It was taking the last of her strength to keep herself upright. Despite that, she was more concerned about Marisa.

"You've spent all your time here," Liz said. "It's five in the morning. You should go home and get some sleep. What's it been? Five hours now? I'm fine."

"Six," Marisa mumbled.

"All the more reason you should get out of here."

Marisa tilted her head, then shook it, taking another sip of her coffee. "I'm good. After the third coffee, who needs sleep?"

Liz laughed, but her eyes dipped down. There was so much pain buried in her gaze. Marisa wanted to do whatever she could to take that pain from her. She couldn't explain why she had this overwhelming urge to take Liz's pain away, but she had never had this strong of a connection with anyone. Not even with her past girlfriend, and that startled her beyond belief.

"Well, I could use some sleep but can't even get my legs to carry me out of the hospital. So, imagine that." Liz tossed back her head as she took another drink.

"I'll help you. If you want to get out of here, you can come back to my place. It's probably closer anyway."

"I have to go home eventually, right?" Liz asked. She got up from her table and walked over to the trash can. She tossed the cup and then hesitated, her back still to Marisa.

"You don't have to be stubborn, Liz," Marisa said, joining her. "I know you're going through some pain. Lean on me. If that's what it takes, I have a shoulder, and you can use it."

"I'm not a weakling," Liz said, turning to her. Marisa's jaw dropped as Liz continued. "I feel like if I have to lean on someone, I'm going to crumble. I don't want to crumble."

"Liz," Marisa started, "it's not weak to have emotions. You are a strong woman. We might not know each other that well, but that much I know. I can see that. So, don't think for even a minute that I think you're weak."

"He's so little. He's Jimmy's age." Liz covered her face and sobbed as Marisa pulled her into her arms.

While Marisa had reservations about getting too close to Liz and was forcing herself to keep her distance, it wasn't the time to quarrel with herself over that matter. Liz needed someone, and if she did have a boyfriend, he wasn't there at that moment for her. This was the least Marisa could do for her. She was going to have to suck it up and be that shoulder for Liz. It was the mature thing to do.

"Let's get you home to my place," Marisa whispered. "You have to get some sleep. Doctor's orders."

Liz opened her mouth, but Marisa wouldn't let her argue. "If you get ill, who's that going to help?"

Liz didn't object after that. Marisa helped her out of the breakroom, and they left the hospital. She motioned toward her car, and they quietly headed in that direction.

"My car," Liz argued, but only once.

"It will wait until you've gotten your rest."

Marisa unlocked the door, and the two of them got in. They were headed to her house in less than two minutes. As she pulled out of the parking lot, she glanced over to Liz. She was already asleep, or at least her eyes were closed. Marisa turned back to the road and tried not to make any sudden movements as she didn't want to jerk Liz awake.

When she turned into the driveway and parked, she considered not bothering to wake Liz up, but the car wasn't as comfortable as the bed would be, so she reached over and gently jerked her awake.

"We're here," Marisa whispered.

Liz moaned and rubbed her eyes, pulling herself up in the seat and looking over to Marisa. "I should have just taken my car home."

Marisa smirked. "You were out cold before I even got out of the parking lot. Doubt you would have made it." She motioned with her head toward the door. "Come on. You need to get some good rest."

Liz eventually reached for the door and got out of the car. They walked to the entrance, with Liz lagging at least two feet behind Marisa. Marisa unlocked the door and held it open for Liz to enter.

"I'll grab you something to wear to sleep in," Marisa began.

"Not necessary. I can sleep in my scrubs, and I'll take the couch. I'm easy."

Marisa rolled her eyes. "You'll recall I said you needed *good* rest, not adequate rest. Again, you don't need to be so stubborn. You're here, so just let me help you to relax."

Liz nodded, and Marisa led the way down a hallway. She stopped at her bedroom and went in to find lounge pants and a T-shirt. She brought them out to Liz and led the way to the spare bedroom.

"Make yourself comfortable and don't wake up until you're ready."

"What about your work?" Liz asked.

"I'm off, as are you. I've already checked the schedule, so get some rest."

Liz nodded, and Marisa slowly backed out of the bedroom. Liz was uncomfortable allowing Marisa to help her out, as she was clearly an independent woman, but Marisa was relieved Liz was finally allowing the help and hoped that she didn't wake for at least three hours. Marisa escaped into her room, ready to fall into bed, the coffee slowly wearing off. She collapsed into bed, but her mind went to the woman down the hall. Liz was so close, in the same house. Thinking about that too much would drive her nuts, so she focused on her breath and let sleep take her.

LIZ'S BODY WAS WARM AGAINST HERS AS MARISA PULLED LIZ closer to her. Liz's breath was warm, too, just as their lips touched. Marisa felt Liz's tongue slowly invading her mouth, and she gasped, grabbing hold of Liz's arms, then trailing her hands down Liz's bare back until the agony of her being so close yet so far away from her came crashing down upon her.

"I need you," Liz whispered, those words echoing throughout Marisa's brain. Was she really hearing those words from the woman who made her body tingle, the woman Marisa was left craving?

Marisa heard those words again.

"I need you, Marisa."

It sounded even better with her name.

She had longed to hear that from Liz. Her heart pounded wildly in her chest as Liz's sweet and innocent body—filled with youth yet so much maturity—caressed hers.

"I need you, too," Marisa groaned. She needed her more than she needed air to breathe.

Just as their lips collided, Marisa's chest caved in. She gasped for air and jolted up, her breathing raspy. When she stared ahead at her empty bed, she felt dread. She was alone.

"Ugh!" she groaned, falling back into her bed and staring up, her eyes darting around the dots that were scattered unevenly across the length and width of the ceiling.

Liz came back into her memory, but not the Liz from the dream that had invaded her sleep. That was hot and sexy, and she desperately wanted to get back to it, but the thoughts she had now were the thoughts of earlier and the struggle Liz was going through.

"Liz!"

Marisa looked at her alarm clock and covered her face. Was it really that late?

Still fully dressed, she jumped out of bed and hurried out of the room, down the hallway to Liz's bedroom. She peeked into the room and she saw that the bed was made and Liz was gone. She hurried back the other way and rounded the corner. She hesitated when she saw Liz standing at the mantle. She had a picture in her hand.

"Who's the woman?" Liz asked.

Marisa entered the room. "My ex," she said. She reached out and grabbed the picture from her. "Guess I haven't gotten around to cleaning my mantle."

She looked down at the picture. It'd been a while since she was able to look at it and not get a pang of regret in her chest—regret that her life didn't work out the way she had wanted it to. But, at that moment, she didn't feel anything but pride at the thought of how far she had come. She laid the picture facedown on the table and looked at Liz. "It was a long time ago."

"Ex," Liz said softly as if turning it over in her mind and making the connection. Now, there was no more hiding that Marisa was a lesbian.

"How long?" Liz asked.

"About a year. Too long to keep the picture hanging around?"

"Well, that depends," Liz started. "Are you still holding out hope that she's coming back?"

"No. That's long past. She's moved on." Marisa shrugged. "And so have I."

Liz looked over to the picture, and Marisa cringed. "I know how this looks, but honestly, I rarely have time to spend in the living room. Maybe I should have cleared away that picture long ago, but it doesn't mean I still feel anything for her. I'm just a lazy housekeeper."

She laughed, hoping to lighten the mood. Liz did get a slight smile on her lips over that comment.

"Enough about me, though. What about you? How are you feeling? Did you get enough sleep? I didn't realize it was so late. Apparently, I needed rest, too."

"Got a couple of hours in. It was much needed. Feeling a little better. I didn't want to wake you. There was a laundry basket, and I dropped your pajamas in there. Hope that was all right."

"Yeah, that's fine. Thanks."

Liz nodded. "I had considered getting an Uber back to my car, but then found myself in the living room."

"Looking at my pictures," Marisa teased. Liz's eyes widened, and Marisa waved her hand in front of her. "I'm only teasing. There's nothing off-limits here. But I imagine you're hungry. I know I'm famished. Do you like eggs? I could make breakfast."

She glanced at her watch and laughed. "Er, brunch," she amended, leading the way to the kitchen.

"That's really not necessary," Liz argued, coming up from behind her. "If anything, I would owe you breakfast. I could buy you something on the way back to my car. Or we could grab something at the cafeteria."

Marisa opened the refrigerator. "Or, you can help me whip us up something. No point in spending money when I have a kitchen full of food."

She looked over her shoulder, and Liz threw up her hands. "Grab a bowl from the cupboard." She pointed, and Liz obeyed.

Marisa smiled as they worked on making eggs and bacon, and even pancakes. It was good to have someone else in the kitchen, helping to do the work and even offering up some good conversation. Cooking helped her to keep her mind off the dream that had woken her up. The more she moved around, the more she was certain she could leave that dream behind her. But the minute she stopped and looked Liz's way, the dream came rushing back to her, causing her cheeks to get red.

Marisa slowly released a breath and pushed on. She flipped the pancakes in the skillet. Liz stood directly behind her, and she felt her eyes on her. "Did you minor in cooking?"

Marisa laughed loudly. "Not hardly. You know what my minor was?"

She placed the skillet back on the stove and turned to look at her. Liz tilted her head, her eyes wide.

"Dancing." She shook her head. "Looking back, I wonder why I went with something like that. I mean, it's not like I'll get any use from it. But then again, that was a long time ago." Marisa turned back to the stove and continued working on the food in front of her.

Liz stepped up next to her and stirred the eggs. Her arm touched Liz's, and Marisa quickly stepped to the side. If Liz got too close, Marisa was liable to give away all her secrets, and Liz would see that she was sexually appealing to her.

"We'll have to go dancing sometime, and you can show me what you've learned," Liz said.

Marisa turned her head to look at Liz, who was still focused on the eggs and bacon in front of her. "We could, but I doubt I remember anything."

She also doubted getting Liz on the dance floor was a smart move. Marisa glanced at the pancakes and picked them up, flipping them once more. "Looks like we're done," Marisa said.

They pulled the food from the stove and put it on the placemats on the counter, then Marisa grabbed the plates from the cupboard and dished the food out while Liz grabbed the butter and syrup from the refrigerator. It was definitely a unique situation they had been tossed into, but it made things even more difficult for Marisa as she was struggling to get that dream out of her mind while having the real thing in her kitchen at the same time.

They sat down and ate, and the conversation stagnated. Liz focused on her food as she took each bite, and Marisa tried to keep her eyes off the woman across the table from her.

Suddenly, Liz snapped her head up. "Hey," she said, reaching across the table to touch Marisa's forearm. "I'm not sure how to fully express my gratitude because you've done so much for me lately. You've given me comfort when I've been a mess and you came to the hospital last night to help. You even let me stay here when I was too tired and emotional to get myself home. It means a lot to me. Thank you for everything, Marisa. I needed you and you came without a second thought. That means so much to me."

As she squeezed Marisa's arm tenderly, Marisa's heart slammed against her chest. She thought of leaning forward and kissing Liz, giving in to her feelings. No one had ever shown such gratitude to her before or recognized her efforts like this.

She shoved a bite of food into her mouth, pulling away from Liz's touch before she did something she shouldn't. She couldn't cross that line. Ever. "You're very sweet," she said. "I'm happy I could help, and you're very welcome."

Liz perked up with more energy than she had shown in a while. The rest must have really helped to recharge her. "What do you like most? Brownies? Cookies?"

Marisa laughed. "Why do you ask?"

"I want to bake you something to show my appreciation. Brownies?"

"You don't need to do that. But, sure. Brownies."

They smiled at each other until Marisa broke eye contact and chugged water. She probably needed to ask Liz to leave soon before anything happened.

The pep in Liz's posture faded and her shoulders drooped. "I wonder what he's doing right now."

"I imagine they're running him through some tests. He's probably nervous, but his mother seems to be a strong influence in his life. He's lucky to have her."

As Liz looked up, Marissa saw there were tears back in her eyes. "He's lucky to have you, too, a nurse who cares a great deal about him."

"I'm sure everyone thinks I care too much. Like, what kind of fruit loop am I?" She shook her head and dropped her fork into her dish.

"You're not a fruit loop." Liz met her gaze, and Marisa continued. "Can I let you in on a secret?"

Liz nodded.

"I've never told anyone this before, but when I first decided to become a laboratory technician and got this job, I thought I was invincible. I thought that if I saw sick people, it wouldn't affect me. I thought I had the backbone and nothing would phase me. The first week I was at the hospital was the first week I realized how wrong I was. I was working in a lab, and a patient came in. She was about thirteen years old. She had labs just like Donovan did. It was a routine checkup. She was seeing a new doctor, and they wanted to run routine blood tests. No biggie. But then things fell apart. It turns out she had brain cancer, and without the lab work, they would have never caught it.

"I watched her for a year of her life struggling and in so much pain, and she was alone. She was a foster child. She was abandoned when she was two and left in the system, and she was fostered out to this family, but the minute she got the brain cancer diagnosis, she was abandoned again. They said they couldn't afford her medical care. I don't know their situation, and maybe that was the case, but I know there are government benefits as a foster parent, and I was angry. Angry that they were leaving this little girl to suffer alone.

"But she was strong. She had the most beautiful spirit, and she didn't let that get to her. While I was angry, she was fighting for her life and still smiling through it all. So as time went on, I had to continue doing regular blood tests on her, and I saw her gradually getting sicker all while being in the foster care system, which, don't even get me started on that..."

Marisa shuddered just thinking about it. "She was alone. So, I attempted to foster her, and the paperwork was going through, but before it was finalized, she took a turn for the worse. We never got it finalized because she wound up passing away—in my arms. And at that moment, I wanted to give up. I didn't think this job was for me, either."

Liz gasped. "Wow..."

Marisa nodded, looking down at her nearly empty plate. "We have more in common than you may ever know. I saw someone I loved dearly die in front of me, and your brother..." Marisa looked up, reaching Liz's gaze, which once again was full of tears. "It might not be the same thing. She wasn't my family, but she sure felt like it."

Liz nodded slowly. "It was the same thing."

Marisa took a bite of her pancake, then slowly ate through it. Liz wiped her tears away.

Marisa considered her nagging thoughts, then sighed. "So, you saw a picture of my past, but what about you? Any significant other? Boyfriend in the picture?"

Marisa braced herself, wanting to know the truth once and for all. If what Hanna had said was true, Marisa needed to keep Liz at arm's length away, even if it was a struggle. It would be easier than getting too close only to get her heart broken even deeper.

Liz stirred her fork in her plate of eggs. "Yeah, but it's complicated. There's someone, but I'm not sure how strong that connection is anymore."

Marisa bit back the smile. So, while there was a man out there, it didn't seem like Liz was too set on him. That was a good sign, even if

Marisa didn't know why she cared so much. So what if this woman who was technically young enough to be her daughter was possibly on the market? She wasn't prepared to be with a woman like that, and she needed to have her brain examined if she felt otherwise. It was best just to push those sexual images clear from her mind because it wasn't happening.

CHAPTER TEN

Liz

Making her way up to Donovan's room was harder than Liz expected. As the doors opened, she considered going straight back down. It had been two days since she had first left him in the children's ward. She was nervous to see him and determine how things were going based on the doctors' projections.

When she reached his room, she released a slow and steady breath. "You've got this," she whispered.

She entered his room and halted when she saw that the sign was cleared of his name; plus, the bed was empty. Liz backed out of the room and went to the nurses' desk. Nadine sat there, staring at her computer.

"Hey, Nadine. I know it's been a couple of days, but where's Donovan?"

She looked up, confused. "Didn't you hear?"

Liz's mouth went dry, and she stared at her. That was never a good thing to hear, especially if you feared bad news. "Hear what?"

"Oh. Nothing like that. Your face just went three shades whiter." She laughed and stood up, then pointed down the hallway. "He was transferred to the oncology service."

Liz released a sigh, feeling the weight that had plummeted in her stomach. "Thank you!"

She hadn't considered they would move him. It made perfect sense, but she was a little frustrated she hadn't heard the news. It would have saved her some heartache. Still, it was better than having to hear the alternative. She walked down the hallway and moved on to the next section. She came to another desk, where a woman whom she didn't recognize sat. Upon a closer glance, she saw the volunteer tag attached to her badge.

"Hi, may I help you?" the woman asked.

"Hi, Crystal. I'm Liz. I work in the ER, and there's a patient up here I was working with and just wanted to follow up on. I don't know if you can give me that access..."

"Sure thing. What's the name?"

"Donovan Prescott."

Crystal looked down at the computer and clicked around, just like someone like Nadine would normally do. Liz had no idea that they had volunteers who could come in and have so much control over what was happening around the hospital.

She looked up and pointed to the door behind Liz. "He's right in there."

"Great! Thank you!"

Liz turned and went to the door. She softly knocked before letting herself in. Victoria was at Donovan's bed, reading him a story, and they both looked over to her as she entered the room.

"Liz!" Donovan cried, jumping up.

"Be careful," Victoria ordered. She jumped up to grab him by the waist.

Liz smiled as she moved closer to bed. "Hey, kiddo." He threw his arms around her neck, already standing on top of the bed. "How are you doing?"

"Good!" he said.

When Liz looked at Victoria, she saw that Victoria had a smile on her face, but her eyes seemed dim and dark. Liz helped Donovan back into the bed, then sat on the corner of his bed. His grin hadn't once faded.

"Just wanted to stop in on my break to see how things were going. I didn't realize you had been moved. When did that happen?"

"Yesterday afternoon," Victoria said. "They wanted to provide him more care."

"Well, that's not all that bad of an idea," Liz added. "You look good, though." Liz tossed a look to Victoria. "He does, doesn't he?"

Victoria's eyes grew wider, and she nodded. "He's doing well."

"Mom was just reading me a new book she bought." He grabbed the book and held it out to her.

"Can't buy a whole lot at the gift shop." Victoria laughed and then looked up at Liz.

Liz saw a cover with a boy in a bed, a bandage around his head, and a basic title. *Scotty Goes to the Hospital.*

"Maybe I can read it sometime," Liz said, smiling as she handed the book back to Victoria. "Are the doctors treating you well?"

"I really like Mindi," he said.

"She's the nurse who's handling his care," Victoria explained when Liz shot a questioning look toward her.

"As much as you like me?" Liz teased.

Donovan giggled. "No, silly."

Liz beamed and put her hand against his forehead. He felt nice and cool, so that was good. She dropped her hand and brushed it against his pillow.

"I'll leave you two to catch up," Victoria said, getting up from the spot next to the bed.

"You don't have to go," Liz argued.

She shook her head. "I think this is good for him. I'll be back."

Liz turned back to Donovan. "Are you comfortable?" she asked.

He nodded. "A little hungry, maybe." He touched his stomach, and it growled, making Liz laugh.

"Give me a sec." She held up a finger and quickly left his room. Crystal remained at the front desk. "Is there anywhere here where I can get pudding or something? Donovan's a tad hungry."

"We have a fruit cup." She reached under the desk and pulled it from a refrigerator, then handed Liz a spoon.

"Thanks!"

Liz went back into his room, holding the cup up like a trophy. He beamed brighter. "Do you like fruit?"

"Love it!"

He reached out for it, grabbed it from her hands, and then tried to get the lid off. He groaned, which brought a smile to Liz's lips.

"Allow me."

She removed the lid and handed the cup back to him. Donovan eagerly dug into it. After a few bites, he looked up. "What's that smirk for?" Liz asked, taking her seat.

"You know what this reminds me of?" he asked.

"Let me see..." She tapped her mouth as if in thought. "When we first met? Taking you out to have some Jell-O?"

He nodded. "You got it."

He took another couple of bites, and Liz just relaxed in the chair, watching him. It was good seeing him smile. She feared that she'd enter the room and find him hooked up to machines or something. But he hadn't started treatment yet. That would probably come several days later after they had all their testing in.

And Marisa had helped so much. Even now while she spent time with Donovan, Liz couldn't stop thinking about how Marisa had been there when she most needed her. It had felt a little odd sleeping at her house but also thrilling. It had given her an even stronger sense of who Marisa was and brought their relationship out into the real world. Liz never imagined that she could feel so comfortable around someone, so important and listened to. She definitely never felt that way around Chad, and he would never drop everything to come be with her.

A knot formed in her stomach. He had sent her a message to say he had landed safely in France, but she hadn't responded to his messages much since. Work was constantly draining her, but she also didn't feel any spark between them. He rarely asked how she was and mostly just talked about everything he was experiencing in France. Part of her felt relieved that she didn't need to put on a fake smile for dates or pretend like everything was okay since he never wanted to talk about anything heavy. The other part of her felt guilty for not being more responsive or missing him.

With Marisa, she was free to be herself. She could express her emotions and get the support she craved. And learning that Marisa was into women had changed everything.

But that was a silly thought. She liked Marisa as a coworker and friend. She did find her attractive, but she was a woman. She was also a lot older.

Liz had no idea what a romantic relationship with an older woman would be like.

Besides, she doubted Marisa would even be interested in someone like her—an emotional wreck.

"Will I ever get to go outside again?" Donovan asked, pulling Liz back into the moment.

Liz looked up and made eye contact. "Of course you will."

That question hurt Liz—to even think he would ask something like that. No kid should need to worry about something like seeing the sun again.

"I'll tell you what. If the weather is nice and you're feeling up to it, sometime within the next week, I'll come back here and take you out to the garden. It's beautiful out there. Just you and me. Deal?"

He nodded. "I like that."

There was a knock on the door, and Liz turned to see a nurse coming into the room. "Hey, I'm Mindi," she said.

"Liz. I work in the ER."

Mindi's eyes lit up. "I've heard a lot about you. This little guy can't stop talking about the nurse before me." She grinned. "I have to run my vitals. It shouldn't take too long."

"Hey, bud. I have to get back to work." Liz leaned in and kissed Donovan's forehead. "I'll be back in a few days."

"Bye, Liz!" Donovan called out.

Liz waved and then left his room. Victoria stood against the wall, her eyes closed. Liz approached her cautiously. "How are you doing?"

Victoria opened her eyes and nodded. "Pretty well, all things considering. He meets with the specialist tomorrow morning, so we'll have a better understanding of what's going on."

"I'll be praying," Liz said. "I mean, I've been praying. But I will continue to."

She smiled. "Thank you! He needs all the prayers possible. He really likes you."

"Your boy is darling. I told him if he's feeling up to it and you're okay with it, I'll come and take him outside. There's a garden on the south side that's breathtaking. I think it could lift his spirits."

"That would be awesome. He would love that and, frankly, it would be nice to have a short break. Never knew just sitting and lying around could be so exhausting."

Liz smiled and reached out to stroke her arm. "He's going to be all right. I have faith that you'll get through this rough patch, and it'll be behind you when he's in remission."

Victoria nodded and then looked past her to Donovan's room. Liz turned as Mindi exited. "I have to get back to work. But I'll be back in a few days."

"Thank you!" Victoria hugged her and then went back inside as Liz headed over to Mindi.

"Can I talk to you for a minute?"

"Sure!" Mindi turned to her.

"How do I go about volunteering on this floor?"

Mindi frowned. "Volunteering? You're a nurse, and surely that leaves you rather busy, especially in the ER. I've heard horror stories. How would you have time?"

Liz shrugged. "Just a couple of days a week. It wouldn't have to be much. I feel compelled to do this, but is it an option?"

She smirked. "This floor could use all the volunteers it can get. There's always a shortage. I'll let my boss know. I'm sure he'll be in touch."

"Great! Thanks!"

Liz left Mindi, feeling better about everything, knowing that Donovan was in good hands and being glad to be a part of it. It was something she felt compelled to do. She loved kids and looked forward to being able to help them instead of looking in from the outside. It was an opportunity she couldn't ignore.

Liz sunk into the seat across from her computer. It had been a long day, and she was ready for it to end, but her shift wasn't over. "Three more hours," she groaned, rubbing her face.

"Wanna go to break?" Sally asked as she popped up at the desk.

Liz jumped. "Didn't see you there."

"I tend to be stealth-like." Sally grinned, plopping down in the seat next to her. "But I saw you zoned out looking at the computer. Thought maybe you were ready for a break."

"Sure!" Liz stood to her feet as the phone rang. "I'll be back in fifteen."

Before she could step around, Sally was already motioning her back.

"Call for you."

Liz frowned, grabbing the phone from her. "Hello?"

"Liz? This is Mindi, Donovan's nurse."

The blood rushed from Liz's face. "Yeah, I remember. Is Donovan all right?"

"Oh, yes. No worries about Donovan. He's hanging in there. He just had his first chemo treatment yesterday, so there are some things he's dealing with, but that's not why I'm calling. My boss, Trace, asked me to give you a call. He has a few minutes this afternoon and wanted to sit down with you. I told him you're interested in working as a volunteer on this floor. If you have a few minutes within the next hour, he would like to chat with you."

"Oh. Okay. I'm working currently, but..." She held the phone away from her ear. "Can you handle the afternoon for a bit? They want to see me upstairs in the children's ward. Shouldn't be long."

Sally shrugged. "Not going anywhere, so sure."

She went back to her call. "Thirty minutes?"

"Sounds good. I'll let him know. We'll see you then." Mindi's cheery voice came through the phone, and then the call was dropped.

Liz placed the phone back into the receiver and considered the conversation. On a whim, she had considered volunteer work, but she was now looking forward to getting up there and seeing what Trace had to say.

"Are you sure you can handle it? This morning has been kind of busy. I don't want to put added stress on you."

"Don't even think about it. I'm fine. Hanna comes in an hour, right?"

Liz checked her watch and nodded. "I'll be back, then. See ya!"

She waved and then went to the elevator to first take her break. As she got off the elevator, her phone rang without fail. Every time she was on the verge of getting a few minutes alone, Chad called or messaged. She felt like maybe he had a camera on her and knew when she was free to chat. She slipped the phone back into her pocket. And just like many other times, Liz ignored the call, trying not to linger on her guilt.

He and I really need to talk about this whole engagement thing. I think we rushed into it.

Chad probably wanted to go on and on about his experiences, so why damper her mood when she would be going straight into a conversation with Trace after her break? Ignoring the call, sadly, seemed like the only option to take.

When she opened the door to the breakroom, she went straight to the refrigerator and pulled out her iced coffee. She sighed, taking a drink. *Perfect!* She turned to walk to a table when she saw Marisa with her head buried in her phone.

Liz smirked. Their paths always seemed to cross. But Liz didn't mind. Despite her confusion about what she felt for Marisa—if it was really more than friendship—there was something about Marisa's presence that made the world feel okay again. She also gave really great hugs.

"Reading something interesting?" Liz asked, taking the seat across from her. When Marisa looked up, she pushed her phone away, then shrugged. "Oh? Not interesting, then?"

Marisa laughed. "You might call it lame."

"Try me." Liz took a drink of her coffee.

"*Lab Weekly*. New articles drop every Monday."

"And yet, today is Wednesday." Liz scrunched up her nose. A soft chuckle came from across the table.

"Sometimes I like to read the articles over again. Get more knowledge that way." Marisa shrugged. "Told you. Lame. But hey, that's where my old person's mind goes." She picked up her cup and took a drink of whatever she had.

"Not my idea of fun," Liz admitted. "But I wouldn't ever call you lame. We all have our preferences."

Liz put her bottle down and reached for Marisa's phone. "Let's see what this is all about." She made a face. "Coagulation and blood clotting? Intriguing."

Marisa rolled her eyes. "How thrilling!"

Liz shook her head and took another sip of her coffee. "So, did you get my brownies?"

"No. What do you mean?"

"Well, I baked brownies to show my appreciation for everything you've done and I left them in the lab for you. Samantha was there when I dropped them off and said you'd be in soon. You didn't get them?"

Marisa frowned. "No. How strange."

"Bummer. I also baked some for Hanna and the other nurses since they've been so patient with me. They all loved them. Well, I'll bake you another batch." Switching subjects, she added, "But I have news. You might not find this all that exciting either." Liz crossed her legs and stared across the table at Marisa.

"Oh yeah? What's that?" Marisa arched an eyebrow and didn't respond further as Liz told her about the volunteering opportunity.

"Just thinking that it's what I need. It will make me feel like I'm doing something to make a change."

Liz beamed, waiting to hear what Marisa felt about that, but Marisa remained quiet. She looked like she was about to open her mouth, but she didn't respond.

"You have nothing to say?"

Marisa tilted her head in response.

"Come on, Marisa. There's something you want to say. Are you afraid that it will upset me? Or maybe you think I'll tell you to mind your own business?"

Marisa laughed. "Are you going to get all high and mighty and respond as such?"

"No, but I can sense that you have something to say, and there has to be a reason you won't come out with it."

Marisa sighed. "I'm not afraid to say something," she began. "Maybe I'm apprehensive, I guess." She shrugged. "Not my call, really. That's on you. If this is what you want to do, then go for it."

Liz's phone rang, and she pulled it from her pocket. Chad's name flashed on the screen again. She quickly pushed it back into her pocket and looked back at Marisa. "I guess I thought you might not find it interesting but would at least be excited for me. You're kind of disappointing me here."

She looked away, then back to Marisa. "Why aren't you excited?"

"It's not that I'm not excited for you. If this is what you want to do, then I think that's great."

"You just don't approve. Maybe even wondering why I would want to do this? Think I'm biting off too much?"

Marisa pointed with her finger. "That's one thing I question. But then, am I wrong, or were you close to calling quits on this profession? You even thought you couldn't handle it. I saw the struggle you felt with one kid. Yet, you're now throwing yourself into the fire? What if you get attached to other patients who just don't make it?"

"That's true," Liz muttered, looking down at her drink and wondering if she could fully throw herself into the flames of working the children's cancer ward and what that would entail. "I like children, and I want to be a force of a good. It's only a volunteer position. You know, two or three days. And if it gets to be too much, I'll pull back."

"Guess maybe I want to be the level-headed voice of reason here. I worry that you're getting in too deep. You can't get attached to all these children and watch the pain they're going through. Remember? I know that."

Marisa was trying to be a mother to her about it, and while Liz wanted to appreciate her thoughts on the matter, it was tough hearing that Marisa didn't think she was prepared for the volunteer position.

Marisa stood up and grabbed her phone, pocketing it. "I have to go back to work, but if you're sure that this is something you want to do, then I trust that you've considered it fully. If you have, then sounds good. See you around."

She left the table, and Liz let those words sink in. She tended to jump into things blindly, and this was one thing she had jumped headfirst into. But the thought of being there for Donovan and all the other kids made her happy. She would be just fine with that.

Her phone rang for the third time. Again, Chad's name flashed on the screen. This time she turned the phone off so he couldn't interrupt her any further. She left the breakroom and went up to the floor where she was to meet with Trace. She saw Mindi at the front desk, so she walked over to her.

"Liz," she began. "He's down the hall and last door on the right. He's waiting for you."

As Liz walked toward Trace's office, she caught a glimpse of Donovan's door, which was tightly closed. Usually, they left it open or ajar. She pushed away any frantic thoughts she had and proceeded to where Trace was. She knocked on the door and waited for his greeting.

"Come in!"

She opened the door and stepped in, ready to impress him. He greeted her with a handshake. "Elizabeth Fletcher, I presume?"

Liz nodded.

"The name is Trace Reece. Have a seat and tell me why you want to volunteer on this floor."

There it was, the question she had to face before she would be able to get the job. A million thoughts went through her mind, but she had to focus on the one thing that was her truth and not think about what Marisa thought about it. She was doing what was best for her, even if she did feel some doubt about it.

CHAPTER ELEVEN

A knock on the door signaled Marisa to look up. Samantha entered the lab and collapsed against the wall. "Hey there. The last patient signed out."

"Yes, thankfully," Samantha replied. "So, I was wondering what you were doing tonight."

Marisa shrugged. "Busy night ahead of me. More Netflix. More wine." She laughed. "You?"

"Well, that's kind of why I'm in here."

Marisa continued to look down at her paperwork, not realizing Samantha was moving closer to her.

"You see, my sister is the only one home, and I'm sure her jerk of a boyfriend will be there. They'll be hooking up to try to move this baby along further."

Marisa looked up as Samantha continued, "That's a whole other story. Anyway, I'm not looking forward to the sounds that will come from them as they're, well, you know..." Her eyes dropped, and Marisa smirked.

"Pretty sure I know. So, would you like to come over?"

Samantha looked up, and her smile deepened as she nodded. "Please."

"Let me finish up here. Give me ten minutes, and I'll be out."

"Thank you!"

"Oh, by the way, did Liz come by the other day to drop off brownies?"

With a poker face, Samantha said, "No. Why?"

"No reason."

As Samantha spun on her heel and went back out to her computer, Marisa frowned. She believed Liz, so why would Samantha lie about something like that?

Dismissing it for now, she turned back to her computer and stared at it for a moment until she pushed her work to the side. It could wait until the next day when she had a clearer mind.

"Are you ready to go?" Marisa asked, throwing her purse over her shoulder.

"That was fast," Samantha said, jumping up from her desk.

"Decided work could wait. I just had paperwork to do anyway. Turn the lights off on your way out, and let's get out of here."

Marisa was ready to dig into a bottle of wine. As she left the hospital, her mind wandered back to Liz. She was most likely gone for the evening. The way things had strayed for them was awkward because she got the feeling that she had said something wrong, at least in Liz's eyes. Liz wanted to hear what she wanted to hear, but that wasn't Marisa's job. Marisa wasn't supposed to tell Liz what would make her feel better. That was the immaturity in Liz, and it came with her age.

It was Marisa's job to be honest with her. And in her honest opinion, Liz wasn't someone who could go running into the fire for a bunch of kids who were in desperate need of help. If she couldn't handle one child having to struggle, how could she handle twenty and all at the same time? Marisa was only thinking about Liz and what would benefit her. She wanted to be wrong, but at that moment, she didn't think she was.

"Do you want to follow me?" Marisa asked.

"Sure! I'm parked right over there." Samantha pointed to a small gray SUV. Marisa got into her car and watched as Samantha got out and pulled out of her parking spot. Samantha drove over to her, giving Marisa enough room to get out of her spot.

One good thing about Samantha going to the house with her was she wouldn't have to face the house alone. As many people have said in the past, it was probably lonely, and that was true. Marisa was caught with the loneliness way too often. She thought she had gotten over that and was dealing with her loneliness just fine, but having Liz stay with her the other night brought all that sadness back to the surface. She needed the company tonight. It didn't have to be a sexual connection, just someone she could talk with so she wouldn't have to be stuck alone with her thoughts running wild.

Marisa turned into the driveway and parked, then got out of the car and waited for Samantha to get there. When Samantha parked and got out of her car, Marisa asked, "White or red wine?"

"You choose. I'm not picky."

Marisa pointed to the living room. "Have a seat. I'll be out in a minute." Marisa grabbed two glasses and a bottle of white wine and then carried them out to Samantha. She poured her a glass, then handed it over. "Enjoy!" she said. "Any preferences as to what we watch?"

Marisa turned on the television and took a sip of her wine, waiting for Samantha to give her suggestions.

"So, you'll think I'm totally weird," Samantha started, "but I'm in love with those reality-type dating shows."

Marisa raised an eyebrow, and Samantha took another sip. "Told you you'd think I was weird."

"Weird is such a strong word," Marisa said. "But I've learned a lot about you recently. You read Harry Potter and love reality dating shows. Are you sure you're twenty-one?"

"Twenty-two, actually. Today's my birthday."

"What?" Marisa jumped up from the couch. "Why didn't you say something? The office could have served up some cake or something. Hold that thought."

She left the living room and went into the kitchen. She opened her cupboard and reached into a box, pulling out a Twinkie. Having known Samantha for three years, she felt bad that she didn't know when her birthday was, but they didn't always have time to talk during work, and that wasn't the type of thing they discussed at the hospital. Still, it both-ered her that she was finding out at the last minute, especially when Samantha was sitting on her couch.

"It's not a birthday cake, but it will have to do." She tossed the wrapped Twinkie to Samantha.

Samantha laughed and held it up. "Thank you!"

"My pleasure, but I'm confused right now." Marisa turned off the television. "Why are you here and not out with some guy or something? Or you could be with your parents. Doesn't make sense to me."

Samantha shrugged, taking a bite of her Twinkie. "My parents had plans, and as you've heard, I'm struggling with who I want to date. So, I guess it just helped that you offered up your place for me to hang out."

"You should have told me it was your birthday, but happy to have you." Marisa took a drink of her wine. "And, since it's your birthday, you'll definitely get your choice of shows. So, reality TV it is." She made a face, and Samantha snickered.

"You'll love it."

Marisa wasn't certain that she would. She had lost all interest in reality TV just the first year that that one show set on an island came out. Getting back into it wasn't her idea of entertainment, but she had to just give it a try for Samantha's sake. She turned the TV back on, started the show that Samantha pointed to, and tried to just focus on her wine.

Samantha jumped up and turned the lights off. "That's better."

"It's not a movie," Marisa teased.

Samantha plopped down on the couch next to her, and even in the dark, Marisa saw her smiling. If she thought about it, it seemed like that was the first real smile she had seen from Samantha in months. To happen on her birthday—all the better.

But as the show went on, Samantha got into it way more than anyone should. She was beaming over the men and women as if she had some sort of stake in whether they made a relationship work. Marisa couldn't help but laugh.

Two episodes in, Marisa had poured herself a second glass of wine, but Samantha had barely touched her first glass. Another two episodes passed, and Marisa stared at her fourth glass and shook her head. If she had any more, she would find herself passed out on the couch. She got up and left the living room to go to the kitchen.

She poured coffee into the maker and leaned against the counter, just watching the coffee maker percolating in front of her. That was more entertaining than the show they were binging in the living room. She glanced at her watch. It was already two o'clock. She would never throw Samantha out of the house, but she did wonder how much longer

Samantha would want to watch TV. That was nothing, though, and definitely not reality.

"You don't much care for the show."

Marisa glanced over her shoulder as Samantha entered the kitchen, her glass in her hand. She took a long drink, then made a face. "Flat."

"It's been sitting for four hours," Marisa replied with a laugh. She grabbed the glass. "Coffee is on. As for the show, it's not all that convincing. Do relationships really work out of these?"

"A few," she replied. "Guess it helps to get my mind off my relationships." She leaned back against the wall, and Marisa stared at her. "It can be entertaining if you get swept up in the characters."

Marisa pointed to her. "You just called them characters. But it's real life, right?"

The coffee timer went off, and Marisa turned to pour them both cups. She handed one over to Samantha, then took a seat at the table.

"When I say characters, I just mean everyone has characteristic traits that come out." Samantha moved to the chair across from Marisa. "I know that it's not necessarily the type of show everyone likes. Me, I would watch all the new ones with my mom as I was growing up. It was kind of our thing. Now that she's gotten older, she doesn't much care for it either."

Samantha took a sip of the coffee as Marisa took one of her own. She winced as the hot coffee touched her tongue. "It happens when you get older, I suppose. Your likes tend to differ from years past."

"So, can I ask you something?" Samantha asked.

"Depends," Marisa teased. "I'm kidding. Of course."

"What type are you really attracted to? What are some deal breakers of yours? What are your turn-ons and turn-offs?"

"Geesh, that's more than just one question." Marisa took a drink of her coffee, giving herself time to consider her answers. Why Samantha wanted to ask these questions was beyond Marisa, but no question was off-limits for her. If Samantha wanted to know, then Marisa would answer.

"I'm inquisitive. What can I say?" Samantha shrugged.

"Does it have something to do with your own relationships, wanting advice and all? You never did tell me who you're crushing on at work. My money is still on Alan."

Samantha sat there for a moment and stared down into her coffee. Marisa felt like that long silence gave her the answer she expected. After a moment, Samantha looked up, avoiding the topic of her secret work crush. "I guess you could say I'm just curious about your love life."

"All right, let's see if I can give you what you're looking for." Marisa took another drink of her coffee, which no longer burned her tongue. "I don't necessarily have a type. If I'm attracted to someone, then I'm attracted to them. Blondes, brunettes, redheads, or even women with purple hair." She laughed, then shrugged.

"Small, tall, dark, light, short, frumpy. All of the above. Things like that don't matter. Deal breakers—hmmm, that's a toughie. I guess the major dealbreaker is if they don't like kids. I couldn't be with someone that didn't love kids. Besides that, nothing stands out. I don't know that I could be with a smoker, but I might be able to get past it."

Why hadn't she mentioned the age gap issue? She had been adamant about not pursuing younger women, but somehow that was changing.

"So, like, your relationship with Shana..." Samantha's words trailed off.

Marisa looked up, waiting for Samantha to continue.

"You both seemed to mesh well together."

Marisa snickered. "We seemed to mesh well together because we did mesh well together. We had just enough differences to keep the relationship interesting. All around, though, we were similar in a lot of ways. We were the same age, had the same style, same mood, same likes, same dislikes..."

Her mind went to Shana, and she shrugged. "Well, other than the fact that she hated coffee. Couldn't understand that one." Marisa held her mug up and took a drink. "Have to have some differences, though. Things would have gotten awfully boring."

"You mention age a lot," Samantha replied.

Marisa shrugged and looked down at the coffee.

"I always thought age was merely a number, but you seem to focus your attention on that."

"Guess I just realize that if your maturity levels differ, things would never work out."

"But can't someone be emotionally mature, yet physically youthful?"

Marisa sighed. "That's true, but I guess I never considered getting physically attached to someone who wasn't within arm's reach of my age. It just never was something I considered."

"Interesting," Samantha mumbled. "So, then, where do you stand as far as the age gap goes? Five years? Ten years? Won't date anyone past sixty? Younger than thirty? Where does it end?"

"Well, now I think you're just reaching." Marisa laughed. "I mean, I never thought about it in terms of I'll only date those who are thirty-five and older, or they can't be older than fifty. Things like that don't cross my mind. I would say sixty is a little too old, though. Don't want a mother."

Marisa smirked, taking a drink from her coffee mug. "I would say somewhere around five years. So, they have to be thirty-seven to forty-seven. Sounds like a good compromise."

Marisa nodded, feeling good about that decision but knowing that struck out the only woman who had brought her some satisfaction in her fantasies. Though Liz was making her question her stance, she needed to stay true to herself.

"I think if you go along those lines, though, you could in essence miss out on a great woman," Samantha argued, glancing at Marisa's lips. "If you hit it off with someone, then that should really be the only thing that matters. I just think people get too caught up with caring how old someone is."

"So, we're back to that, huh? This guy must be either super old compared to you or super young. In your case I would say that eighty is way too old and I wouldn't go younger than eighteen. Mainly because you don't want to have to deal with his parents." Marisa snickered, finishing off the rest of her coffee. She got up from the table and went back to the coffee pot. "Do you need another cup?"

"No, I'm fine," Samantha softly replied. "I really don't think you understand where I'm taking this."

Marisa turned to look at Samantha. Samantha's eyes diverted to Marisa's now-empty seat. "I had the perfect birthday planned in my mind."

"What was it?" Marisa asked.

Samantha's phone rang, cutting into the tension in the kitchen, and Samantha groaned and grabbed it from her pocket. She shook her head. "Hello?"

Marisa turned back to her coffee and finished pouring herself a cup.

"Where's Brett?" Samantha asked. "Come on, Chelle. Are you sure?"

Marisa turned back to find Samantha getting up from the table. "I'm on my way. I said I'm on my way. Bye."

"Everything okay?" Marisa asked.

"My sister thinks she's in labor. I have to go."

"Do you need me to follow you or something?" Marisa reached for her car keys, but Samantha shook her head.

"I'm fine. We'll talk later. Thanks for tonight and the Twinkie."

Marisa followed Samantha out of the kitchen and to the front door. "Happy birthday!" Marisa said, hugging Samantha goodbye.

It may have been her imagination, but it seemed like Samantha lingered too long in the embrace. When she pulled back, she hesitated, staring into Marisa's eyes intensely.

Marisa took a step back, and then Samantha gave a quick wave and left. She closed the door once Samantha was out of the driveway. Their conversation replayed in the back of her mind. She got the sense Samantha was trying to tell her something, but what?

———

MARISA SHOOK HER HEAD AS SHE PULLED UP IN FRONT OF THE club. She wasn't sure why she had even agreed to be there. While several hospital staff wanted to get together for some drinks and fun after work on a Saturday night, she wasn't convinced that she should have agreed to go. This wasn't her scene. The only reason she was going with it was that she knew Hanna would be there and they were the same age. Yet even that seemed like a skewed reason to make her appearance. She hadn't spoken to Hanna since Hanna had awkwardly asked if Marisa was sexually attracted to Liz.

But there were bound to be others in the same age group as her, or at least in the rough vicinity. So, she forced herself to make an appearance. She only needed to have a couple of drinks before deciding to leave.

When she stepped out of the car, she looked down at her attire. She didn't look half bad, at least in her shaky opinion. One thing was certain —she didn't want to cause any friction with the staff, who might be wondering why she wasn't going out with the rest of them.

When she entered the club, she looked around. The music that played over the blaring speakers wasn't a song she recognized but people were already dancing out on the floor, gyrating to the music, like it was the sexual presence that pulled them together.

In two seconds of being there, she considered turning around. Then she spotted Samantha. At least she could have one person to share a pleasant conversation with. On the other side of the floor was Hanna. She was going to avoid her—at least, until she was forced to have another awkward encounter.

She saw others from various floors of the hospital, some she spoke to often, and brief acquaintances whom she didn't have too many conversations with. She waved to a few who looked in her direction.

This wasn't so bad. When a waiter passed, she grabbed a beer from the tray and took a long swig. A few more of those and it might be possible she would forget she didn't want to be there. She took another sip, then cast a glance toward Samantha. She headed over in that direction to talk to her, as she hadn't had the chance in the week since Samantha's birthday. Working opposite shifts had made it difficult to carry on with their interrupted conversation. Plus, she did want to know how things had turned out with Samantha's sister.

"Hey, Marisa. Long time no see."

Marisa stopped when she saw Liz. It wasn't surprising that Liz was there, but she hesitated briefly. She had done fairly well making sure she didn't have to face Liz, but now there was no avoiding it. Liz was right there. And she looked stunning.

Marisa put on a smile. "Hey. How ya doing?"

"Good," Liz answered. "Over the past week I kind of got the feeling like you've been avoiding me. Funny, right?"

No, because I have been avoiding you. "Not sure I would call it funny, but I guess I wasn't sure if you'd really want to see me. I mean, we didn't

271

really agree on whether you should volunteer and I thought maybe you wouldn't want to see me."

"Oh." Liz stepped back from her, dropping her gaze to the club's floor. "Well, I did start volunteering and I really think it's where I'm needed. If you don't agree with that, then I don't know what to say."

"You don't have to say anything, Liz. If that's how you feel, then great. I'm happy for you if you feel it's the right choice. Really."

Marisa looked over but Samantha had moved somewhere else. She'd have to find her later. "How's Donovan doing?"

"Not great," Liz replied.

Marisa frowned. "He's not? What's going on?"

"I haven't been able to see him. He started chemo this week, and it's taken a toll on his body. Even though I'm volunteering, they only want the actual staff to be around him. So, there's that. Just hoping I can see him soon."

"I'm sorry," Marisa quietly replied. The pain in Liz's eyes was undeniable, and she wanted to pull her into a hug, but that would derail the distance she was putting between them.

"Just praying," Liz replied. "I wanted to talk to you about it but felt that maybe I should give you some space."

"I wouldn't have turned away from your call, Liz. You should know that."

"I do now," Liz said. "Do you want another beer? My treat."

Marisa nodded. "I'd like that."

Maybe Marissa could take a night and just forget about the distance and sexual tension she felt between them. The one-sided sexual tension. She had to constantly remind herself that Liz had a boyfriend and she was straight. Marisa enjoyed Liz's company, so what did it matter if she had one night that she didn't have to think about anything else?

That's what she decided and stuck by as the night went on. She had a few drinks and hung close to Liz. She spotted Hanna looking in their direction a few times, but even that didn't make Marisa pull away. People would believe what they would believe and there wasn't anything that was going to change that. She just wanted to enjoy Liz's company.

"I love this song!" Liz said after they had both emptied their glasses onto a waiter's tray. Before Marisa could fight it, Liz grabbed her hand and pulled her onto the dance floor.

"I don't even know this song!" Marisa yelled over the music.

"Just follow my lead," Liz replied, smiling even wider. Marisa watched her but found it difficult to follow the steps. It didn't seem to matter as they were both laughing and just moving around the floor. The whole dance floor was filled, and everyone seemed to know the dance but Marisa, but that didn't change the fact that she was enjoying herself.

When the song ended, an announcer spoke through the speaker. "Ladies and gents," he started. "As you've been patiently waiting, I'd like to inform you that the entertainment is here and ready to please you all."

Everyone applauded, as did Marisa, but she was still confused. Liz screamed and Marisa frowned. The speakers blared out another song, then in a blur, the dance floor cleared, and five men jumped off a stage and started to dance in front of them. As the crowd cleared to give them room, everyone cheered for the dancers. Liz seemed to be divulging in the cheering louder than most.

Gradually the dancers all scooted around the dance floor, grabbing women who wanted to dance with them. Marisa moved out of the way as one man came up and pulled Liz onto the dance floor. Together they started to dance, with the man grinding against her. Liz was laughing and moving like it was the easiest thing to do.

Marisa looked away, unable to indulge in watching them. Watching Liz act that way and go nuts over male dancers only reminded her of their insurmountable age gap. If this was what Liz wanted, then they would have never gotten a chance to be together. This wasn't something Marisa could see herself getting caught up in and she surely didn't want to watch the woman she was attracted to grinding against a man.

Marisa reached out and grabbed a glass off another tray, tossing some money onto the tray. She took a long sip and tried shaking the image out of her head.

"Not enjoying the show?"

She turned to see Samantha. "Not exactly," Marisa mumbled.

"Yeah, not really my thing either."

Marisa laughed. "Interesting. Another thing I'm learning about you.

You're the perfect age for this. I would think you'd be out there with the rest of the young women."

Samantha shrugged.

"I was going to ask you earlier," Marisa continued, "how's your sister? New baby?"

"Nope. It was a false alarm." Samantha laughed, then shrugged again. "A shame I had to leave your house in a rush. Her loser boyfriend, a.k.a. the father of this baby, took off because they got in a fight. I was the only one she could call."

"No need to apologize. It was late anyway. I'm sure you would have had to go sooner than later."

"Would have preferred later," Samantha softly replied. Her words were so low that Marisa thought she heard her wrong. She opened her mouth to ask, but Samantha said, "So, going back to the age gap issue we discussed before. Correct me if I'm wrong, but I would say Liz isn't in the vicinity of what you're looking for."

Marisa snickered. "Your point?" She took a sip of her beer and looked at Samantha.

"Come on, Marisa. It's pretty obvious you're into her. Maybe you don't want to admit that and that's fine, but you can't fool me. Or half of the hospital, for that matter. But then when you see that..."

She pointed to the dance floor, where Liz was now getting a lap dance from the male dancer. "I don't see how you couldn't be turned off and see that she's not the woman for you. Liz is looking pretty into the guy's moves, if you know what I mean. So, why put yourself through the heartache?"

Marisa's stomach churned, but she didn't want to admit that Samantha was right. "And I'll tell you, as I've said before. You're reading the signs wrong."

Samantha nodded. "If only that were true. Then maybe others would have a shot."

Marisa laughed. "Others? I don't see anyone kicking down my door. I'm staying single and I'm fine with that, but I'm telling you that Liz and I are merely friends." *And at this point, I'm not even sure if we're that.*

"Are you just oblivious?" Samantha asked. "You've been around and can surely see the signs that I've been directing your way. And maybe I'm not in your age bracket either. Heck, I'm even younger than she is. But I'm mature for my age. If memory serves me, you've even told me that once or twice. So, sometimes you just need to let nature take its course."

She grabbed onto Marisa's arm and pulled her close. In a matter of seconds, Samantha kissed her, and Marisa wasn't sure if it was the adrenaline rush or the pure shock racing through her system, but she didn't pull back. Even as she could feel everyone's eyes on them, she allowed the kiss to linger. Her mind was mush and suddenly everything she thought she knew was thrown out the window.

CHAPTER TWELVE

Liz

The fresh air hit Liz straight in the face as she wheeled Donovan into the garden. Her hands gripped the handles of the wheelchair, with a picnic basket tucked in the bottom of the chair.

"How's this spot?" she asked, pulling him up. They were right next to the roses, and she could smell the scent coming off the flowers around them. Sadly, they didn't lift her mood. Ever since that night at the club, she had to force smiles and chug energy drinks to get through the day. It felt like storm clouds had rolled in and were drenching her with rain.

"Nice," Donovan said.

When she sat down on the bench next to him, she looked over in his direction. Color had returned to his cheeks. Maybe this was exactly what he needed as part of his treatment. It had been tough getting him out there, but since he had been getting stronger, she had taken the first opportunity to do so.

"Do you want turkey, bologna, or ham?" she asked, digging into the basket.

He laughed. "You brought all that?"

"Are you kidding me? For you, I'd bring the world."

The smile on his face was bright and infectious—certainly, something that couldn't go unnoticed. Liz was so happy that everything worked out. Not only was the weather gorgeous, with a ray of sunlight cascading over the garden, but she had gotten the clear to get him out there. She wouldn't have been able to pull it off if even one person had objected. Victoria was ecstatic for Liz to take him on a picnic, and the doctors all agreed, since he had gone forty-eight hours without barfing. He needed to have fresh air and sunlight in his diet. It'd been almost two weeks since he'd been stuck inside, and that was ten days too long. Everyone—but most of all, Liz—was ready to see him outside of his room. Whatever was going on in her personal life didn't matter. She needed to be here for Donovan.

"Turkey," he said. "No, ham." A sly grin popped on his face. "Bologna?"

Liz laughed. "I know exactly what you need. Give me a minute." She tore three sandwiches apart and put meat from each one until she had made a sandwich piled so high that she wasn't sure he would be able to handle it. She was mistaken as his eyes went wide and he took a bite. He took a moment to chew it, but the grin that played on his face was magnetic.

"This is so good," he said, chomping down on the rest of that bite.

Liz was proud of herself for coming up with something that made Donovan happy. "Glad you like it."

She took a bite of her turkey club, then reached into the basket and pulled out a variety of chips. Donovan was quick to grab a bag of barbecue, and she ripped it open for him.

"Orange or apple juice?" she asked.

"Apple," he said between bites.

They both settled into a routine of just enjoying the meal. They were the only two out there, so it was a great, relaxing experience, and Liz, for one, couldn't take it for granted. Donovan wasn't the only one who needed that. She took a bite of her sandwich, then popped a chip into her mouth.

When she looked over at Donovan, his eyes were drawn to his food, and he looked uneasy. His lips were curved into a frown. Liz hesitated but couldn't hold off any longer. "Everything okay, bud?" she asked. "You're not sick now, are you? Too much food?"

He shook his head, then looked up. "No. I'm good. But thank you. This means a lot to me."

He turned his gaze away from her, and she followed his eyes as he scanned the garden. "You're the only one..."

He stopped talking, then took in a deep breath. Liz reached out and touched his shoulder, waiting for him to continue. "The only one who doesn't treat me like I'm going to break. It's nice."

Liz reached out and touched his knee. "Remember when we spoke that first night at the hospital? I said a mother's job is to worry, or something like that. But if you feel like your mom is all over you, you should talk to her. She only means the best."

"I don't want to make her sad. She cries enough."

He took a bite of his sandwich. Liz understood that. It was tough having to watch the one you love suffer. And if something happened to take away that life, it left you a shell of yourself. She had seen that first-hand with her own mother.

"Donovan, your mother would hate to know you're feeling this way. You should talk to her. Trust me."

He nodded, then grinned. "Look at this."

He put the small bag of chips up to his mouth and downed them in one swoop. He laughed as he munched on the crumbs that were left. That was what Liz liked to see. She wanted to see him in his element, being a kid, laughing and enjoying himself. So far, she was succeeding.

"I can do that, too," Liz said, flipping the bag up and pouring the crumbs into her mouth.

Donovan's eyes went wide, and his face went red as he continued to laugh. He then started to choke, and Liz's laughter died.

"Are you okay?" she jumped up and considered pulling him out of the chair and doing the Heimlich if needed, but he started to laugh again, easing her mind.

"Got you," he said.

"Donovan Prescott! That wasn't even funny."

He giggled, wadding his napkin up and tossing it at her. Looking at him at that moment, no one would have been able to guess that he was sick. It had been several days since Liz had last been able to see him, and from what the doctors and Mindi had said, he was so sick that they weren't sure he'd ever regain his strength while fighting through the chemo treatments. Through the prayers, it looked like something was actually working.

Liz turned to look toward the garden entrance just as another person stepped out toward the roses. *Marisa.* As their eyes locked, Liz inhaled sharply, her insides a mix of butterflies. There was a squeezing pressure on her chest. She broke eye contact, looking down.

She hadn't seen Marisa since the Saturday night at the club. She still couldn't shake the image that played through her mind as Marisa and Samantha made out in front of everyone. It was awkward, but everyone else seemed to be happy to cheer it on.

Liz had felt ready to cry.

Seeing that kiss had changed something in her. She had no idea Samantha and Marisa were involved with each other, and it filled her with envy. In that moment, she had realized she wanted to be the one Marisa kissed. She wanted to know how Marisa's lips felt and what it would be like to trace her hands along the curves of her hips.

She had slipped out of the club silently and went home to lie in bed, awake all night, staring at the ceiling. She'd never felt this way for another woman. What did that mean for her and Chad? What about the age difference? The gap didn't matter to Liz, but was it a problem for Marisa?

As Liz's cheeks burned, Marisa cleared her throat.

"Oh. I'm sorry. I didn't know anyone was out here." She started to turn away.

Liz felt a strong urge to just let Marisa go back inside, but she didn't own the garden and it wasn't her place to turn her away. "No need to rush off. We were just enjoying the scenery."

Liz glanced at Donovan, whose joyful and mischievous demeanor had suddenly become reserved. She remembered all too well how he had appeared shy and recluse when they had first met. "Marisa? This is Donovan. Donovan, Marisa."

Marisa smiled, then nodded. "We met. When I did his blood, remember?"

Liz's cheeks flamed up. How could she have been so dumb? Of course they knew one another. And here she thought she was being considerate by introducing the two.

She covered her face. "Oy, duh."

Marisa smiled. "How ya doing, Donovan?"

"Good," Donovan said. "Liz made lunch!"

His eyes brightened, and he didn't look reserved any longer. Maybe he was afraid that Marisa would stick him with more needles.

"Cold meat sandwiches." Liz shrugged. "Nothing major."

Marisa gave her a genuine smile, then looked over to Donovan. "That's nice. You're looking good. I heard you haven't been feeling too well, so I'm glad to see you looking well."

She knelt next to him, and Liz caught herself watching their sweet encounter. While Marisa talked to Donovan, Liz moved her eyes to look at Marisa. There was a light behind Marisa's blue eyes, and it choked Liz.

She quickly diverted her eyes down to her hands. Why she got caught up staring at this woman's eyes was beyond her. But they had slowly gotten closer over the weeks. Yet, some moments seem to separate them, such as the club. They had been getting along, so she thought. Then Marisa had gone off to Samantha and started kissing her in front of everyone. It left Liz confused. Marisa didn't seem the type.

"Are you guys best friends?" Donovan asked, tearing Liz's eyes back to him.

Marisa turned and met Liz's gaze, her lips in a straight line. On one hand, she looked to be smiling with her eyes, yet her gaze was also blank.

It was Marisa who spoke up. "Liz is a very good person. Anyone would be glad to have a best friend like that." That was an easy response. "Do you have a best friend?" she continued.

Liz released a breath. Getting his attention off them was the best route to turn.

"Joey," Donovan replied simply. "Haven't seen him since I got here. I miss him."

"And I'm sure he misses you, too," Marisa softly replied. She stood to her feet. "I have to get back to work. But it was good to see you." She rested her hand on his shoulder before turning to Liz. "Both of you."

"Good to see you," Liz replied, standing up from the bench. "We have to get back inside as well."

"Do we have to?" Donovan groaned.

"Sorry, buddy." Liz smiled. "We'll do this again sometime."

"Do you wanna come, Marisa?" Donovan asked, piping in.

Liz opened her mouth to break off that suggestion right away, but before she could, Marisa smiled and nodded her head. Liz snapped her mouth shut, then kept her eyes off Marisa as she said, "I'll be sure to let you know when we do this again."

It was probably best not to have Marisa tag along next time. What if Liz's feelings started to become more obvious before she even had a chance to make sense of them?

"Sounds good. You both take care." Marisa walked past her, and Liz turned to watch her leave. She was gone before Liz could utter a response.

"I like her," Donovan said.

"Yeah, she's nice." Liz turned back to look at him and grab the items to put back in the picnic basket. "Are you ready to head back in?"

"No," he grumbled.

Liz smirked and piled the basket into the bottom of his wheelchair. She couldn't wait until they got back out there or even went down to the cafeteria again. Just getting Donovan out of his room was something that Liz would continue to do whenever she got the chance.

When they got back up to his room, Victoria was still sitting next to his bed. Her eyes were closed, and Liz maneuvered him so that she wouldn't wake up. However, as he slipped into the bed, Victoria moved. She opened her eyes, and Liz cringed.

"Sorry. We tried to be quiet."

Victoria shook her head and sat up straighter. "No problem. Did you guys have a good time?"

"It was beautiful, Momma," Donovan eagerly replied. "You should see it sometime."

"I'll do my best." She shot a look at Liz and mouthed, *Thank you!*

Liz nodded and moved closer to the bed. "I'd better get out of here. I have some things to do once I get home."

"How are things with volunteering and your full-time job?" Victoria asked. "I'm sure you have little time to do anything else."

"Enjoying every minute of it. Wouldn't trade it for anything."

Liz meant it, but she was also exhausted. Sometimes, she was so exhausted that she caught herself falling asleep in the parking lot before she could even get home. Yet, she really didn't want to change anything about that.

"Just glad to do what I'm doing," she replied. "I'll see you both around."

She waved and then left Donovan's room. Before she headed to the elevator, she stopped at Gina's room. Gina was the newest patient brought into the ward, newly diagnosed with Wilms' tumor, a kidney cancer. She knocked and waited for someone to call out to let her enter.

"Yes?" Gina's mother's voice echoed through the door.

Liz peeked her head inside. "Just heading out but wanted to see if either of you wanted or needed anything."

Gina, who had just celebrated her tenth birthday the previous day, put on a weak smile. "I'm fine," she mumbled. Her eyes were tearing up, and that wasn't because of a side effect of cancer. Liz knew she had interrupted at the worst possible time.

She walked into the room and brushed her hand against the girl's forehead. "Heard they got a new flavor of pudding," Liz offered.

Gina shook her head. "Stomach feels sick."

"All right, honey. If you need anything, your mother has my number. Have a good evening."

She looked over at Gina's mother. It wasn't easy seeing so much pain in children, but Liz knew this was the absolute thing she needed to focus her attention on. Knowing that she could help kids in a volunteer capacity when she wasn't working made her feel fulfilled, as if she had been given a unique opportunity.

Liz left the hospital, and a weight lifted off her shoulders. Donovan was getting the care he needed, and that was what she had to believe in— the power of a doctor's hands. She got into her car and sighed, leaning back against the car seat.

Her phone rang, and she pulled it out of her pocket. Chad's name flashed on the screen. She had been working hard to ignore all his calls, knowing it was only pulling them further apart. But how could she face him considering she'd developed an attraction for someone else?

"Hello?"

"Is this Liz? Really?" Chad laughed. "Didn't think I would ever reach my love."

Liz remained silent.

"I imagine you must be working hard on wedding preparations."

That hadn't really entered her mind, but telling him so would surely put another wedge between them. "Work has been rough," Liz replied. "And I'm doing some volunteering in the cancer ward for children. But I sent that to you in text."

"Right. I recall seeing that."

You do? Because I don't recall getting a text back commenting on the matter.

"Yeah, so it's kept me occupied."

Liz looked down at her unadorned finger. The thought of promising her love to him for the rest of her life wasn't even on the forefront of her mind, and it killed her. If she said yes to a marriage proposal, she wanted to believe that it would always be forever. Yet she just wanted to figure a way out.

A tear dropped from the corner of her eye, and she quickly flicked it away. "How's France?"

"Good. Busy. We're close to a deal, though. It shouldn't be too much longer. Doing what I can to get home to my baby."

She forced a smile, but when it wouldn't touch the corner of her lips, she felt a pit growing in her stomach. "I'm sorry, Chad. I have to get back to work. Only had a few minutes to take this call."

"Oh. Sure. Well, I hope we can truly talk in the next few days. Maybe we can video chat."

"Yep, sounds good. Talk later." Liz quickly disconnected the call.

She wanted to grow stronger in love with her fiancé, but with him gone, it only cemented their distance, which was hard to overcome. It also didn't help when every facet of her life was now surrounded by anything but planning for a life of marriage. Donovan needed her attention, for one.

Liz's mind shifted back to Marisa, the one adult she could tell her troubles to and not fear that she would be questioned or judged. But Marisa had her own life and her own romantic relationships and Liz wanted to respect that. All she needed was to find a way back to the easiness she felt when Marisa and she were just growing as friends. And to get rid of all these strange feelings that seeing that kiss had stirred in her.

Without her friendship with Marisa, she felt like she lost everything. That fact scared her even more.

LIZ WAS SITTING ON HER COUCH, STARING AT MARISA'S NAME on her phone. Should she call or not? That was the question that had been in her mind for two days now. After seeing Marisa in the garden, she knew that she wanted to hold on to their friendship above all else. She needed to chat with someone about her relationship with Chad, because at that moment she was confused and conflicted about how she wanted to work out her engagement woes.

She sighed and finally made the call. A text would have been better, but it was way too informal to resolve the situation. The phone rang several times and then went to Marisa's voicemail.

"You've reached Marisa. I'm away from my phone, so leave me a message. I'll return your call as soon as I'm able."

The beep sounded. "Hey, Marisa, it's Liz. So, just thought I'd reach out and see what you're doing tonight. Thought we could get together and chat about something. No rush to call me back. Just—if you're available. Talk soon."

She hung up and stared at her phone. It was all in Marisa's hand from that point on. If she didn't call back, then she knew that Marisa wasn't interested in working on their friendship.

Thirty minutes later, Liz's phone rang; Marisa's name flashed on the screen.

"Hey, Liz," Marisa replied after Liz answered the phone. "Sorry I missed your call. As for tonight, I'd like that, but I work until eight. It'd be a late dinner but if you're up for it, we could meet at the cafeteria."

The cafeteria didn't appeal to Liz, as she knew that they could be interrupted and overheard by other employees.

"Eight o'clock would be fine, but what about meeting at Char's right down the block? If that doesn't work we could do the cafeteria, but just thought this would be different."

"I'm fine with that," Marisa commented. "I'll see you no later than eight-thirty."

"I'll be there waiting. See you then!"

Liz hung up the call, got up from the couch, and headed to her room. Now to just think about what to wear. She didn't want to wear anything that would be revealing, but she also didn't want to look frumpy. After cycling through several outfits, she opted for blue jeans and a simple pink blouse. Then she spent way too much time than was necessary on her makeup and hair.

Looking at herself in the mirror, she frowned. *What am I doing? We're just hanging out as friends. Just friends.*

She misted her hair so the curls loosened and then tied her hair in a ponytail. Then she wiped off some of the makeup. She wasn't going on a date. Just meeting a *friend*. She was dressed an hour early, but at least she was prepared ahead of time.

The clock ticked slowly by, but that was to be expected. She had a list in her mind of everything she wanted to get off her chest. For starters, it was time to tell someone about her engagement. To make it real. Sure, she and Chad had some things to work out, but she cared for him. They had been together a while, so it was probably time to move the relationship forward. Getting the engagement out in the open might help bring back some of their spark, and she might start to feel close to him again. What she felt for Marisa were just feelings. She didn't need to act on them. She needed to turn her focus back to Chad and her relationship with him.

Despite her thoughts, her heart wasn't convinced that was what she really wanted.

She dropped the engagement ring in a pocket of her purse and left for dinner.

At eight-fifteen Liz walked into the restaurant. Marisa was already seated in the corner booth, her eyes locked down on the menu. She went to the table and Marisa looked up.

"Hey."

"You're here early," Liz replied, taking her seat.

"Wanted to make sure I got out of there. Sometimes the lab gets backed up and I end up staying longer. When Angie got in, I told her I had to finish up paperwork and needed to get out of there. Your call sounded important." She closed her menu and slid it over to Liz.

Liz grabbed it and opened it, but then closed it right back up. "Didn't mean for it to sound that eager."

She snickered, though, in truth, she had been pretty eager. Getting out the truth was going to be a weight lifted off her and she was anticipating that moment. If Marisa were a true friend, then she would understand where Liz came from and why Liz had kept Chad's engagement from everyone.

A waitress walked up to the table. "Are you ready to order?" she asked. "The name is Tiff, and I can start you out with drinks."

"I'll just take water," Liz said.

"Same." Marisa nodded in agreement.

Tiff left and Liz turned back to Marisa. "How was work?"

Marisa heaved a sigh. "Some days I think it's time to retire, but it was all right."

Liz dropped her purse on the spot next to her in the booth. "I have a ways to go before I can even dream of retirement. But, hey, I have some days like that, too."

Marisa nodded, but her eyes shifted to where Tiff stood with their waters. They placed their orders, and once Tiff left again, Liz knew it was time she should just get it out there. She felt it would be better to say everything at the beginning of the meal, giving Marisa time to process it and discuss why Liz was so hesitant about Chad.

"So," she started.

"I was surprised to get your call," Marisa said, interrupting her. Liz looked away from her purse and back to Marisa. "After the club, I thought maybe something had changed with you. It just seemed like you didn't want to talk to me. I saw you a few times in the cafeteria and once in the breakroom and you totally ignored me."

"I did?" Liz asked. "I'll be honest, I don't recall seeing you. If anything, I thought maybe we were just on opposite schedules. While we used to bump into one another often, it didn't seem to be the case anymore. Then I thought maybe you were avoiding me because…"

"Because why?" Marisa asked.

Liz shrugged. "I don't know, really. Maybe because everyone from the hospital saw you." She latched down on her lip. "You know, at the club."

"Oh. You mean with Samantha?" Liz nodded and Marisa's cheeks turned a shade of red. "That wasn't supposed to happen."

"It doesn't matter. You don't have to explain it to me. You can kiss whoever you want to kiss."

"But, Liz, hear me out," Marisa started. "I didn't want to. I mean, it wasn't me..." Her words trailed off as Liz took a drink of her water.

Somehow the conversation had flipped to the kiss and Liz wanted to shift it quickly. She wasn't there to ridicule Marisa for kissing someone. If they were having a secret rendezvous, she couldn't judge her. She didn't want to judge her.

"Please. That's not why I came here," Liz pleaded. "The truth is, I had something to tell you and wanted to get it out there before we got too far into dinner. That's all, and it wasn't because I felt the need to talk about Samantha. Wasn't even in my thoughts."

That was a lie. Truthfully, Liz couldn't get the kiss out of her mind. She couldn't stop thinking about switching places with Samantha and...

She shook her head. That's not why she wanted to talk to Marisa. She needed to focus.

"There's just something I wanted to talk to you about so I can get your advice. That's all."

Marisa nodded as their food arrived. "Thank you," Marisa said to Tiff.

"Thank you," Liz added softly.

When Tiff was gone, Marisa looked down at her food.

"Ever try the fish here?"

"Nope. I'm a pretty plain person." Liz pointed to her plate. "I'll take chicken any day, but the fish looks good."

Marisa smiled, which tugged at Liz's heart. Suddenly all conversation about Samantha ended, along with thoughts of speaking about Chad. She bit her bottom lip, trying not to stare at Marisa and how pretty she looked.

"So, while I really didn't mean to ignore you at the hospital, it really was an oversight. I was so focused on Donovan's health that my mind didn't seem to be all there over the past week. If I blatantly ignored you, or you thought I saw you and I just didn't greet you, I apologize. If we cross paths, I wouldn't intentionally ignore you. That's not my style."

Marisa nodded. "Well, if I was worried about it, I should have come over to you. So, for that, I'm just as to blame." Marisa took a bite of her fish and Liz watched her.

"Good?"

"Excellent." Marisa took another bite, then continued. "But on a better note, Donovan looked good when I saw you both a couple days ago."

"He looks stronger than I expected. I was happy about that. And I was super happy I was able to take him outside. He needed it. I needed it."

"Do you know what his treatment plan is going to be?" Marisa asked.

"I know that they're doing chemo every other week. That will hopefully get him to feeling much stronger when he has to have his next one."

"That's good and promising. Still keeping him in my prayers."

"Thank you!" Liz took a bite of her potato, then another bite of her chicken. Talking to Marisa was easy. She didn't have to think about what she was saying, she just could be herself. *Maybe now isn't the right time to mention Chad. I will in a little bit...*

She just wanted to have this moment in which they could talk back and forth like they used to before things got complicated.

They shifted the conversation to the weather and even that didn't seem strange. It was relaxing and Liz cherished it. When the meal was close to coming to an end, with neither one having much on their plates, Liz took a sip of her water and swallowed the lump that had come back to her throat. It was time. She reached into her purse to pull out her ring.

"So, can I be honest with you about something that's been nagging at me?" Marisa asked, dropping her napkin in front of Liz.

Liz dropped the ring from her finger, and it went back into the pocket. "Sure. What is it?"

A reprieve from having to divulge her own deepest secrets.

"So, I've worked with Samantha for over three years and never saw her as anything more than a coworker, with the potential for being a friend. We just weren't that way. For one, she just turned twenty-two. That's way too young. With that twenty-year age gap, the thought of being with her in any way other than a friend has never crossed my mind."

"Marisa, you don't have to explain."

"But I do. Stepping into that club on Saturday night, I was reminded just how much older than everyone I am."

Liz smiled. "Stop it. You're not old." She quickly realized that Marisa wasn't laughing. Her seriousness wiped the smile from Liz's face.

"I'm older than all of you. And when those dancers—strippers, really —came out on the floor and all of you were gyrating against them..."

Liz tilted her head. "We were having fun. Nothing happened. Our clothes were still on."

Marisa nodded. "I'm not a prude, or never thought I was. But in that moment, I felt uncomfortable on so many levels." She shrugged. "It just hit me that I didn't belong."

"Don't feel that way," Liz quickly interjected, trying to get through to Marisa. "You belonged just as much as anyone else did. I know many people were happy you were there."

Marisa shook her head, and Liz paused. She thought she would get through her soon enough, but Marisa continued.

"So, when I was talking to Samantha, she said that however I felt about age at that moment wasn't a big deal because she had feelings for me. Then she kissed me. That's how it went down. I didn't expect it and I definitely didn't want it. I was taken aback, so, yeah, I let it linger. But the thing is, in the perfect world, I would have wanted to be there kissing someone else. If age weren't a factor, it wouldn't have been Samantha that I would've chosen. Sometimes you just do things because it's easier than stopping them."

Liz frowned. So, Marisa wanted someone else, but age was a factor? "Have you talked to this woman?"

Marisa snickered. "That's why I like you, Liz. There's a certain naïveté about you. In many ways I'm just as naïve."

Liz furrowed her brows. *What is she getting at?*

"It's you, Liz. And I know you have a boyfriend, and the age would never be something we could get over, but I'm forced to be honest. I just hope one day you can understand that you can't help who you find attractive. Furthermore, I hope you realize that I can put my feelings aside and I hope that we can somehow find our way back to a friendship."

Liz's jaw dropped as she processed what she'd just heard. How could she have missed this? Chad was struck from her mind; she no longer had any intention of bringing up that conversation to Marisa. She was struggling to find the words to speak.

"I'm sorry," Marisa whispered. "You don't have to say anything."

Liz watched as Marisa tossed some money down on the table and stood up from the booth. "Sorry," she said again.

She then hurried out of the restaurant.

Liz stared at the empty space in front of her, Marisa's bombshell playing on a continuous loop in her head. She closed her mouth and looked over her shoulder, but Marisa was gone. *Marisa!* They had to talk about this. She tossed some money down on the table as well, way more than what would pay for the bill, then grabbed her purse and ran out of the restaurant.

Outside, it had started raining, and Liz glanced around the full parking lot but couldn't see Marisa anywhere. How could she go home and just ignore what Marisa had laid out on her? She walked back to her car, her head foggy with disbelief.

She unlocked the door and started to open it when she heard her name. "Liz!"

Liz turned and Marisa stood inches from her. Without another word, she pulled Liz toward her and kissed her. Liz dropped her purse and, without hesitation, wrapped her arms around Marisa and just let Marisa's tongue slip into her mouth and take over all her cognitive senses.

Liz gasped and Marisa pulled back from the kiss. "I couldn't leave without doing that."

She turned and walked away from Liz. Only two words came to Liz's mind. *Come back!*

But Marisa was already gone.

CHAPTER THIRTEEN

Marisa

I f Marisa had gotten a phone call from Liz, then she would have at least felt better leaving her with the kiss still haunting her lips. She had gone back for a kiss to see if she would feel anything coming from Liz. She had. Liz had responded, giving reason enough to tell Marisa that maybe the age difference wouldn't interfere with a potential relationship. But not once had Liz called her or even texted her. A response would have been nice, but Marisa knew what was going through Liz's mind.

There was a light tap on her office door and Marisa looked up to see Samantha. A week had gone by and she had been able to avoid Samantha after the kiss at the club. Ironically, while she had anticipated a call from Liz, one would imagine that Samantha was doing the same with Marisa. She stayed silent because she didn't want to face the awkwardness that would ensue from the aftermath of the kiss.

She knew the truth already. She didn't have to debate over it. Samantha was a nice woman, but that wasn't where her heart leaned. If she were going to be with someone, regardless of age, she would embrace her feelings for Liz. Samantha was a year younger than that, and it was foolish to go with something just because someone else wanted you to. She couldn't hide her feelings for someone else, despite what Samantha wanted. Besides, in the three years she knew her, never once had Samantha expressed being into women. So, maybe she just wanted to experiment, but Marisa wasn't the type to be with someone who wasn't ready to go all in.

"Hey," Marisa said, slipping her hands into her pockets. "Thought Brooke was working the front desk today."

"She was but went home sick. So you're stuck with me."

Marisa nodded. "Is my next patient out there?" She moved toward the door.

Samantha reached out and touched her arm, making Marisa slip her gaze to Samantha's.

"Are we going to talk about it?" Samantha inquired.

If Marisa had her way, then she would rather not hash over what had happened. She couldn't change it, and it was best just to ignore it altogether.

"I don't know what to say," Marisa admitted. "Do you really feel something?"

"Yeah," Samantha said. "I've been trying to deny it, but those feelings are there and to deny them would be denying who I am. I don't want to do that any longer. I'm sorry if that puts you in a strange situation, but I'm just trying to be honest."

"Look, Samantha," Marisa started. "I appreciate that you're trying to put your feelings out there and you're a great woman, but..."

"You have feelings for someone else," Samantha proceeded.

"Believe me, I'm trying to fight that. With our age difference, it's not going to pan out well. So, I'm doing everything I can to ignore those feelings. But with you, I would still have the age difference."

And then the kiss happened with Liz and now I'm not sure what's going to happen.

When Samantha had kissed Marisa, there were sparks of passion there, but Marisa's heart wasn't fully into it. The kiss with Liz, however, had electrified her. It was like fireworks and hard to ignore.

"I don't want to hurt you, but if I'm being honest..." Her words trailed off. However she spelled it out to Samantha, she was destined to say the wrong thing.

"It's just that if I choose to pursue something with you, it would be because I didn't want to be alone, and you deserve way better than that."

Samantha nodded. "Maybe I should have talked to you when I first started getting these feelings, and then maybe I wouldn't have put myself through all this." She shrugged. "I'll get over it."

The bell rang at the front desk and Samantha moved toward the door of her office. "I had better get to my patient."

"I'll prep them. Thank you."

Samantha left the office and Marisa sunk back down in her desk chair. It wasn't the hardest conversation she had ever had. That would come if she could ever talk to Liz. She got up from her chair and went to prepare the lab for her patient.

The day turned busy after that patient, and it left her little time to think about Liz and the kiss and what the kiss meant. That was the good thing as far as that went. She cleaned the lab down from the previous patient when she spotted Samantha peeking her head into the lab.

"You have a call on line two," she said. "Children's oncology ward."

"All right. Thanks!" She grabbed the phone and hit the line. "This is Marisa."

"Hello, this is Jamie, a volunteer on floor four, children's oncology. I'm calling because we have a patient who needs lab work done."

"Patient name?" Marisa asked.

"Donovan Prescott."

Marisa looked up from her computer. *Donovan?*

"Have the orders been entered into the computer?"

"As far as I know. I'm just a volunteer."

"All right. I'll be right there."

Marisa looked up the orders on the computer. She decided she wouldn't bother to alert the phlebotomist and would draw the blood herself. She grabbed her supplies, then hurried past the front desk. "I have an urgent draw. I'll be right back."

Her breath hitched as she got on the elevator. She was anxious to get upstairs, as she was just as worried about Donovan as Liz was. The elevator seemed to sneak up the floors, but finally, the door opened. When she got off, she spotted Mindi at the desk.

"That was quick," Mindi said.

"Had a lull in patients." Marisa shrugged. "Donovan needs his blood drawn? Do you know why? This seems sudden. I hope he's okay."

"Yeah, they're looking at transferring him to the university hospital. They're going to enroll him in a clinical trial. The specialists at the hospital want an updated set of labs. He's in there." She motioned to the room.

Marisa considered what she had just heard, then looked back to Mindi. "Does Liz know he might be transferring?"

She shrugged. "Not sure. Excuse me, it's been a hectic day."

She then rushed off as Marisa turned back to Donovan's room. She knocked on the door, then entered the room. Donovan looked over at her, a wide smile on his face.

"Marisa!"

"Hey, bud," Marisa said, walking over and hugging him. She looked over to Victoria, who was beaming. That was a good sign. She knew that Victoria was emotional whenever given uncertain news, so it was a blessing that she didn't appear upset. "You know the drill. This will only take a second."

She pulled the cart over to the bed and Victoria reached out for her son's hand. Marisa would get the blood drawn and call Liz to make certain Liz knew that Donovan might be relocated. She knew that Liz would want to be there to say her goodbyes. She decided to finish off her schedule and then worry about talking to Liz later.

When her shift ended, Marisa walked out of the hospital and sighed as the cool air hit her face. She loved the spring air, when it was much warmer than winter and not as hot and humid as the summer months. She pulled her jacket tight across her chest and headed off toward her car. As she stepped into the parking lot, she spotted Liz walking no more than ten feet in front of her.

She thought about what she needed to tell her about Donovan and decided it was just as good a time as any. "Liz!" she called out.

Liz hesitated and turned to look over her shoulder. Marisa picked up her pace to meet up with her, but Liz turned and moved faster to get away. When it was evident that Marisa wouldn't reach her before she got in her car and drove away, she stopped trying. Liz got into her vehicle and hurried off, leaving Marisa literally in her dust.

Marisa didn't want to be upset by Liz's reaction. She understood that kissing her was out of a brief lapse in judgment. Yet, down in her gut, she had this gnawing feeling and felt like she had ruined everything. She wanted a chance at friendship, but there was looking to be little chance of that.

CHAPTER FOURTEEN

Liz

Liz woke and rolled over in her bed, staring out the window. She could still hear Marisa calling out for her and running up behind her, like Liz couldn't wait to have a chat with her. How could Marisa expect Liz to be open for discussion when Liz could barely process the thoughts that the kiss had brought up?

You wanted the kiss, Liz. Just admit that.

Her subconscious was smarter than she was. Yes, she had wanted the kiss. What was even harder to admit was that she had needed the kiss. She had needed to feel Marisa's desire for her. It freaked her out in many ways. Marisa was the only one who made her feel seen and accepted as she was, and she now longed to explore her feelings for Marisa in a physical way.

Liz got up from the bed and went over to her jewelry box. After digging through her box, she realized her ring wasn't there.

"Where could it have…" Her words trailed off as she left her room. She had forgotten she had stuffed it away in her purse when she had intended on clarifying things with Marisa and telling her the secret she had been hiding.

Downstairs, her purse still lay on the couch, where she had left it when she first got home. She grabbed it and plopped down on the couch, then dug through the purse into the compartment she had placed the ring.

She pulled her finger out, but the ring wasn't there. Liz tipped her purse over and slid her hands around, looking for the one thing she needed to have back in her possession desperately.

Gone. In just ten minutes of frantically digging, she was positive that the ring was no longer in the purse. For good measure, she went back through the contents again, then dug through the crevices of the purse. Nothing.

Liz cupped her mouth, stunned that she had lost the exorbitantly priced ring. Chad was one to brag about spending his money, and while she didn't know the exact amount, she was confident enough to believe that he had spared no expenses when deciding to propose to his wife.

Liz felt the tears coming. She covered her eyes and closed them tightly, willing herself not to let any tears fall down her cheeks.

He would understand, right? No. How would he possibly understand that I wasn't wearing my ring? He's going to know something is wrong. He's going to think I'm having second thoughts about this whole thing.

Her hand fell from her face, and she stared straight ahead, even more confused than before. She was having all sorts of doubts, and it wasn't a huge leap to think that he would think those things.

The last place she knew she had it was at the restaurant. It was a long shot that anyone would actually turn the ring in, but maybe some saint had come across the ring and decided to do the right thing.

Liz called the restaurant, waited for someone to answer. Finally, a woman came on the line. Liz released a breath as the woman greeted her.

"Hi, so I have a crazy request. I lost a ring when I was there the other day. I just realized it's missing, and it's the last place I know for certain I had it. Someone didn't by chance turn it in, did they?"

"A ring did get turned in. Just a minute; I'll go double check on that."

Liz's breath hitched. Was it possible? This would be the best news ever if they truly had her ring. She waited for the woman to return to the line. It felt like forever, but finally, she came back on the line.

"Sorry for the delay."

"No worries. Do you have it?" Liz held her breath.

"Yep. We have a ring. It's a mood ring, right?" the woman asked.

The minute she said that, Liz's heart fell. She was seconds from thinking that something was actually working in her favor, but now there was little hope.

"Actually, no. But that's all you got?"

Liz hated that her hopes were dashed, but it wasn't the woman's fault. She was destined to have to tell Chad that something tragic had happened.

"Yeah. Sorry," she said. "I can take your name if something turns up."

Liz rattled off her number, then quickly hung up. It was hopeless and there was only one thing she could do. It was either bite the bullet and do it now or wait until they were face to face. That was an easy decision to make. She didn't want to see Chad in front of her as she told him she had lost her engagement ring. She pulled up his name and dialed his number.

The phone rang three times and was just about to reach voicemail when someone answered.

"Hello?"

Liz's mouth hung open as a woman's voice echoed through the phone. It came again. "Hello? Anyone there?"

"Babe, who's on the phone?" Chad asked. The sound of running water sounded in the background and Liz held her breath, waiting for some sort of plausible explanation.

"Guess nobody," she said, then the phone went dead.

Nobody? She had to have seen the name flashing on the screen of his phone. Did she not know who Liz was? More than that, who was *she*? One thing was for certain. When Chad came back, they had a lot to talk about—none of which was about how excited she was for their nuptials. At this rate, the likelihood of marrying Chad just kept getting lower and lower.

TEARS STUNG LIZ'S EYES AS SHE SAT HUDDLED UP IN THE corner of her couch, distraught over hearing the woman's voice. She groaned and sat up, rubbing her eyes raw, trying to get rid of her tears. Who cared if Chad was sleeping around on her? It wasn't like she hadn't considered just calling the whole thing off. She hesitated, that thought still looping through her mind. It was true. The thought had crossed her mind every day since she had accepted his proposal. *If you're not happy, then run.*

Still, the mere thought that Chad was out there having sex with another woman had Liz's skin crawling. Mostly because of the deception behind it. He must've wanted to marry her. Otherwise, why go through the charade? His mom expected it? She supposed that was plausible.

She got up from the couch and started frantically pacing back and forth. She was upset that she had practically caught them in bed together. The fact that she had heard the woman had her skin crawling, and she shivered, pulling her arms across her stomach, which felt queasy, and holding them there.

Liz fell back down on the couch and shook her head. There wasn't anything to do about it. Without talking to Chad, she didn't know what else to think. They were most likely sleeping together. At least a 95% probability. Yet, even if there was only a 75% probability, why even indulge in thoughts about him? And who knew when he would be back to Chicago again and able to discuss with her all the reasons she should believe him? Besides, why should she buy anything he ever told her again?

Liz groaned and stood up from the couch. There she was, still thinking about him. "What good is that going to do? He betrayed my trust by having another woman in his hotel room. And to call her babe? Why? Who is she?"

Liz shook her head. "Stop torturing yourself!" She leaned against the couch and closed her eyes. It was all going to somehow work itself out. She only wished she knew when that would be.

Her phone started ringing, and she quickly grabbed it, half expecting Chad's name to flash across the screen. Instead, it was Marisa. Instantly the kiss came flooding back into her mind and she couldn't stop herself from answering.

"Hello?"

"Uh, hey, Liz," Marisa started. "Wasn't sure if you would answer."

Neither was Liz. There was a greater part of her that was surprised by the way she had quickly picked up Marisa's call. Yet, in that moment, she couldn't get the images out of her mind how Chad was enjoying himself in France and Liz was stuck having to think about what it was he was doing. But her kiss still played in her mind, making her unsure how she could continue to avoid Marisa.

"Yeah, sorry I rushed off like I did earlier."

"Oh, that's okay. I get it. I mean, it's understandable with the way things ended and all at the restaurant. You know…" Marisa released a breath, and Liz could hear it echoing through the phone. "Now I'm rambling, and I promise I did have a reason to call you. I have something to tell you. Do you have a few moments?"

"Sure," Liz responded, sitting back down on the couch. After the blow from hearing that woman's voice, she wasn't going anywhere, and she could take any distraction. "What's up?"

If Marisa mentioned the kiss, that might send Liz into full-blown panic, but they would have to face it eventually. So, why not the present?

"Have you heard any news about Donovan?"

Liz's heart pounded. What was it that Marisa knew? Her tone sounded concerned—overly concerned, even. "No, not lately, anyway. What's happened? Is he all right?"

"Oh, yeah. Right now he's fine. I don't want you to be concerned or anything. Just wanted to see if you knew the update. That's all."

"Oh, okay." Liz sighed and leaned back in her seat. Unfortunately, she had gotten too engrossed in other issues, and she hadn't visited Donovan as often as she had wanted to. "I haven't seen him in a few days."

"I had to do labs on him earlier today. I was curious, so I inquired with the staff, and they said they feel he'll benefit more at another facility. They're transferring him to Tennessee."

Liz released a breath. It wasn't horrible news, because at least this meant they were working to get him the best help they could for him. That was great. But there was a hole in the pit of her stomach. Once Donovan was out of the hospital, she would lose all contact with him. She hadn't had enough time getting to know the kid, and for that, she was sad.

"I'm happy if he can get the help he deserves—the help he needs. But, sure I'm sad. That's just my selfish side. I don't know what I'll do without him around."

"I just wanted to make you aware. In case you weren't."

"Thank you," Liz quietly replied.

She wasn't yet ready to end the call. Marisa's voice was too comforting. "So, um, what are you up to?"

She didn't want to be there, in her home, alone and think about her missing ring. She didn't want to have to think about her failing engagement. She just needed someone. Anyone.

Don't lie to yourself, Liz. You know Marisa is the one you need.

"Probably wine and Netflix. My typical weekend night."

Liz swallowed, almost too shy to ask. "Well, I have both wine and Netflix. If you want to come over."

There was a long pause on the other end of the line, so long that Liz had to rest her hand from holding the phone. She shook her hand out, waiting for her reply.

"I don't know," Marisa started.

"If I'm being honest, I think that I need us to talk about what happened between us—clear the air and all that stuff. I enjoy being around you Marisa, and I don't want that to end."

Plus, I just need to figure out this stuff happening in my life right now.

Liz sighed. "Look, there are just some things I think we need to talk about. That's all."

"See you in fifteen," Marisa replied softly.

When Liz hung up, she knew having a talk with Marisa was the right thing to do. And clearing the air with her about Chad would finally have everything out in the open. What she didn't account for was that the mere thought of telling Marisa about Chad would go out the window fifteen minutes later, when she showed up.

"There's wine chilling in the fridge and Netflix already on. Go pick a show and I'll be right out."

Liz grabbed two glasses, the bottle of wine, and a corkscrew, then carried it all out into the living room, where Marisa was relaxing on the couch and staring at the television screen.

"Did you find us a show?" Liz asked, placing the glasses on the coffee table.

Marisa looked up and shrugged. "Don't really feel like Netflix." She shrugged again and looked over to the glass.

"Wine, on the other hand..." She picked her glass up and looked up to meet Liz's gaze. "Yes, please."

Liz tilted her head. She was confused as to why Netflix didn't much appeal to Marisa, despite that it the one thing—well, one out of two, including the wine—Marisa said she wanted to do that night. She put in the corkscrew and started to turn it, then popped the cork out and poured Marisa a glass.

"Thank you!" Marisa replied, taking a drink before Liz could pour her own glass.

"It's good, I hope," Liz replied, putting down the glass. "Didn't even get in a toast."

Marisa laughed, taking the glass away from her lips and nodding. "Just what I needed. Now, if you want to say a toast, go for it."

Liz looked down at her glass, then sat down on the spot next to Marisa. She looked over to Marisa, who now held a curious stare. Nerves suddenly shot to Liz's stomach. What kind of toast could she make? *New friendships? Old relationships coming to a screeching halt?*

She raised her glass and met Marisa's stare. "Here's to people getting to know each other and overcoming obstacles, and to finding one's purpose."

Marisa arched an eyebrow. "I'll drink to that. And to being honest with yourself and others."

She tossed her head back as she downed half her glass. Liz watched her, curious by that last statement. When Marisa finished her drink, she turned to Liz and Liz quickly took a sip.

And to finding out what Marisa meant.

She put her glass down on a coaster, then slid another coaster over to Marisa.

Marisa laughed.

"What?" Liz asked.

"I don't know. That was just a mature thing to do. Heck, I don't even know that I could find my coasters." She smirked as she put her glass down on the offered coaster.

"So, you're calling me old?" Liz teased.

Marisa held up a hand. "Not old, mature. It isn't often that someone of your age would even think about using a coaster."

"Probably something my mom instilled in my brain." Liz laughed as she picked her glass up and took a sip. "I would say that has something to do with one's upbringing."

"Yeah, I suppose you're right," Marisa replied.

The living room turned quiet, and Liz looked over to the television, the Netflix home screen still pulled up. She grabbed the remote and turned the TV off, then put it back in its basket.

"There's something I need to tell you." Marisa's words came out in a rush as Liz turned back to her.

Liz opened her mouth, but Marisa held out her hand and touched her arm. "Let me get this out there before I lose my nerve."

Liz nodded.

"So, I like you, Liz. I have tried to push those feelings aside because you're so much younger than me. But the truth is, it's becoming impossible. When I kissed you, it was out of instinct. I wanted to know what it would be like to feel your lips on mine."

Liz's cheeks filled with heat, but she didn't interject. Hearing Marisa's words left her feeling something inside of her that she thought was dead. It was something she hadn't felt in a long time, even with Chad. She felt renewed hope that maybe something more was out there for her. She felt even excitement that welled up inside of her.

"The age difference is something that I feel is too hard to get past, but then when you do something like the coaster thing, I think maybe I'm just being crazy or even maybe I'm the immature one."

Liz tilted her head. "So, just the mere act of using a coaster has you thinking that, oh, maybe I'm not so young after all?"

"Look at me, Liz."

Liz slowly turned to look in Marisa's direction. Liz's breath hitched as she stared at her, not sure if she should continue to look or force herself to look away. Her heart was in play, and she knew that if she continued staring, she would do the inevitable and kiss her.

"If I thought for one minute what I'm feeling would never be reciprocated, then I'd turn away. I'd never look back. But seeing your eyes locked on mine, and having felt your lips against mine, without one ounce of hesitancy..." Her words trailed off.

As Marisa's eyes dropped to Liz's lips, Liz sucked her bottom lip instinctively. Just the thought of Marisa kissing her again excited her and made her feel a longing that she didn't know existed. In this moment, though, there was more. Heat built up inside of her, and she couldn't pull herself away from that.

Marisa reached out and slowly grazed her hand over Liz's cheek. Liz locked eyes with her, and it was Liz who slowly moved in, capturing Marisa's lips against hers.

Hold me. I want to feel your arms around me.

The words echoed through Liz's head as she scooted in closer to Marisa.

Marisa's tongue swooped in, claiming a moan that was deep inside of Liz. Marisa said breathlessly, "Once we go there…"

Liz dropped her gaze to Marisa's, waiting for Marisa to go on.

"There's no going back."

"I wouldn't want to," Liz whispered before she crashed her lips onto Marisa's again.

She pulled herself up and straddled her legs around Marisa's waist, breaking from the kiss only long enough for Marisa to slide her hands under Liz's shirt and pull it up and over Liz's head. Liz frantically went back in for another kiss, not wanting to take a moment away from pressing against her soft lips. She felt Marisa's hand at her bra, and there wasn't any doubt this was right where she craved to be. Marisa removed her bra with a flick of the wrist, and Liz slipped out of it, her breasts touching Marisa's. She wanted nothing more than to be right there, in Marisa's arms, and seeing what their future could hold. She could worry about the aftermath later.

CHAPTER FIFTEEN

Marisa

Marisa shifted in bed and her arm wrapped around the warm and naked body beside her. She opened her eyes, smiling as the images of Liz came tumbling through her mind. With lovemaking like that, who could even fathom that age even mattered? She shifted next to Liz and turned to look at her. The cover was draped loosely over Liz's petite body. Marisa pulled back the covers and kissed the inside of Liz's cleavage, which made Liz let out a groan that only intensified the heat inside of Marisa.

Marisa tossed the cover back and moved in, splaying several kisses down Liz's body until she reached the core of Liz's femininity. Liz groaned, giving Marisa the motivation to move in. Marisa took in a whiff of Liz's scent and smiled to herself. She could definitely get used to this. No way was age going to deter her at that moment, when Liz's satisfaction was at the brink of all of Marisa's desires.

Her breath brushed against Liz's opening, a place she had spent much of the night before sleep overtook them. Before she could even caress that very spot, Liz moaned and shifted in bed.

"Marisa?" Liz whispered.

"Right here, babe," Marisa replied, shifting between Liz's legs to look up into Liz's expectant stare. Liz closed her legs and her eyes dropped.

Marisa frowned at that. Was something wrong? Was Liz regretting their time spent getting to know one another intimately?

"Something wrong?" Marisa asked, pulling herself up and plopping down into the spot where she had been sleeping only minutes earlier.

Liz glanced over at Marisa and her face looked as white as the sheet that was on her bed.

"You regret it." Marisa quickly looked away. "That's fine. I should have known it was possible. I mean, this is all new to you. You were simply exploring. No need to say anything." She tossed the covers to the side and slipped out of bed. "I'll just find my clothes and get out of here."

"Marisa, will you hold up for a minute?" Liz reached out and trailed her finger down Marisa's arm. Before her hand could reach Marisa's, Marisa pulled back.

She shook her head. "It's easiest if I just go. No one needs to feel awkward. It is what it is. Happens all the time."

Liz pulled her hand back and her eyebrows furrowed into a straight line. Marisa tossed a look to Liz, who nodded. "Happens all the time? Okay, then. Must've been no big deal to you."

Marisa's jaw dropped, pain resounding inside of her when she heard those words. She slowly backed away from the bed, tripping over her shoe as she tried to reach the door. Tears stung her eyes, and that infuriated her because she was supposed to be the regal one, the one mature who didn't let some simple statement rattle her. Yet, there was a lump in her throat and her vision was blurred.

Do not let her see you like this.

Marisa spun on her heel and grabbed the shoe from the floor, then picked up her panties and bra, hurrying to get out of there. When she reached the door, she turned around to face Liz, her jaw clenched. Before she could leave, she had to get this out there or she was liable never to have the chance.

"Is that what you think?" Marisa asked. She pulled on her bra and brought her panties back up, still gawking at Liz over on the bed. "You think that it meant nothing and that I'm just flippant about what happened between us? If that's so, then you don't know me at all."

Her breath hitched, and she mentally cursed herself for showing her pain to Liz. She turned around and said, "It's fine and all, but that's not how I feel," before leaving.

"Marisa. Wait!" Liz called out before Marisa could get to the stairs. Before Marisa stepped onto the top stair, she felt Liz's hand on her shoulder. When she looked over at her, Liz's face softened. She now was in just a T-shirt.

"I'm sorry if I offended you. It's just, it seemed like you were saying it was no big deal that we had sex. Not just once, but multiple times. I guess I was protecting my feelings."

"You were protecting yours?" Marisa turned and faced her. "I was protecting mine. You were filled with regret, and I didn't want you to think that it was breaking me down inside. But the truth is..." Marisa swallowed the lump that had never left her throat. "It was."

"If you saw regret in my eyes, I can't deny that."

"Great! A fantastic way of boosting my ego. Thanks a lot."

Marisa looked away from Liz. She wanted to bolt, get out of there and never look back, but something kept holding her steadfast to the top of those stairs.

"It's not what you think, though. Please...Come back into the bedroom so we can talk. I'm begging you."

Before Marisa knew it, Liz grabbed her hand and was pulling her back through the bedroom doorway. Liz sat down on the edge of the bed and tried to pull Marisa down to the spot beside her, but Marisa leaned against the dresser.

"I'm good here," Marisa mumbled.

"Suit yourself," Liz softly replied. Marisa met Liz's gaze and Liz's eyes went dark before she looked down at her hands. There was something she was hiding. Marisa could sense that from even all the way across the room. She was fidgety, and when she looked up, a tear trickled down her cheek.

"I haven't been honest with you," Liz whispered.

Marisa didn't even attempt to reply. She just watched her. Waiting. Waiting for whatever it was that Liz felt she had to get off her chest. The waiting was slowly killing her inside, but Marisa didn't move. She just waited.

"I don't know that you'll ever forgive me."

"Just tell me," Marisa stated.

Her words pleaded for Liz to go on. Nothing could be that hard, right? Yet, there was so much angst and anxiety in Liz's eyes that Marisa worried she was wrong on so many levels. "I don't know that I can wait another minute, or even second. What's going on here?"

"I'm engaged to be married, Marisa," Liz yelled out.

The blood drained from Marisa's cheeks as Liz slid down the bed and brought herself to her heels. She had to have heard her wrong. This was some kind of joke. It was the only explanation she could focus on. Please, someone tell her this was some big mistake and Liz didn't just utter those words. Liz didn't move to explain herself and Marisa knew that she wasn't dreaming. Her world had just come crashing down around her.

CHAPTER SIXTEEN

Liz

From across the bedroom, Marisa stared at her bottle of water. Somehow, the two had switched places: she was now sitting on the bed and Liz was standing across the room. Liz opened her mouth to say something, but then slowly shut it again. She was relieved Marisa hadn't bolted out of there the minute she dropped the bombshell. She hadn't meant it to come out like that, but it seemed like she couldn't stop the words from sounding the way they did. Marisa needed to know. But like this? She wasn't so sure that had been the way to go. She nibbled on her lower lip and waited for Marisa to do something.

As if in response, Marisa lifted the bottle to her lips and took a swig. Not quite the action Liz had wanted.

"Are you going to say something?" Liz asked.

Marisa snickered. "I don't know what you want me to say, Liz. You're getting married. I just had sex with someone who is about to walk down the aisle. Yay me."

She took another drink and her eyes dropped to the top of the bottle. Liz's chest caved, and she wanted to rush over there and pull Marisa into her arms. Still, she continued standing.

"It isn't like that," Liz started, wanting to scream at herself. How could she have done this to the one person she'd connected with? It was hard to fathom that she could actually be forgiven. "It wasn't like this was on a whim."

"Oh? It wasn't?" Marisa looked up, her eyebrow arching. "Explain that to me, because from where I'm sitting, it looks exactly like that. It looks like you were set to see where things could go, not thinking about anyone else's feelings. Not thinking about how it would affect me. Isn't that right?"

"No," Liz blurted out. "Will you please let me just explain my side of things? Please."

She pleaded with her because the thought of Marisa running away from her at that point would only bring Liz back to the state she was in when she first heard the woman on the other end of the line.

Marisa glared at Liz, finally giving her the attention Liz had asked for. It was now or never. "Yes, I'm engaged. I'm engaged to a man. I won't try to deny that."

"You really can't. You just blurted that out to me fifteen minutes earlier."

Marisa glowered at Liz and Liz slowly nodded. Marisa tossed her head back, downing the rest of her water.

"It's in name only," she said.

Marisa frowned, but Liz quickly explained. "Chad is someone my mother pushed for. My parents would have had me married five years ago if they had their way. Chad was the guy who could give me what I wanted. Or, rather, what they wanted me to have. Sure, I looked for a relationship that would reflect the one I saw in my parents, but it was Chad that my parents wanted for me. When he proposed, I honestly thought I had no other choice."

Marisa sighed and stood up from the bed. "You really don't need to explain yourself. If I was some last-minute fling that you wanted to see if you were ready to commit to your fiancé, then so be it."

"Listen to me, Marisa. Please. Because that's not it at all."

Liz pushed herself off the wall and started to move toward Marisa. Marisa crossed her arms and dropped her eyes to the floor before sitting back down on the bed. It was a defensive way of pushing Liz away and Liz understood that. Liz turned and walked over to a chair, then sunk down into it.

"I didn't plan this, thinking that I would hook up with a woman and try to see what I was missing. You just happened to be there. I'm sorry that was the way it happened, but I don't regret it."

Marisa looked up, her gaze landing on Liz's. "Then why? Why me?"

Liz shook her head. "I planned on telling you at the restaurant, but then the timing just never seemed to be right. I even brought my engagement ring to tell you everything, but we got to talking and I realized that telling you could mean losing your friendship. I had spent so much time hiding this that I didn't want you to think I didn't know to be truthful."

Marisa smirked. "So, you didn't want me to see how you truly are. Is that it?"

Liz dropped her gaze. She felt a tear slowly sneaking up on her and she willed it to go away.

"That came out all wrong," Marisa softly stated.

Liz shook her head. "No. It's understandable. I let the kiss linger when I should have stopped it right there. Then tonight was unthinkable. I allowed us to have sex all while knowing this truth. But, you see, before you called, I realized that I had lost my engagement ring. Somehow it had fallen out of my purse, and I called Chad to tell him what happened. Then I realized he's not on a business trip alone. He's with another woman. I was feeling lonely, and it's not some horrid excuse, but it's the truth. I was lonely. You called, and all I thought was how I needed to see you. How I wanted to see you. You were in the right place at the wrong time, but Marisa, I needed that."

Marisa's eyes softened, and Liz had a brief glimmer of hope, of Marisa walking over to her and pulling her into her arms, telling her everything would be okay, and possibly kissing her to comfort her. She held onto that feeling, but Marisa's eyes hardened, and she scoffed.

"What bothers me the most is at the time, I planned on throwing caution to the wind and saying screw all the fears about age and who cares about anything that might have divided us. I let my guard down. I allowed myself to open myself up to feeling this way. I allowed myself to let go and just relax and then this happens. I can't even say I regret that because it *was* time for me to open myself up to feelings like this. And I needed that. I regret that you're not available, but it is what it is."

"But I am," Liz argued. "My engagement is over, as far as I'm concerned."

Marisa's eyebrows furrowed, and she stood up from the bed. "But you're not. You're not free and I'm not going to be the other woman. I deserve more than that. And as the mature one in this duo, I have to walk away."

Liz swallowed the lump that had formed in her throat. "I'm sorry if I hurt you."

Liz stood up as Marisa started to move past her. Marisa reached out and touched Liz's shoulder.

"Don't be sorry. Goodbye, Liz."

She walked past Liz and Liz turned to watch her leave. She opened her mouth to plead with her to stay, but as she walked away, she knew that it was right to let her go. She fell into the chair and felt her heart aching as Marisa closed the door. She waited a second before she jumped up, hurried out the door, and ran down the stairs. By the time she got the door open to run out and beg Marisa to stay, she saw her backing out of the driveway. It was too late, and Marisa was heading further away from her.

Liz turned and went back into the house. She fell back against the door as she closed it behind her. Her phone started ringing, and Liz thought that maybe Marisa was calling her. When she reached the table where her phone lay face down, she grabbed it and spotted Chad's name. Her heart fell as she answered the call.

"Hello? Chad?"

"Hey, babe," he started. "Funny thing, I left my phone at a board meeting and just got it back. One of the women there said she answered your call. Gosh, babe, I miss you."

Another lie. Liz sat down on the couch, her heart racing from her conversation with Marisa a few moments earlier. Right now wasn't the time or place to get into it with Chad, but that moment would come. She was getting stronger to finally have that conversation.

LIZ WALKED UP TO THE DESK AND MINDI LOOKED UP AND smiled. "Hey, Mindi!"

She nodded. "Hey, it's been a few days."

Liz nodded. "Too long. Just came to see the little man. Hear he might be headed off to Tennessee soon."

She started to walk past the desk and toward Donovan's room.

"No one called you?" Mindi asked, bringing Liz's attention back to the front desk. "Thought Victoria might reach out or something."

"What do you mean? I haven't heard anything, outside Donovan going to Tennessee."

Mindi shrugged. "Guess they thought it would be better to have a clean break. But he's already gone. They had a clinical trial opening, and he needed to be there today."

Mindi's phone rang, and she grabbed it across the desk as Liz stared at her, tears already threatening to fall. He was already gone? How'd this happen? Why didn't someone call her? She looked away from the desk and her breath hitched. If she hadn't talked to Marisa, she wouldn't have even known that he was leaving the hospital. At least she was forewarned. She turned away when she heard her name.

"He did write you this letter."

She reached out as Mindi handed her the letter.

"Thank you," Liz mumbled. It wasn't the same. Liz tucked it into her pocket, not wanting to read it until she had some privacy. She was off for the day, and she found herself heading out to the garden. It was the last place she had been with Donovan—just the two of them. She now considered it their place. She was relieved to see she was out there alone and sat down on one of the benches. When she opened it, she braced herself; she knew the note would make her emotional.

Dear Liz —

I want to thank you. Thank you for being you. I have enjoyed our time together, no matter how short it might have been. Know that you have helped me. You have helped my mom, too. I will never forget you. And whatever happens to me, know that you have been a smile that I've loved. So, thank you! You are my sunshine, Liz. I hope that I've been yours.

Love,
  Donovan

Liz wiped the tears that had fallen down her cheeks as she folded the note and put it back into her pocket. Donovan was a strong boy, and she wanted to be just as strong for him. She stood up from the bench and turned to head back into the hospital.

Marisa walked out of the hospital and Liz spotted her first. When Marisa's gaze went to hers, Liz wiped the tears away and opened her mouth to say something. It would come out all wrong, she knew. But she didn't even get the chance to. Marisa turned on her heel and hurried back into the hospital.

Liz looked down at the ground, steadying herself and hoping she didn't fall to her knees. Life was turning out way too hard and she couldn't stand there and watch everything fall apart around her. She grabbed her phone from her pocket and closed her eyes, anxious for the tears to stay away.

A voice answered the call after the first ring. "Hello?"

"Hey, Mom," Liz spoke, the tears thick in her throat.

"Liz? Are you crying?"

Liz released a forced giggle. "Of course not. Just wanted to let you know that I'm coming for a few days to visit."

Her mom squealed into the phone and Liz pulled the phone away from her ear. At least her mom sounded excited to have her there.

"What's the occasion? Are you coming to start working on the prep for the wedding?"

The excitement laced through her mom's voice was like a dagger to Liz's chest. She could already see the disappointment on her parents' faces when she told them the wedding wasn't going to happen. Then again, she still needed to tell Chad that. But first things first, she needed a break from the hospital and a break from reality.

"Nah, just wanted to see you guys. That's all. Any problem with that? I can get a few days off work and no better time than the present. Might as well, right?"

"Of course, honey. And that doesn't have to stop us from talking about wedding plans. I'm so excited to see you."

"Yeah, I'm looking forward to it, too."

She collapsed against the building, prepared to break down in tears. She bit down on her lower lip and heaved a sigh. "I have to go, but I'll be heading to Indy in the morning."

"Sounds good. I'll prepare your old bedroom."

Liz smiled. "Love you, Mom."

"Love you, too."

Liz quickly hung up the call and stayed there for a moment. She felt like she was running around. In a sense, maybe she was, but her heart ached that she now didn't even have Marisa to talk to.

Can you blame her? You had sex and then said, "Oh and by the way, I'm getting married."

Liz covered her face and shook her head. She would be devastated, too, if she was Marisa. It was awful that she had played with her heart in a way that she couldn't ignore.

Liz entered the hospital and took the elevator to the ER floor. Sally sat behind the computer and stared absentmindedly at it. She yawned, covering her mouth, then looked up and met Liz's gaze. She smiled as she pulled her hand away.

"I didn't know you were still here," Sally said.

"You look exhausted."

Sally nodded. "Rough day already."

Liz looked around the empty waiting room. At least Sally had a break in action at that moment. "Just about to head out, but I have a question. How do I put in a request for some time off?"

Sally arched an eyebrow. "For how long?"

Liz shrugged. "A few days maybe. Some things are going on at home and I really could use some time away. I know that puts everyone in a bind, but I don't see a way out of it. Whom should I speak with?"

"Frank, I'd say." Sally smiled. "There's a lot of us looking for work, so I doubt it will matter. But I saw him headed to his office. He's probably still here."

"Thanks!" Liz turned, but Sally's voice made her jerk her head to look over her shoulder.

"I hope everything is okay. I know all too well about family drama. I'll be thinking of you." She got up from her desk and gave a genuine smile.

"Thanks, Sally." Liz turned and headed straight for his office. Things would be fine if she took just a few moments to herself. She had to get away from thoughts of Chad and her feelings for Marisa. It was the only way she would be able to clear her head and figure out where her heart really belonged.

CHAPTER SEVENTEEN

Marisa

The computer screen blurred as Marisa stared at it, the words suddenly losing focus. She looked down and covered her eyes. Had the day been that long that she couldn't even focus on what was right in front of her? No, she knew the truth. She just couldn't get her mind off the woman down in the ER. Marisa opened her eyes and stared at the screen once more. If she kept this up, she would be forced to end her shift and head home.

She had a couple more hours to get through. Then she could drown her sorrows in as much alcohol as she wanted. Forget the Netflix; it would be alcohol, her tears, and her bedroom. It'd been three days since she'd last seen Liz out in the garden and she still pictured the way Liz had looked. Her eyes were red. She was crying. But for what? Her? She didn't want her to look so down and out. Marisa turned and looked away from the computer as the other monitor dinged a notification that her next patient was there.

"Perfect timing," she groaned. Now if she could just keep her tears at bay, she would be able to get through the next couple of hours. Marisa stood up and went to the cabinets to pull out the vials for her patient's labs.

Once she had her work area ready, she left the back room and went out to the front. Samantha sat behind the computer and looked over to meet Marisa's stare. Marisa gave her a weak grin. Since they had their last conversation about how Marisa didn't feel the same way Samantha did, they had kept their relationship strictly professional. It wasn't fair to Samantha when it might only confuse the situation. Yet, Samantha usually smiled at her in passing, so maybe she had moved on and realized it was a frivolous attempt when Marisa gave no sign that she felt the same.

"Lucile?" Marisa called out, turning her eyes back to the waiting room. The only woman there got up and walked over to greet Marisa. "I'm Marisa and I'll be drawing your labs today. How are you doing?"

"Nervous," the older woman said. She smiled, but her eyes seemed droopy. "Don't like getting my blood drawn."

Marisa smiled. "I've got you. We'll get through this together." It was what she needed to get Liz out of her mind and focus her attention on the woman who needed her attention and support right now.

Marisa talked to Lucile softly as she prepared the woman's arm to get her blood drawn. She kept the conversation going while she drew the four vials of blood, then pulled the tourniquet off as the woman looked up.

"You're all set," Marisa said.

The woman's jaw dropped. "Really?"

Marisa nodded. "Your doctor will have your results within two days. Enjoy the rest of your day."

The woman clapped her hands together. "That was the best blood draw I've ever had."

Marisa nodded. She liked to hear that. She waved to the woman and carried the paper to the computer to finalize her portion and get the labs ready to be processed. She heard the door open as she finished putting the last vial in the envelope for it to go out through the mail.

"She seemed happier than when she got here," Samantha said, leaning against Marisa's desk.

Marisa snickered. "That's my job, right?"

Samantha nodded. She didn't move to leave, so Marisa looked back over at her.

"So, can we talk?" Samantha asked.

"Don't you have patients to triage?"

"Don't have any scheduled for almost an hour. I think I'll be fine, and it won't take long. But I feel like I owe it to myself to say something."

Marisa nodded. There it was. They were going to be forced to have an awkward conversation, and she wasn't prepared for that. She closed the envelope and looked up. "You gonna make this all cringeworthy and awkward?"

Samantha scrunched up her nose, then laughed and shook her head. "Not unless you want me to. Honestly, I was going to say that I get why things wouldn't work out with us. I mean, we work so closely together and I'm much younger than you. I can think of a million reasons why you and I wouldn't work out. Not to mention, I'm not sure I'm really a lesbian. Or, maybe I am, but you probably don't want someone to experiment on you. I get it."

Marisa quickly looked away. Samantha had literally described things between her and Liz. Coming from an outsider's perspective, Marisa figured that maybe she was only trying to have something that would never have worked out. It was disheartening, but then maybe it was good for her that Liz wound up being engaged.

You don't buy that for a minute. Marisa sunk down in her chair. She couldn't fool herself, so why try to fool anyone else. She looked up and Samantha smirked.

"You want to know the main reason I know you and I wouldn't work out?"

"I'm all ears," Marisa mumbled.

"Because you've got it bad for someone else. I couldn't compete with that. And I realize this. So, yeah, it's troubling to have to take myself down a few notches, but it's really the only thing that can happen. What's confusing is the fact that you're all about the age difference and I'm literally just a couple years younger than her, so yeah, that hurts a bit. But, hey, you just aren't into me in that way. It is what it is. But I can see there's been a change and I'm thinking maybe she's also shown you that she likes you. So, this is no longer a one-way street."

Her infectious smile lit up the room and Marisa sighed with relief.

"Wanna talk about it?" Samantha asked.

Marisa smirked and looked away from her. "So, it's that obvious, huh?" She looked back as Samantha stepped back and leaned against the wall.

"It wasn't. Or, maybe I was just trying to ignore it. But there's been a sudden shift in how you're holding yourself, and I saw how you would light up whenever Liz was around. It would take a blind person not to see that. What I worried about was the fact that Liz is definitely not a lesbian, and she didn't look like someone that would swing your way." She held out her hand and quirked up an eyebrow. "No offense."

"None taken. And I get it. I thought that, too. But then..." Her words drifted off and an image of Liz's naked body pressed into the back of her mind. She shuddered, wanting that image to dissipate. "It just would never work out."

"Well, that look on your face tells me otherwise," Samantha quietly replied. "So, I'm guessing that you attempted it."

"We attempted it," Marisa mumbled. "Then everything fell apart. Because what she had failed to mention to me was that she's engaged. To a guy. So, there is nothing that points to us working out in any sensible fashion." She shrugged. "So be it."

"You wanna know what attracted me to you in the first place?"

Marisa scrunched up her nose and Samantha laughed. "Don't worry. It has nothing to do with your looks."

Marisa felt her cheeks burning. Was it smart to have this conversation? Not really, but she wasn't going to turn from it. Not when Samantha seemed invested in getting her point across to her.

"It's the fact that you're so confident about everything. You carry yourself in a way that makes anybody feel like they can do anything they set their mind to. And I believed that. That's sexy to me. Even more than looks can be."

Marisa blushed, focusing her attention back on her computer screen. Samantha wasn't through talking. "You don't find that in too many people. I know for certain that I don't have that. I was drawn to your self-confidence, and I was drawn to your maturity. So, it bothers me that you're just giving up."

"I'm not giving up," Marisa argued. "But how can I compete with a guy that she's known a lot longer and agreed to marry him?"

"Have you asked her that? Is she happy?"

Marisa looked up. Was that important? Liz hadn't been honest with her. That was what she couldn't get past. Yet, Marisa didn't know whether she had been able to give her the chance to be honest with her. If she was hiding her fiancé, then clearly she felt she had a reason to. Was that enough, though?

"You're pretty smart for being a young'un."

Samantha laughed. "Maybe I'll find someone as mature as you are someday. But I know that if you want something or someone, you need to try to make it work. Fight for what's important to you. It's the only thing you should want to do. Do you think Liz is worth that?"

Marisa didn't hesitate as she nodded.

"Then you know what you need to do."

Marisa looked down at her envelope with the vial of blood. "Can you handle it up here for fifteen minutes?" Marisa asked.

"I'll manage," Samantha said.

Marisa grabbed her phone and the envelopes meant for the mail slot and hurried out of the office. The moment she got in the elevator, she called Liz.

"Hi, you've reached Liz," Liz's voice stated, going straight to voicemail.

Marisa pushed the button for the main floor and stared at the numbers as they slowly descended. It was best not to dwell on what she would say and just blurt it out once she got there. Finally, the door opened, and she rushed into the ER. She slowed her pace as she walked straight to the desk. Hanna sat behind the desk at one end and looked up when Marisa approached her.

"Hey, I can see you're busy," Marisa started.

Hanna nodded. "It's been a crazy day and we're short-staffed and..." She sighed. "Don't want to get into all of that. Do you need something?"

"Um." Marisa looked around the waiting room and her eyes trailed down the main hallway. Things were still different with Hanna because Hanna didn't understand Marisa and her attempt to be friends with Liz. Now Marisa wondered if that was because she knew about Liz's fiancé.

Hanna cleared her throat, bringing Marisa's gaze to her.

"Is Liz working?" she blurted out.

Hanna sighed. "I wish, but she took off a few days. A few usually means three, right? Well, it's been three days and not a word. So, who really knows? It's some family business, apparently. Gotta get back to work, but if you hear from her, be sure to let her know we're anxious for her to come back."

Hanna rushed off and Marisa gawked at the front desk. She was gone? Gone where? Family business? She turned and headed to the elevator, then looked at the envelope in her hand. She took a detour down another hallway to the mailroom. When she entered, she was alone.

She looked over to the mail slots and saw that Liz's slot was jammed full of papers. She frowned, confused. Maybe she had rushed off to be with her fiancé. Nothing would have surprised her at that moment.

She dropped the vial into the mail slot for the outgoing mail and looked over to the door. She walked over to Liz's slot and started to reach for her mail, but quickly pulled back her hand. What would rifling through Liz's mail even change? It wouldn't explain where she was or why she had left.

She left the mailroom with just her own mail in her hand. She took the nearest elevator back to the lab. The moment she stepped into the lab, Samantha looked up.

"That was fast," she said.

Marisa shrugged. "Apparently everything I thought I knew is no more. Liz didn't even care enough to tell me she was taking some time off." Samantha opened her mouth, but Marisa shook her head. "Don't want to talk about it."

She shut the door behind her and slumped down in the nearest chair. Things would never be able to go back to the way they were. Not now. Not ever.

MARISA WALKED UP TO SAMANTHA AS SHE LOGGED ONTO HER computer. She looked over and gave Marisa a tentative smile.

Marisa shrugged. "I'm not going to break. I've been through a lot more heartache than this right here. It just wasn't meant to be."

"Great! Glad you're feeling so positive over it."

Marisa smirked. Positive wasn't exactly the right word to use for it. She had been upset over the past two days since finding out about Liz, but it was what it was and she wasn't going to think about it. If she did, then it was likely that she would crawl into a hole and never want to leave. What good would that do?

"Wanna go grab some coffee?" Samantha asked.

"How about beer?" Marisa asked, grinning.

Samantha laughed and shrugged. "Whichever. I'm game."

"Great! Let's get out of here."

"Do you work tomorrow?" Samantha asked as they left the lab and Marisa locked up behind them.

"Nope. I might sleep the day away," Marisa teased.

"Me too, girlfriend."

Samantha laughed and Marisa put a genuine smile on her face. Before this drama had happened, she could see herself hanging with Samantha as a friend, so maybe that was where this would bring them. Since things weren't awkward between them, it was at least a start. The door of the elevator opened, and they saw Sally standing in the elevator.

She let out a sigh as she got off the elevator. "I'm relieved you're still here," she said.

"You have a patient?" Marisa asked. She tossed a look over to Samantha. "Might have to take a raincheck." She turned back to Sally.

Sally shook her head. "No, but Liz is probably going to kill me."

Marisa frowned. "Liz?"

From the corner of Marisa's eye, she saw Samantha quirk up an eyebrow.

Sally held out a piece of paper that was folded into four squares. Marisa took it from her and saw her name scrawled on the side of it.

"I didn't read it," Sally said quickly. "But she asked me to give it to you and then I forgot and then I lost it." She shook her head. "My head has seriously been a mess lately. I'm really sorry about that. If you could please try to protect me, I'd appreciate it."

"No problem," Marisa said, still looking at her name, carefully written across the paper. "Thanks, Sally."

Sally turned and got back in the elevator. "Are you going down?" she asked.

Marisa looked up as Samantha got onto the elevator. Samantha smiled softly and nodded. "I am. You on the other hand...Have a good weekend, Marisa."

Marisa waved and then looked back at the note as she carefully opened it.

Dearest Marisa —

I don't know where to start. The truth is, I've literally started this note a hundred times and every time I get to the end I throw it away. What it boils down to is I can't think of what to say to you because there's so much I want to say. I know that sounds so cliché and maybe it is, but what isn't cliché is how I feel about you. I didn't expect it. I didn't anticipate it. And I certainly didn't look for it. I didn't know what I was looking for, but I knew I was always looking for something to put my heart back together. It was you all along and I didn't even know it.

Yes, I'm engaged. Am I happy? No! Truth is, I haven't been happy for a long time. When I talk to you, that's me at my happiest. Why would I run from that? Because I'm scared, that's why. I should have been honest with you. You are the one person I have in my life I feel I should always be honest with. I don't have that feeling for Chad and that also scares me.

Do I have things to work out? Heck yeah, I have things to work out. I don't know where I can take this or even if you'll ever forgive me to make things right with you. I wouldn't blame you if you never wanted to see me again. But I beg you to at least give me the opportunity to tell you how truly sorry I am. If you have read the letter up to this point, I feel I have some chance.

As I'm sure you have already figured out, I've taken some time away. I needed that, and I went to my parents' house in Indianapolis. It might just be the break I need. But I won't be gone long and I hope that we can talk things through. Please just forgive me. I need to know I haven't screwed things up so much that I've permanently messed things up between us.

When I get back, I will know exactly what's in my heart. But I can tell you what I feel now and it's every kiss we have shared. It's the warmth you bring to my body when I think about you. And it's every smile you bring to my face. Am I getting cheesy? Probably. But just thinking about being with you brings me the warmth and desire I need in my life.

I look forward to having some deep conversations with you.

Sincerely,
Liz

Marisa stared at the heart that followed Liz's name and she couldn't keep the smile from trailing her lips. She held the letter to her chest and closed her eyes. It was everything she would have said to her if given the chance. She thought Liz was running from her. She was upset that she didn't get the opportunity to talk to her because she was already gone. But soon. Very soon. She just might get that happiness after all.

CHAPTER EIGHTEEN

Liz

A knock sounded on the bedroom door. Liz groaned and tossed her legs over the side of the bed, pulling herself into a seated position. "Yeah?" she called out.

Her mother peeked her head into the room. "Are you hungry? I made soup and sandwiches."

Liz shrugged. "Not really."

Her mother frowned, coming further into the room. "Are you sure? You've been here a week and have hardly eaten anything. I'm worried about you. Something isn't right. Are you still up for wedding dress shopping?"

No!

Liz looked up and met her mom's gaze. "If I say no, can we put it off?"

That brought a frown to her mother's face. "I don't understand. You've done virtually no planning on this wedding. Are you going just to stay engaged forever?"

Liz's phone rang, and she anxiously reached across the bed and grabbed it. She frowned as she saw Chad's name. She had been waiting for —even expected—a call from Marisa. The last thing she wanted to do was hash over what she had to talk to Chad about. She slid the button on her screen to ignore the call and tossed her phone to the side.

"Did you and Chad have a fight?" her mother asked.

Liz looked up and gawked at her mother. "To fight would mean that we've talked. We don't talk, Mother. If you took the time to actually see what I wanted, then you would realize that."

Her mother's eyes bugged out, and Liz sighed. "I'm sorry. I shouldn't have spoken to you like that. No, we didn't have a fight per se. But, Mom..."

She covered her face, fearing the tears that she had tried to keep hidden for as long as she could would finally fall. When her mother sat down beside her, she leaned her head against her shoulder.

"I don't mean to be so emotional. It's just that..." She wiped her face and shook her head. "Forget I said anything."

"I can't do that," her mother said, sitting down beside her. "What's going on? You're scaring me."

Liz felt the weight on her shoulders as she stared at her mom, desperate to get it off her chest yet scared that her mother would try to tell her that she was being paranoid, that the thoughts that maybe Chad really was having an affair were all in her mind.

"There's so much going on. I don't even know where to begin," Liz poured out.

"Best to just start from the beginning. You're happy, right? With Chad?"

Liz shrugged. "I wanted to be. I've pushed to be happy. Yet, it's suddenly becoming so clear that what I thought was happiness was just me merely getting by. It's overwhelming and I feel like I can barely breathe."

"Talk to me," her mother said, reaching out and brushing her hand over Liz's shoulder.

Liz held up her hand. "Haven't you noticed I haven't been wearing the ring?"

Her mother dropped her gaze to her daughter's ring finger, then looked back at her, shocked. "Guess I really didn't."

"I lost it."

Her mother's jaw dropped, and Liz continued. "Obviously it wasn't planned. But I was out, and it came off," she lied. "I called the restaurant where I had lost it, and no one found it."

"Have you told Chad?"

"I tried," Liz mumbled. "But when I did, a woman answered the phone. He called me later and said he had left his phone at a board meeting."

"If that's what he said, then that's what happened. I'm sure of it."

Liz tilted her head and shook it. "Mom, I heard running water. His voice was in the background. He lied to me. Why? Because he's f…"

She sighed. "He's sleeping with someone else. That's blatantly obvious to me. Maybe they work together, but that doesn't change the truth."

"He wouldn't," her mother said.

Liz leaned forward, covering her face. There wasn't any doubt that her mother would want to defend him. Both her parents already thought of him as their son. But Liz trusted her instincts.

"He isn't my one and true love. I'm sorry, but that's the truth."

She jumped up from her bed and went to the mirror. When she looked at her reflection, she saw that her eyes were red from the tears she had already cried. She turned around and noticed her mother's lips were drawn into a thin line.

"I've met someone else."

Her mom's jaw dropped. "You can't be serious. Are you saying that you're the one having an affair? Are you just trying to make yourself feel better about finding someone else?"

"Mom! No!" Liz argued. She went back to the bed and sank down on it. "I didn't plan on this. There's just something about this person that makes me think that there's no one else I'm meant to be with. And believe me, no one is more surprised than I am."

"I don't think you want to ruin your engagement, though."

Liz groaned and shook her head. "This is what you and Dad want. If you took a minute to listen to me, you would see that Chad doesn't make me happy. Chad has been in France for a month, and I've literally talked to him only a few times. What kind of engagement is that? I don't love him. It's Marisa I love."

The words came out in such a rush that Liz couldn't stop them. Once they were out there, though, she could heave a sigh. She had said it and there wasn't any going back.

Her mother's jaw dropped. "Wow. Didn't see that coming."

Her mother looked away from her and Liz prepared herself to see her mom's heart break right in front of her. Instead, she turned and looked at her daughter.

"I don't want you to think that I don't want you to be happy. That's truly my biggest hope—that you'll find happiness and hang onto that. So, I'm surprised to hear this coming from you, but it isn't totally unexpected. Like mother like daughter, right?"

Liz frowned. "I'm confused."

"Honey, I wasn't always happy and in love with your father. It took work. The only difference is that you didn't even dare try to stay with a woman back in my day. Looking back, if I had, then you and your brother wouldn't have been here."

Liz's jaw dropped. Her mother's eyes lit up and there was a smile on her lips. "Her name was Penny. Or, is Penny, rather."

"What happened to her?"

"She's living in Houston with her husband." She smiled and reached out, stroking Liz's arm. "It was a long time ago. Just know that I know where you're coming from and if you can follow your heart, then I think you should."

"Even if it means ending things with Chad?" Liz asked.

Her mother simply nodded. "You have been here a week and I've been trying to get you to open up. I just feel that it's clear your heart or mind isn't with your fiancé."

"Are you upset?"

She shrugged. "Disappointed. But I only want you happy. Chad was your father's and my dream. That's no way to live your life."

She pulled Liz into her arms, and they embraced in a warm and loving hug. All Liz could think about was getting out of there and home to Marisa, hoping it wasn't too late to fix things.

LIZ SMILED TO HERSELF AS SHE DROVE. SHE WOULD BE HOME soon, and everything would be just as she wanted. Her phone started to ring, and she spotted Hanna's number on the line.

"Great minds," Liz replied, answering the call.

"Oh really? You were thinking of me?" Hanna asked.

"Thinking of you and Capmed."

Mostly, Marisa.

The thought left a permanent smile on her lips. "Just getting back to Chicago, so, yeah, you crossed my mind. How's work going?"

"Um, good. Busy," Hanna said. "You sound good."

"Better than I've been in a long time. It's amazing what a week can do. That's for sure. But I'm sorry you guys have been busy. I know I left you sort of stranded. My apologies for that. Just a few more days and I'll be back to work in full force."

"Um, so, yeah, there's something I need to tell you."

"Go for it," Liz replied, turning the radio down to a low murmur.

"I don't know how to tell you, but it's like this. While you were gone, it put us in a pretty big bind. And the department was forced to get someone from another department to fill in."

"Ugh. Sorry about that. Hope it wasn't too awful. A newbie?"

The ER was too difficult to have a new person filling in and Liz could already imagine the frustration in some of the nursing staff. They would hopefully get over it and be happy that she was coming back better than ever.

"No. Not really. There's a waiting list for the ER staff. Did you know that? Turns out people want the high-anxiety-type jobs. Who knew?"

Liz laughed. "Well, then it probably all worked out."

"Listen, Liz," Hanna started. "I didn't want to be the one to tell you this, but we're friends. And frankly, I would want to know if things were reversed. It's why I feel you deserve to know. You get that?"

"Uh, yeah, but what are you trying to tell me?"

Hanna sighed on the other end of the line. "They went out on a limb to hire you for the ER. They went and moved you to the top of the list. And when you weren't here, since they had to get someone else, they decided that they would replace you."

"Wow!" Liz's heart sunk a little. "So, I'm not working in the ER now. Are they putting me back in the pulmonology department? That's all right. Not the most exciting gig, but it works. It still pays. I'm not going to get upset over that. I needed to take this time away."

"I don't think you get it, Liz. Since you took the time off and it was an unexcused absence, they have decided to term you."

Liz's jaw dropped. "Seriously? You're joking, right?"

"I wish I were. And I wish I didn't have to be the one to tell you this, but again, you deserved to know. You have to be working here for longer than a year in order to have personal time like that. So, I'm sorry."

Liz shook her head, a tear hanging at the corner of her eye. If they had told her that, then maybe she wouldn't have stayed away for so long. But she thought that everything would work itself out. She might have been out of a job, but she was on her way to the house of the one person she wanted to share the news—any news, for that matter—with. There was something in that.

"Thank you for telling me, Hanna. I'm sorry I wasn't there for you guys."

"Don't say that, Liz. I'm glad you're feeling better. And you didn't let us down. We all tried to defend you. But they made up their mind."

In one week they had dropped her like she was a burden to them, so it was clear that she wasn't someone they felt they needed to protect. If that were the case, then she would have to find someone else who had her back.

"It's all right. Thanks again, Hanna. I have to go."

"Bye, Liz." Hanna's voice sounded so far away as Liz hung up. She pressed the button to call Marisa.

"H...hello?" When Marisa answered, Liz was relieved.

"I'm so glad you answered," Liz replied, a smile tugging at her lips. "Are you home? I need to see you."

"I am," Marisa replied without hesitation.

"I'll be there in five minutes. See you soon." She disconnected the call and turned down the main road that led to Marisa's house. A few minutes later she turned into Marisa's driveway. When she got up to the front door, Marisa opened the door before she could knock.

"I'm sorry," Liz said immediately. "I ran off because I was scared. I was scared that falling for you would mean losing a part of myself. What I didn't anticipate was that not being with you would bring me to the darkest places of my mind."

"You meant what was in your letter?" Marisa asked.

Liz nodded. "Every word."

Marisa reached out and grabbed Liz's hand, pulling her into the house and closing the door behind her. Marisa kissed Liz hard, and Liz's nerves vanished completely.

"Are you ending things with Chad?" Marisa whispered, parting from the kiss.

"As soon as he's home," Liz replied.

Marisa wrapped her arms around Liz and embraced her as Liz kissed her, her tongue swooping in to claim a moan from Marisa. She wanted to stand there forever and kiss her, her heart racing, pounding, rolling like thunder in her chest. She grabbed Marisa's shirt and slowly pulled it up, over her breasts. When she was with Marisa, everything felt right, and it was time to forget her doubts and just embrace the love she felt for that woman.

CHAPTER NINETEEN

Marisa

Marisa pulled the beaded necklace from Liz's jewelry box and stared at it. Liz stepped up behind her and she felt the warmth of her lover's breath on her skin. Her body got goosebumps as Liz softly kissed Marisa's neck. Marisa tilted her head and allowed the kiss to linger. She closed her eyes and released a soft moan.

Liz snickered, pressing her lips hard enough that Marisa wouldn't have been surprised if she had left a hickey behind. "I love when you moan," Liz mumbled.

Marisa turned around, holding onto Liz's waist. "Then maybe we should just stay in. Who needs to go to the restaurant anyway, especially when we have one another?" She wrapped her arms around Liz's neck and swooped in to capture Liz's lips on hers.

"Our reservation would go to waste then, hon. We wouldn't want that, right?"

Marisa laughed. "Well, if I had my way, I would miss all the reservations if it meant getting you back in bed. You disappoint me, Liz." She winked and pulled back from the embrace. "But, if you would rather save the lovemaking for dessert later, then so be it. Have it your way."

She held up the necklace. "I like this necklace. What do you say?" She held it up against her neck. "After all, gotta look the part when the woman I love is so much younger than me."

Liz smirked and tilted her head. "You love me? Were you going to tell me that or make me guess?"

Marisa moved in and touched her finger along Liz's lips. Liz closed her eyes and leaned into the touch. "Thought you would have figured that out by now. I love you, Elizabeth Fletcher." She dropped the necklace back onto the top of Liz's dresser.

"I love you, Marisa. So much." She touched her lips against Marisa's. "But you can't wear that necklace," Liz whispered.

"And why not?" Marisa pouted.

"Chad gave it to me," Liz replied.

Marisa made a face and Liz nodded. She stepped forward to Marisa and pulled her into her arms. "Who needs jewelry? Or clothes, for that matter?" Liz asked.

She kissed Marisa hard, then pushed her back against the wall, nearly knocking Marisa's head against it. They kissed in a feverish and impassioned embrace. Marisa grabbed onto Liz's leg and wrapped it around hers, Liz's skirt inching up higher as Marisa pressed her hand on the inside of Liz's thigh, running her fingers up and under her panties. The warmth of Liz's sex touched Marisa's skin, and she flicked her tongue into Liz's waiting mouth.

"I want you," Marisa moaned.

Liz parted from the kiss, a sexy grin on her lips as she grabbed Marisa's hand and pulled her toward the bed. Marisa smiled. What was one reservation, anyway? Liz pressed her hand against Marisa's chest, knocking her back onto the bed. Marisa watched her as Liz straddled her legs, then moved down to kiss her. Marisa wrapped her hands around Liz's body, feeling around for the zipper on her back. As they kissed with a hunger that ignited the flames inside of them, the doorbell rang.

Liz groaned, breaking from the kiss. Marisa's mouth hung open. Talk about a buzzkill. She was left desperately hanging for the thrill that had been interrupted.

"You go ahead and look for a necklace. Any other one will do." Liz winked. "I'll get rid of whoever's at the door and we should just about make our reservations."

Marisa groaned as Liz reached for her hand and pulled her up. "Get rid of them and we could resume where we left off." Her eyes popped up and Liz laughed.

"You and I know it's hard to get into this restaurant. So, we should make it. But there's always dessert." She winked and then turned away.

Liz had this way about her that told Marisa everything would be all right. Marisa couldn't get rid of the images playing in her mind of Liz on top of her. They were, enough, for now. She just hoped she could make it to dessert.

With Liz gone, Marisa went back to the jewelry box, replaced the necklace that she wouldn't wear, and then grabbed another. She looked at her reflection and shifted her head from one side to the other, then back again. She liked it. She kept it in her hand and left her room, heading down to the foyer, where she could only make out soft voices.

"What about this one, babe?" she asked, entering the foyer.

Liz turned toward her, and her mouth dropped. Marisa glanced at the door to find a man standing there. His gaze darted between the two women. Liz uttered, "Marisa, this is Chad. Chad, Marisa."

Marisa felt all the blood drain from her face. She never meant to be introduced to Chad, let alone when they were moments ago in the throes of passion. She opened her mouth, but no words came out.

"I should go," Marisa said.

"No. I don't want you to." Liz reached out and touched Marisa's arm. Marisa caught the way Chad's eyes darted to her arm, and she felt uncomfortable.

"I'll go," he said, turning on his heel and rushing from the house. He got into his car and tore away from the house, the squealing of tires following after him. Liz looked at Marisa and shrugged, but all Marisa could do was gawk at her. Was this really something Liz was ready to work through?

THE TIME SLOWLY TICKED BY AS MARISA LOOKED OVER AT LIZ. They had been sitting in the living room for what felt like hours as she waited for Liz to say something. Anything. They had shared a few awkward glances and that was all. Marisa fidgeted in her chair.

"Listen, Liz. I don't want this to get any weirder. Maybe I should just go, and you should run after him. I think you guys have some serious things that you need to hash out."

"It's not weird," Liz argued, shooting her a glance.

Marisa laughed and looked away from her, then down to her watch. "We've been sitting here for fifteen minutes with no more than two looks between us. It feels sort of weird. I'm not gonna lie."

Liz rubbed her face and made a guttural groan. "I'm sorry. I don't want things to be weird or awkward or anything like that. I wanted tonight to just be about us. I had no idea he was back in Chicago, and I certainly didn't expect him to pop in like that."

Marisa tilted her head. "When's the last time you talked?"

"Two weeks ago? Something like that. Guess I lost track of time. Once I set my heart on you, nothing else mattered."

Marisa quirked up her lips in a smile. She blushed and looked down at her clasped her hands. Liz knew exactly what to say at that moment. Marisa got up and went over to the couch to sit next to her. She reached out and held Liz's hand in hers. She traced her finger down her fingers and Liz smiled and cast a glance her way.

"Whether I stay or leave, it doesn't change that I'm here for the long haul, Liz. I've gotten past any insecurities about us being in a relationship. You are the one I want, and I will wait for you to get your baggage behind you. You have to know that."

"My baggage is behind me," Liz whispered, moving in.

Marisa didn't object to the kiss, but she kept it short and touched her fingers to Liz's puckered lips.

"Your baggage isn't truly behind you until you tell Chad that it's over."

Liz smirked. "I think he got that message when you came down the stairs looking like that."

She traced her finger under Marisa's chin and Marisa closed her eyes to her touch. How had things gotten to the point that they felt their chemistry finally coming alive?

Marisa opened her eyes and smiled. "You are the one woman who keeps me guessing and I love that. I love you." She gave a simple peck on Liz's lips, then stood up. "But, serious question coming your way. Are you ready for it?"

She tossed a look over her shoulder at Liz, who looked like a little kid huddled in the corner of her couch. She shrugged, which made Marisa turn to face Liz. "I don't know if I should ask it, then. I need you to be prepared to be honest."

"I'll be honest, Marisa. You don't have to worry about that. I'm not about to be anything but honest with you. You can trust me."

"I'm glad to hear that," Marisa said, kneeling down in front of Liz. "But there comes a moment where some answers might be difficult to come by."

"Such as?" Liz asked, leaning forward, her breath on Marisa's hands as Marisa rested her elbows on her knees.

"When you saw Chad this evening, did you have feelings?"

"Feelings? As in?" Liz scrunched up her face, a look of agony in her eyes.

"Feelings. You know, like maybe you were second-guessing your decisions. Like maybe you were fearing that what you felt for Chad was more than you were letting on?"

"Are you serious?" Liz asked, leaning back in her seat.

Marisa kept her gaze locked on Liz's. Liz shook her head. "No. Never. If anything, when I saw him, it made me realize that everything I'm feeling with you is true and real. It made me realize that my feelings for him were never genuine."

Marisa smiled, her heart warming up to those words. "I needed to hear that."

Marisa pulled herself up and sat next to Liz, pulling her in her arms. She kissed the top of her head and just held her. Liz helped Marisa to feel young again, a feeling that had long been forgotten and was everything Marisa wanted to get back to. How could she have ever turned away from that?

"Maybe we can get into our reservation just a little later," Liz whispered.

Marisa turned her head to see Liz's wide grin. "I just want to sit here with you," she replied.

She snaked her hand around Liz's and pulled her to her. They would have forever to spend going out as a couple. As long as they wanted one another, they would be there for each other. They parted from the kiss and Liz rested in the crook of Marisa's arm as Marisa held her closer. No matter what Liz needed from her, she would give it. Whatever it was, she was there to be her protector, and she was ready for whatever that entailed.

CHAPTER TWENTY

Liz's phone rang as she sat in the parking lot of the corner diner. She checked the clock on her dashboard. She had been watching for Chad for the past fifteen minutes and now wondered if maybe he had stood her up. He had seemed a bit hopeful on the phone when she called him earlier about meeting so they could talk. Yet, she still hadn't seen his red Camaro pull into the parking lot; maybe he had backed out.

She grabbed her phone, not recognizing the phone number. "Hello?"

"Hello, is this Elizabeth Fletcher?" the man on the phone asked.

"Yes, this is she."

"Hi, the name is Braxton Shaw. I got your name from your mother."

Liz frowned. "Okay..."

"The reason I'm calling is I am opening a pediatric clinic in Indianapolis. It's all in the preliminary stages, but I'll be looking for two to three nurses to help manage it, along with me, of course. Your name comes highly recommended."

Liz laughed. "By my mother? Is this a joke?"

He snickered on the other end of the line. "I can assure you, it's no joke. I've made a few calls as well, and can assure you that I'm not just taking your mother's word on this matter. I'm looking forward to building an empire here. You can do an Internet search for my name, and you'll see I'm not some sort of stalker."

Liz put the call on her speakerphone and pulled up a search engine. She entered his name and a picture came up, along with various charities he had worked with.

"From the silence, I assume you're looking at my picture right now."

She turned her attention back to the call. "So, you're interested in me. What now?"

"Well, that's up to you, really. But in the next few months, I'll be starting the hiring process. The building will be up and running in six months. If all goes well, that is. I would like to know if you would be interested if I were to call you back in three months."

Liz spotted Chad's car turning into the parking lot. She opened her door and stepped out of the car. "Give me a call. I just might be intrigued."

"I'm glad to hear that. You'll be hearing from me. Goodbye, Ms. Fletcher."

"Bye."

She disconnected the call and slipped her phone into her purse. Exactly what she needed—a job. Yet, she hesitated to take it. What would that mean for her relationship with Marisa? Would she be willing to uproot her own life for Liz?

She had to push that worry out of her mind as she entered the diner. Chad was in the corner booth, and she nodded her greeting to the waitress at the counter, then head over to where he sat. He looked up but didn't acknowledge her by standing up.

"Good afternoon," she said.

"Hey!" He closed the menu he had been looking at and smiled, but it appeared forced. "Let's order and then you can tell me why you brought me here."

His words were tense, and he didn't even look in her direction. It wasn't going to be an easy conversation to get through, but she was more ready than ever to make sure it happened.

They placed their orders and, once the waitress had left, Liz looked across the table. "Will you please at least look at me?" she asked.

He slowly looked up, but his eyes were dark. It wasn't the typical

Chad that she was used to seeing. He appeared reclusive and quiet, like maybe he had been crying. But Chad didn't cry, and even if he had, Liz didn't care. He had been unfaithful.

"I won't take long. I just felt our relationship deserved to have some closure, if you will."

He clapped his hands in front of him. "If that's what you want to call it. Go right ahead."

"Chad," Liz started, "you don't need to be a jerk about this. I mean, come on. If you're being honest, you know that we would never have made it. Be honest with yourself if you don't want to be honest with me."

He dropped his gaze to his hands, and she saw she was breaking him down. "Exactly! So, it is what it is. This is as good for you as it is for me. Because I'll tell you right here and now, Chad. I don't buy for one minute that you left your phone at a meeting. I heard you. The shower was running, and you called her babe. So, don't go giving me that."

He looked up, his eyes wide. "So, that's when you thought you would go out and have your own little rendezvous? 'Serves him right' sort of thing?"

Liz huffed, wanting to break into laughter, but it wasn't the place or time. "I didn't get with Marisa for revenge. That just happened."

"A woman." He shook his head. "And I thought I knew you."

"You thought you knew me? I thought I knew you. I thought you'd never cheat on me. But surprise, I was wrong. I didn't go out looking for Marisa. It did really just happen. But I was missing something. Marisa filled that void."

Again, his eyes dropped. Liz fought the urge to reach out to take his hand. There was no point in trying to show him compassion; it could lead to the wrong idea. She waited for him to look back up, but his eyes rested on the table.

"I never wanted to hurt you. And I want to believe you never meant to hurt me."

He looked up and shook his head. "Never! It, it, well, it just happened."

Liz nodded, smiling, knowing how that could happen. "If we were meant to be, then it wouldn't have just happened. Not for either of us. And that's the truth."

He sighed and looked away from her. "When you're right, you're right."

He chuckled and even grinned, and Liz felt relief overwhelm her.

"I knew something was up," he said. "You rarely took my calls and then I got a call that blew things out of the water."

Liz frowned as he reached into his pocket and pulled out a ring box. He opened it up and pushed the ring toward Liz. "A friend of mine owns a pawn shop and called me when this beauty showed up."

"How did he know?" Liz asked.

"The inscription." He pulled the ring out of the box and turned it over. "I had told him when I got the ring but I never in a million years thought you would pawn it. I mean, that's not very classy. Not the woman I grew to know and love."

Liz's cheeks burned with embarrassment. "I didn't," she said. "I lost it and I called to tell you but then the woman answered. That was the turning point in our relationship—at least, in my opinion."

"Wow." He shook his head. "Guess it's a good thing it showed up in the right place, or else who knows if we would have ever found out what happened to it."

The waitress returned with their food, placing it in front of them.

"Thank you," Liz mumbled.

When the waitress left, she looked back at Chad. "I'm sorry things didn't work out, Chad. I really am."

"Neither of us was perfect. It happens. I wish you happiness, Liz." He reached out and touched her hand. A smile crossed her lips.

"I wish you the same, Chad."

With those words, one path ended. Liz was ready for the full realization of everything she could have with Marisa, and she looked forward to that journey.

LIZ STEPPED INTO THE HOSPITAL AND SPOTTED HANNA heading to the front desk. She gave a wave when she saw Liz, but her eyes lacked their usual shine. Liz forced a smile. "Hey there. How are you?" she asked.

"I'm good. You?" Hanna fidgeted from one foot to the other. "I'm sorry about how things went."

"Don't be," Liz said. "Could be for the best." She thought of the call she had earlier and forced a smile. "Trust me, I'm not upset about it."

Hanna sighed. "Good. I didn't know if I should call you. I didn't want you to be mad at me or something."

"It's not your fault," Liz replied. "Don't worry about it."

"Okay." Hanna nodded. "Hope you're not needing to be seen today or anything."

Liz shook her head. "Came to see Marisa. But we definitely need to catch up soon. I have a ton to tell you."

Hanna smiled wider. "Sounds good. Take care." She pulled Liz into a hug before she went to call her patient.

Liz watched her as she grabbed the patient, a feeling of irritation coursing through her veins. No matter what she said to Hanna, she did feel upset that she had lost that job. She just had to believe that something better was out there. She turned and headed to the elevator. Once the doors closed on her, her phone rang. She took it out of her bag and noted the lack of bars at the top right corner of the phone.

"Hello?" she quickly answered.

"H...Li...how..."

Then, silence.

"Hello? Can you hear me?"

"Liz..." Then silence.

"Hold on. I'm on the elevator," Liz yelled into the phone. She looked up at the numbers on the elevator, then finally reached her floor. When the doors opened, she rushed out of the elevator. "Hello?"

"Liz? Can you hear me?"

"I can hear you."

"Good. This is Victoria, Donovan's mother."

The blood rushed from Liz's face as she fell back against the wall. Beads of sweat piled up on her forehead. It felt like an eternity since she had last spoken to her. Why was Victoria contacting her now?

"Hey, Victoria." She braced herself for the worst. "I'm surprised to hear from you."

"Well, it took a while before I could get someone to give me your number. I finally got ahold of Marisa today at the hospital and she was eager to give me your number. How are you?"

"I, I'm fine," Liz stuttered. "But, more importantly, how's Donovan?"

"Well, that's the reason I'm calling."

Liz held her breath. Was that nerves that she heard coming from Victoria? She wanted to start crying already, but she had to be strong for Donovan's mother.

"Yeah?" she asked.

"Donovan and I went to Tennessee for his treatment, as I'm sure you heard. There's a specialist here that the staff at Capmed thought could work well with Donovan. Well, it turns out they were right."

Liz released the breath she was holding. "They were?" she asked.

"Yep. Treatment is going well and they're even talking about him being able to go home soon and continuing his care on an outpatient basis. His leukemia is in remission. You were the first one he wanted to call. And he's here right now, anxious to talk to you."

"I'm so happy." Liz covered her face, tears—happy ones, this time—threatening to fall.

"Liz?" Donovan came onto the phone, and everything she had feared about his condition was washed away with the tears that streamed down her cheeks.

"Donovan! I'm so happy to hear from you. Not a day has gone by that I haven't thought about you. You and your mom. How are you?"

She wanted to talk to him about so many things, but just hearing his voice was more than enough. She had feared that she would never find out how he was doing. Now that she had their number, she wouldn't have to worry about that anymore.

Unfortunately, they couldn't stay on the phone long, as Donovan had therapy he had to get to, but even the fifteen minutes they had put Liz in a better place.

"Call me again soon," she said to Veronica as Donovan handed the phone back to her.

"I will. But thank you for everything."

"It's been my pleasure."

Liz disconnected the call, wiping away the rest of her tears. She put her phone away and headed toward the lab. Samantha sat at the front desk and looked up the moment Liz walked into the lobby. She gave a weak smile.

"Hi," Liz said. "Is Marisa back there?"

Samantha nodded. "Head on back."

Liz smiled and went through the door. Marisa looked up and got up from her desk. "Well, to what do I owe this pleasure?" she asked.

"Just got off the phone with Victoria," Liz replied. "You gave her my number?"

"I knew you'd want to take that call." She shrugged. "Great news, wasn't it?"

"The best." Liz wrapped her arm around Marisa and pulled her to her. They kissed, and when Marisa pulled back, Liz brushed a strand of hair behind Marisa's ear. "I love you so much!"

"I love you more," Marisa whispered.

"I saw Chad today, and I have officially put that all behind me. We've realized that our relationship would have never worked. You, on the other hand, were always meant to be my destiny."

"Oh, is that so?" A sexy grin rested on Marisa's lips.

Liz bit her lower lip and nodded. She looked over to the door and then back to Marisa. "What time is your next appointment?"

"Twenty minutes," Marisa quietly answered.

"Then we'd best hurry," Liz replied. She kissed Marisa, pressing her back up against the desk. The heat had already gone straight to her inner thighs, and she didn't even care if someone walked in on them. Why hold back when she had everything she needed right there?

Grab the thrilling epilogue by scanning or clicking on the QR code below:
[or Type or Click here: https://BookHip.com/JVXRGHZ]

Happy Reading,
Morgan
P.S: Thanks, www.kindlepreneur.com, for the QR code generator, and www.booklinker.com for the universal links.

PROTECTING HER *Heart*

BOOK 3

HEALING HEARTS
A *Lesbian Medical Romance* Drama Series

MT CASSEN

CHAPTER ONE

Bella

T he halls of Capmed were filled with people running every which way, giving Bella Strong a bad case of nerves. Her heart raced, and she scanned her eyes in several directions. Did she know what she was truly getting herself into?

She put on a wide smile and approached the registration desk. "Name and reason you need to be seen?" the woman at the desk asked, barely looking up to make eye contact.

"Hi, I'm Bella Strong. I have an appointment with Margo Smythe. She's with the—"

"Hold on, please," the woman said. She swiveled her chair away from Bella and turned to her phone.

Bella snapped her mouth shut and waited for her to come back around. She was currently in the last semester of her university's nursing program and working at Capmed was the next step in her life plan. Bella ran through her plan in her head again, as if she hadn't done it a million times before. Graduate at twenty-two. Get a full-time nursing job at Capmed. Marry Jackson. Start a family. And it all needed to happen before she turned thirty.

The woman turned around, her eyes refocusing on her computer.

"Take hallway E down until it T's, then take a right, followed by another right. She's in office number one-four-two."

"Hallway E?" Bella asked. Her voice trembled slightly. Now wasn't the time to break. She was about to have her first day, and if she faltered too many times, they would laugh her right out of the hospital.

The woman looked up and gave a weak smile. "Right behind me. It's labeled E. At the end of the hallway, take a right, followed by another right. And then..."

"Office one-four-five," Bella completed for her.

The woman glanced up at her with a frown. "No. One-four-two. She'll be waiting for you."

Bella swallowed at her blunder. "Got it. Thank you very much!" Bella exclaimed.

She turned and released a breath. She could do this. She was born to be a nurse, just like her mom, and she was ready to prove that to her family —but most importantly, to herself.

———

As Bella walked toward Margo's office, she recalled how she had met the woman. Her sister Veronica's best friend, Brittany, just happened to be the daughter of Tabby, one of the nurses at Capmed. When Veronica had mentioned that Bella was in her last semester going for her bachelor's in nursing, Tabby had seemed enthusiastic and had mentioned a new program that she had helped develop at Capmed. The rest was history. Now, Bella was about to meet Margo, the woman who could give Bella the opportunity she was looking for. She prayed she wasn't making the wrong jump in her career. But Capmed was an amazing hospital, so it must be the right choice.

Bella followed the path to the office, just as the woman behind the reception desk had laid out to her. When she reached Margo's door, she exhaled and knocked.

"Enter," a woman's voice hollered.

Here goes nothing. Bella entered the office, prepared to release any negative feelings and make the best impression she could. What she hadn't anticipated was immediately being thrown into the fire as Margo took her up to the pediatrics ward without so much as a welcome or any other information.

"This is Dr. Whalen," Margo said, motioning to a man standing at the receptionist's desk as she made her introductions. "I think we'll have you round with him." She held up her hand to shield her mouth before she added, "His bark is way worse than his bite."

"I heard that," he responded, his voice booming out from underneath his mustache.

Bella smiled at the gleam in his eye. "I'm Bella Strong. It's a pleasure to meet you, Dr. Whalen," she said.

"The pleasure is all mine. Now, Margo, if you'll leave this young protégée to me, I'll have her working the halls of this hospital like a pro."

Margo smirked. "I have all the confidence you will." She reached out and touched Bella's arm. "It was nice to meet you. Know that we are one big family, and you are going to excel here." She winked at Bella, then turned and left.

It was nice to hear those words, and they put Bella at greater ease.

"Follow me," Dr. Whalen said. He started walking away, and Bella hurried to keep up. She couldn't be known as a dawdler or straggler. She had to make sure he saw that she was putting in all the effort she could muster.

They approached a woman. "Ms. Strong," Dr. Whalen started.

"Bella," she quickly interrupted. "Just Bella."

He nodded. "All right, Bella. This is Tori Mitchell, and she's one of the lead nurses on this floor. If you can't find me, you go to her. If you can't find her…" He hesitated. "Then send out the troops because we're all in a heap of trouble."

Tori laughed. "He makes jokes. That's why we keep him around." Tori reached up and touched his arm, and he gave a gentle chuckle.

Bella had to remind herself that Margo did say Dr. Whalen's bark was worse than his bite. As far as she could see, he was just a giant teddy bear—maybe even the papa of the floor. She made a mental note, anticipating that he would also be the one she frequently reported to. After all, he did mention that. Right?

Bella grimaced to herself. She had a notebook full of notes that she had taken during orientation and studied up on, but what with the fast-paced nature of Capmed, Bella worried she wouldn't be able to keep up.

Bella's stomach churned. This position was something that could either make or break her. If she could keep up with the accelerated BSN program, she could have a secure job by the end of it. If she couldn't handle studying and working, she would be a major failure and her entire plan would be thrown off. And then what? She'd be a nobody, which is exactly what her high school bullies had told her she'd be. She had been a little awkward back then and had struggled with her grades, but she was so much better now. She *had* failed one class in her first semester of undergrad, but she'd been working her butt off since then, and everything had been fine. She was on the path to a wonderful, successful life, to proving all of her old peers wrong. She wasn't a screw-up. She could do this.

She only needed to avoid having a panic attack on her first day.

Tori had a frozen smile on her face, waiting for Bella to respond. "Um, hi," Bella said, snapping out of her inner spiral. "It's nice to meet you, Tori."

She nodded. "Same to you. Good luck around here."

Before Bella could walk away, Tori said, "Oh, and just so you know..." She reached across the desk and held up a folder as if it were a trophy. "You'll want to get accustomed to this folder. This is where you'll find all your information about what rotation you're on. But don't worry about all that. It'll gradually come to you."

Bella nodded. "Thank you!"

Another thing to go on in that notebook of hers. Should she bring it to work and carry it around to refer to and take notes, or would that be seen as a weakness? She certainly didn't want to give her coworkers the wrong impression, like she wasn't capable. But what if she forgot something important and they told her to leave?

No. That wouldn't happen. She'd remember everything, and she had the folder Tori gave her for help.

Fifteen minutes down and just eight more hours to go. She could do this. She already was. She hoped.

Bella's cellphone rang, and she groaned. It was the way Dr. Whalen said he could best reach his nurses. What she didn't account for was the fact that he needed to reach his nurses every fifteen minutes. She grabbed her phone from her pocket and answered it. "Hello, Dr. Whalen."

"Four-zero-six needs meds. The script was written on his chart. And four-one-two needs his vitals taken."

"All right, I'm on it," she said, hoping her voice came across as chipper.

Bella stifled a yawn as she disconnected the call, then checked her watch. She groaned. It was already nearly three o'clock in the morning, and she had intended on getting out of there by two. She had a test at eight and would need to get up no later than six to freshen up. She hadn't prepared herself for this part of her responsibilities.

She retrieved her patient's medication from the automated dispenser and delivered it to room four-zero-six with a cup of water. Then, Bella quietly stepped into the other patient's room to get a full set of vital signs. By the time she had everything documented, it was almost three-thirty. She grabbed her phone from her pocket and stared at it. Just like clockwork, it started to ring.

"Hello, Dr. Whalen." She released a breath, then inhaled and held it, waiting for him to rattle off another list of patients who needed her assistance. She was exhausted, and surely these pediatric patients could hold off until later in the morning when another nurse came in.

"Just noticed the time. You should get out of here. Job well done, though. See you next time. Make sure you check the schedule on your way out." Bella opened her mouth to inquire about that, but Dr. Whalen beat her to it. "It's in the folder that Tori showed you when you first got here."

"Ah, thank you, Dr. Whalen. See you later."

Bella had given her class schedule to Capmed, so she was hopeful whoever was responsible for her schedule didn't mess anything up. When she checked the folder, she was relieved to see that her schedule did fit around her schoolwork, though it didn't give much time beyond that. She took a picture of it and shrugged. It was what it was. This wasn't going to be forever. Only four more months and she would be finished with school. She'd be able to stop the juggling act and focus solely on work. She only needed to survive until then.

Her stomach twisted. *Could* she survive until then? She had to, or the ideal life she'd designed for herself would be ruined.

Bella hurried to the locker room and grabbed her purse and bag, then left the hospital as quickly as she could. The sooner she got home to her apartment, the better chance she would get to fall asleep and have at least some time to relax before she had to get up for her classes.

The good thing about working into the morning hours was missing all the traffic, and Bella made it home in record time. She collapsed into her bed, not even bothering to get out of her scrubs. It felt like no sooner had she closed her eyes than her alarm went off.

"This can't be right," she mumbled.

She opened her eyes and looked over at her clock. Sure enough, six o'clock flashed on the LED screen. She reached over and shut the alarm off, then fell back in bed and stared up at the ceiling. Somehow, her eyes closed, and by the time she opened them again, they were looking at a clock that read seven-thirty.

"Crap," she cried.

Bella jumped up from her bed and worked double-time to shower and get dressed. She had her hair pulled up into a messy bun and was out the door with only a granola bar in fifteen minutes. Still, even that didn't get her to her campus on time. She rushed into the classroom fifteen minutes late.

Immediately, Professor Julian looked over and stared at her. The whole class remained quiet, and Bella felt her cheeks grow instantly hot.

"So glad you decided to join us today, Ms. Strong," he said in his heavy Italian accent.

"Sorry for the interruption," she mumbled. She moved in, brushing past a chair that made a loud screech across the floor. She paused as students giggled all around her. She wanted to crawl into a hole and never be seen again, but she had to carefully maneuver her way up the bleacher steps to reach an empty seat. She fumbled with her bag as it clumsily fell to the floor, making another loud noise echo through the auditorium room. *Shoot me now.*

She looked up and met her professor's gaze, as he hadn't said a word the whole time she was fumbling her way to her seat. "Are you ready?" he asked dryly.

She nodded, a yawn escaping her, which caused her to squeak in embarrassment and him to arch an eyebrow in her direction. "Sorry," she whispered, covering her mouth.

"Where was I before the interruption?" the professor asked.

Hands shot up all around her, as the rest of the class was eager to impress. Bella rolled her eyes and pulled out the required textbook for her accounting class. She just wanted the class to be over, but more importantly, she wanted to make sure she didn't nod off to sleep. That was the last thing she needed in a day that had already started horribly.

What was wrong with her? Was she slipping back into the high school girl she'd fought so hard to change? If she kept this up, she'd fail her last semester, which would set her back. Then she wouldn't get married by twenty-five and have kids by thirty. What would she be then? A failure, that's what.

The day had to get better. Her life had to get easier. She had to prove to herself and everyone else that she could do whatever she set out to do and that she *was* capable. Otherwise, what good was she?

CHAPTER TWO

Bella

The restaurant was busy when Bella entered and glanced around for Jackson. When she saw him, she smiled, her worries and awful morning washing away. He was the only person she looked at as she approached him.

He pulled her into his arms and murmured, "Good afternoon, beautiful."

"Good afternoon," she replied, squirming a little. She didn't like when he called her beautiful. It wasn't because of any low self-esteem; it just never made her melt when he said it. He was her boyfriend, though, so she needed to get more comfortable with him calling her that.

She smiled, finally able to take a small break. She was no longer exhausted as she sat down across from him in the corner booth. He gave her second wind, and her morning of being late and belittled by her professor was instantly forgotten.

"I needed to lunch with you," she said, grabbing her glass of water and taking a sip, then sighing.

He tilted his head. "That's obvious from the way you're looking. You seem a little frazzled."

She reached up and touched her messy bun, grimacing when she felt that half her hair had already fallen out of the elastic band.

She cringed. "I probably look like a mess."

He reached out and grabbed her hand, offering her a wink. "Babe, you look beautiful. Just saying that I can tell when my honey is stressing."

Bella nodded. "And I absolutely am." She leaned forward and flipped her menu open and looked through it. "We can discuss that later. Have you decided what you're going to order?"

"Chicken and pasta sound good," Jackson offered.

Bella smiled and looked up. "I'm good with that."

As if on cue, the waitress approached them and turned her attention to Bella. "My name is Jess and I'll be taking your order. Do you want anything besides water?"

"Water is fine. Thanks," Bella said. "And I do believe we're ready to order." She motioned to Jackson, and he placed their order. Then the waitress was gone, and Bella closed her eyes. "Where to begin," she started.

"The beginning is always a good start," Jackson replied.

When she opened her eyes, she saw that he had a hint of a glimmer in his eyes. She smiled. He knew her better than any other person did. They had met in the jewelry store he owned. She was there to get a bracelet clasp replaced from a bracelet she had inherited from her grandmother. He had fixed it easily while explaining that he had taken over his father's jewelry shop and came from a long line of jewelry makers. He intrigued her, and they had developed a solid friendship. When he said he had feelings and wanted something more, she decided it was perfect timing. He was a good guy and would make a good father, and she cared for him. They didn't have a passionate relationship, but it was enough. And she no longer needed to date because Jackson fit into her life plan.

It also helped that her parents loved him. So why not choose Jackson?

They had developed a solid bond over the past two years, and he hadn't been fazed when she told him about her plan. He had agreed that she needed to get her degree and secure a great nursing job, and then they would marry and have at least one kid by her thirtieth birthday.

As Bella told him about being late to her first class, he listened intently. His eyes were focused on her, and he seemed completely zoned in on every word she had to say. There wasn't any indication that he was judging her. She liked that about him.

"Everyone's late at some point. It just happens. I'm sure your professor doesn't blame you for that."

Bella smirked and sipped her water. "Spoken by someone who doesn't know Professor Julian. His eyes can bear daggers into a person's soul."

Jackson laughed and shook his head. "Well, if that's how he is, then I would say who needs him. You'll be finished with this class in a few months and be able to look back and sigh with relief."

At that moment, Jess returned with their food. "Thank you," Bella replied, quickly digging in. She munched on her meal and nodded. "You are so right."

He smiled. "That's what I like to see. That beautiful smile on your lips."

She nodded, ignoring how his words didn't cause butterflies—or anything at all. She looked down at her food and took another bite. "Pretty good," she said, wiping her mouth and then taking a sip of her water.

"So, how was your first night at the hospital? I was worried about you. It seemed like too much, getting off so late and then having to head to class."

"You don't even know the half of it," she mumbled. "I got out late and might as well have only had an hour to sleep. By the time I had unwound and closed my eyes, my alarm was already going off."

Bella shook her head, thinking back to earlier that morning. It was overwhelming, but somehow it brought a feeling of exhilaration inside of her. A few more nights like that and she was sure she would get used to it.

Jackson listened as she dished on her experience working at the hospital, and when she was done, he tilted his head. "And this is a part-time gig, right? Don't want you overstretching yourself."

She smiled. "Thank you. You're always so sweet to me."

He reached out and brushed his hand against her cheek. "Well, I love you."

"Me, too," she responded. She'd never been able to get the L-word out for Jackson, but love wasn't necessary to have a good life and relationship. They had mutual respect, and she cared for him. They made a good team.

"I won't overstretch, I promise," she continued. "I'm going to enjoy it.

Sure, it's going to be a lot, but I didn't expect this to be easy. Nothing worthwhile ever is, right?"

He shook his head. "You always amaze me, babe."

As Bella opened her mouth to respond, her phone started ringing. She reached into her purse and saw *Capmed* spread across the screen. She looked up and gave him a sheepish grin.

"Speaking of..." She held up the phone to show him the name that was flashing on the screen. He arched his brow as she answered the call. "This is Bella."

"Hello, Bella. This is Tori Mitchell. We met late last night. I'm the lead nurse in the pediatrics department."

"Of course," Bella said. "I remember."

"Perfect. Anyway, there was a call-in for this evening. I know that you had a late one last night, but I checked your school schedule, and it seems you only had morning classes today. I was hoping you could come in tonight. It would only be for a few hours. Five or six tops."

Bella shook her head in disbelief. *She called that a few?*

"Um, well..." She hesitated, glancing across the table at Jackson's expectant stare.

"You would be helping me out greatly. I understand if you're not free, but I'm kind of in a bind here."

Tori hesitated a bit before continuing. "I know this kind of puts you on the spot, and technically you're only a nursing assistant, but this will look great on your resume, whether you choose to stay with Capmed or go somewhere else." She laughed on the other end of the line. "I'm begging you here. We had two more pediatric patients come in this morning, and we're stretched thin."

"You don't have to beg, Tori. I'll be there in twenty minutes."

"Really?" she squealed. "Thank you so much!"

"My pleasure." Bella disconnected the call, and Jackson's jaw dropped.

"Babe, you're exhausted."

"I'll get some sleep," Bella argued, standing. She saw Jackson's gaze drop to her half-eaten food. "I'll finish this during a break."

She waved Jess over to the table. "Can I please get a to-go box?"

Jess quickly left and returned a moment later with a box in her hands.

"Thank you." Bella packed her food and looked up to find Jackson's eyes still on her. "Listen, the more I help them out, the more they'll be willing to help me out, right?"

"I suppose," he mumbled. "Just don't overexert yourself. That won't be good for anyone."

Bella leaned in and kissed his cheek. "I won't. I'll call you later." She turned with her food in her hands, then looked over her shoulder. "Thanks for lunch." She held up her box, then hurried out of the restaurant. She had to get to the hospital and start her second shift, whether her body was ready or not.

As Bella approached Tori, the lead nurse looked up. Tori's hair was a mess and a smidge of her blush had streaked on her face. She sighed and practically collapsed into a chair across from Bella.

"I'm so glad you could come in. You have no idea how much I appreciate this."

Bella put on a wide grin. "Happy to help."

She glanced over to where a woman had just exited a room with Dr. Whalen. Bella couldn't help but stare. The woman was stunning and oozed confidence. She looked to be completely in her element, waving to a nearby nurse. Though she was just wearing a lab coat and scrubs, she had an elegance that stole Bella's breath.

She pulled her eyes away so she wouldn't be caught gawking. She looked at Tori, motioning to the woman and trying to seem disinterested. "Who's that?"

Tori looked, following her gaze, then smiled. "Oh, that? That's Dr. Leona Guillano. She just transferred here from New York City." Tori handed a folder to her. "And your next patient is waiting in his room. He needs fluids and is in major need of some rest. He was brought here from Indianapolis this morning. Six years old."

She started rattling off other information, then smiled. "You've got this. Same drill from before. Dr. Whalen couldn't praise you enough."

Bella looked up from the chart and arched an eyebrow. "Really?"

"Yep." Tori got up from the computer and grabbed another chart.

"Said you were on top of things. That's high praise for him." She laughed. "Anyway, best get to it. No rest for the weary.

She started to leave, then snapped her fingers and spun on her heel. "Almost forgot—Karen won't be in until six. I hope you don't mind staying. And I'll be out of here in an hour."

Bella's jaw dropped. What happened to only a few hours?

"You're a lifesaver," Tori added. She turned and entered a room, accidentally knocking Bella back in the process.

She shook her head. She hadn't even gotten a chance to argue against it. It was like Tori had this way of making Bella feel like it was her idea to stick around three hours longer than intended. She chewed her bottom lip and looked down at her chart, checking the room number. What had she gotten herself into?

Before heading to her patient—Brad, the chart said—she glanced around for Dr. Guillano, but the woman had disappeared. It was strange how drawn Bella was to this doctor. She shook the thought from her head. She was tired, and the doctor was beautiful. That was all.

She knocked on Brad's door, waiting for someone to welcome her in. When she didn't hear anything, she knocked a little louder. "Hello? May I come in?" she asked, peering her head through the door.

"Come in!" Brad looked up from his book.

Bella looked around the room, expecting that a mom or dad would be just a couple of feet away. Instead, the kid was alone. She turned back to him, noticing his wide brown eyes.

"Hello," he said, his voice chipper.

"Why, hello there." Bella grabbed her stool and pulled up next to him. "Are you Brad Carver?" she asked.

He nodded, his cheeks rosy and his eyes bright. He then leaned forward and coughed hard, choking as he fell back onto his pillow. Bella jumped up and grabbed him his glass of water, then helped him take a few sips.

"Are you okay?" she asked.

He looked up, tears leaking from the corners of his eyes. He nodded. "The doctors said I have a virus. But the doctors here are the best. That's what they told me."

"Who's 'they'?" Bella asked, taking her seat back on the stool.

361

"Kimberly Blackstone."

Bella swiveled her chair at the sound of a woman's voice. The woman in question wore a black pinstripe skirt and blouse, and she walked with purpose. Her tanned features were almost as dark as her jet-black hair that cascaded over her shoulders.

"Hello," Bella said, shaking the woman's offered hand. "And you are..."

"I work at Chesterhill Children's Home in Indianapolis. I'm sorry I was away, but Brad is one of two kids I have here."

Children's home? At least that explained why there wasn't a mother or father by Brad's side.

"Nice to make your acquaintance. I'm Bella Strong, the nurse who's been assigned on Brad's rotation this afternoon."

Kimberly nodded. "So, what's the verdict? We hear it's 'just' a virus, but since Melody Jane had to come here for her cancer treatment, I thought I would get Brad checked out."

"Well, it could very well be just a virus. Dr. Whalen will be coming in shortly and will make sure to get Brad all checked out. I see some of Brad's symptoms are fever, cough, upset stomach, and tremors. Anything else to note?"

Kimberly shook her head. "That just about covers it," she said.

"I've been monitoring his BP, and it seems normal. His pulse is a bit elevated, but nothing too erratic to worry about." Bella turned to face the boy and grabbed her thermometer. "Let me get your temp. Open your mouth."

She slipped the thermometer under Brad's tongue and waited for it to beep before checking it and nodding. "One hundred point five. A little higher than I'd like, so I'll get him some acetaminophen."

She stood up from his stool and frowned. There was something else she was supposed to do, right? She thought she had recalled Tori mentioning something, but she skimmed over the chart and shrugged. "I'll let the doctor know you're ready and get you that medicine to cut the fever."

"Thank you," Kimberly said.

Bella left the room and went over to the medicine cabinet. She measured out the appropriate dose of acetaminophen and documented the release of medicine on the cabinet, just as she was shown the night before. At least she had remembered this important step. Little by little, she was getting the hang of things, but she still felt so slow and not on top of things as she normally was. What if she couldn't do this job?

She pushed those thoughts away as she carried the cup back into Brad's room. "Go ahead and drink this all up. Here's some water to wash it down. The doctor will be in with you in just a few minutes. Until then, I'll be right outside these doors if you need me."

"Thank you," Brad said before lying back against his pillow.

"You are very welcome. Feel better soon."

She turned and left his room. Bella looked up and down the hallway, waiting for Dr. Whalen to come out of one of the hospital rooms. Instead, it was the new doctor, Dr. Guillano, who emerged, heading straight toward Bella. She had her hair pulled back into a ponytail, giving her a younger look, although Bella would guess she was in her mid-forties. She didn't have wrinkles to prove that, but the way she moved when she walked showed she had years on Bella. Her stature was one of independence and maturity, not like the awkward girl Bella sometimes felt she portrayed.

"Is that chart for me?" the doctor asked, approaching her.

Bella realized she had been gawking, lost in the woman's eyes. Bella looked away. "Uh, I mean, um..." Bella swallowed and looked over the chart. "Um, it should be for Dr. Whalen."

Dr. Leona Guillano frowned. "It's not Brad Carver?" she asked.

Bella's insides tensed. It was, but she was supposed to be working with Dr. Whalen. That's how things were done, right? Work with the same doctor repetitively, so you would get used to how they operated. She chewed her lip. She was so confused.

"It is, but..." Her words trailed off when Leona grabbed the chart and smiled.

"Yep. It's mine." She started to turn but stopped herself and looked over her shoulder. "Silly me. I'm Dr. Leona Guillano. I believe you'll be working with me this shift."

She grabbed a piece of paper from her pocket and held it up to show it to Bella. Bella's name was written underneath the doctor's. Dr. Guillano smiled. "The patient in room four-zero-two needs an extra blanket."

"Yes, ma'am," Bella replied, still in slight shock.

Dr. Guillano turned and headed to Brad's room, leaving Bella in her dust. There was a hurried tone in her words, but a small smile showed on her lips. It made her a woman first, a doctor second. She didn't look much like the doctors Bella had met. She had dimples that touched the corners of her smile, and she wore makeup, even though it was lightly done. But she had this way about her that got people's attention. Maybe it was her stride. Or maybe it was the way her eyes homed in on Bella that made her feel seen. Being in Dr. Guillano's presence also gave her a warm sensation in her core, something she'd never felt with Jackson or with anyone else.

She sighed. She needed to ignore whatever crazy things were happening in her body because of this doctor. The last thing she needed was to develop a crush when she was already struggling with work and school. Besides, Dr. Guillano was a woman. An older woman. And Bella already had her future mapped out with Jackson.

She hurried toward the room that the doctor had come out of but hesitated at the door. Was that 402? Or 404? She stared at each room, confused as to which one she was supposed to get a blanket for. After a moment, she stepped into 404.

A young girl looked up from her bed. She looked to be in her early teens but frowned when she saw Bella. "Are you cold?" Bella asked.

The girl shook her head, her eyes still wide. Bella put on a smile. "Anything I can get you?" she asked.

"The remote?" Her voice was so small as she made her request.

"Sure," Bella said. That couldn't be a hard thing to come by. But try as she might, Bella couldn't locate it. She dug through drawers, checked under the bed, and even looked through her closets. She frowned, turning around.

The girl giggled as she held up her hand. "Oops," she said.

Bella smirked and shook her head. "Guess you found it," Bella replied.

"Guess so!" The girl shrugged. She turned on her TV and leaned back in bed.

"You can holler if you need anything. The call button is right on your bed."

"Thanks," she said.

Bella left her room and nearly bumped into Dr. Guillano. "There you are," she said. "What are you doing in there?"

"Helping, um..." She hesitated, not sure what the girl's name was. "She couldn't find her remote."

Dr. Guillano tilted her head. "Did you get our patient his blanket?" she asked. "Tye?"

Bella cowered, acid rising in her throat. How could she have made yet another mistake? "Um, well, you see, I couldn't remember the room number."

Dr. Guillano shook her head with a frown. "I can see we have a lot of work to do to get you whipped into shape. One, the blanket. And two... You haven't started the IV fluids for Brad."

Bella winced. That was what she needed to do. "I'm sorry, Leona," she started. "I mean, Dr. Guillano." Bella's eyes widened. "It won't happen again."

She turned around and hurried away from her, worried that Dr. Guillano would already have a bad impression of Bella as a nurse. Somehow, though they had just met, Leona's opinion of her mattered. She was just about to reach the supply closet when she remembered the blanket. She turned around to go back to room 402 but saw Tori was already headed into the room, a blanket in hand.

She groaned and turned back around, then headed to the supply closet to get the items she needed for the fluids. She could picture everyone already talking about her behind her back, joking that she would never make a good nurse if she didn't get it together. Her mind went right back to high school—the teasing, the taunting, the practical jokes. Her peers insisting that she was just plain stupid and had no future doing anything of importance.

She swallowed away the tears and the painful memories to focus on what she needed to do. Just one step at a time. *You got this.*

Still, those thoughts kept running through her mind as she worked on getting Brad's IV started. She reviewed the steps in her mind as she wiped down the back of Brad's left hand with an alcohol wipe. "You'll feel a big pinch," she said, but he didn't even wince. Perhaps he was used to the discomfort that a needle brought on. Quickly, she connected the IV tubing, taped down the cannula with a sense of pride, and entered the fluid rate in the IV pump.

"I'll be back in an hour to check up on you," she said, then squeezed his hand and left his room triumphantly. She was back to feeling a sliver of confidence that she could master this job.

Once she left, she spotted Tori at the computer. There was no better time than the present to see what already was being said about her. She cleared her throat, making Tori look up.

"Hey, Bella," she said.

"So, how upset is Dr. Guillano?" Bella asked.

Tori quickly waved her hand. "Don't worry about it. It's your second shift. Everyone has a few mishaps when they first start. It's how you deal with them that will determine how far you go. Just remember that."

Bella tilted her head. "Thanks for getting the blanket."

The nurse's station light lit up, and Tori looked over and shook her head. "I would ask you to get that, but that wouldn't be fair to you."

Bella leaned over and saw that room 404 was lit up. She frowned. "What do you mean?"

"Isabelle likes to call the nursing staff into the room just because she gets lonely. And if I have to look for her remote one more time when she already has it, I can assure you I might just scream." She laughed. "It's what happens when your mother has to work, leaving you here alone."

The alarm sounded again, and Tori put on a smile. "Just put on a happy smile, and away you go." She turned to go, and Bella watched her. She now was glad she knew the tricks that Isabelle liked to pull, and hopefully she wouldn't fall for it next time. She spotted Dr. Guillano headed her way and quickly jumped behind the desk. If she looked like she was just standing around, that would be another mark against her.

"Hey, Bella, listen," Dr. Guillano started, approaching her. "I don't want us getting started on the wrong foot. I didn't transfer hospitals so I could be the hospital bully. That's not who I am or what I'm about. The truth is, I would like to believe that once you get to know me, you'll realize that I'm just a nice woman who's only trying to help."

Bella nodded, and Dr. Guillano's smile faded slightly. "With that being said, I believe to be the best, you have to learn from the best. And I don't want to sound conceited, but I'm one of the best. And I don't support mistakes. We all have to be better every minute, every hour, and every day than we were the day before. So, I'll be sure that you live up to my beliefs. Do you understand?"

"Yes, ma'am," Bella said, feeling like she needed to salute or something.

"Very well." Dr. Guillano turned from Bella. "For the record, just call me Leona."

She then left, never looking back to make sure her point had gotten across, but Bella heard her loud and clear. She needed to step up. If she tried hard enough, maybe she could be half as confident as Dr. Guillano— Leona. She still wasn't exactly sure how to take the doctor, but she was surely going to do her best to live up to whatever her expectations were.

As she watched Leona walk away, an overwhelming mix of emotions flooded through Bella. Part of her was giddy about the prospect of seeing Leona again, or her possibly becoming Bella's mentor, and the other part was weighed down with self-doubt. Moments of feeling like she had everything handled were brief and always replaced with the nagging thought: What if I'm not good enough? What if I majorly screw up and everything falls apart?

Bella returned to work. She had to prove those thoughts wrong.

CHAPTER THREE

Leona

When Leona first caught a glimpse of the nurse on duty with her, Bella, her thoughts went to how young she looked. She couldn't possibly be any older than twenty-one years old, right? She wasn't like the nurses Leona was used to seeing in the hospital she worked at in New York. But Leona could tell she had determination, despite her faults. She was also alluring. Leona couldn't deny that she had checked out Bella's figure under her scrubs. She had ample curves and a lovely smile, which had made Leona's heart flutter slightly. She was at work, though, and knew feelings like that were inappropriate.

"Four-zero-seven needs some ice." Leona reached out to take Bella's arm as Bella hurried past her. "And her mother needs two extra pillows. It's going to be a long night for her."

"Yes, ma'am," Bella said, her tone soft. She looked up and met Leona's arched eyebrow. "Leona," she corrected.

Leona let go of her arm and watched her as Bella stepped into the room before letting a small smile play across her face. There was a definite hesitation about Bella, like she was waiting for Leona's next slap across the wrist. She didn't want to hold that kind of power over Bella, so she would need to tread carefully so Bella saw her as more of a coworker. Leona sighed and turned, heading to the front desk where Dr. Whalen stood.

"How's your shift going?" he asked.

"For Bella or me?" Leona asked, smirking.

He dropped his gaze to hers, then chuckled. "For both."

"I'm not in Kansas anymore," Leona teased. "Or, I should say, definitely not New York City."

He crossed his arms around the chart he was holding, pulling it to his chest. "Come on now," he started. "Chicago can't be all that different. Maybe we don't have the high-tech mumbo jumbo machines you have in The Big Apple, but we do pretty well. Heck, it's been just over a year since they remodeled this place. You should have seen it back then."

Leona smiled. "Nah, your hospital is fine. I'm only teasing—more or less. It's Bella, though. What's her story? She seems a bit wet behind the ears if you know what I mean. I get the feeling she's been a nurse for about a day."

He laughed, checking his watch, then leaned against the counter. "You aren't far off. She started last night." Leona's jaw dropped, which brought on another round of laughter. "You see, she's part of this program that we run at Capmed, which is only in its second semester. But if you're in a nursing program and you're in your final semester, you can apply for a position here. It's like a nursing assistant program, through which we shape the way these individuals become nurses. Each floor gets two to three individuals that are welcomed into Capmed to take part. If they succeed by the end of the semester, then typically we try to have a position waiting for them."

"Interesting. So she really is brand new to the field. It's kind of like an externship."

"Except they get paid. They do it along with their schoolwork, so life can get challenging. But that one..." He hesitated, and Leona followed where his hand pointed. Bella had just exited the room and pulled her hair from her ponytail. It cascaded down her shoulders, and Leona had an urge to run her fingers through it. She wanted to smooth the tangled strands, tying it back in a sleek up-do. Then her fingers would trail to the exposed nape of Bella's neck. Then her lips...

"Don't you think?" Dr. Whalen asked.

Leona blinked. She had gotten lost in her fantasy—one she wasn't supposed to be having. "I'm sorry. What was that?" She watched Bella set her hair back up into a tighter bun, then went on along her way.

"I see great potential in her." Dr. Whalen repeated.

"You do?" Leona asked, turning to him.

He smirked. "Let me guess; you don't?"

She shrugged. "I do, but there have been a few issues. She seems a bit forgetful. And I would say her youthfulness isn't going to win her nursing points. For example, there's this one patient that practically had her scouring the room, looking for a remote control that the patient had in her hand."

He laughed. "Isabelle. That's one thing about the pediatric floor. You always have to be on your toes. Otherwise, these patients will run you ragged. Tori still falls for the remote trick." He threw up his hands and shrugged. "It happens. But what I've noticed is Bella Strong has heart, which goes a long way in the nursing profession. I can see that she would be a great asset to this team. I wouldn't count her out just yet." He patted Leona's shoulder, then left to tend to a patient. Leona stared after him, musing on his words. She looked down at her clipboard, then headed toward Brad's room.

She knocked on the door and Bella's voice rang out. "Come on in!"

Leona opened the door and entered the room. She didn't recall telling Bella that Brad needed anything. She herself had only stopped to check in on him. Bella looked up as she finished fluffing a pillow behind him.

"Just getting Brad more comfortable. That huge basketball game is on. Isn't that right, Brad?"

Brad's eyes and rosy cheeks were bright as he nodded eagerly. "That's nice," Leona said.

She cast a look over to Bella, hearing Dr. Whalen's voice in her head. He was right. What Bella had going for her was the compassion she could give to patients. That was something you couldn't train for or be taught. Suddenly Leona didn't want to worry quite so much about the mistakes here and there. She just wanted to help Bella. She wasn't used to monitoring a new nurse, but she also remembered her first days. Medical school had been rough, and she had been a bit clumsy when she had first started working with patients. For that reason, she had a lot of empathy for Bella and wanted to see her succeed.

She watched as Bella interacted with Brad. If she wanted to have kids one day, Bella would make a great mother. Leona's heart squeezed as she ached about her own desires for motherhood. She had always wanted a child, but somehow it had never worked out. And now that she was in her forties, that dream was fading more each year.

She smiled at Bella, pushing her own longings aside. Leona had a feeling she would really love working at Capmed thanks to a certain nurse.

Two hours into the shift, Leona and Bella left another room. Leona looked over to Bella as the young nurse released a yawn. Bella's eyes widened as she covered her mouth. "Excuse me. I'm not quite used to the work schedule yet."

"Well, it has only been like twenty-four hours since you started this routine, right?"

Bella arched an eyebrow, which made Leona smile.

"Let's go grab some coffee."

"What about our rounds?" Bella asked.

"It's called a break. I'm sure even Chicago allows breaks."

Bella's cheeks turned a dark shade of red as they got into the elevator and took it down to the cafeteria. "So, how'd you know?" Bella asked as the elevator dinged and the doors opened.

"Know what?" Leona replied, leading the way.

She noted that Bella picked up the pace to keep up with her, indicating she didn't want to be left in the dust. That was a good sign, and she admired that.

"That I've only worked here twenty-four hours," Bella responded. "Is my work ethic that obvious?"

Leona smirked, turning to face her. "Well, there are obvious things that you need to learn, but that comes with time. No one becomes

Florence Nightingale overnight." Leona snickered. "You probably don't even know who that is. You're a young'un."

Bella laughed. "I don't live under a rock. I am in nursing school, after all."

They turned and entered the cafeteria, and Leona continued. " I like to learn who I'm going to be working with because it helps me know what I need to do as the practitioner for my nurse and what my nurse will be able to handle."

She stopped at the coffee cart and put two fingers up for the guy manning the cart, then glanced over at Bella. "Make sense? I'm not simply wanting to be nosy or anything. I just feel it's my due diligence to make sure I know what I'm getting into, as far as a working relationship goes."

Bella nodded. "Can't see anything wrong with that. But may I ask what you've figured out so far? I mean, I know we didn't get off to the best start with me, um...Well, you know." Bella's eyes dropped as Leona paid for the coffees.

"Again, you'll improve as the days, weeks, months, and years go on. That much is clear. I would say there's definite work to be done, but in due time, if you stick with me, you'll be ready to run this place." She handed Bella her coffee.

"You didn't need to pay for my coffee. I can manage." Bella reached in her pants pocket and pulled out a few dollars.

"Keep your money." Leona turned from her and led her way to a corner table. "Everyone makes a few mistakes at the beginning. If I had known you were fresh into this job, I would have expected those mistakes. Going forward, it's what you do to learn from your mistakes. You can always work to be better. That's the goal, and that's what I intend on helping you with."

Bella nodded. They sat in silence for a few minutes as they both sipped on their coffees. Bella's cheeks were flushed and she kept averting her gaze, which gave Leona an opening to really take her in. She watched Bella's full lips perch on the edge of her cup, taking small, timid sips, and she lingered in the dark hues of Bella's eyes as they darted around the room. If she was really going to be working with Bella more and helping her find her place at Capmed, she needed to get this attraction in check.

After a moment, Bella finally met her gaze.

"May I ask a question?"

Leona arched an eyebrow. "On one condition." She scrunched up her lips into a small pucker. "Make that two conditions."

"Which are?"

"One, if I don't like the question, I don't answer it."

"I suppose that's acceptable. What's the second condition?"

"If I agree to answer the question, then you have to answer a question of mine." Leona grinned. "And you can't decline to answer it."

"That hardly seems fair," Bella replied, scrunching up her nose, which elicited a soft chortle from Leona.

"Those are my conditions. So, do we have a deal?"

"Fine. Deal." Leona nodded and motioned with her hand for Bella to proceed. "Why move to Chicago, when you were based in New York City?"

"Now who's checking up on who?" Leona softly replied.

Bella shrugged. "Tori happened to mention it. That's beside the point, though. What brought you here from New York?"

Leona looked down at her pool of black coffee, then lifted it to her lips and sipped. They had known each other only a short time, and she wasn't ready to dive down that rabbit hole with anyone, but she could answer the question without giving Bella a comprehensive picture.

"Have you ever just felt like you needed a change?" Leona asked. Bella gave her a blank look, which made Leona drop her gaze. "Probably not, because you're still a child."

"I'm not a child," Bella argued. "I'm twenty-two years old. That legally qualifies me as an adult, by anyone's standards."

Leona saw she struck a nerve, but she didn't feel the need to apologize. "I'm forty-five," Leona said quietly. "So, by my standards, anyone under thirty is a child."

She paused. "I'm sorry. I won't call you a child again. But...Have you ever felt you needed a change?"

Bella nodded, then hesitated. "I guess maybe I haven't quite gotten there, but I think I know what you mean."

"Then, yeah, I was just at that point. So here I am." She rubbed her hands together. "And on that note..."

Bella's eyes widened. "I think it's time to go back to work now, isn't it?"

Leona chuckled. She would give Bella a reprieve, but when the opportunity arose, once they had gotten to know each other a little bit, she would make sure ask all the questions she wanted the answers to. For now, Leona was just looking forward to spending more time with her.

CHAPTER FOUR

Bella

Bella's phone rang as soon as she stepped foot into the hospital. She gave a weak smile when she saw Jackson's name on the caller ID, requesting a video chat. It was bittersweet for her. While she was glad to get the chance to speak with him, it'd been two weeks since they had last seen each other, and she worried that he would soon get tired of this. What shocked her the most, though, was that she'd barely thought of him during that time. He was the one always calling and texting to try to get them to spend time together. She was...indifferent. Or simply too frazzled from school and work.

His call reminded her that she had yet another thing to juggle: her relationship. Now that she was headed into another shift, she would only be able to spare two minutes. Not nearly long enough to sustain a healthy connection with Jackson.

"Hey," she said, stepping into the elevator.

Wrong move. Immediately his face flickered on the screen, and then he froze. Bella groaned and she quickly punched the button for her floor. "Give me a minute. I'll get off the elevator soon and—"

Her call dropped, and she groaned, falling back against the wall of the elevator. When the doors opened, she stepped off onto her floor and dialed Jackson's number.

"Hello?"

"Sorry, I got in the elevator and lost connection."

"So, you can't do dinner tonight," he said. Just hearing the pain in his voice tore at her chest a little bit. "You're at work."

"I'm sorry," she said. She felt like she had said sorry so many times over the last two weeks. But with her demanding school and work schedules, all free time was devoted to her coursework and sleep. Things had been busy from the beginning, but these past two weeks had her running in circles at twice the speed. "Are you still there?" Bella asked, as Jackson hadn't responded to her apology.

"I'm still here. I'm sorry. I just miss you. That's all."

A weight shifted in her chest. "I know." More guilt ate at her because she realized she didn't feel the same. She did miss hanging out, but not as much as he seemed to miss her. She looked over to the desk where Leona stood, her face immediately warming. It was like she ran a fever every time Leona was around. What was wrong with her body?

She sighed. Another minute standing there, and she'd be late to her shift. She couldn't stand there and chat on the phone, especially when she knew others were looking in. She didn't want to give anyone a reason to think she wasn't doing her job. "I'm sorry, but I have to get going."

"It's all right, I understand," Jackson said flatly. "Have a good day at work."

"I will."

"Love you," he said.

She disconnected the call and hurried over to where Leona stood, who arched an eyebrow and looked up and down at Bella. Bella looked down to see her purse still hanging around her. In a rush to answer Jackson's call, she had come to the floor without dropping her things off in her locker.

"I'm sorry," she mumbled. "I was in such a rush that I didn't stop at the breakroom."

"That call must've distracted you. Was it your boyfriend or something?" Leona asked, turning from Bella.

For some reason, Bella couldn't say yes. She didn't want to talk about Jackson with Leona. "Uh, I'll hurry to the locker and be right back."

"Don't bother," Leona replied, opening up a drawer. "You can lock it up in here."

Bella didn't object as she locked the drawer and turned back to Leona. "Ready for duty," she said, like she was a soldier standing at attention.

Leona nodded, tilting her head slightly. "We have a full day," she said. "For starters, room four-zero-four needs a breathing treatment. Room four-zero-seven needs to be taken down for an X-ray. Room four-zero-two..." She stopped and looked at Bella. "Don't you think you need to take notes?"

"Oh. Right," Bella said, hurrying around the desk to grab a notebook and pen.

Bella jotted down what Leona had told her, ready to add this to the stack of notes she had at home. Despite reviewing her notes before passing out each night, Bella didn't feel like she had gotten that much better at this job. She needed to remind herself that she wasn't an incompetent woman destined to make a mistake at every turn.

There was also the fact that even after three weeks, Leona flustered her. It was most likely because Leona held a seniority position, and it worried Bella that she would mess up in front of Leona and screw up her chances for getting a job at Capmed after her program ended. That, and the sensations Leona stirred in her body.

They got to work, with Bella running around like she did most nights, with very little time to complain about her feet being tired or worry about time creeping to a crawl. That was one definite thing she could say about working at Capmed. There was little time to focus on the day dragging by. That was the best part about the job.

It was when she sunk in a chair to relax during a break that she realized how tired she truly was. She grabbed her water after opening a bottle of aspirin, then downed two pills and sighed. In thirty minutes, the pills would kick in, and she would have some more energy. She stifled a yawn, shaking her hazy head. At least, she hoped so. She tore into her granola bar and flipped open her economics workbook.

"It's not a lifestyle everyone can handle."

Bella looked up when she heard Leona's voice. She gave a weak smile and shrugged. "I'm working on it. Doing what I can to accomplish all my dreams. Isn't that what life is all about?"

Leona quirked up an eyebrow, then let it fall. "I would say so. I should leave you to it."

She turned, and Bella watched her elegant strides. She paused to look over her shoulder, turning her beautiful eyes to Bella. "When you're off your final break, we have an evaluation to get to."

A jolt shot through Bella's spine. "Evaluation?" She stopped mid-chew, gawking at Leona.

"Nothing major. Just something that needs to be done every few weeks. I checked the calendar, and they have me down as your evaluator." She smirked. "I guess it's because I've been the one working with you these last few weeks. This is new to both of us. It shouldn't be too bad, and I'm confident you'll get through it. Enjoy the rest of your break."

With that, she left the breakroom, but the damage had been done. Now she had to focus on what it was that Leona would want to talk to her about. Or how Leona felt about her work habits.

What did Leona really think of her? Probably that she was the clumsiest, most forgetful nurse she'd ever seen and would fail horribly in the end.

Bella closed her eyes and took a breath. It wasn't even about succeeding to prove it to herself and all her old bullies anymore. She wanted to make Leona proud. She felt warm and giddy when Leona smiled at something she'd done well. She wanted more of that smile.

She closed her workbook and stared blankly down at the title. The past three weeks had been a blur. She knew she wasn't being a good girlfriend and she wasn't excelling at work. He grades were also iffy. Though her anxiety often got the best of her, and she knew sometimes her fears were only in her thoughts, what if she really did end up failing? What if she was headed for *the* most epic fail of her life, losing Jackson, her job, and her degree all at once? Her life plan would be ruined.

She needed to stop getting so lost in her worries. Evaluations and tests always did this to her. If she thought too much about something, she would become overanxious.

Fifteen minutes later, she was headed back to work and in search of Leona. Instead, she found Jacqueline, a fellow nursing assistant in the same program as Bella. She stood at the desk, staring at the computer, and when she looked up, she heaved a sigh.

"Bella, you have no idea how glad I am to see you," she said. "The computer froze, and I've tried everything."

"You tried rebooted it?" Bella asked.

Jacqueline nodded. "Even that. But nothing." She slammed her hand down on the desk, frustration etched on her face. "Dr. Whalen asked me to print this patient's chart, and he's already been waiting ten minutes. I'm going to fail this task for sure." Her voice was filled with a despair that Bella had felt so many times.

"You'll be fine. Let me look."

Bella hurried around the desk to inspect the computer as Jacqueline scooted back to make room for Bella. Bella pressed a few keys, then tried the Esc. key, and suddenly, the mouse zipped across the computer. Bella held up her hands and looked over to Jacqueline.

"Not stuck anymore."

"You're a lifesaver," Jacqueline responded, moving up to take a look. "What'd you do?"

"Hit a bunch of keys and said a little prayer," Bella replied with a snort. "Who knows? As long as it's working again."

"Truth," Jacqueline said. The printer whirred to life, and she looked over to Bella. "I'll just get this printed, and Dr. Whalen will be a happy camper."

"So, have you had your evaluation by any chance?" Bella asked.

Jacqueline looked at Bella in horror. "Evaluation? Are you serious? I feel like I'm messing up every thirty seconds, and now I need to be evaluated over that? This can't be for real. How'd you hear about that? *What* did you hear?"

"Don't stress!" Bella quickly retorted. "I'm sure it's no big deal. Leona, I mean, Dr. Guillano just told me that she needed to see me after break to have my review. Something about how we need an evaluation every few weeks. Guess they want to see if you're on track to completing the Capmed program. Who knows?"

She stifled a yawn, then shook her head. "You started a week after me, so yours is probably coming up. But, I have a question…"

Bella's words fell off as she waited for Jacqueline to look at her. Jacqueline nodded at her, and Bella asked, "Are you finding it difficult to have a social life while doing this and going to school?"

Jacqueline laughed. "What social life? I didn't have one before all this landed in my lap. So, to answer your question..." She grabbed the papers from the printer. "Haven't noticed a difference. I'd better get these to Dr. Whalen."

She hurried away from the desk, and Bella thought about what Jacqueline had said. If she didn't have Jackson, then she probably could have said the same, but having a boyfriend really complicated things. *Future husband*, she reminded herself. Jackson would be the father of her kids someday, which made him even more important.

Bella looked toward Leona's office and groaned. She was already ten minutes over her break. She just hoped she didn't get lectured about tardiness. When she reached Leona's office, she lightly tapped on the door. Leona kept her head down at a chart she was reading. "A few minutes later than I expected," she said in greeting.

"I'm sorry. I, uh, you see," Bella stammered. Leona looked up, gawking at her as she responded like an idiot. "Jacqueline had computer issues, and I was helping her out."

"I see," Leona said. "Close the door behind you."

That was never a good sign. Was she about to be yelled at for her inability to handle the job? She thought she was doing well enough, but if that were the case, why did the door need to be closed?

She probably just doesn't think everyone should hear what stellar work you're doing. It might make people jealous. That was one way to look at it. It sure sounded much better than the alternative.

As Bella sat down, she crossed her legs, then uncrossed them. She fidgeted in her seat, then sat up straight. Her body felt restless as she stared straight ahead, just hoping that the whole thing wouldn't be a bust.

"No need to be nervous," Leona said.

"You can tell?" Bella said, releasing a nervous giggle.

"The fidgeting gave it away." Leona smiled, leaning across the desk to grab a notebook. "As mentioned, I'm not even sure what to expect out of this. So, we're just going to wing it together. Sound like a plan?"

"Oh, yeah, sure." Bella stared.

How was Leona always so confident and easygoing about everything? It was a trait that never failed to draw Bella toward her. If relaxed is what Leona wanted her to be, then that was what she was going to be. But even the easy tone of Leona's voice didn't do anything to soften Bella's worry. Hopefully, that would work itself out once the evaluation began.

"I'm going to ask you a few questions, and then we'll sort of go into any thoughts, worries, or brutal beatings."

"What?" Bella squealed.

Leona snickered. "Kidding. Just relax. I'm not here to belittle you as an employee or as a person. There's nothing I can say that can cause you harm if you don't let it. Got that?"

Bella thought about it. No, she wasn't sure she quite understood it, but she simply nodded.

"Great. Shall we begin? For starters, tell me about Bella Strong."

Bella's eyes wandered nervously around the room. That seemed like an offhanded question, not to mention extremely vague. What was the point of Leona asking that? How was it related to her evaluation?

She hesitated for what felt like ages, her face warm from the beating lights that shot down on her. Was she sweating? She felt like she was sweating. Again, she started to fidget, but that was because Leona had a way of looking at Bella and making her feel like Leona was boring holes into Bella's mind.

Bella cleared her throat. "Tell you about me? Like, what are you looking for?"

Leona leaned back in her chair, clasping her hands together. "Shall I rephrase the question?"

"That might be best," Bella mumbled.

"All right. What made you want to become a nurse? Your influences, your ambitions, your passions, etcetera. Does that help?"

"Somewhat," Bella whispered. "Well, I guess I would start with my mom. She's a nurse. Or was, I mean."

"She got out of it?" Leona asked.

"It's not that she got out of it, exactly. She loved being a nurse, or so I was told. She decided to start a family and thought nursing would take away from her passion of being a mom. But she's told me stories about helping people, and that intrigued me to give it a shot."

"How many siblings do you have?"

"There are three of us. My older brother, who's just about to turn thirty, then me, then my younger sister, who's fourteen."

"Gosh, seems like the family tree spans over several years as far as the kids' branches go." Leona arched an eyebrow. "I would guess there's a story there as to why she waited so long between your brother and you and then again from you to your sister." Her eyes darted away. "Not that you need to share that story if you don't want to."

"I don't mind. As I've heard it, my parents wanted to spend time with each of their children before bringing another one into the mix. They wanted to make sure all of us felt loved. They might have had another after Veronica was born, but an accident changed that."

Bella stopped speaking after that and looked down at her hands, which were clasped tightly together. She unlatched them and looked back up; Leona's gaze had drifted at the same time Bella's had.

Leona cleared her throat and nodded. "I see." She looked down at the notebook in front of her, then back up to Bella. "So, it looks like you had a fine upbringing that led you to help people. That makes sense."

"It does? How so?"

"Well, when I see you interact with the patients, it's like you're speaking to their soul. That's one thing you excel in, and I can assure you that it's a quality that doesn't go unnoticed."

Bella felt her cheeks getting warm. That was nice to hear. Now, if only they could say the same about her nursing abilities. She knew she had a ways to go before she could be called a stellar nurse. After all, she was still learning so much. But she was always willing to adapt, and she hoped that would account for something.

"I do have concerns, but they are limited, " Leona continued. Bella grabbed onto her chair, bracing herself for what Leona was about to thrust upon her. "I saw the way you were with the foster kids that were here a few weeks ago, but there are only so many places empathy can take you. You also need strong skills to succeed in a hospital. I'm not trying to sound cruel but...Are you sure nursing is the right profession for you?"

Bella faltered. She had always wanted to follow in her mother's footsteps, no matter how hard it was. Maybe Leona was simply trying to build her resolve.

"Well, those kids didn't have anyone," Bella began. "So I wanted to spend more time assisting them. I'm sorry if I spent too much time with them."

Leona waited for Bella to answer her question. When she didn't, Leona repeated, "Are you sure nursing is for you? Some people just aren't cut out for nursing, and that's entirely okay."

"So, you don't think this is something I'm capable of?"

"I didn't say that," Leona started. "Everyone is capable of everything if they put their mind to it. But does that necessarily mean you should strive for that? Why not put yourself in a place that you would shine?"

Bella looked down at her fists. "I want to be a nurse," she stated firmly. "I can be a nurse. All I've wanted is to follow in my mom's footsteps and help people." She stopped short of going into a rant about how much her bullies had hurt her and how she just wanted to do her part to take away other people's pain.

Leona sat back in her chair and smiled. "Good. Remember that. On days when you feel you've made a lot of mistakes, remember your reason for being here. Prove to me that you really want this. Otherwise, you should consider a new career path."

Bella looked up, surprised. She felt inspired and crushed at the same time. Could she prove she belonged here? She hoped she could. Changing careers wasn't in her plan.

———

Two days had passed, and Bella still couldn't get what Leona had said out of her mind. Was she fighting a losing battle and attempting to do nursing only because it was her mother's passion? She did want to help people, but there were other careers through which she could do that. The way the evaluation had ended had left Bella determined but a bit shaken. While Leona had said that there wasn't one major issue with Bella's work habits, she *had* said that Bella needed to reconsider her drive. Bella didn't want to back down from her goals, especially when that would mean revising her whole life plan. And trying to pivot now would be admitting defeat, that she wasn't good enough to be a nurse.

"You look like you have a world of thoughts lying on your shoulders."

She looked up to see Tori at the desk, her eyes homed in on Bella. Bella had been staring at the computer screen and aimlessly tapping her pencil in time to her thoughts. She dropped her pencil and let out a little laugh.

"You've got that right." She covered her face and shook her head, hoping that she wouldn't burst into tears right there in front of Tori. That was something she definitely wanted to avoid. "Can I talk to you about something? Maybe a few things?"

"Sure. I have time. Want to go in my office?"

Bella looked around the empty corridors and shook her head. "Here's fine. First of all, why did I get put on Dr. Guillano's rotation instead of Dr. Whalen's? I thought that we worked well together, Dr. Whalen and I. I know it was only one shift, but even you said he said I had potential, right? So, why the change? Jacqueline could have easily been placed with Dr. Guillano when she started. I just don't get it."

Tori frowned. "Is something wrong? Are you and Dr. Guillano not meshing well together? I thought it would be something that would work, especially since she asked for you to be on her rotation."

"She asked for me?" Bella asked, her jaw dropping.

Tori nodded. "You were only supposed to be with her for one night. Dr. Whalen was off the rest of the week, so when Jacqueline started, it was intended that you would switch back to Dr. Whalen because he thought it was a good fit. However, Dr. Guillano insisted, and Dr. Whalen, being as chill as he is, didn't object. He even thought that maybe you would be better off with her because she came from New York and could teach you some of the finer things. He thought it would be a good move for you, and we didn't think anything of it. It was a mutual decision, and it was an easy transition to keep you with Dr. Guillano and put Jacqueline with Dr. Whalen. But if you feel that it isn't the right fit, then maybe we need to do some adjusting."

"It's not that," Bella quickly commented. She leaned against her chair. In reality, she thought that maybe Leona would have been better off without her. She was still making a lot of mistakes and probably causing Leona a lot of headaches. Was Leona just feeling sorry for her? That thought made her queasy. She didn't want her pity.

"I just had no idea. I thought it was something you decided based on the schedules. But if she asked for me, then maybe I'm mistaken."

"Something has clearly happened, though. Wanna talk about it?" Tori leaned against the desk, her eyes locked on Bella's.

Now, Bella wondered if maybe she was opening up a can of worms that she wasn't prepared for. It was best to leave it unsaid, right? But keeping her thoughts and emotions bottled up inside could derail her progress in her training, and her training meant everything for her.

Bella took a deep breath, steeling herself for what she was about to say.

"The other day, I was in Dr. Guillano's office to go over my evaluation." Tori raised an eyebrow, but didn't interrupt, so Bella continued. "Ultimately, she had nothing negative to say, but some of her comments got me thinking...like if nursing is right for me. I'm starting to doubt my choices. I want to help people, but I've focused on being a nurse mostly because that's what my mom did. And it fits well in my life. Plus, I've put four years on hold to be a nurse. But what if I'm just not suited for this and everything I've worked toward is a waste? Because I..."

Bella stopped short of saying she was a failure. She had achieved a lot over the years, but somehow her self-doubts always crept back in. And being so clumsy at nursing so far wasn't helping.

"But why would Dr. Guillano make this suggestion?" Tori asked. "She must've felt she had a reason to say something."

Bella sighed. "I don't know. She said that I show a lot of empathy with the patients. Like when the foster kids were here from Indiana." She shrugged. "I love children, and I don't see why that can't mean I would make a great pediatric nurse. I was left a little confused, like she was hinting that nursing isn't for me."

Tori scrunched up her face. "Looks to me like maybe you didn't take the time to try to get some real answers from her. Ultimately, though, I would say she's only trying to help. All communication I've had with Dr. Guillano has been positive. I really wouldn't worry too much about the matter. But if you want answers, sometimes you just have to insist on them."

Tori looked at Bella oddly before continuing. "But I'm also a little confused about one thing. Did you say your evaluation? What evaluation?"

"The one that we have to go through every few weeks." Bella shrugged. "I don't know, she said it's to make sure we're on the correct path or something."

Tori tilted her head. "I know nothing of that. Guess I'll be looking into that myself. The only evaluation I know of is the end-of-the-program evaluation. That's when they'll either recommend you for a position or see about placing you elsewhere."

Tori's phone started ringing, and she looked down at it. "I have to take this, but I would say you should talk to her. Couldn't hurt." She then answered the call and turned away from the desk.

Bella got up from the nurse's station and headed straight for Leona's office. She had plenty to discuss with her—for starters, why she felt the need to lie to her about the evaluation. Something was wrong, and she wasn't leaving her office until she had all the answers, whether good or bad.

CHAPTER FIVE

Leona

A knock sounded on her door. Leona looked up from her work and saw Bella, whose eyes seemed to have darkened instantly. Leona felt there was a strong sense of urgency as to why Bella was there.

"Bella!" she exclaimed. "Do you need something? I thought I'd just head downstairs to the cafeteria for lunch. Wanna join me?" Leona stood up from her desk, but Bella remained standing by the door, her expression stony.

"I need to get this out there," Bella said, taking two steps into her office. "Why did you want me on your rotation and what was that fake evaluation all about? I talked to Tori, and she knows nothing of an evaluation save for the end-of-program one."

Leona dropped her gaze to her desk. Well, this wasn't exactly something she thought she would have to rush right out to explain. But it was out there, and she couldn't back down from it. If Bella needed answers, then she would give those answers.

"How about you let me get you lunch, and I'll explain?" Leona moved around her desk. "It's my treat, so what do you have to lose? An hour of your time having a meal with me?" She laughed. "And I'll give you the answers you need."

Bella looked over her shoulder, like she was looking for someone. Leona stepped in closer to her and Bella finally turned back around and nodded. "Fine, but I hope this isn't a trap."

Leona moved past her and out her door. She was going to have some serious explaining to do, and she just hoped that Bella wouldn't be upset once she spilled everything out to her. She didn't think she was being mischievous in her attempt to have Bella assigned to her.

She supposed, looking back, it might seem like she had been deceptive, but her intentions were good, if not a bit misguided. Bella had intrigued her, from her looks all the way to her compassion for her patients. She had a yearning to get to know Bella, an interest she tried not to think about too much since it was beyond work appropriate. But she liked to think she could separate her personal and professional life. Above everything, she wanted to mentor Bella and help her gain more confidence so she could succeed. Plus, she had just ended a relationship three months ago and wasn't eager to jump into another one.

They each got their food and headed to a table, where Bella seemed quiet and reserved. She had barely spoken two words when they were ordering their lunch.

"You're not very talkative," Leona began.

"Just processing, I suppose," Bella quietly remarked. "Not sure what you're going to tell me in order to explain the secrecy and all, but I guess I'll soon find out. Right?"

"That's the plan," Leona replied, taking a bite of her salad. She slowly chewed on her food, then swallowed it. Bella didn't strike her as someone who would wait too long to get the answers she wanted. It wasn't like she could wait for Bella to forget about it.

"So, what'd you ask?" Leona joked. Bella looked up, making Leona laugh. "I'm kidding. You want to know why I wanted you on my rotation?"

"Or, rather, why you didn't tell me that you purposely asked for me," Bella responded. "That would be a nice start."

Leona shrugged. "I guess I didn't think it was that big of a deal. When I first started here, I felt like it was a huge change. I was coming into new surroundings, and I guess a part of me didn't want to be the new one in town. You know? When I heard good things from Mitch...Dr. Whalen, it seemed to click that maybe you were the one I should have working rounds with me. It was out of respect that I felt compelled to pull you on my rotation. I didn't tell you because I didn't think it was something I had to say. Plus, I thought that maybe you wouldn't want to work with me every shift. I didn't want you to think I was forcing you to do something you didn't want to do."

"I suppose I can understand that," Bella responded.

Leona exhaled, happy that explanation was enough. Was she doing the wrong thing, putting herself in closer proximity to a nurse she had romantic interest in? No, she was only trying to help Bella. She could ignore the attraction. And Bella might be in a relationship, which made everything complicated. Bella seemed stressed, and revealing her interest in her young mentee would only stress her out more. They were coworkers and that's how it would stay.

"Happy to hear," Leona said, digging into her salad and ignoring the fact that Bella's eyes were still on hers. As the minutes dragged on, she couldn't ignore it any further. "Oh, yeah," she mumbled. "You had another question."

Bella nodded. "Tori knew nothing about said evaluation. She's the head nurse, and I would think that she would know what evaluations needed doing. So, I'm guessing that was only a ruse. What I don't know is, why?"

Leona dropped her fork and took a long swig of her water. "I believe, in the beginning, I told you that I like to get to know the people I work with. A few weeks ago, we were talking, and you seemed to not want to give any answers or be open personally. This was my way of getting to know you a little bit more." She sighed, taking another drink. "I'm sorry for making it happen in a not-so-normal manner. I shouldn't have lied to you. For that, I sincerely apologize."

Bella shook her head, staring down at her fries and sandwich. It looked like she was processing the news and not sure how to take it. "I don't want the fact that I falsely said you were being evaluated to cloud our working relationship, Bella. I really am sorry."

Bella sighed. "What I don't get," she began, looking up for the first time since Leona apologized, "is how you don't think I'm cut out to be a nurse. That upset me."

"I did not say that," Leona argued. "I wanted to know your reasons for being a nurse and help you be open to the possibility that there are other careers out there. There's a learning curve here, but it's also okay to consider a different option if things don't work out. I only said that because you always seem so stressed, and nursing should be your passion. And again, that's not a negative thing. That's all."

Bella looked like she was going to say something, but Leona held up her hand. "Let me finish, please. I think you're a hard worker and that you've grown as an employee over the past few weeks. That's saying a lot. I worked with a lot of people in New York, and I would definitely say they would be better off not working in a hospital. You told me why you decided to become a nurse, and I admire your reasons. I absolutely think you could make a fine nurse. Don't believe that I'm saying you're not capable, because I don't feel that way—only that you should remain open to new possibilities. I would give that advice to anyone."

She paused when she saw Bella's eyes softening quite a bit. "If I hurt your feelings in any way, I'm sorry." She wanted to reach out to touch Bella's hand but stopped herself. That wouldn't be a very coworker-like gesture.

"Thank you," Bella replied.

In that moment, relief washed over Leona; Bella even held a slight smile on her lips. Maybe they could get into their meal and just relax and enjoy it. Bella's phone buzzed, and she checked the screen, rolling her eyes.

Leona couldn't resist probing because she didn't get a definite answer last time she fished for information about Bella's personal life. "Boyfriend trouble?" she asked casually.

Bella gave a slight nod, focusing on her food again.

Though Leona's stomach sank, she was glad Bella was in a relationship. It might help Leona keep her distance.

Before she could think of how to change the subject, her phone vibrated and she checked the message, frowning.

Trauma alert in the ER department. Young male bicyclist, hit by a car. Patient, Bradly Carver.

Leona looked up, her eyes wide.

"Something wrong?" Bella asked.

Leona hesitated, then nodded. "It's fine, though. Finish up your meal and I'll see you back at work in fifteen. I have to take care of this."

"Is it a patient? I can come back early and clock in." Bella stood up, but Leona needed first to see what she was coming into. If this was the Brad Carver they had seen a few weeks ago, she didn't want Bella to walk headfirst into the scene without knowing what they were up against.

"It's all right. You enjoy the rest of your food. No need for you to come." Leona got up and grabbed her salad. "See you upstairs."

She hurried and dropped the food into a garbage bin and briskly walked out of the cafeteria and to the elevator, hoping that Bella wouldn't see the urgency in her movement.

She took the elevator up to the main floor to the ER and didn't stop until she reached the front desk. "Where is he?" she asked.

"Trauma room three," the woman behind the desk said. "The trauma team is evaluating him, but I saw on the chart that he was in your service the last time he was here. I thought you should know."

"Thanks." She quickly moved away from the desk and headed to the room.

When she entered, a man was looking down at Brad, speaking firmly but kindly. "You're going to be okay, buddy." A surgeon in scrubs was examining the boy while a nurse stood at his side, assessing the wounds on his body.

"My name is Dr. Leona Guillano. I took care of Brad last time he was here. Can you tell me what happened and what relation you are to the patient?"

The man turned to her, his eyes glossy. "My name is Shane. I, I'm..." He turned back to look at Brad. "I'm the one that hit him." He shook his head. "I don't know what happened. It was all a blur."

"Everything's going to be all right," Leona responded. "Just please wait outside."

As Leona turned to Brad, the trauma surgeon began barking out orders for X-rays and blood work. Leona's heart started racing. She'd help the trauma team get the situation under control and then let Bella know what was going on. There would be plenty of time to ask questions later.

LEONA GRABBED THE PHONE, THEN DROPPED IT BACK INTO THE cradle. How was she going to start the conversation? *Hello, Bella? Brad was brought to the emergency room and just transferred to the ICU.*

It still felt so unreal. How could a young child like that be playing one minute and the next, fighting for his life? If anything, that only showed how fragile life was. There wasn't a minute to waste in telling Bella the news.

She grabbed the phone again and dialed upstairs to the pediatric ward. She was surprised Bella hadn't already gotten the news, but if she had, Leona was confident Bella would have rushed downstairs to see Brad for herself. Bella had compassion like that.

"This is Tori," a voice answered.

"Hey, Tori. It's Dr. Guillano. Is Bella around?"

"Ummmmm...Oh yes, there she is. I'll grab her for you. Bella, it's Dr. Guillano."

Leona tapped her fingers on the desk and stared down at the counter. When she noticed her tapping, she quickly stopped and slipped her hand into her pocket to get rid of her nerves.

"Hello?"

"Hey, Bella. I need you to come down to the ER for a minute."

"Is everything okay? Are they short-staffed? What's going on?" Bella rattled off at least a dozen more questions in the time it took for Leona to release a breath.

"I'll discuss it with you once you get down here. Please."

"I'll be right there," Bella said, just before Leona dropped the phone back into the cradle.

While she waited for Bella to arrive, Leona recalled how she had quickly left the cafeteria to get to the ER when she got the text about Brad, but things had seemed to be improving slowly over their conversation. That was a relief, because it meant that hope wasn't all lost for them to find a good working relationship.

It wasn't long before the elevator doors opened and Bella stepped out of the small enclosure. She headed over to where Leona stood, and Leona quickly grabbed her arm and escorted her away from the main lobby.

"Now you're scaring me," Bella mumbled.

"Sorry, I just need to do this away from everyone," Leona said, pulling her into a small and secluded office. After she closed the door, she turned to Bella's wide-eyed expression. "Do you remember Brad Carver?" Leona asked.

"Yeah. The little boy from the foster home in Indianapolis. How could I forget?" Bella's eyes bugged out. "Is he sick? Is he here?"

She started to push past Leona, but Leona reached out and touched her arm. "Hold on, Bella. He's here, but you can't see him quite yet. He was involved in a vehicle-pedestrian accident. A truck didn't see him and rounded the corner. He rode his bike right into this man's path and he was rushed here, and he's in critical condition."

Bella turned and stared at Leona; tears stuck in the corner of her eyes. "I don't understand. What's he doing in Chicago?"

Leona shrugged. "All I know is that they decided to keep him in Chicago in case he had any more health issues and the Indy foster home was overrun with children. A family fostered him immediately once he got put into the system. Unfortunately, this family has six kids already, many of whom are fighting health issues, and they weren't observant enough when he went out on his bike."

"Where is he?" Bella asked.

"He was just moved to the ICU. He'll have some of the best doctors supervising him, but both of his legs are broken, and he has broken ribs. He also has a head contusion. It's a bumpy ride for him, but they're all confident that they'll be able to nurse him back to health."

"And his foster parents?" Bella asked.

"They're here and being questioned, as is the guy that hit him. He didn't run, so that's a good thing. If he hadn't gotten him to the hospital in record time, we could have had a much worse situation."

"I want to see him," Bella replied quietly.

Leona nodded. She knew that Bella would want to have a chance to visit him, but Leona had to prepare her first. "You aren't used to seeing patients like this. You have to be certain you're prepared for that."

"I want to see him," Bella said again, with no hesitation.

Leona led the way out of the room and headed across the hallway. When they walked into the room, they were the only ones in there. She looked over to Bella and saw that Bella's eyes were red. Leona reached out and touched her arm.

"You have to be strong for him. Understand that?"

Bella nodded.

"I'll give you a few minutes."

Leona left, allowing Bella some time alone. When she got out into the hallway, she looked over to the waiting room, where the couple that currently fostered Brad was sitting. They were talking, and she even saw a few smiles and chuckles shared between the two of them. Those smiles bothered her.

When she approached them, the woman looked up and her face turned solemn. "How he's doing?" she asked.

"Mrs. Chadwick, with all due respect, I question if you really care."

Mrs. Chadwick's eyes bugged out and her jaw dropped. "How dare you?" her husband bristled.

"He's six years old. How could you leave him outside by himself, long enough that he would dart into a street? Anything could have happened, but you were too bothered to even pay attention to the littlest child that needed you."

"You don't know us," Mrs. Chadwick said, standing up from her chair.

Leona didn't flinch. "I know that I saw you two laughing just now. This child might not ever laugh again. If he dies, that's on you, and I know for a fact CPS will revoke your foster license."

"Is that a threat?" Mr. Chadwick asked.

Leona tossed a look over to him and shook her head. "No threat, just saying that if I have my say you won't ever get the chance be the cause of any other child in pain again." With that, she spun on her heel and hurried back to the hallway, just as Bella stepped out of Brad's room. Bella met Leona's eyes.

"How is he?" Leona asked.

"He looks so fragile." She looked past Leona and Leona saw a darkness in Bella's eyes. "Are those his foster parents?" she asked.

Leona nodded and Bella started to walk toward them, but Leona pulled her back.

"I took care of it," she said. "I'm sure they got my message."

Bella shot a look to Leona, and they stood there for a short while, their eyes locked on each other.

Leona slowly pulled her hand away from the place on Bella's lower back. She had felt heat radiating up her spine when she touched her, but she had to force herself to step away from her. "I'm sorry I had to be the one to tell you the news."

Bella slowly nodded. "I'm glad you did, though." She sighed and looked over to the room. "We should probably get back to work."

"You don't have to stay, you know. If you feel you're not in the mood, I can cover for you. You're free to get out of here."

"If I leave, I'll probably get stuck thinking about Brad the entire time I'm home, so I might as well just stay."

Leona understood that, but she wasn't sure Bella would concentrate as they worked the rest of the shift. But she wasn't going to be the one that pushed her to leave, especially when Leona wanted to keep tabs on her and make sure she wasn't falling into a depressed state. If this was how she could watch out for Bella, she wouldn't complain about that.

CHAPTER SIX

Bella

B ella kept her hand on top of Brad's. The longer she stayed there, the smaller he seemed to get. It'd been three days, and he still hadn't opened his eyes. The doctor said it was normal, as his brain was healing, and she shouldn't worry about it, but that was all Bella could do. Worry. She bowed her head.

"Lord, he's too young to come to you. Please watch over this little guy."

She opened her eyes and stared at Brad's little face. The swelling had gone down, so that was a good sign. Another thing the doctors had told her. She brushed her hand across his cheek. She just wanted to see him open his eyes. She looked down at her watch and groaned. If she didn't leave, she would be late for her class.

"I'll see you tomorrow, Brad," she whispered. "Rest well." She squeezed his hand, then got up from the bed. She turned just in time to see Leona turning to leave. Bella cleared her throat, making Leona turn to look at her. "I didn't hear you come in," Bella said. Leona kept the door open and Bella stepped through, Leona following after her.

"Didn't mean to interrupt. I thought you left work an hour ago, though."

"I didn't have to be at school quite yet and thought I would check up

on our patient. Well, not our patient, but you know what I mean..."
Bella's voice dropped, and Leona simply nodded. "That doesn't change
the fact that you were about to leave, like you didn't want me to know you
were there."

Leona gave a weak smile. "It wasn't that I didn't want you to know I
was there. I just wanted to give you ample time to spend time with him.
Any change?"

"In three days, there hasn't been a single change. But Dr. Boxell said
that's not necessarily a bad thing. No change also means he isn't getting
worse. So that's promising."

"Right," Leona replied, her eyes a tinge brighter. "Gotta look at the
positives."

Bella nodded. "Are you still working?" Bella asked. "It was nice of you
to check up on him."

"Well, I just thought that I would check to make sure his health wasn't
getting worse. Didn't expect to bump into you." She lifted her gaze to
Bella's. "You really should get home, though. You look exhausted."

Bella groaned. She felt exhausted. Every bit of her body ached, and she
would have done anything to crawl into bed at that very moment, or at
least slip into a nice warm bath. "Class starts in twenty minutes. I don't
think I'll be getting rest anytime soon. But that's okay because in the end
it will be all worth it, right?" Bella laughed and covered her face in dismay.

"It will be worth it, if you don't work yourself into the ground. That's
the fine line you're fighting."

Leona reached out and touched Bella's arm. Bella dropped her hands
from her face, making eye contact with Leona. There was an instant
spark the moment Leona touched her. Bella tried to steady herself, but
the warmth of having Leona near was undeniable. It seemed to grow
every shift they spent together, and they even seemed to be growing
closer.

But Bella feared that maybe they were getting too close. Leona was a
woman, and Bella couldn't be having these kinds of reactions. On the
other hand, maybe it was the lack of sleep that was quickly making her
mind all weird. Yeah, it was definitely just her being delusional and sleep
deprived. Bella was sure.

"I'll do my best to get some rest, but I'm sure I'll be fine," Bella said, quickly stepping away from Leona. "I really should be getting changed and heading to class."

"Of course. I'll see you tomorrow?"

Bella nodded. "I'll be here, bright-eyed and everything." Bella smiled, which seemed to bring a smile to Leona. Bella waved goodbye and turned, heading to the elevator. Once she was inside and the doors were closed, she leaned back against the elevator wall. Leona's smile still played in her mind and part of her didn't want to push that image away.

The doors opened, and she headed to the breakroom, relieved no one was in there. She reached her locker and pulled her clothes out, able to change in private.

She grabbed her purse and bag of scrubs, then slammed her locker shut. The sooner she got out of the hospital, the sooner she would be able to get Leona out of her mind. Or so she hoped. It slowly felt like Leona was the only thing she could think about these days.

As Bella pulled into the parking lot of her school, her phone started ringing. She looked over at the caller ID on her Bluetooth and her face fell —which made her instantly regret that feeling. "Hey," she said, answering the call.

"I've missed you," Jackson said, making her heart tug even harder. That wasn't what she wanted him to say, especially when she had her mind focused on another person. But it was the one thing that made her push Leona out of her head.

"I know. I promise we'll get together soon. Work is even more hectic than before. There's this boy and...Well, we'll hopefully be able to discuss that soon."

Jackson sighed. "It feels so long since we've seen each other. But I know your heart. And while it's a struggle now, it's only short-lived. Before we know it, you'll be graduated and we'll be able to spend all the time we have together. Right?"

Bella fell back against her seat. Jackson was so supportive, and it only made her guilt about not being able to plan dates worse. With everything going on at the hospital, she hadn't even thought of graduation. But it was true. With only three months and two days to go until she graduated, they would have every reason to believe that they would be able to be together every minute after that. Sure, she would hopefully still have a job, but it wouldn't be the mountain of work she was currently experiencing.

Then there would be marriage and children, and everything would fall into place, just the way she had planned. Somehow, that thought didn't give her as much comfort anymore.

"Right?" Jackson asked again.

"Oh. Of course. We'll have the rest of our lives together after just a few more stressful months. Unfortunately, I have to run to class now. Sorry I can't talk longer. I don't want to be late and have everyone stare at me again. That's never fun." She gave a light laugh. "But I hope to see you soon, Jackson. We'll talk later."

"Okay. Love you. Bye."

She hung up and hurriedly jumped out of the car to run through campus, stepping foot inside her classroom two minutes before her class would begin. It was time to refocus her thoughts on her schoolwork and put both Jackson and Leona to the side.

"There's something I need to tell you, Bella."

The way Leona looked at her had Bella clenching her jaw. What was it that Leona wanted to tell her? And where were they? Everything seemed...surreal? But Bella didn't have time to think about that as she moved closer to Leona, feeling the heat from their bodies intertwine. What would it be like to kiss Leona? Would her lips be soft?

Jackson always had dry lips. His kisses were nice, but somehow Bella imagined a kiss from Leona would be on a new level. Electric.

"I'm all ears," Bella gasped.

Leona looked ready to pounce, which sent Bella's mind reeling with fantasies she never let herself admit to. She couldn't be thinking these dirty thoughts about her superior, yet all she wanted was to crash their lips together, give herself completely to this kind, confident, and charismatic older woman. Leona always listened to her and kept her grounded, even when she freaked out about yet another work mistake. Leona gave her confidence, and it was making Bella's urges for her more intense. Maybe it was time to finally give in.

Leona moved closer, whispering, "There's a girl in room four-one-two that needs ice water."

Bella frowned. If Leona kept things this heated, then Bella would also need ice water. But Leona turned away from her, and that only confused Bella even more. Maybe she was reading the signs all wrong. Had she been that crazy to think that Leona would ever be sexually attracted to her?

Bella went to grab the water and ice, which had suddenly appeared on a table that had come out of nowhere. She shook her head, heading to the room with glass in hand. She was there to do a job and needed to remind herself of that as many times as she had to. She wasn't there to fantasize over the doctor, as if she were reading one of those erotic romance novels.

When she got to the room, she saw that it was all...pink. There was no patient, only a big, plush bed. She saw Leona standing in front of her. She was naked from the waist up. Bella's jaw dropped, and she dropped the glass, which shattered.

"What are you doing?" Bella stuttered, though she wasn't opposed to whatever it was that was going on. Leona was sexy and alluring.

Leona had this sensual smirk on her face as she moved closer to Bella. "Do you think it's gone unnoticed the way you look at me? Because I can assure you it hasn't. Those eyes of yours have been locked on me every minute for the last week. And I've loved it."

She grabbed Bella's hand and pulled her closer. With one tug, she placed Bella's hand over her right breast and squeezed. "How does that feel?" Leona whispered.

Bella could only let out a soft moan before Leona passionately pulled her into a kiss. Leona sat down on the bed, pulling Bella down on her. Bella straddled her legs, and they enthusiastically made out with one another inside the hospital room. The front of Bella's pants were already warm and moist from the way Leona passionately kissed her, embracing her and then slowly groping her. Their tongues thrashed wildly against one another. Bella cupped each of Leona's breasts in her palms, kneading them thoroughly between her fingers as Leona made energetic noises of pleasure.

Leona pulled away from the embrace as Bella flicked Leona's nipples between her fingers. Leona's jaw clenched, and she smiled.

"Now what?" Bella panted.

"You should get your phone," Leona said, licking her lower lip.

Bella frowned. Her phone?

She then heard the faint sound of her phone and jerked awake. Bella stared at the books that sat open in front of her, the fog of sleep slow to clear from her mind even as her heart erratically pounded inside her chest.

It was only a dream, even though it had felt so real.

She reached out and grabbed her phone. Jackson's name flashed on the screen. After the heated dream she had just woken up from, the last thing she wanted to do was talk to Jackson. But that was also the reason she had to answer the phone. She felt guilty that it wasn't him featuring in her erotic dreams. Why was she getting so obsessed with another woman?

"Hey," she answered, stifling a yawn. "Good thing you called me because I fell asleep studying and I have a test in a couple of days that I need to focus my attention on."

He laughed. "That's my job," he said.

That brought a slight smile to Bella's lips. "Anyway, good to hear from you."

"Well, thought I would call and see if you had school or work tomorrow evening?"

Bella leaned back in her seat. She had a twelve-hour shift and then expected—or hoped—she would get a full eight hours of sleep before she had classes the following day. But hearing him inquire about her plans left her thinking. Maybe, to get out of her head, she should do what she could to make sure they did get together.

"Were you thinking dinner?" she asked.

"You guessed it. I just think we could use this. What do you say? I won't pester you about it, but I hope it works out."

She couldn't turn down those words. Even though she needed the rest, she had to do something to salvage her relationship with Jackson. "I'm free. Let's do this."

"Great! I'll text you the details after I get a reservation. Can't wait to see you."

"Same." She hung up and nodded to herself. That was the best option to get together with her boyfriend, and then she could stop fantasizing about another person, especially her older female boss.

Bella looked at her anatomy book, which was opened on the kitchen table. She tried focusing on the words on the pages, but the dream invading her mind. She closed the book and sighed. There wasn't any use. If she couldn't get Leona out of her mind, she might as well go to bed and study tomorrow during her breaks. Hopefully, the dream would be out of her system and she wouldn't get caught up in more crazy thoughts by then. At that moment, there wasn't much hope in that.

CHAPTER SEVEN

Leona

"**A**ny pain here?" Leona asked as she pressed on Cassidy Black's stomach. The twelve-year-old winced, and Leona smiled. "Got my answer. I'll have a nurse get the surgeon prepared. We'll get that appendix out tonight."

"Mom!" the girl said, shooting a panicked look past Leona.

Leona chuckled and looked over her shoulder at the concerned expression on Cassidy's mother. "The sooner we get this appendix out, the better. We don't want it to burst. The surgeon on call is one of the best." She winked at Cassidy. "You're going to be just fine."

"Thank you, Dr. Guillano," her mother said, stepping up to her daughter's side.

"My pleasure." She looked back at Cassidy. "I'll leave you alone for a while. Just imagine how much better you'll feel this time tomorrow. Trust me. You'll be thanking me."

Cassidy simply nodded, and Leona left her room. She walked to the front desk, where Tori sat, on the phone. Tori looked up just as she approached. "Just in time. This call is for you."

Leona grabbed the phone from her. "Will you let the surgeon know we have the surgical consent for Cassidy Black and she's ready to go? The sooner the better."

"Oh, sure." Tori left the nurse's station as Leona took the call.

"This is Dr. Guillano," she said.

"Hey, Leona. It's Dr. Redding. I just wanted to let you know that little Bradly Carver has woken up. CPS has banned his foster parents from seeing him, at least for the time being, and I think he would feel better seeing a familiar face."

"That's amazing news!" Leona said. "Give me a few minutes and I'll be up." She dropped the phone into the receiver and hurried to the stockroom where she had last seen Bella.

Bella looked up when Leona burst through the door. "Just finishing up here, then I'm off duty. But if you needed something..."

"I just got off the phone with Dr. Redding from the ICU. He tells me that Brad is awake. I thought you'd want to see him before you go."

"What?" Bella squealed. She stood up and threw her arms around Leona. Leona instinctively wrapped her arms around her, and they held onto the embrace, both emotional about the news. She was excited to see Brad awake, as was Bella. It felt like he'd been unconscious for too long.

Slowly Bella pulled her arms down from the embrace. "I...I'm sorry," Bella said.

Leona shook her head. "Don't apologize. It's great news. You wanna go?"

"Um, yeah. Let me get clocked out and then I'll meet you at his room."

Leona nodded and left the room. As Bella brushed past her, Leona stared at her backside, her mind racing. Just the feel of Bella's arms around her left her wanting more. She shivered, trying mentally to shake that feeling. She knew too well how much she wanted to keep that feeling going, but for so many reasons, she was forced to ignore the inner heat that coursed through her body.

She took the elevator up to the pediatric ICU. Leona waited just outside Brad's door, not wanting to see Brad before Bella had a chance to get to the room. Ten minutes later, Bella got off the elevator. She was dressed in a skirt and low-cut blouse. She wore a blazer over the blouse, but it didn't hide the cleavage that stared Leona straight in the face. Leona quickly looked away, willing her lips to not quiver. Why was Bella dressed like that? And would Leona ever have the opportunity to see her dressed so provocatively again?

She let her eyes lift long enough to brush over Bella's breasts and then to her eyes. "You're dressed, um..." Her words died and Bella tilted her head.

"Dressed um, what?" Bella asked.

Leona shrugged. "Just not used to seeing you in anything but scrubs. That's all."

"Do I not look okay?" Bella asked; her eyes dipped down to her cleavage and Leona was forced to follow Bella's gaze. Her breath hitched, and she mentally groaned. *Stop it, Leona. It will only cause you heartache.*

"You look great," Leona said, then bit down on her tongue. "I mean, you look fine. We should get in there so you can go wherever you need to go. It's obviously not anywhere in the hospital," Leona mumbled, pushing through to Brad's room.

Brad was seated in his bed and already looked a million times better even with the swelling and the oxygen coming out through his nose. "Hello, Brad." Bella smiled brightly. "Do you remember us?"

His eyes lit up, and he nodded. "Bella and Lona," he said.

Leona laughed. "Close enough." She reached out and ruffled her fingers through his hair. "How do you feel?"

He frowned. "Sore." He winced and touched his head.

"That will be something you'll be feeling for a few days," Leona reluctantly told him. "But before you know it, you'll be ready to jump right out of this bed."

"And ride my bike outside?" he asked, his eyes lit up.

Bella tossed a look over to Leona and Leona smirked. "If that's what you want," Leona answered.

Bella grabbed a chair and pulled it up to his bed. "Do you remember much of what happened?" she asked.

He frowned and shook his head. "They said I was hit by a car, but I don't remember."

"That's all right," Bella said. "You might get your memory back at some point."

"And if you don't," Leona continued, "that's all right, too."

Bella nodded in agreement. The door opened and Leona heard footsteps behind them. She turned and saw a woman entering the room. The woman smiled and approached the bed.

"Candice Gordon," she said in greeting, holding her hand out to Leona and then Bella.

"I'm Bella and this is Leona—Dr. Guillano. We're the nurse and doctor that helped Brad when he was here at the beginning of the month," Bella explained.

"Yes, I have you down on my list. I'm the social worker here in Chicago that will be helping Brad while he's in the system, which, unfortunately, he'll be going back into once he leaves the hospital."

Leona looked over at Brad; his eyes were slightly closed. "Hey buddy, you should try to get some rest. We'll be in later to see you." She looked over at Bella, who nodded.

"Goodbye for now," Bella said, leaning in and kissing his forehead. "Rest well."

"Thank you Bella and Lona." Brad yawned and shifted in the bed as Bella moved to Leona's side.

"May we speak to you for a moment out in the hall?" Leona asked.

Candice nodded, and the three of them left his room. It was Leona who was first to speak once the door was closed. "I'm assuming that his foster parents are out of the picture?"

Candice smiled gently. "With all due respect, I can't explain the case to you. I can just say that we're making sure we're doing what we can to keep that little boy safe."

"And we appreciate that," Bella said.

Leona looked over at Bella and they met each other's gaze. There was a smile on Bella's lips that made Leona respond with the same. Somehow this connection between the two of them had suddenly become much more magnetic.

"I should get back in to be with him. He's in good hands, I can assure you."

"Thank you, Ms. Gordon," Leona replied, turning her attention back to the social worker.

"It's just Candice," she said with a smile before going back into Brad's room.

Leona turned back to Bella. "Well, it's good to see that he appears to be doing well."

"The best news ever," Bella replied. She looked down at her watch and winced. "I'm going to be late," she said, looking back up to Leona.

It was obvious she was ready to head out on a hot date with her boyfriend. Leona wouldn't lie and say she wasn't jealous, but she wasn't going to show that. "Enjoy your night, Bella."

"Thank you. I'll be seeing you." Bella gave a slight wave and headed to the elevator.

Because Leona didn't want to get stuck on the elevator with Bella, she settled on using the stairs. She took a leisurely walk down the steps, her thoughts getting locking onto Bella. She caught herself smiling as those thoughts floated through her mind. She hesitated at the door to the pediatric floor and stood there, clutching the handle. If she ever caught herself hugging Bella again, she didn't think she would be able to pull herself away. She would have to make sure that didn't happen.

She opened the door and stepped into the corridor of the ward. As she rounded the corner, Jacqueline looked up and immediately waved her over. She released a huge sigh as Leona reached her.

"I wasn't sure where you were and the desk is swamped and Dr. Whalen has me..." She stopped and took a breath as Leona gawked at her. "Sorry, you have a phone call." She thrust it out in front of her and Leona smiled.

"Thanks, Jacqueline."

Jacqueline was a bit too flighty for Leona's liking. It was another reason why she had chosen Bella as her mentee. It was obvious, though, that the main reason was the attraction that Leona felt for Bella.

"Hello?"

The line seemed dead as Leona pulled the phone away from her ear and stared at it, like it would miraculously tell her who was on the other end. She put the phone back to her ear.

"*Hello*?" She spoke again.

"Leona?"

Leona fell against the counter. She clutched the phone tightly between her fingers so that she wouldn't drop it. "Why are you calling me? How'd you find me?"

"I, I, you see..."

Leona's breath hitched as she continued clinging to the phone.

"I tried every hospital. I didn't think I would ever be able to reach you. Yet here you are."

"Here I am, wondering why you're calling me. The way we left things..." Leona released a breath. "You aren't supposed to be calling me."

"I miss you, Le. Don't you miss me?"

Leona shook her head, angered by how Cicily apparently felt it was fine just to reach out because she thought Leona missed her. They had broken up. It was supposed to be a clean break.

"I'm not ready to talk to you."

"I said I'm sorry. Doesn't that account for anything?"

It'd been three months since Leona walked away from New York and left that life behind her. That included walking away from Cicily, the one woman she thought she might settle down with. Now, getting this call from her, Leona was reminded how much pain and anger she felt toward this woman. Cicily hadn't crossed her mind even once in the past three months, other than in the periphery, when Leona thought about how grateful she was to have a clean break. While there were still some complicated, residual feelings, Leona wouldn't tell her she missed her and give Cicily false hope.

"I've forgiven you, Cicily. Even before you asked for it. But I see things clearly, and what we had wasn't forever. I'm moving on and I suggest you do the same."

"Leona!" Cicily argued.

It pained Leona to hang up when she heard the way Cicily's voice broke. She didn't want to hurt her, but the sooner Cicily knew she wasn't holding onto their relationship, the better off Cicily would be. She turned to Jacqueline.

"If she calls again, tell her I'm not here."

Jacqueline nodded, her eyes wide.

This call was actually what Leona needed, to know she was on the right track and there was only one woman who occupied her thoughts day and night. Unfortunately, that woman wasn't available. That was the pain that hurt the most. So until then, Leona would just have to find a way to get over Bella Strong.

CHAPTER EIGHT

Bella

Bella rushed into the restaurant. She was sure she was going to be late and have to apologize repeatedly to Jackson for not being there, but she made it with two minutes to spare. Spotting Jackson at a nearby table, she waved and rushed up to him.

"I thought I wouldn't make it on time," Bella said.

Jackson stood and pulled her into his arms, kissing her with a hunger that took her by surprise. She froze, doing her best to kiss him back, but not feeling the same intensity.

She finally pressed her hand against his chest. "That was a warm welcome," she said.

"That's what happens when I miss you," he replied.

She blushed and took a seat, letting the weight release from her chest. "It's good to be sitting down. Today was a rough day," Bella said. She smiled and added, "It got better as I was about to clock out."

"You knew you were coming to see me?" Jackson asked, a teasing grin on his lips.

"Well, that, and you know that foster boy I told you about who got hit by a car?"

Jackson nodded, then took a sip of his water.

Bella beamed. "He woke up today. He's going to be fine."

"That's great news, babe," he said. "Oh, and by the way, we're not going to be dining alone tonight."

Bella frowned and turned around to look where his eyes had wandered. Her jaw dropped as her mom, dad, and sister approached the table. "Mom? Dad? Veronica?"

She jumped up and hugged each of them, surprised and confused why they were there. They were all smiles, but when she looked over to Jackson, she saw that his grin was the biggest. "What's going on?" she asked.

"Can't your family just want to come see you?" her mom asked. "It's been forever. Or at least feels like it's been forever."

Her mother's grin widened, and Bella had to admit it was good to see all of them, even if she had been kept out of the loop. It wasn't like Jackson to take the initiative to do something like this. His wide smile showed that he was proud of himself.

"I'm just happy to see you all," Bella admitted. They sat down and she grinned and shook her head. "I should have known something was up, since we're at a larger table. You're so sneaky, Jackson." She reached out and touched his arm.

As she touched him, Bella realized again that she didn't feel the same spark she had felt when she had hugged Leona earlier. When she and Jackson had kissed moments ago, there had been this deep passion in their embrace that had come from him, but she hadn't felt the chemistry pouring from them like she had around Leona. That struck her to her core. What in the world was wrong with her? Jackson was part of her plan, not Leona. She brought her hand back and proceeded to look down at her menu, trying not to let her unsettled feelings distract her from an evening with her family.

After they ordered, Veronica, her parents, and Jackson got caught up in conversation, with Jackson focusing his attention on her sister. Veronica was just talking about cheerleading and a book report, but Jackson acted as if Veronica was talking about the most thrilling things. He seemed intrigued by it all. Seeing him like that couldn't help but put a smile on Bella's lips.

Jackson was a good man by anyone's standards. When they got

married, she would be the luckiest woman in the world. When had that wound up not being enough?

"What are you thinking about, honey?"

She jerked when her mother reached out and touched her arm. She turned and looked at her, then gave a slight shrug. "Nothing. Everything." Bella smirked. "You probably know more than anyone what I'm going through. Tired and not sure which way is right and which is left."

Bella reached out and grabbed her glass of water. She held onto it for a moment, suddenly feeling overwhelmed.

"I'm sure it's extremely intense," Bella's mom said. "But you have to remember, I didn't have to worry about school. I had already graduated when I started working at a hospital. You're ahead of the game. It's exciting, though, right?"

Bella nodded. "And overwhelming," she whispered. Her mother squeezed her hand.

"It will get better. Trust me on that." Her quiet words were meant to reassure Bella, and Bella wished she could believe them.

The waitress brought them their food and Bella spent time just focusing on eating and not making small talk. She looked up when she noticed there was a lull at the table.

"So, Veronica..." Bella started. "How's school going?"

Her sister groaned and scrunched up her face. "Depends on what part of school you're referring to," she said. "Classes? Ugh!" Her sister dipped a fry into her ketchup. "As I was telling Jackson, the highlight has been cheerleading, and this summer I plan on going to cheerleading camp." Her eyes lit up.

"That's cool. But you know, school is really where you need to make sure you keep your grades up. If they fall, then the pyramid will tumble, because you won't be there to hold it up."

Veronica nodded. "That's what Mom keeps saying." She rolled her eyes. "But really...What am I going to need all this math mumbo jumbo for?"

Bella laughed. "When you're done with school, where do you see yourself? I mean, when you go off to college."

Veronica shrugged. "I thought maybe I would be a vet tech or something. I love animals."

Bella waved her finger. "And that's exactly why you'll need math—calculations for medicine, or even at the register. I wouldn't count out your education just yet. Down the road you may see that you were way off in your calculations."

Veronica smirked. "I see what you did there." She shrugged. "I'm doing my best to keep my grades up. I study every night and I do like most of my classes."

"That's good to hear," Bella said.

The table went quiet as they all enjoyed their food. Before Bella knew it, Veronica and Jackson were talking about other small topics. Bella appreciated being able to just listen and not have to participate in the conversation. But in that small time frame, her mind wandered back to Leona. She wondered what she was doing at that very moment. Possibly still at the hospital.

"Honey..." Jackson reached out and touched her arm. She jerked and looked over at him.

His eyebrows furrowed. "You look like you've seen a ghost." He laughed. "I was talking to you and you looked like you were somewhere far away."

I was. And with another woman.

"Sorry." Her face flushed, and she touched her cheek. It was warm. "What were you saying?"

"Just that it was good everyone was able to get together tonight."

Bella smiled and nodded. "All thanks to you," she replied.

He slipped his fingers around hers and squeezed her hand, then looked around the table as Bella's eyes dropped to their intertwined hands. Bella's mom cleared her throat and Bella looked over to her. Her eyes narrowed and she arched an eyebrow at her daughter.

Bella forced a smile onto her face. "It was great to see you all," she said, and she meant it.

"Let's just hope we're able to get together again before too much time has passed," her dad commented, and everyone agreed.

Ten minutes later, they were all outside the restaurant and hugging one another, giving their goodbyes. "Love you, Mom," Bella said, hugging her tighter.

When she started to pull away, her mother rested her lips to her ear. "I think you need to talk to Jackson," she whispered.

Bella frowned and looked at her, and her mom gave a weak smile. At that moment, Bella knew her mother completely seen through her during their time together. She wondered how much her mother had figured out. She wasn't ready to have any deep conversation with Jackson, either easy or hard. She couldn't. It would throw everything off. She just needed to concentrate again on what she wanted out of life and stop thinking about Leona.

"Love you all," Bella called, waving at her family as she and Jackson turned away and headed toward her car.

"I'm parked over here, too," he said, pointing.

"Yeah, I saw your car when I got here," Bella replied.

When they reached her car, she turned to him. "Tonight was nice. Thanks for thinking of it."

He grinned. "I'm glad you enjoyed it."

He wrapped his arm around her and pulled her to him. As they kissed, she felt the hunger coming from him, and she pressed her hand against his chest, ending the kiss. It wound up a bit awkward, but she thought about what her mother had just said to her. She always knew Jackson felt stronger emotions for her than she did for him, and she figured that would grow with time and dedication to their marriage. But after experiencing that intense spark with Leona, something she'd never experienced before, nothing felt right anymore. Life with Jackson didn't feel right, and that was a huge problem.

"I should head home," she said.

"I could follow you," he offered, a teasing grin on his lips. "After all, I'm not ready for the night to end. Are you?"

Her jaw clenched, and she quickly searched for reasons she couldn't have him coming back to her place. She opened her mouth and released a yawn. He frowned. "I'm sorry. I'm just so tired. I wouldn't be the best company tonight."

He nodded. "I understand. There's always another day." He kissed her softly and she let it linger so her feelings wouldn't be conspicuous. "Love you."

"Me, too," she said.

She opened her car door and looked over her shoulder. He stood with one hand holding onto her door, waiting for her to climb into the car. She paused, opening her mouth to possibly explain where her head was, but no words would come. Instead, she said, "See you," waving and quickly sliding into her car.

As she drove away from him, Bella's heart broke a little. Stringing him along wasn't the right thing to do, but telling him that it was over was even harder. How could she just let go of the vision she'd had for her life for so many years?

———

BELLA'S MIND WAS TOO FOGGY TO GO HOME, AND SHE DIDN'T want to be alone with her thoughts. Thankfully, she didn't have any early classes, so she decided to stay out a little longer and go somewhere familiar with lots of activity. Anything to distract herself from the mess her life was becoming.

She drove to a small cafe near Capmed, one she sometimes stopped in for a quick bite to eat before and after her shifts. The staff there was chatty, so maybe they could help ease her mind with some kind of gossip or general small talk. As she pushed open the door to the bustling interior, though, her gaze immediately zeroed in on a familiar face. Leona.

She was sitting on a stool at the counter, sipping from a mug and reading a book. Bella thought of leaving, but before she could, Leona looked up, as if she had a sixth sense that had told her Bella had entered. Bella forced a weak smile, waved, and then joined Leona at the counter.

"Hey," Bella said, feeling awkward.

Leona smiled, her eyes warm and inviting. She had a vulnerability to her that Bella didn't see when they were at work. "Hi. I just got off shift and thought I'd grab some hot chocolate and do some reading to help me relax. Stressful day. Somehow, being in a busy atmosphere helps me unwind more than being at home alone."

Bella nodded and relaxed as her eyes darted over the casual jeans and shirt Leona wore. Meeting her outside the hospital like this was so different, and it sent a thrill through her. "Me, too. I've had so much on my mind, places like this always help."

They sat in silence for a few moments, both lost in their own thoughts. Bella ordered some tea, wondering if she should say something or just let Leona keep reading. Before she could make a decision, Leona spoke up.

"How was your evening out?" she asked, not looking up from her book.

Bella tensed. "It was...fine."

Leona glanced up, eyebrows raised. "Just 'fine'?"

Bella shrugged. The server brought her tea, and she mindlessly stirred it with a spoon. "Yeah. I mean, we had a nice time and all, but...I don't know. I guess I just haven't been feeling it lately."

"Are you talking about your boyfriend?"

Bella nodded.

"Well, I'm a good listener."

Bella hesitated. Was it okay to be sitting here telling Leona about her life? Leona was her superior, so shouldn't they maintain certain boundaries? There was also the whole feelings situation.

"I understand if you don't feel like sharing," Leona said when Bella didn't respond. She looked a bit sad, which tugged at Bella's heartstrings. Leona really cared about listening to her vent?

Bella gave in and let everything out. She told Leona about Jackson and her life plan and how uncertain she was feeling lately about all of her choices.

Leona nodded slowly throughout Bella's rambling as if she understood exactly what Bella was going through. When Bella finally finished with a sigh and sipped her tea, Leona said softly, "Sounds like you're dealing with a lot. I know how you feel."

Bella looked up at her, surprised. "You do?"

Leona nodded again and gave her a small, sad smile. "Yeah. I've experienced my share of uncertainty in my life as well as relationship problems." She reached out to touch Bella's hand. "Just know that you're not alone."

Bella didn't move her hand, letting Leona's touch linger and letting her words sink in. Bella felt a sudden wave of comfort wash over her. It was nice to know she wasn't alone in feeling this way.

"So what did you do?" Bella asked. "How did you deal with the uncertainty and your past relationships?"

Leona shrugged and took a sip of her drink before answering. "I guess I just decided that I deserved better," she said simply. "I deserve to be with someone who ignites something strong and beautiful within me. Life is too short to settle, which sounds like what you're doing. Forgive me for being bold, but you don't have to stick to your plan if what you want starts to change. It's okay to take chances and go after what truly fulfills you in life. Sometimes what we need turns out to be different from what we wanted."

Bella nodded, understanding. She had been feeling the same way lately, but hearing it from someone else made it feel more real. More possible.

"Thank you," Bella said quietly. "For talking to me, I mean. It means a lot."

"Don't mention it," Leona said. "That's what friends are for."

Friends. The word echoed in Bella's mind. "You really see us that way? As equals?"

"Of course. I know we work together, but we're not at work now, are we?"

Bella grinned, her first genuine grin that entire evening. "I'm so relieved. I've felt a lot of pressure to live up to your expectations. You're my superior, so I do feel a bit awkward right now talking about my life so much, but...I also admire your confidence and like your company."

She blushed and looked away. Leona had gotten her to open up, but now she might be overstepping and letting too much out.

Leona hesitated and then touched Bella's hand again. "I enjoy your company, too. I hope that, moving forward, you can see us more as equals at work. I want to mentor you, but that doesn't mean I'm your superior. Just a friend trying to help you out, okay?"

Bella nodded, moving away from Leona's touch to lift her mug. Heat had spread through her entire body and the cafe had suddenly become *very* stuffy. But Leona wanted to be friends, not something more.

They spent some more time together chatting about lighter topics, and soon Bella felt too tired to keep the conversation going. She really needed a good night's sleep and to process everything that had happened that evening. Driving home, she thought about her conversation with Leona. At least she had someone who understood what she was going through and could offer some advice. For the first time in a long time, Bella felt hopeful. Maybe things were finally going to start looking up.

———

BELLA TAPPED LIGHTLY ON BRAD'S DOOR. "COME IN," Kandice's voice rang out. Kandice was a social worker and Bella was glad Brad had someone who was going to uphold her promise of keeping him safe.

"Hey, Bella," Kandice greeted her. "Just in time."

"I am?" Bella asked.

Kandice nodded. "I have a meeting with a possible foster for Brad. I didn't want him to wake up and not find anyone here, so I didn't want to leave him alone. He had a painful night."

She then registered that Bella was in her scrubs. "Oh, silly me, you're probably here for work. I guess you won't be able to stick around in case he wakes. That's fine; I'll just let the nurses know."

"I have an hour or so. Thought I would just check up on my favorite patient." Bella looked over to Brad, who was sleeping soundly. "But you say you have a possible foster lined up for him?"

She nodded. "A couple, actually. They don't have any children but are looking to foster. They live about two minutes from here and I'm doing a house call. It won't be long. If I'm not back, just let the staff know."

"Okay. Sounds good. See you, Kandice." Bella sat down in a chair next to the bed. She looked over at Brad, noticing the slight smile on his lips. Bella reached out and touched the wisp of curl that hung at his eyes. When she pulled her hand back, she felt a slight pain in her chest. The thought of Brad leaving the hospital and going to live with another family bothered her. She wanted to make sure she got to see him again. But right now, there was little guarantee.

Bella fell back in her seat and watched Brad's chest slowly rise and fall as he slept so soundly. He had been improving greatly over the last week and it was a relief to everyone. His bones were healing nicely and his external wounds were slowly fading. Bella just hoped whatever family got to raise Brad would keep him safe and that he wouldn't have any reason to stay in the hospital again.

Bella had been watching over Brad for twenty minutes when he slowly rustled himself awake. He shifted onto his left side and opened his eyes. A smile broadened on his face. "Bella," he said happily.

"Hey, bud." Bella got up and helped him sit up. He held out his arms, and she hugged him tightly. "How are you feeling?"

"Good!" He nodded eagerly. "Do you know when I'll be able to get out of here?" There was a slight frown etched on his forehead.

"Well, I think they just want to make sure you're stronger first. While you appear strong on the outside, they need to ensure you aren't having any problems. Do you understand?"

He nodded, but then shook his head. "I'm okay. I just want to go home," he whined, his young age showing. Bella's heart ached for the boy, imaging how confusing it all must have been for him.

"I know you do." She looked down at her watch. Time was slowly ticking by. "You wanna go for a walk?" she asked.

His eyes widened, and he nodded vigorously. She held up her hand and then quickly disappeared out of his room. "Hey, Jess," she said. "Would it be all right if I just pushed Brad around the hospital for a minute? He's anxious to get out of his room."

She smiled and nodded. "That'd be great. I'll get you a wheelchair." A few seconds later, she returned with a chair.

"Thanks." Bella went back into the room, where Brad was already sitting on the edge of his bed. He groaned. "You said we were gonna take a walk."

Bella laughed. "Sorry. I'll walk, you'll ride. It's best this way."

He grumbled but allowed Bella to help him into the chair. She pushed him out of the room and straight to the elevator.

"Where are we going?" Brad asked, his eyes still bright.

"You'll see," she said mysteriously. She grabbed a blanket from a shelf and placed it over him. "Just in case you get a chill." Bella pushed the button to call the elevator and they waited for it to reach their floor.

"It's taking forever," Brad mumbled.

Bella smirked. "Good things come to those who wait."

When the doors opened, Leona stood there, leaning against the wall of the elevator. She straightened up when she saw them. "Hey," she said.

Bella's heart fluttered. "Hi."

"Lona," Brad said. "We're going for a walk. Wanna come?"

"I'd love to," Leona said with a smile.

Bella looked down, one thought immediately coming to mind. *Good things come to those who wait.*

CHAPTER NINE

Leona

L ater that day, Leona rounded the corner and spotted Bella at the nurses' station. Her head was resting against her hand and her eyes were closed. It was a quiet evening, so no one was pressing Bella to take care of patients' needs, but Leona laughed to herself. Never had she caught a nurse napping on the job. But Bella was something special, and she worked so hard.

Really, Leona wasn't surprised to find her napping. She had noticed how exhausted Bella had looked when they had been on their walk earlier. Speaking of the walk, she hadn't expected to enjoy the silence so much. It had felt like they were just out on a stroll, with no cares in the world. For a moment, it had even felt like they were a family. Leona had longed for a family for so many years, she had just let herself fall into the moment and simply enjoy the fantasy.

When she'd first met Bella, their age difference had stared her right in the face. But as she grew closer to Bella and got to know her, she found that the gap no longer mattered. She saw how determined and hard-working Bella was, and how she always pushed through despite any setbacks or errors.

Bella had a lot of resilience despite doubting herself so much. And she had such a kind, caring heart that Leona knew she'd make a great mother one day. Thanks to their unexpected meeting at the cafe a few days ago, Leona now knew that motherhood was something Bella wanted and had already planned for. It made Leona's feelings for her grow. Now she was getting into riskier territory, especially since Bella was questioning her relationship with her boyfriend.

Leona had loved the walk and the feeling that this could be her family, or that she could have something similar in the future. Did she want that with Bella? When the walk had ended, Leona had dismissed those thoughts. Just because Bella was on uncertain ground with her boyfriend didn't mean she was interested in women, or older women. Or Leona.

She stepped up to the desk where Bella was napping, hating to wake her up. She looked so peaceful. But at any moment, someone else could round the corner, like Tori or a head of the hospital. Either way, it wouldn't look good if someone else happened to catch Bella asleep.

Leona lightly cleared her throat. When that didn't jar her awake, she tapped her on the shoulder.

"Bella!" she whispered.

Bella's eyes flew open, and she jumped up from her chair. "Was I asleep?" she asked, her eyes wide and her cheeks flushed.

"It's fine. You obviously needed the rest," Leona pointed out.

Bella looked away from her, her eyes hazy as she quickly shook her head. "That's so embarrassing. It's not fine. You're my boss and..."

"Whoa, slow down," Leona said, reaching out for her arm. Bella dropped her gaze to her hand, grasped around Bella's arm, and Leona slowly pulled it back. "I'm not going to tell anyone. As far as I can tell, I'm the only one who saw. No harm, no foul." She threw up her arms. "I swear."

Bella looked up and frowned. "But why? Shouldn't I be written up or something? This can't possibly be all right." Her eyes were still bugging out.

That was true. But Leona wasn't going to report her. She knew how hard Bella worked.

"You want to be written up? I can get the chief of staff right now. Your call." Leona pretended to turn away, but Bella was quick to reply.

"Well, no, but..." Leona grinned and turned back around, and Bella chuckled in relief. "You were teasing. Of course you were."

"It's really all right, Bella. It could happen to anyone." Leona hesitated and scrunched up her face in thought. "Although, I do worry you're pushing yourself too much. Maybe you should go take your break."

"But it's not time," Bella argued, looking down at her watch.

"There are no set break times," Leona replied. "You could freshen up or take in a few more z's. Your call. I just think that you need to get off your feet."

"I guess you're right. I'll be back in ten." Bella turned to leave.

"Make it fifteen, Bella. Don't push yourself. If you do, you're liable to make yourself sick and that helps no one. Understood?"

Bella looked over her shoulder, holding Leona's gaze. Finally, she nodded, then went to the elevator. Once she was gone, Leona turned back to her list of patients she needed to follow up on. She entered a room where one of their oldest patients, seventeen-year-old Martina, lay. She had her eyes peeled on the TV screen, but when Leona entered, she groaned.

"Finally!" She turned, then rolled her eyes when she saw it was Leona. "Thought you were Bella. She was supposed to get me ibuprofen like an hour ago. My arm is throbbing."

"She was detained," Leona quickly replied. "I'll go grab you something." She turned and left her room, then walked to the medicine cabinet.

"Have you seen Bella?" Jacqueline asked, coming out of a room.

"She's on break," Leona replied, putting the pills into a cup and grabbing an extra bottle of water. "You need something?"

Jacqueline hesitated. "Well, you're the doctor and this is trivial, so I guess I'll just do it. But I have Dr. Whalen waiting and really shouldn't detain him..."

"It's fine, Jacqueline," Leona cut in. "I don't mind. What do you need with Bella?"

"Tommy was supposed to be taken down to CT twenty minutes ago. My patient is next and has been ready, but they're still waiting on Tommy."

Leona cringed. That wasn't good, but with the way Bella was feeling, she felt compelled to support her. "That's my fault. I put Bella on a project and told her I would move the schedule to accommodate it. I'm sorry."

Jacqueline tilted her head and shrugged. "It happens."

"I'll call down to radiology and tell them we're moving your patient in front of ours. Thanks for the heads-up."

Leona turned away from her and hurried back to Martina's room. "Here you go." She handed over the cup and water and waited for Martina to take her medicine. "Need anything else? How are you feeling?"

"Pretty good, other than the pain. Thanks!" Martina turned back to her TV and Leona slipped out of her room. She went over to the receptionist's desk and called down to the radiology department.

"This is Pete."

"Hey, Pete. It's Dr. Guillano. There's been a misunderstanding. We're moving Dr. Whalen's patient in front of mine. Call the floor once you're ready for us."

"Sounds good. Thanks for the update."

Pete hung up and Leona leaned against the desk and sighed. She glanced at her watch and frowned. It'd already been twenty minutes since she sent Bella on her fifteen-minute break. She went to the elevator and took it down to the breakroom.

When she entered the room, she stopped. Bella sat at the only occupied table. Her head was down and she looked completely knocked out. Leona cleared her throat, which jogged Bella awake. "Where am I?" Bella asked, jumping up.

"Bella, look at me." Leona knelt in front of her. Bella's eyes slowly refocused on Leona. "You're exhausted. You need one night off where you don't have work and you don't have school. You need to go home."

"I can't," she argued, shaking her head. "I'll get a coffee and be fine."

"You're not fine, Bella. I'll cover for you. You go home and get some sleep. And this isn't a request. It's an order." Bella frowned and looked down at her clenched hands. "You'll be fine. I promise."

Finally, Bella nodded. "Thank you."

"Just get that rest so tomorrow you'll be better. Take care." Leona left her in the breakroom and headed back to the elevator. When the elevator doors opened, she saw Kandice, who looked up and greeted Leona.

"Hey," Leona said in greeting. "Headed out for the evening?"

"Yeah, Brad is resting and in good hands tonight. I hear he could be ready to leave the hospital by next week. Great news considering I think I found the perfect foster parents for him."

"Oh really?" Leona asked, her chest heavy. "Bella did mention you have a prospective couple. Are you sure you've given it plenty of thought? I would hate for him to get involved with another couple incapable of handling his care."

She smiled. "I appreciate your concern. Both you and Bella have been great for Brad and I've appreciated both of you worrying about the little guy, but I'm confident. This family has no kids, but they have a dog and are looking to expand their family. Unfortunately, they can't have a child of their own. So, there's potential they could adopt him in the end. That's what we all want, right?"

Leona nodded, but she was sorry to think that Brad would soon leave the hospital. Who knows when they would see him again? "That sounds good then. He's a lucky guy."

"He will be," Kandice said. "His life hasn't been so lucky, so he deserves this. Anyway, I should head out. See you later, Leona."

Kandice waved and Leona watched her go. There was still a knot that rested in her gut. In a short amount of time, she had gotten attached to Brad. She wanted a family, and that was more obvious to her now. Hopefully she'd have that one day soon.

The thing is, Brad wasn't the only one she had gotten attached to.

LEONA SIGHED AS SHE STARED AT HER CELLPHONE. *JUST CALL her. You'll feel much better if you do.* After staring at the phone for what felt like forever, she finally pressed the number in her contact list. There went nothing. She just hoped she wouldn't be seen as a stalker when she was merely trying to be thoughtful. She quickly hung up the phone before it could ring. Leona cringed, hoping Bella's phone didn't get a notification.

Leona fell back in her seat and stared at her phone again. She was being a chicken, but why? After several more minutes, she grabbed her phone again and hit the Call button. The line started ringing, and it was too late to hang up again. She had to go through with the call.

"Hello?"

"Uh, hey, Bella. This is Le...Leona. Are you busy?"

"Um, hey."

There was some hesitancy behind that greeting, and Leona waited for the tension to break, but it felt even more awkward as the seconds ticked on without either of them speaking.

Bella broke the silence. "How'd you get my number?"

Not exactly what Leona was hoping she'd say.

"Well, since you have a landline, one search and pulled it right up." Leona laughed nervously. "I hope that's okay. Don't want to give you stalker vibes or anything."

"Well, no, it's fine. Just surprised to get a call from you on my home number. That's all."

"I honestly wasn't sure I'd reach you. I thought maybe you'd have school or something this morning. But I'm glad to chat you up." Leona cringed again. *Chat you up?* Who even talked like that?

"Anyway, the reason I'm calling is that I just wanted to check up on you. You know, given the way you were last night. You were so tired and all. I wanted to make sure you made it home and got plenty of rest."

There, that seemed like a sufficient explanation.

There was a pause, then Bella said, "Oh, well, that's sweet of you."

Leona smiled and sat down in the nearest chair. That was a good sign. She found it sweet and not the least bit stalkerish. "I'm a doctor. It's my job to care."

An exhale sounded on the other end of the line, and Leona opened her mouth to say that it didn't come out at all how she wanted it to. It seemed crass, like she was saying she only cared because she was a doctor. It wasn't genuine and frankly the furthest thing from the truth. "I mean..."

"I get what you mean," Bella replied, interrupting her. "And it makes perfect sense. In the profession you're in, you're expected to care. So, thank you for doing your job well. Anyway, I have to go. I have laundry and a million other things to do. Thanks for calling, Leona—or, I should say, Dr. Guillano."

"Wait, Bella, that came out all wrong, really. Yes, I'm a doctor. That fact is very true and can't be changed. But it isn't the only reason I called. I was concerned about you, not as my nurse, but as a friend. I just didn't want you to hang up thinking that I was merely calling because I felt it was out of duty or something. That would be the furthest thing from the truth."

There was a long silence and Leona leaned into the call, waiting, holding her breath, trying to hear any kind reaction on Bella's side, whether it was hesitation or warmth. She released a breath and waited some more.

"Are you there?" she finally asked.

"Yeah, I'm here. I get what you're saying. I just took it the wrong way. I do feel much better than I was last night. I'm rejuvenated and ready to go to work this evening."

Leona felt relieved to hear that. "That's great to hear."

"Yep. And I don't have classes today, so I plan on just laying low until tonight. I'm assuming you're on duty tonight?"

"Yeah, I'll be there at eight. What time do you come in?" Leona asked, settling into the smooth conversation between them.

"Also eight."

A thought came to Leona. "So, if you don't have anything else planned, would you like to grab a bite to eat before we go in?"

"You mean like in the cafeteria?" Bella asked.

Leona released a laugh, then bit down on her lower lip, not expecting it to have come out as loud as it did. "Well, the cafeteria has good food and all, but I was thinking more along the lines of outside of the hospital. There's a seafood restaurant around the corner and I've been meaning to try it. Or, if that's not your thing, we can go somewhere else."

"I love seafood," Bella replied.

"Okay, then. Six o'clock?"

Belle immediately agreed and Leona hung up the phone, slightly taken aback by her own bold attitude. Was she pushing things too far? She was simply trying to be friendly. They could be friends despite her growing attraction—right?

Regardless, the only thing that mattered was that Bella had said yes, and while she couldn't go as far to say it was a date, she could say that she was excited about getting to know Bella a little more.

CHAPTER TEN

Bella

I t felt too close to an actual date, even though she showed up at the restaurant wearing scrubs. Ever since Leona had suggested grabbing a bite to eat, Bella couldn't stop thinking about what that would entail. What would they talk about? How would she feel? It frightened her in a way that startled her.

She arrived at the restaurant to find Leona already sitting down in one of the booths. Bella approached the table and Leona looked up and greeted her with a smile. She had a sincere look about her, one that completely fit a woman who had enough empathy to dig up her number and call to check up on her. She had jumped to the conclusion that Leona had only made the call because she was Bella's superior, but it wasn't a fair conclusion to jump to. Leona had said just as much, and they were friends. Or trying to be. Bella still felt a little awkward calling a superior that. But looking back, she was glad that Leona had explained herself. Otherwise, Bella would've kept thinking Leona was only calling out of duty, and Bella didn't think she'd be able to handle that.

"Hi there," Leona said, standing to her feet.

"This place has some of the best shrimp you'll ever find," Bella said. "If that's your thing."

"I'll keep that in mind. Thank you."

They both sat down, and Bella opened her menu and peered down at it, feeling Leona's eyes on her. When Bella looked up, Leona looked back down. It was something that was probably just in her mind, but it was like there was a way that Leona's eyes often followed her. She shook the thought from her mind. It was merely a coincidence, she was sure.

The waiter came to their table, and they ordered their drinks, followed promptly by their food. When he was gone, Bella looked across the table. Again, Leona's eyes were dancing.

Leona cleared her throat and sat up straighter. "So, I ran into Kandice last night. It was shortly after I sent you home."

"Oh yeah? Did she say how Brad's doing?"

"He's doing well—well enough that he should be discharged soon. She said sometime next week, by the looks of things." Bella nodded, happy for Brad.

It was great news, but Bella needed to know the whole story. Leona continued, "She said that there's this couple that is super excited about fostering him, possibly even fostering to adopt. And she said that they're good people. That's promising."

Bella nodded again and looked down at the empty spot in front of her. If it all sounded good, which it did, then why did she feel this sadness radiating through her body?

"You don't look too happy," Leona observed.

"I'm happy for him. I'm sad for me." Bella let out a sigh. "I mean, I feel like I've known him a while and I just hate the fact that after he leaves the hospital, we might lose contact completely."

Leona's expression fell. "I had the same thought. So, I would say it's sad for us."

Bella liked knowing there was someone else concerned about the little guy, someone that she could talk to about Brad. She liked that she didn't have to worry about droning on about something she couldn't change to someone else.

Leona continued. "The funny thing is, I even considered looking into fostering. I would have said something to Kandice, but it seems like everything has already been figured out." She shrugged. "As long as he's happy."

Bella perked up. She was touched that Leona would have even considered fostering Brad. If Bella had one ounce of time, then maybe she would have as well. But there just wasn't any time with school and work and trying to maintain her relationship with Jackson.

Leona smiled at her, eyes playful. "What are you grinning about?"

Bella touched her cheeks. She had been grinning like a fool at Leona. She laughed at herself. "Oh, sorry. I just...Well, there's this softer side of you that I'm seeing more of. You're always so confident and self-assured, and a little firm at work, but you also have this soft spot. Considering how you've encouraged me, I know you'll be a wonderful mother." She bit her lip. It felt rude to pry into it too much, but she was curious about Leona's past.

Leona blushed and avoided eye contact. "Thank you, Bella."

"So, why—"

She was interrupted by the server bringing their food. After poking around her plate a bit, she found the nerve to try again. "Why did things never work out for you?"

"You mean motherhood?"

Bella nodded.

Leona let out a long sigh, as if she'd been holding it in for years. "The wrong partners, I guess. I settled, just like I told you to be careful to not do. I know how it feels to think you have limited options, but I can tell you from experience that there's a big world out there and sometimes life takes you in different directions. My last relationship was a disaster, so I moved here for a fresh start. I don't think my body can handle a pregnancy anymore, and it was tough to come to terms with that, but fostering can help a child already in this world who needs a stable, loving home. I've decided I can do it on my own."

Bella touched her chest. "That's so amazing you would do that. And I'm sorry things didn't work out. Men are tricky, aren't they?"

"Women."

Bella almost choked on her food. "What?"

Leona gulped water and then said, "My past relationships have been with women."

Bella stared, even though she didn't mean to and knew it was probably rude. Leona's admission sent her insides whirling. If Leona was interested in women, that changed so much—mostly, Bella's chances with her. But that was silly to think of, because Leona wasn't interested in Bella in that way. Right?

"Oh," Bella said. "That's...I'm sorry for assuming. I guess relationships are just tricky period, no matter who you're with."

Leona nodded silently and focused on her food.

Thankfully, their conversation turned to work.

As Bella ate and the conversation got easier between them, Bella became more assured about speaking her mind instead of being hesitant to say things she wanted to say.

"Can I ask you something?" Bella asked halfway through the meal.

Leona looked up, catching her eye before dropping her fork. "I'm a little nervous as to what you're going to say, but ask away." She laughed, sipping on her water.

"When you gave me that evaluation, you said that I wasn't the type to have nurses' skills. Do you still feel that way?"

Leona set her napkin down on the table. "I didn't use those words. And I can honestly say that you *are* fit to be a nurse. I was concerned at the beginning, but after working with you, I'm confident you can do it. My concern now is that maybe you're pushing yourself too much. I've been in this field long enough to know when someone isn't giving themselves ample time to rest. And I believe I was right to think that."

"But I won't always have school and work trying to share equal time," Bella pointed out.

"You're very right in that aspect. But nursing is a gig that takes a lot of time and energy even if you don't have school. I just want to prepare you for that, as your mentor."

Leona smiled and went back to eating. "This food is delicious. This place might just be one of my top three restaurants so far."

Bella looked down at her food, not fully satisfied with Leona's response. She had danced around the question more than she had answered definitively.

"I'm dedicated," she said.

Leona looked up mid-bite and nodded. "I have no doubt you are. If you put the hard work in, then you'll make a fine nurse. But know that if it doesn't work out, that's all right, too. You have other options."

She continued to eat while Bella sat there, thinking about Leona's words. There wasn't any way Bella would let failure be an option.

Since they were so openly talking about things, more words flowed easily between the two of them. Bella realized how strong her interest in Leona had become. Though she wasn't going to act on it, she liked the idea of them being friends. But something still nagged at her. "Is this okay? Us hanging out together outside of work?"

Leona gave her a concerned look. "Of course. Why wouldn't it be?"

"I'm having trouble separating the fact that you're my boss at work but not my boss in this setting."

Instead of looking more concerned, Leona smiled. "You show a lot of maturity."

Bella's eyes shot to Leona. "I do?"

"Mm-hmm. You're sharing what's bothering you and not keeping it in. That's a level of maturity I don't always see in people my age. So many of my past relationships..." She stopped, clearing her throat and switching gears. "I can understand how you might be struggling. Instead of me being your boss, what if you think of it as us simply being on a team, trying to do what's best for each patient? We each have different skills and roles, and we work together for a greater cause. I know it may feel like I'm bossing you around, but I really don't want it to be like that. We're just communicating with each other about what needs to be done."

Bella considered her words a while and then finally nodded. Thinking of them as teammates helped a lot. "I like that idea."

They smiled at each other, their gazes lingering too long for two people who were supposed to be just friends.

They finished their meal, and Bella tried to enjoy her time with Leona and not worry about anything else. She knew Leona was trying to help by suggesting there were other options out there for Bella, like a different career and different future, but it still nagged at Bella's mind. She really didn't want to give up nursing, so she would continue to do her best. Outside of nursing, though, was she getting more comfortable with letting go of her life plan and considering a different future? That thought was both terrifying and thrilling.

THE ONLY TWO PEOPLE WORKING THE FLOOR THAT NIGHT were Bella and Leona. Luckily, they immediately got into their shift and Bella didn't have time to think too much about all of their recent interactions outside of work. And the doubts Leona still had about her. She knew Leona had only the best intentions, but it still hurt that she thought Bella was pushing herself too hard and needed to consider new options or take time off. Bella could handle anything and everything. She was capable. She wasn't a quitter, and she wouldn't fail.

"Bed four-zero-five needs a fresh bag of IV fluids rehung. Bed four-one-two needs a bath, and bed four-zero-eight needs his labs drawn." Bella nodded, jotting down the notes, feeling like a walking zombie, as she had been feeling the whole night. She just wanted Leona to look at her with confidence and say that she was handling everything and doing a stellar job. Was that too much to ask? "And four-five-zero needs a story read to him."

Bella frowned and looked up. "Huh?"

Leona smirked. "I was worried that you weren't paying attention." She leaned against the wall and arched an eyebrow. "Seems like ever since we got to work, you've been a tad distracted."

Bella shrugged. "Nothing I can't work out for myself. I'll get on this." She held up her notes and hurried about doing the tasks that Leona gave to her.

After getting through her tasks, Bella rounded a corner, spotting Leona coming out of another room. "What's next?" Bella asked. "Another bath? Another lab draw? Perhaps I really should read the patient in room four-five-zero a story."

Leona grabbed her hand and pulled her toward a closet as Bella resisted, digging her heels into the ground.

"What are you doing?" Bella asked as Leona shut the door behind them. When Bella tried to reach for the handle, Leona slid into her path.

"No...What are you doing, Bella? What did I say this time to irk you? Because something has clearly messed with your mind. The sooner you tell me what it is, the better off we'll all be."

Bella crossed her arms, putting up an invisible barrier between them. Leona arched an eyebrow.

"Fine...I'm hurt, all right?"

Leona frowned. "Hurt? About what?"

Bella turned away from her, creating some distance. When she twirled back around, Leona was still looking at her. "Hurt that you still doubt that I can handle myself. You doubt my ability to juggle work and school. I'm surprised you haven't gone to the board and said that they should revoke my privileges here."

Leona's jaw dropped. "What? Are you serious?"

Bella sighed. When she got like this, that little voice in her head started playing on loop, reminding her of every time she had failed in the past and how she would always be behind and be a screw-up, just like her peers used to tell her. Then that self-doubt would make her say things she would later regret.

"You just think that I'm some little girl playing nurse or something. You have no confidence that I can do this job. I want to prove you wrong, but with you knocking me down every chance you get, I don't see how I could."

Leona shook her head. "I know you're more mature than this, Bella. What's going on?"

"Are you telling me I'm wrong?" Bella asked.

"Bella, I am your biggest cheerleader here. I want you to succeed." Leona hesitated, then continued. "I didn't want to tell you this, but yesterday, when you were tired, you missed some steps with patients. I'm only telling you this now to prove to you that I'm on your side. It happens, and I covered for you because I want you to succeed. You are a passionate and gifted worker when it comes to communicating with patients. You can do anything you set your mind to. I know this. And I do think you're going to make a wonderful nurse. But you have to practice better self-care and know your limits."

Bella winced. "I *was* tired, but you shouldn't have covered for me. I don't want you to feel like you have to do that."

Leona moved closer. "I help people out when they matter to me. And you matter to me. Why can't you see that?"

Bella's breath caught, all the fight leaving her body. "I matter to you?"

"Yes. A lot. Why can't you see that?" Leona repeated. She moved closer, so close Bella could feel her breath on her cheek. "But you've raised concerns about feeling like I'm your boss and I don't want to cross any lines. I don't want you to feel pressured or like you have to—"

Bella grabbed the sleeves of Leona's lab coat and pulled their bodies together. She kissed Leona with a passion that surprised her, feeling half out of her mind for doing something like this. Being this bold wasn't like her at all. She had plans that she wanted to stick to, and Leona wasn't part of that. But she couldn't hold back any longer. So much uncertainty and confusion about her life was eating away at her insides and she needed the comfort of Leona's arms.

To her relief, Leona kissed back, resting her hands on the sides of Bella's waist. Bella's knees went weak, and she nearly collapsed. Her head was spinning. The world faded as Bella closed her eyes and just let the kiss sweep them both away. But she wasn't content with just standing there and letting the kiss continue to deepen. She wanted to wrap her fingers through Leona's hair and embrace her with a hunger that continued to leave her knees shaking.

She slowly lifted her hand to Leona's chest, Leona's heart racing beneath her fingers. "Leona," Bella gasped, slowly pressing her back.

"I know," Leona said. Her cheeks were flushed but her eyes were soft. "You have a boyfriend. We shouldn't."

Bella fell backward. She had completely forgotten about Jackson. She certainly hadn't been thinking about him while she has been passionately kissing Leona. What kind of girlfriend was she? She shook her head, her heart shifting as she stared into the eyes of the woman she just wanted to throw her arms around.

"That wasn't what I was going to say," Bella whispered.

"What were you going to say?" Leona's eyes lit up. There was a sweet, sexy grin on her lips.

Bella opened her mouth but was unable to get the words out because Leona's phone decided to ring. In one swift second, the moment was gone. Leona's eyes darkened as she read the message.

"I'm needed in the ER. There's a pediatric trauma patient coming. Can we finish this talk later?"

Bella nodded and watched as Leona rushed from the room, the memories of the kiss unable to fade from her mind. She needed to let Leona know that Jackson wasn't someone who could turn her away from Leona. Still, she would need to tell Jackson the truth. Her heart grew heavy with that burden, but there was no other way around that.

CHAPTER ELEVEN

Leona

T he elevator dinged and Leona slowly got off, entering the pediatric floor. It'd been a long night, and she still had two hours to go. How was she going to make it? She had tried so hard to save her last patient but...She felt a tear escape from her eye and closed her eyes.

Be strong, Leona. You still have a job to do. She wiped away the tear and opened her eyes. If she kept telling herself that, maybe she would eventually believe it.

As she rounded the corner, she spotted Bella. Bella rushed up to her, and Leona wanted Bella to just hold her, but they were in the middle of the ward, and that would have raised too many questions. Instead, she simply nodded.

"I was wondering if you would ever come back up here," Bella said, her voice lighthearted and airy.

"What are you still doing here?" Leona asked, barely making eye contact. "I thought you were off at three."

"I was, but Dr. Whalen needed help with a breathing treatment on a patient, Joey. He couldn't get to sleep and started having an asthma attack. It was sort of last minute. I didn't mind staying, though. I'll get home in plenty of time to get three hours of sleep before I head to school."

Leona gave a weak smile, knowing this was a sore subject for Bella. "Remember, just don't push yourself too hard."

"I won't," Bella replied. "How was your trauma patient?"

Leona looked to Bella, and she couldn't stop the tears from falling. Bella's eyes grew wide, and she grabbed Leona's hand and pulled her toward the room they had embraced in. The place they had passionately made out in was now a place Leona would crumble in front of Bella.

"What happened?" Bella asked.

When Leona looked up and met Bella's concerned stare, Bella pulled her into her arms and hugged her. There was a warmth in that hug that left Leona feeling safe and secure, despite the heartache that was crushing her chest.

"I lost her," she said. "Only two years old and I couldn't save her. Maybe I'm not the doctor I thought I was."

Bella pulled back from the embrace and met Leona's eyes. She shook her head. "I'm sure you did everything you could to save that little girl. What happened is not your fault."

"But—" Leona started to argue.

Bella brushed her hand against Leona's cheek and Leona closed her eyes, moving into that very touch. Why was she feeling all these things that were wrong in so many ways? She knew Bella wasn't available and she should have backed off from her deep desires. Instead, she clung to them like they brought her life. It was wrong, and now she was paying the price for that. She was destined to have another heart broken—hers.

"You were *not* the problem, Leona. I wasn't there, but I know that in my heart."

Leona swallowed the lump in her throat and nodded. It was harder to believe than that, though. She was the one sent there to assist in taking care of the little girl. But the trauma was too much. The girl had fallen into a pond and had been without air for too long. By the time she had gotten to the hospital and was rushed into surgery, she was gone. Her brain had been unable to handle the blunt trauma.

Leona wiped a tear away from her eyes and nodded, wanting to hold on to Bella's words. "You shouldn't have to take care of me," Leona argued. "You only have a few hours to rest up."

Bella shook her head. "I'm not worried about that." She once again reached up and stroked her warm hand against Leona's cheek. Leona thought she saw passion behind that stare of Bella's. It felt nice. She also remembered Bella's hand on her chest, pushing her away from their earlier kiss. No matter how much she wanted to kiss Bella again, she resisted. She didn't know what Bella wanted or what any of this meant for them.

Bella didn't initiate anything, either. They only stood there in an embrace, gazing into each other's eyes as Bella touched Leona's cheek. As Bella parted her lips to say something, a voice came from behind them.

"Oh...Pardon me."

Leona pulled away and turned to see Stella, one of the late-night housekeepers, standing there. She had a wide-eyed stare and her jaw was hanging open. "I'll come back," she stuttered.

"No need," Leona said. "We were just leaving."

As they left, Leona had a slight smirk on her lips, despite the pain she felt in her heart. She could only imagine what thoughts were roaming through Stella's head over finding Bella and Leona in that intimate embrace on the hospital grounds. Once out in the hallway, she turned to Bella. "I hope that wasn't too awkward for you."

"Surprisingly, no," Bella said. There was even a grin on her lips. She then frowned. "I'm so sorry about your patient, though. I know that must not be an easy thing to go through."

Leona shook her head and started to open her mouth when she spotted Dr. Crowley headed her way. Leona looked down at her watch. "You're early," she said. Heather Crowley was the doctor set to take her place when she was off the clock. She still had well over an hour and a half to go.

"I heard the news," she said. "Thought maybe you'd want to head out early."

Leona nodded, sighing with relief. "I appreciate that." One thing that caused her anxiety was having to finish her shift after losing a patient. "Thank you."

Heather nodded. "Happy to help, and I'm sorry about your loss."

Bella and Leona went to the elevator and took it to the main floor to get their items from their lockers. As they were leaving the breakroom, Bella turned to Leona. "I don't think you should go home alone. Come with me."

Leona frowned. "You need your rest."

"Sleep is overrated and right now what matters is being with you."

Leona smiled and followed as Bella led the way to the stairwell. Leona didn't inquire as to where they were going as they walked up one set of stairs after another. Finally, Bella opened a door, and they stepped outside to the roof. The whole sky was lit up with stars.

"Wow," Leona gasped.

"Found this place by accident when I came to the hospital for my interview. Isn't this amazing? Rumor has it that just over that horizon you can watch the sun rise. Some say it's the most magical thing you'll ever witness."

Leona nodded, her eyes cast over to where Bella pointed. Silence hit them as they looked far off into the distance. It would be a while before the sun would rise, and Leona didn't want to hope that they would still be out there. After all, Bella did have classes to attend and couldn't possibly waste her morning with her.

"Wanna talk about it?" Bella asked gently.

Leona sighed and slowly turned her eyes toward Bella. "Losing a patient is never easy. When I worked in New York, I was with geriatric patients for a big part of my career. The last two years, I moved into pediatrics. I've lost a few kids—ten, to be exact. It never gets easier."

"I can't imagine losing a child. It's heartbreaking, and not just for the parents."

Leona nodded, swallowing the lump that had come back to her throat.

"I'll pray for the family and for you," Bella said softly.

Leona smiled. "Thank you."

She turned and looked back to the spot that Bella had pointed out to her, feeling Bella's eyes on her the whole time. "It's one of the reasons I asked you to simply entertain the possibility of another career." She turned and met Bella's eyes and she continued. "I've been doing this job for a while, and I love it. I wouldn't want to do anything else but be a doctor. But that's me, and not everyone feels that way. You're young and I wanted to save you the heartache. There are days even worse than this when it feels like the whole world is falling apart. It's hard watching other people go through so much pain and suffering, especially children."

Bella nodded. "I get that. And I appreciate you trying to keep me from having to experience this, but you see, I'm not as weak as I look. I can handle it—the heartache, the sadness, and everything in between. I'm in it for the long haul, wherever the job wants to take me. And I'm sorry for how I reacted earlier. I'm not mad at you. You've made me rethink a lot of things in my life and it's been difficult. I'm struggling with changing my whole idea of the future and I don't know where to go from here."

"I can see that," Leona said. "And I don't think you're weak." Leona reached up and brushed a strand of hair behind Bella's ear. "I don't want to complicate your life, Bella."

"You're not. You won't." Bella shook her head.

"You have a boyfriend," she said.

Bella nodded. "For now," she said. "I know in my heart that I need to end things with him. What you said is true. I've been settling because I've been stuck on this one vision for my life. He's a good man, but my desires have changed. I never expected to meet you."

Bella pulled back a little, hesitating.

"What is it?"

"Will this get us in trouble? Is what we're doing inappropriate? Plus, I don't even know what you want, and—"

Before Bella could fall into a spiral of anxiety and worry, Leona pressed her lips against hers. There were a lot of questions that needed answers and the two of them had a lot to sort through and figure out. But in that moment, none of that mattered. What mattered was that they were in this moment together, alive, safe, with so many possibilities in front of them. Maybe everything around them would crash and burn, but right now, their kiss was the only thing that existed.

———

I CAN'T BELIEVE WE STAYED OUT HERE AND WATCHED THE *sunrise*, Leona thought as she headed into the hospital later that afternoon. But she had to admit that watching the sunrise with Bella was the highlight of the past four months. If she was being completely honest, it was the highlight of her past year. There was something so raw and real about their conversations together and she couldn't turn from them.

Bella had been there in her hour of need and that meant more than anything.

She didn't want the morning to end there, but Bella had to rush off to school. Leona only worried that Bella would fall asleep at the wheel, as Bella had little sleep to go on and five hours of classes that was sure to exhaust her even more.

Leona couldn't stop worrying and sent a text to check in on Bella.

Just checking in with you to make sure you haven't slept through all your classes. I needed this morning. Thank you for being there.

Moments later, Leona's phone vibrated with a response. *I needed it just as much and surprisingly I'm doing pretty well. I don't work tonight, so I'll be sure to get plenty of rest.*

Leona smiled, relieved. *Glad to hear. I'll miss working with you tonight, but please get lots of sleep.*

Bella ended their conversation with a heart-shaped emoji that brought a big smile to Leona's face. There was a sweetness about Bella, which Leona needed in her life, though she knew they both needed to sit down soon and talk about everything and what they each wanted.

Leona's mind stayed steadily on Bella the whole time she went to her locker and took the elevator up to her floor. The moment the elevator doors opened, Jacqueline was there to greet her.

"I'm working with you tonight," she said.

Her voice was high-pitched, and Leona sensed the energy coming from her. Leona mustered up a smile.

Jacqueline continued. "They just brought a patient from ICU to the ward—Brad Carver. He'll only be here a couple days and then he'll be discharged."

"What room?" Leona asked without hesitancy.

"Four-zero-two," Jacqueline responded.

Before Jacqueline could say anything further, Leona was hurrying toward the room. She wanted to see how Brad was doing. She knocked on the door and entered, seeing Kandice and Brad.

"Leona!" Kandice exclaimed.

"Hi, Lona," Brad said, grinning as he saw her.

"I heard my favorite patient had been moved from the ICU and wanted to see firsthand how he was doing." Leona moved over to the edge of his bed and laid her hand against his forehead. Aside from some yellow bruises and the fact that his arm was in a cast, she could barely tell he had been involved in an accident. And the grin on his face was always a pleasant sight to see.

"I'm doing great!" he said. His infectious grin brought a smile to Leona.

"I'm so glad to hear and see that." She knelt at his level. "Do you need anything? Blanket? Something for pain? A book? Anything?"

Kandice's phone rang, and the social worker stood up. "I have to grab this." She left the room and Leona turned her attention back to Brad.

"Anything at all that will make you more comfortable. You name it."

"A juice box? If it wouldn't be too much trouble. And maybe a pillow to rest my arm."

"At your service. I'll be right back."

She left his room just as Kandice was hanging up. Kandice turned, and Leona saw something in the woman's eyes that alarmed her.

"Just grabbing Brad a pillow and juice box. Everything all right?"

She shook her head. There was a sparkle of a tear in her eyes. "I promised that little boy a home to go to when he leaves here. He expected that and now I'm going to have to break his heart. Which breaks my heart."

Leona frowned. "I don't understand. I thought there was a couple that was excited to bring him to their home. What happened?"

Kandice shrugged despondently. "They seemed so perfect. I thought our little guy would have a shot at real happiness. Looks can be deceiving, though. The guy, turns out, has a previous record. They did the background check, and he didn't pass. Guess it was a minor offense, but the law is that if they have a failed background check, they aren't eligible for the program."

She heaved a sigh. "I should have been more cautious. When things are too perfect, something is bound to happen and screw it all up. There goes that opportunity. And here goes me telling a five-year-old that once he leaves here he'll be going back to a children's home."

Kandice shook her head. "This part of the job sucks. All I ever want to do is help children, not see the pain in their eyes when things like this happen." She turned and went back into Brad's room.

Leona stared at the door, Kandice's words resonating with her. It was all the same, from seeing kids going through pain at the hospital to not surviving their diseases or injuries. But in the end, she did it, because that's what she knew how to do. That's what she loved, even when things didn't always work out in the child's favor.

She grabbed the juice box and pillow and headed back to Brad's room.

"Do you want me to do that?" Jacqueline ran up to her, reaching out for the items in Leona's hands.

"That's all right. I got it," Leona replied.

Jacqueline frowned. "But...you're the doctor..."

"Don't worry Jacqueline; I've got it," Leona reassured her.

She entered Brad's room, aware that Jacqueline was still confused by the fact that Leona was doing something so trivial. Maybe she would understand Leona's ways in due time, but at the same time, she really didn't need to because Bella was Leona's nurse of choice.

"Here you go." She handed Brad the juice and tucked the pillow under his arm. "Better?"

"Much! Thank you!"

She smiled and looked over at Kandice. "Hey, can I talk to you for a minute?"

"Sure." Kandice got up from her chair and followed Leona into the hallway. "Is there a problem? Not with Brad's labs, I hope." Her eyes were wide, and Leona was quick to assure her.

"No. Nothing to do with labs at all." She slipped her hands into her pockets and looked over to his room. "Have you talked to him yet? Tell him that the couple fell through?"

Kandice sighed. "I figured I would give him one restful night. No need in telling him this news when he's just glad to be out of ICU."

"Maybe you don't have to tell him," Leona said, turning back to look at Kandice. Kandice arched an eyebrow, and kept Leona talking. "What if another person came forward to foster him?"

"A person? Or a couple?" Kandice asked.

"I believe that it shouldn't have to be a couple. If someone loves the little guy, isn't that what really matters? Can't a single man or woman come forward and foster?"

"There are no rules against it," Kandice replied. "But who is this person? You?"

Leona nodded. "I don't want to see Brad put in another rough situation. I can take care of him with all the love he could need."

As she spoke, Leona felt her heart swelling. If she didn't do this and Brad ended up getting into another dangerous situation, she'd never forgive herself. That was a fact.

CHAPTER TWELVE

Bella

When Bella got to the hospital the next day, she heard the news that Brad was in one of the rooms and ready to be discharged in a couple of days. She was surprised that Leona hadn't texted her and told her, or, even better, called her. But then again, with the way they had left things, she wondered if maybe Leona was regretting their night together.

She had two objectives once she got to work: Find Leona and gauge where her thoughts were and check on Brad. Stepping off the elevator she looked around for Leona but couldn't find her. Disappointed, she headed straight for Brad's room and knocked.

"It's open," he called out. She entered the room and saw he was alone. "Hey, Bella." He met her with his cheery grin.

What a sight to see, Bella thought happily. "Hey, bud. How's it going?"

"Good!"

"I'm so glad to see your smiling face. Is everyone treating you well?"

"Yep! Lots of loving."

She grinned. "I'm glad to hear that. I went to your old room, and they told me you were here. Super stoked to hear that. And I hear you'll be leaving us in a couple of days. I bet you're looking forward to getting out of here."

"I like the people here," he said. "But yeah, I won't miss this place."

Bella laughed. "I don't blame you. But the food isn't so bad, right?"

He shrugged. "Chicken nuggets are good. And French fries. I also love the juice boxes." He held up one. "This is my third."

"Then you probably have to go to the restroom."

He giggled. "Just got back to the bed."

"All right then. You should be good for a few minutes at least." She ruffled up his hair with her hands. "I have to get to work, but you know how the button works. Let me know if you need anything."

"I will." He took a sip of his juice.

Bella looked over to the empty chair. "Where's Kandice? Has she been here?"

He shrugged. "She's in a meeting or something. I'm fine, though."

"All right, hon. I'll just be right outside your door. Holler if you need anything."

Bella left his room and went to the nurses' station. She grabbed the folder that listed everyone's schedule and flipped it open, scanning her eyes over the schedule. Her jaw dropped when she saw the schedule had been flipped and Jacqueline was scheduled with Leona, leaving her with Dr. Whalen. It was worse than Bella thought. Leona must've really wanted to make sure they wouldn't grow any closer. Her gut tightened, and she closed the folder and sighed out of frustration as she walked out to start her shift.

"Hey, Bella!"

She turned, spotting a smiling Tori at the desk. "Hey. I noticed I'm with Dr. Whalen today. I thought..." Her words trailed off, and she shrugged. "Guess it doesn't matter."

"Oh. You're wondering why you're not with Dr. Guillano?" Bella simply nodded. "She had some things she needed to do today and wouldn't be able to be in until later. They switched, that's all. I'm sure next week you'll be back to being on her schedule."

Tori turned and left to attend to someone, but Bella frowned at the explanation. She wasn't as confident that it was just that simple. What if Leona was afraid that Bella would continue to pursue her and didn't want that? That would complicate them working together, so she almost understood why Leona would change the schedules.

Yet, deep down, she wanted to believe that it was only because Leona had some engagements she couldn't get out of. That would explain everything. Even though that nagging suspicion still dance around inside her mind. All she could do was go about her day and hope that her thoughts would drift from Leona.

It didn't work. At every turn, she caught herself thinking about all the reasons Leona might have pushed Bella off her rotation, and none of them were positive. When Leona came in at the end of Bella's shift, Bella was prepared to tell her that she was sorry and didn't mean to cause any discomfort in their relationship.

Leona walked up and approached her like nothing was wrong, which only confused Bella further. "Wasn't that awesome that Brad was moved out of ICU?" she asked with a wide grin that halted Bella's fears.

"Uh, yeah. Great. I'm a little surprised that you didn't call to tell me. Even a text would have sufficed. You know how much he means to me."

Leona's face fell. "I'm sorry. I guess I wanted it to be a surprise. We were busy last night and it just slipped my mind to let you know. I knew you were going to be here today, though."

Bella nodded. "Would have been nice to have the heads up and all. That's all."

Leona frowned. "I apologize. I should have told you."

Bella released a breath. "It's all right. I was just surprised. That's all." She turned from her. "But I hope you have a good night."

Leona reached out and surprised Bella by grabbing her arm. "You seem upset with me," she said.

Bella looked over her shoulder to see a concerned expression written all over Leona's face. "Just tired, and I guess my thoughts got carried away. I was surprised you weren't working with me. And if I'm being honest, I guess a little disappointed, too. I thought maybe it was because..." Her voice dropped. "Never mind."

"I had some meetings, but I'm sorry. I should have told you. It had nothing to do with what happened between us. Nothing." She had a small smile that helped ease Bella's anxiety. "But I do have some things to discuss with you. Maybe we can have dinner or something this weekend."

"Yeah, sure. We'll compare our schedules. Have a good night." With that, Bella left her. She felt a little rattled by guilt because she sounded like she was still upset, but she did believe everything would be all right between them. As long as she was open to listen to whatever it was Leona wanted to say.

CHAPTER THIRTEEN

Leona

I t was a quiet night as Leona worked her rooms and dictated a few orders to Jacqueline, leaving the young nursing assistant to focus much of her time stocking rooms and sterilizing instruments. Leona walked off the elevator from her break at midnight and spotted Jacqueline at the nurses' station. She looked up when Leona approached her.

"I was just about to make my midnight rounds for meds. Will you look and verify these before I go around?"

"Sure."

Leona sat down in front of the computer and looked through the patients and their prescribed medicines. When she got to room four-one-two, she frowned. "Isn't Malcolm allergic to penicillin?"

"Um, I don't know." Jacqueline sat down at the other computer, typed in her credentials, and skimmed through the medical records. She nodded. "Yeah, at eight he had a severe allergic reaction. Nearly died."

Leona shook her head. "Jacqueline, we can't make these kinds of mistakes. If I would have missed that and approved these orders, you would have given it to him, and he could have died." She shook her head. "We're going to have to note this error to the hospital's safety team."

Jacqueline frowned. "But I didn't," she argued. "Most of those meds were put in before I even got here tonight. It wasn't me." Leona saw tears spring to Jacqueline's eyes.

Leona turned back to the orders and scrolled down until she spotted Bella's name. Her eyes darkened, and she knew there was only one person to blame over this matter. Maybe Bella had been too tired or distracted. Either way, she had missed the order, which could have resulted in grave consequences.

"It was me," Leona said.

"Excuse me?" Jacqueline asked.

Leona turned to her. "I had just gotten here. I've been distracted because I lost a patient a couple days ago. I rattled off drugs and I distinctly remember telling Bella to put Malcolm down for penicillin to fight his infection. It was all my fault."

Jacqueline's eyes narrowed and she nodded.

Leona turned back to the computer and made a few changes before signing off on the meds. "You're good to go." She got up from the computer and hurried away.

She was going to have to talk to Bella about this mistake, but how? She didn't want to come across as accusatory, even if Bella needed to understand her mistake could have had dire consequences. At least she had caught it, but she shuddered at the thought that she could have faced another child's death, only this time at the hands of one of the nurses, and over something that could have been avoided.

Even though she tried to not think about it until she could actually have a conversation with Bella, the thought of what could have happened wouldn't stop plaguing Leona's mind. Errors happened all the time, but those types of errors that you could avoid changed the game. Leona couldn't just keep it to herself when it was something that could have significant implications.

When seven o'clock rolled around, Leona wasn't just physically exhausted, but emotionally exhausted, too. She yawned, heading to the elevator to go downstairs, grab her things, and leave for the day. She was looking forward to getting home and trying to put the night behind her. She spotted Tori heading to the desk, the staff schedule folder in hand.

"Next week's staffing schedules?" Leona asked.

"Yep. Hot off the press." She laughed, then tilted her head. "You look like you've been run over by a truck, then walked a million miles. Rough night?"

Leona reached up and touched her hair. It was a mess, she was sure of it. Not to mention the dark circles under her eyes. Before she went home, maybe she needed to stop somewhere for a massage.

"Yeah, you could say that." She dropped her hand from her hair. "Ready to get home to a glass of wine. Or a massage; that would be nice."

"Before eight o'clock?" Tori's eyes widened.

"Tells you the kind of night I had." Leona let out a breath and grabbed the book from her. "But I'll probably wait at least until two. Don't want to cause too much hysteria. Have a good day, Tori."

"You too, Dr. Guillano."

Leona looked down at her own schedule and was glad to see Bella was back on it. For one, she could have an easier time meeting up with her, and for another, she could ensure that Bella knew her mistake wasn't going to change how Leona felt about her. They would both just learn from it. She closed the folder and put it back, then headed to the elevator.

When the doors opened, Brian Chandler, the CEO, stood there. "Good morning," Leona said. She glanced at her watch. "You're here early." Not to mention out of his own plush office, which she hadn't seen often since starting her job at Capmed.

He nodded firmly. "Had a few things to take care of this morning. Do you mind sticking around a bit so we can talk?"

She frowned and shook her head. "Not at all."

"Let's go to my office."

That elevator ride was slow and painfully awkward. He didn't speak to her, and she was too confused as to why he was even there that she didn't know what to say to him. But finally, they did reach the floor, and he led the way to his office. Leona couldn't help but notice that a few of the employees coming in for their shifts looked over to her like she was walking to the guillotine. But why? Did they know something she didn't?

They entered a room, where three other men, none of whom she knew, were already sitting. She glanced between everyone, even more confused by the turn of events.

"Am I in trouble?" she asked.

Brian looked over to her. "Have a seat. We just need to discuss something with you."

Leona sank into a chair, feeling like a little kid getting ready to be scolded. Leona scanned her eyes between the four men, waiting for one of them to go first. Her hands started to sweat, and she feared she'd hyperventilate if they didn't start soon.

In all her years of being a doctor, she'd never feared she would be reprimanded at her job. Then again, Capmed was a whole new realm for her. She just hoped she didn't start crying when they gave her the metaphorical slap on the hand over whatever it was they were there to discuss with her.

"It has been brought to our attention," Brian started, meeting Leona's gaze, "that you entered an order for penicillin to a pediatric patient that happens to be allergic to penicillin."

Leona gawked at him. "And it was resolved before the error was carried through."

He nodded. "So we were told, but it doesn't change the fact that an adverse event nearly happened and that kid could have been deathly ill as a result. At Capmed we don't tolerate those types of errors. If we get word of it, then we are required to take remedial action."

Leona's mouth snapped closed. "By action...meaning, what?"

"It will go on your record as a point. Once you hit three points, then we'll be forced to seek termination." He shifted a pile of papers and then slid one paper in front of her. "You will be required to sign this, stating you understand that you've been spoken to and will be more careful next time."

Leona released a heavy sigh. Unfortunately, it came out as a haughty laugh. "This isn't a laughing matter," one of the men said.

"I'm sorry. I wasn't laughing, and believe me, after I caught the error, I couldn't think much about anything else. I know how serious this matter is and can assure you I wouldn't laugh over this." She took in a breath. "I lost a patient a few days ago. Losing a patient is never easy, but I would say it distracted me a bit. I usually am on top of things, and it pains me to think about what could have happened."

She looked down at the paper and pen before her. It was a simple form, just describing the policy of Capmed and then one line for her signature and date. She looked back up, this time turning to Brian. "So, Jacqueline told you, right?"

He returned her stare. "We can't disclose the whistleblower in this situation, and I believe you understand that."

She nodded but knew that was the only logical explanation. Had Jacqueline wanted to get Leona in trouble to ease the stress of the mistakes she had made herself? She couldn't blame her if that were the case, but it was a messed up situation. She looked back down at the paper and grabbed the pen. She wouldn't fight it because it beat the alternative of Bella getting raked over the coals. Leona could get out of this situation, but she was an established doctor. Bella was just a nursing assistant. Perhaps that was another reason Jacqueline wanted Leona to get in trouble over the matter.

"It won't happen again," Leona said, pushing the paper toward Brian.

"We have all heard amazing thing about your performance so we're confident it won't. Thank you."

She nodded. "Am I free to go?"

He nodded and all the men got up from the table and watched her as she left the room. She wasn't sure why the other men had to be there, unless they needed some sort of board to acknowledge that she did, in fact, sign the form. But it was over and done with, and she would have to try to forget that it happened. She went and grabbed her purse from her locker, then left the hospital.

As she got to her car, she sat in the driver's seat for a moment, pulling her phone from her pocket to text Bella. The sooner they got together, the better she would feel about everything she had to tell her. Before she could start the text message, her phone rang.

"This is Leona," she started.

"Hello, Leona. It's Kandice. I was hoping you had some time this morning for us to could sit down and chat."

Leona stifled a yawn, feeling the heavy weight from all that transpired, but she needed to take this meeting. Then she would know exactly how she could proceed.

CHAPTER FOURTEEN

Bella

Bella looked up from her anatomy book and stared straight ahead. It was only two, but she was already dressed for her seven o'clock work shift. Still, she thought of a million reasons she should call out. She could tell them she was sick. Surely they wouldn't want someone that was running a fever to come in and work.

But then you'd be lying.

She hadn't seen Leona since they had passed one another during the shift change, and she had definitely felt an awkwardness between them. If they couldn't even acknowledge their intimate encounters, what did that say for them?

Before she could make the call, her phone rang, and she saw Jackson's name. "Hey, Jackson." Her head started pounding, and she massaged her temples.

She'd been avoiding him, but there were only so many times she could ignore his calls before facing the facts. She wanted to talk to him in person, but everything was starting to wear her down too much. She didn't know where her life was headed or where she stood with Leona, but she knew she needed time to breath and figure out her life without Jackson in the back of her mind. Her stomach churned as she considered what she was about to say.

"Hey, babe." Bella could practically see Jackson beaming on the other end of the line. "Just was thinking about you. Are you free tonight so that we can meet up for dinner or something? I've missed you."

If she called in sick, she could meet with him and have the conversation she needed to have with him. Then again, she would have an absence on her record. She needed to get this out now. Then they could have a longer talk in the future.

The words came out of her, raw and blunt. "Jackson, I need a break."

"Uh, from school or work? If you want to take a weekend trip somewhere—"

"No. I want us to take a break. I'm sorry I can't tell you this in person. Everything is...I'm so overwhelmed and I need some time to think about everything. I don't know how I feel about us anymore and I feel awful about it, but this isn't fair to you. We need to take a break from our relationship so we can both think about what future we want."

Jackson was silent for so long, Bella worried the call had dropped. Finally, he said, "I don't understand. What changed? The plan was always to get married and have kids. I still want that. You don't?"

"I don't know what I want, but right now I need time, so can we put a pause on us?"

"Can we at least talk about this in person?"

"I wish I could, but I have to work and...I'm sorry."

"I'm sorry, too."

She felt a pang of regret for letting him down, but she couldn't keep stringing him on like this. "I want to talk in person. I just don't know when. I'm sorry, I have to go."

"I love you."

"Bye."

She ended the call and wiped tears from her cheek. Had she done the right thing? Jackson had been with her so many years, and she didn't even know what Leona wanted. Maybe asking Jackson to go on a break was wrong, but a weight had lifted from her that she hadn't realized she was carrying.

A text message came through and she looked down to read who it was from.

Leona: I need to see you. Can you come over in two hours to my house?

Bella: Text me your address.

After already having one difficult conversation today, why not go for two and get it over with? At least she'd know where Leona stood one way or another.

Bella wondered if she should dress in normal clothes, but that would look strange, especially when she wasn't sure how long she'd be there. She decided to stay in her scrubs and headed over to Leona's house an hour and a half later.

Leona lived in a subdivision thirty minutes from Bella's apartment. When Bella pulled up in front of her house, her jaw dropped. It was much more lavish than the apartment Bella lived in. Not that she would have expected anything less from a successful doctor like Leona.

When Leona opened the door, Bella started taking off her shoes, but Leona just laughed. "That's not necessary."

Bella moved into the foyer and gawked at the furnishings surrounding her. "You have a nice place here," she commented.

"Thanks. I was lucky. I saw it on the market two weeks before I was to start the job. Placed an offer sight unseen. I was the first one. They accepted the offer and I just hoped that I wouldn't regret it. I have to say that it could have turned into my biggest regret."

"But some things actually work out," Bella concluded.

"Yep, and this is one of those things." Leona looked around her home and then glanced back at Bella. "How are you doing?"

"Doing fairly well. Got plenty of sleep over the past day and a half, so that's promising. School has been busy, but when is it not?" She slid her hands into the pocket of her scrubs, then shrugged, forcing the words out to see how Leona would react. "And I told my boyfriend I wanted a break."

Leona looked up, her face unreadable. Her lips faded into a straight line, and she motioned toward a hallway. "Would you like some coffee?"

Not the reaction Bella had hoped for. "Sure."

Bella followed Leona down the hallway and to a kitchen, where a pot had already been brewed for them. Leona poured her a cup, then they moved over to a table and sat down. It was after two sips that Leona cleared her throat and looked up.

"I want to start by saying that I know things have been rough on you.

You've had a tiring and exhausting schedule. I don't even know how you've been managing. So, when I tell you what I'm about to tell you, know that I'm not here to scold you. I'm not here to make you feel bad about yourself. And in no way do I want you to take this as criticism because I know you've been struggling. This is a learning experience and I know that once we work through this, you *will* able to grow from it. We're a team at work, so I'm telling you this as your teammate who only wants the best for you."

The more Leona spoke about how she didn't want Bella to take offense to whatever it was she was about to say, or how she didn't want to sadden Bella or make her mad, the more uneasy Bella grew. Her muscles tensed. Leona was spewing a lot of words without saying much at all. That meant that Bella had something to worry about.

"You're giving me a complex. Just tell me what's going on. Please."

"Yesterday you left the hospital with a penicillin order for one of your patients. They're allergic to penicillin. Please tell me that Dr. Whalen told you to order it."

Bella's jaw dropped. "Who's the patient?"

"Malcolm Little."

Bella looked down at her coffee mug. The flood of memories came rushing back to her, starting with how Dr. Whalen had run through the list of patients she should prescribe meds to. Malcolm had been one of them, but she had specifically recalled reading his allergy for penicillin. Dr. Whalen had ordered erythromycin instead. She must have inadvertently put in the wrong medication when she had transcribed the orders.

Bella fought to explain herself. "I, I guess I was tired. And I had a lot on my mind." She met Leona's gaze, which had significantly darkened. "I was worried that you were regretting that we had gotten close and when I didn't see you on my rotation, I suspected you had changed your shift to avoid me."

She wiped a tear that had escaped from her eyes. "I'm sorry, but what does this mean? Am I dropped from the program? Am I barred from becoming a nurse? Have these last four years been for nothing?" Panic rose inside of her as the questions tumbled out.

"Malcom didn't get the medicine, I hope." She jumped up from the table and started to pace back and forth in front of Leona. "I should apologize to his parents. How could I make such a huge mistake? Maybe I really am not cut out to be a nurse and—"

"Bella, calm down," Leona spoke. "This is precisely what I wanted to prevent. I didn't want you panicking. It's true this was a grave mistake and could have cost Malcom his life. But all is well. I spotted the error and I defused the situation. He got his meds—the right ones—and there's no reason to fret over that. But..." Her words trailed off. Bella stopped pacing and turned to her. "Jacqueline caught the error."

Bella groaned. "So she's one-upped me. Now I'll be the one that they say doesn't deserve to stay on at Capmed when the program ends."

Leona shook her head. "I told her that I gave you the orders to put the penicillin in. She thinks that I'm the one that caused the issue."

"You shouldn't have covered for me like that. I don't want anyone to think negatively of you. And I don't want your pity. If I made a mistake, I'll own up to it and suffer the consequences."

Leona shook her head. "It's too late to worry about that. Jacqueline went to the board and told them about what happened, and they reprimanded me for it. If things change now, they'll wonder why I covered for you. Frankly, that would be a worse situation to be in. We'll just leave it at that.

"I'm fine with the way it went down, but I just wanted to make sure you knew what had happened. And again, I want to stress that you *need* to get your rest. I believe in your abilities as a nurse, but anyone who is so severely sleep deprived, as you've been, will make mistakes. This isn't from a lack of ability. It's from a lack of cognitive function because you're not allowing your body to recover."

Bella's jaw clenched. She was annoyed that Jacqueline would have willingly done something to get Leona into trouble. She was also upset that it was all her fault. She shook her head.

"It's not right. This is on me. I need to do better. I can do better. I can't imagine you taking the blame for it. Let me do something to fix this."

Leona reached across the table as Bella fell back into her seat. "There's nothing you can do now. I am telling you that if you say something, they'll question why I covered for you, and I could be fired. This is the best option. Remember, we're a team, so it's okay that I took the blame for this."

Bella was startled by the tenacity in Leona's eyes, but when she spoke like that, Bella knew she was right. She couldn't watch Leona get fired over her trying to protect her. That would make for an even harder thing to face.

"Did you get yelled at too badly?" Bella asked, looking down to see that Leona's hand was still in hers. Leona didn't pull away, and neither did Bella.

"It wasn't too harsh. I had to sign a letter and got a point in my chart. But I know that it would have been harder to go through if you would have gotten the lashing. They probably would have thrown you from the program."

"And it would've been well deserved," Bella mumbled.

Leona slipped her fingers between Bella's and moved in closer to her. "Don't say that. I'm glad you're at Capmed and I don't want you to get fired over something like this. I know that you'll remember next time to double and triple check your work. It's something we all have to be mindful of. But as far as anyone knows, I'm the one that ordered this drug, and you were only going on my orders. Got that?"

Bella nodded. "But what about Dr. Whalen?"

Leona shrugged. "I thought of that, too. He would know that he was the one who ordered it, but it's against protocol for the hospital to disclose when doctors get reprimanded, especially with their peers. I don't think that Jacqueline will go running her mouth, because frankly, that was poorly done on her side. No one would take it too kindly if they realized Jacqueline was the hospital snitch. That would stay with her."

It made sense, but Bella was still upset that she had messed up and gotten someone else in trouble for it. She didn't want Leona to always have to take the fall for her. Yet, she appreciated that Leona had done so without hesitation.

"I appreciate that you covered for me. I really do. Thank you."

She smiled. "There wasn't even a doubt that I would." She slowly pulled her hand back. "But on that note, that's not the only thing I have to tell you."

Bella groaned. "Should I start cringing already?"

Leona laughed loudly. "I don't think so. I think you'll be surprised, but hopefully pleasantly so. I have to say that I'm a little shell-shocked myself."

Bella tilted her head, anxious to hear what it was. It wasn't long before Leona started excitedly chattering away.

"I'm not sure what you've heard, but Brad's foster family fell through."

Bella's jaw dropped. The thought that Brad wasn't getting his temporary home killed her, but she waited for Leona to continue, hoping she would say something positive.

"The man didn't pass the background check. But that's only half the story, and frankly, it gets better."

Bella sighed. "That's a relief."

"Because there wasn't another family readily available and because Brad is set to go home tomorrow, I inquired about being his foster mom."

Bella jumped up, gawking at Leona. "Are you serious?"

Leona frowned. "That's a good 'are you serious,' right?"

Bella laughed. "The best, but *are* you serious? You would foster him? How would that even work, with you being a doctor with such erratic hours? He would be left home alone a lot."

Leona grinned. "I've covered all the bases. There's a day care at the hospital. When he's at school I can work around their schedule. I want a family, and I think that ideally, I'll foster him with the plan of eventually adopting him."

Bella grinned. This was by far the best news she'd had in a while. "I think this is a fantastic idea," Bella said. "And I think my sister would love to watch him, too, if you're ever too busy." She paused. "But are we getting our hopes up too soon? I mean, you inquired about it, but it doesn't necessarily mean it will go through, right?"

"I got the call yesterday morning. It's official."

Without a second thought, Bella grabbed Leona by the arms and pulled her up, then threw her arms around her and pulled her into an embrace. "I'm so happy for you."

"You can see him whenever you want," Leona whispered. She moved into the embrace, kissing Bella with the same enthusiastic passion Bella had felt their first kiss.

The news was exciting for sure, but the way she felt in Leona's arms was even more so, and Bella wanted to be nowhere else. All of the unknowns between them, though, made her break the kiss.

"Wait," Bella said. "I just need to know where we stand. I've spent the past few days lost and confused. And I can't promise anything. I don't even know what I want right now, but...I do know that I like you."

Leona smiled. "I like you, too." She stepped away, the brief moment of joy on her face replaced by seriousness. "Things are complicated, aren't they?"

"Yeah. I told my boyfriend we need a break, but I haven't decided what future I want. It's been hard enough just getting through school. And I know it's not fair to you to string you along. Even if I want for us to...Well, I don't know if my heart..."

Leona took Bella's hand. "I understand. Honestly, I'm a little hesitant, too. My focus needs to be on Brad for now. But I still want to spend time with you."

"Even if we don't know what the heck we're doing?"

Leona smiled. "Especially that."

They kissed, a soft kiss that made Bella feel like everything would work out, even if she had no idea it would.

BELLA ENTERED BRAD'S ROOM TO SEE LEONA LOOKING OVER the guy, who was still sound asleep. Leona looked like the doting mother Bella knew she would be. Leona turned to Bella, grinning, and Bella motioned for her to follow her into the hall.

"I have to go because I have class, so I won't be here when you get to take him home. But is he super stoked?"

Leona grinned. "Extremely. I think he can't believe that he's leaving the hospital and going to a loving home. I can't wait until he sees his bedroom. We're going to decorate the spare room together. I'm going to make sure he feels that he's loved every day he's there with me."

"He's one lucky boy," Bella replied. "I called Veronica on break and told her I might have a babysitting gig for her. She can do it when she's not at school. She's really excited. I told her that it was a doctor I work with."

Leona's eyes fell, and Bella reached out to touch her arm. "I haven't told my family yet about Jackson."

She looked up and nodded. "I get it."

Bella sighed with relief. "Well, I'd better go, but I'll call you later. I hope things go smoothly when you get him home."

"I'm sure they will. Thanks, Bella." Leona looked past her, her eyes darting around the hospital.

Bella glanced over her shoulder. The hospital was empty of people. Leona grabbed her hand and pulled her back into Brad's room and closed the door. Then, she moved in and captured a kiss without having to worry about being watched by anyone, including the hospital cameras.

"I'll talk to you soon," Bella said, pulling from the kiss.

As Leona turned back to her foster son, Bella left the room and went downstairs to get her purse and leave the hospital to get to her class. She yawned several times on the way to the hospital, suddenly laden with how tired she truly was. It was going to be a long four hours, but she would have to somehow muddle through them.

At least she was on time. She took her seat before her professor came in and took his place at the front of the class. "Today we are continuing where we left off the last class, finishing our study on the cranium. Turn to page one-oh-two. I want you to study this diagram in its entirety, as we will have a quiz on it next period."

Bella stared at the picture and started to zone out, only vaguely registering the professor's words. Before she knew it, her eyes drifted shut, and she withered into a relaxing sleep.

"Ms. Strong? Ms. Strong, are you paying attention? Answer me, Ms. Strong."

Bella jerked awake when Anthony, the guy in the seat next to her, kicked her foot. "Huh?" she asked, jumping up from her seat. She felt saliva on her lip and quickly wiped the drool away, her classmates laughing all around her.

"I asked you a question. And since I know you were deeply concentrated on it, I look forward to hearing your response."

"Um..." she looked over to Anthony, hopeful he would send her the response telepathically. He smirked and shook his head. She turned back to look at Professor Finch. "The right lower quadrant?" she asked.

"Is that a question?" he asked. Again, students laughed around her, and she shook her head.

"No, it's definitely the right lower quadrant."

Professor Finch looked down at his book, then back up. "Well, if we were discussing the abdomen, then you might be right. Have a seat and see me after class."

Bella sat back down and looked at the book. *The cranium. Ugh. Could I have been any more wrong?*

In a mixed blessing, class went by quickly, but as everyone filtered out of the room, Bella didn't rush to get her things to see what Professor Finch wanted to say to her. She, however, did think of the million things she wanted to say in her apology, but he was a short and curt man who didn't seem to have an empathetic bone in his body, and it wasn't going to suffice him for her to apologize.

"Ms. Strong," he started.

Bella interrupted, "I know what you're going to say and I'm sorry. It's just I've been busy with work and school and I'm not getting much sleep at all. I worked twelve hours and came straight from the hospital. I'm trying here, Professor Finch. You have to believe that."

"Do you know that when I was going to college, I worked sixty hours and did full-time, all the way up to the time I got my doctorate? That's tough work, yet I managed."

Bella dropped her eyes. There was no point in trying to continue her argument. She already knew where it would go. She let him do his own rambling.

"We all have things that keep us busy, but we have to press on if we have any hope to succeed in life. You have to persevere if you want to achieve greater things out of life. A person is their own worst enemy, and if you choose to fail, then you will fail."

"I'm not choosing to fail," she argued.

"Your coursework would beg to differ. Your grades are struggling and if you don't do better, you *will* fail. You have to fight and work even harder if you want to succeed. You can do it, but only if you want it."

"Am I free to go?" She looked away from him.

"Just one more thing. Do you want to achieve bigger and better things out of life? Or do you prefer mediocre?"

"Professor Finch," she stated. "Of course I want that, but maybe I'm not cut out for that. I believe in my heart I'm doing the very best that I can. If that isn't satisfactory then I guess I'll have to live with my failures. But I'm trying."

"If you don't try harder, you might wind up failing this class. Without passing this anatomy course, you won't graduate. Think about that." He handed her a past assignment and she looked at the D written in a bold-faced capital letter. "You say you're better than this? Then prove it."

She yanked the assignment from him and slipped it into her folder. "I'm not a failure and I will show everyone that I can make it through this class." She turned and hurried out of the room.

Bella didn't know how she had gotten a D. She had the book right in front of her when she was going through the assignment. She shook her head and stormed out of the school. She was going to prove everyone wrong. If they didn't think she could do it, then that was on them. Bella was out to make sure she could.

CHAPTER FIFTEEN

Leona

Leona grabbed her phone and flipped through it, checking to see if she had somehow missed Bella's text or phone call. She saw nothing. A day and night had passed and still no contact from her. She knew that Bella had said she would meet with her when classes were through the previous day. Leona had practically been attached to her phone, waiting for a message or call that had never come.

"Lona?" Brad asked, approaching her from behind. She turned to him and lifted him onto her lap.

"What is it, bud?"

He had a serious look on his face, one that melted Leona's heart. She held him closer to her, just thankful to have him there.

"Now that I'm living with you, what should I call you? Should I still call you Lona? Or what?"

She grinned. "Well, what would you like to call me?"

"Mama?" he asked, eyes wide.

Leona grinned, wrapping her arms around him. "I would like that very much, if that's what you feel comfortable with."

He nodded. "Mama Lona."

She laughed, pulling him into her arms. The best two words strung together. "We need to get going so I can get you to the day care."

"Will I be going to school?" he asked. "In the foster homes I was never there long enough, but now...I was just wondering."

"Is that what you want?" He was quick to nod.

Leona smiled, knowing she was going to do whatever she could to make sure Brad grew up happy. Within reason, of course.

"We'll make that happen. But for today, day care."

They got in the car and headed to the hospital. She had plenty of time to get him in the right room and head up to her floor to start her shift. Brad seemed happy and excited to be going to the day care until he reached the room and she was just about to drop him off. He backed up to the wall and just waited. She looked over her shoulder and walked over to him.

"Are you nervous?" she asked.

He nodded, slightly. "What if no one likes me?"

Leona knelt in front of him. "You know, when I first started here, I worried about that, too. I was coming to a new place and thought it would be awkward if I couldn't make any friends. I worried all night about that, but then, when I started, it just felt right, and I've made great friends. Plus, you're a charming young man. I would say you're going to have the kids falling all over you."

He looked up, his grin infectious. "I had a friend, once. Kyle." He looked down at the floor. "Back at my first children's home. Someone adopted him and I haven't seen him in a long time."

Leona nodded. "I understand. It's hard to lose friends that you've made, but I promise you that you're going to make new friends. You have my word on that."

He looked up and his smile grew wider. She grabbed his hand and escorted him into the room. A woman stood with a baby in her arms and another one knelt in front of a little girl as they played with the blocks.

"Who do we have here?" the woman holding the baby asked.

"I'm Dr. Guillano. I work on the pediatric floor. This is Brad. He'll be coming here for a bit, until I can get him signed up for school. I just started fostering him and haven't had a chance to work out a lot of details. I hope this is okay."

"You bet it is," the woman said. "My name is Sheila, and that's Heidi.

We work at the day care during the day. How long will we have him today?"

"'Til about midnight," Leona answered.

"Marla does the third shift most nights, so she'll be here when you get here. What time is his bedtime?"

Leona considered that. The previous night he was in bed by seven, but was that his usual bedtime? He had just seemed exhausted, as things had been hectic for him. "Sevenish, I suppose. I won't be one of those parents that have to stick to a regime, so I understand if something happens."

Sheila smiled. "I'm sure we're going to get along just fine. We just need you to sign a waiver that documents the rules, etcetera, but that will be just about it."

"Sounds good. I'm pretty nervous leaving him and all. I just hope he gets along with everyone."

Sheila smiled. "I would say so far, so good." She motioned with her head toward Brad, who was playing with Heidi and the girl with the blocks. A flood of relief washed over her. "How long have you been fostering him?

"About twenty-four hours," Leona mumbled.

Sheila arched an eyebrow and Leona laughed and nodded. "Wow. That's amazing. I know kids need parents just like you. So, kudos to you."

Leona followed Sheila over to the desk, where the woman fumbled around for some paper, all while keeping the baby jostling in her arms. She sighed and looked down at the baby, then to Leona. "Do you mind?"

"Not at all." Leona grabbed the baby and held the little girl in her arms. She was so small. "How old is she?"

"Twelve weeks. Her mom just went back to work a couple days ago. I send her pictures often, but it's not like the real thing. Here we go." She whipped out a sheet of paper and motioned to where Leona could sign. "I'll fill in the rest of the information for you," Sheila replied. "But you're good to go."

"Thanks a lot." Leona turned to Brad and walked over to where he was playing. She watched him for a minute, then leaned in and kissed the top of his forehead. "I'll see you in a bit."

"Bye, Mama Lona," he said.

She smiled and waved, then looked over to Sheila, then Heidi. "Thank you both."

As she left the room, she felt some guilt. Maybe she shouldn't have left him so soon. He had just been put in her care, and it felt like she was finding reasons to leave him. She turned and looked at him through the door, but he seemed happy and looked like he was enjoying himself. When she turned around, she bumped into a woman who was holding a boy's hand.

"Excuse me," she said.

"No worries." The woman escorted the boy, who looked to be Brad's age, into the room, and Leona felt assured that Brad would find some friends and be just as happy when she picked him up. At least, she hoped that'd be the case. Now all she needed to do was get to work and see Bella. She still questioned why Bella hadn't reached out to her the previous day.

She dropped her purse off at her locker, then headed to her floor and tried looking for Bella. She looked toward the nurse's station, but Bella wasn't there.

Uneasy, Leona went to her office and logged into her computer. She skimmed through the charts to check out the latest things that were happening. She saw that Bella was logged in, so she knew she was at least at the hospital. She got up from her desk to go to her first patient or see Bella—whichever came first.

When she rounded the corner, she finally spotted Bella. That didn't take long. Bella looked up from her notebook and looked straight at Leona. She then turned and darted into the closest room. Leona frowned. Bella was avoiding her. But why? Looking back on their previous encounter, Leona thought nothing would have kept Bella from wanting to see her. Unless something happened after the fact. Or maybe it was because neither of them could commit to being in a relationship or knew how to define whatever it was they had together.

Bella looked like she had been studying while on break, so Leona didn't go after her. Hopefully, they'd get to talk before the day was done.

LEONA SLUMPED DOWN IN HER SEAT AND GLANCED AT HER computer. It'd been four hours since they had started their shift and the only times she could get Bella to talk to her were when they concerned patients. She was starting to get a complex, thinking that maybe she had overlooked something she had done wrong.

A knock sounded on the door. She looked up to see Bella.

"Misty needs an approval on meds." She thrust the order out matter-of-factly, and Leona cautiously grabbed it.

"All right." She looked down, surveying the orders, then looked up. "This is something you could have easily approved yourself."

She shrugged. "Don't want to give something I shouldn't have inadvertently."

Leona handed the orders back to her, arching an eyebrow. "I thought we've been through this," Leona began. "I don't want any craziness between us. You made a mistake with your other patient, but it's done, and we have to just move on."

"Fine. Am I free to go?" Bella asked, a look of annoyance streaking across her face. Leona nodded and Bella turned and hurried from the room.

That was odd. Leona had no idea where that came from. Even though they had already talked about it, could Bella actually be upset that Leona had called her out on the medication error?

She sat at her desk, staring at her computer, looking for answers. Answers that weren't there. Her phone started ringing, and she grabbed it. "Dr. Guillano."

"Hey, Dr. Guillano. It's Marla. I'm the third shift director here in the day care."

"Yes, of course. Is everything all right?"

"I'm having a little trouble getting Brad to lie down. If you were here to talk to him, then maybe he would be able to relax. I'm sorry to bother you. I know you're busy and all..."

"No worries. I'll be right there." She dropped the phone into the receiver and jumped up, hurrying out of the office. Bella was sitting at the nurse's station and looked up when she approached. Bella jumped up from her chair, surprised.

"I have to run to the day care," Leona said hurriedly.

469

"Is everything all right with Brad?" Bella asked, her sour attitude softening.

So she did still remember that Brad was coming to live with her. And yet, she hadn't once inquired about him. They hadn't talked about how Brad factored into any possibility of a relationship between them, but maybe Bella's lack of attention meant she wasn't ready for motherhood right now. And Leona couldn't get involved with someone who wasn't going to stick around. It would be too damaging to Brad.

"He can't sleep, so they're asking for my help. Hopefully I won't be long."

Bella opened her mouth to say something, but Leona turned away and left her standing there. She got into the elevator and watched Bella staring after her until the doors closed her in. She collapsed back against the elevator wall, confused.

The day care was quiet when she reached it. The only people there were a woman and Brad. The woman knelt next to Brad, the two of them looking at a book. She looked up when Leona approached them.

She stood and put on a smile. "I'm Marla," she said.

Leona held out her hand. "Dr. Guillano. You can call me Leona."

She immediately knelt in front of Brad. "What's wrong, bud?"

Marla left them alone, and Brad looked at Leona shyly. "It's quiet here."

"The best way to get rest is by having quiet." She rubbed his back, and he looked around the empty room.

"Too quiet," he said.

Leona followed his gaze and then looked back at him. "Too much like a children's home, perhaps?" she asked.

He looked back at her and slowly nodded. Leona sat down on the floor and pulled him onto her lap. "I'm not going to ever send you back there. You know that, right?"

He shrugged and looked down at his hands. She kissed the top of his head, then grabbed the book he had been looking at. She opened it up and began to read it. Before she knew it, he was nestled against her chest, following along. Leona smiled, happy that Brad already seemed so comfortable with her. She continued to read, and twenty minutes later, he was fast asleep. She carefully shifted him so he was resting on a sleeping bag with his head on the pillow.

Leona stood to her feet and looked down at him. He rolled onto his side, turning away from her. She smiled and turned, looking over at Marla. She walked over to her, checking on Brad one more time over her shoulder.

"I'm not sure what you've heard about our situation," Leona began, turning back Marla.

"That he's a foster child," Marla replied. "Really, that's about it."

Leona nodded. "He just came to live with me, and I think his nerves are getting the better of him. He just needs to be reminded that I'll never leave him."

"That makes sense."

Leona looked around the day care. "Will he be the only one here until midnight?" she asked.

"Yeah, I have one child coming in at two." Leona's mouth opened in surprise. "That tends to happen. Babies need to get woken up just to come into the hospital with their mothers or fathers."

"Wow. Well, I'll be back to get him in a few hours."

"No problem. See you then. I'm not going anywhere." Marla smiled and turned to some paperwork on her desk.

Leona watched Brad as she left the day care. She just hoped he didn't wake up, frightened by his surroundings. She couldn't worry about that, though. Not now. She had to get back to work.

When she reached her floor, she didn't see Bella, so she headed straight for her office. It was quiet in there, with Bella the only nurse working the evening shift. Hadley, a cleaning woman, worked also, but that was it. Luckily, it wasn't a busy night.

Leona sat back down at her computer and opened a drawer, where she had stored her water and sandwich in a lunchbox.

She took a bite of her sandwich and leaned back in her chair, releasing a yawn. She closed her eyes. *Nothing a five-minute cat nap couldn't fix.*

When she heard the clearing of a throat, her eyes snapped open.

"I didn't know if you were back," Bella replied, her voice soft.

Leona sat up in her chair and put her sandwich down on her desk. "It didn't take long to get him to go to sleep."

"That's good. I thought I would run and get something to eat. If you think you can handle it, that is."

Leona smirked. "We only have three beds filled. I doubt I'll run into any issues."

Bella started to turn, then looked over her shoulder. "Want anything? Besides that bologna sandwich, I mean."

"No, but thank you."

Bella turned to leave, but Leona couldn't stop herself from speaking. "Are you going to tell me why you're having an attitude with me all of a sudden?"

Bella turned and opened her mouth, but then looked down at the floor. Leona stared at her as Bella started to sob. At first, Leona thought she was misreading the signs, but she saw that Bella's face was bright red and tears were running down her cheeks.

"Bella!" She jumped up and hurried to the door, closing it so they had privacy, even though there wasn't anyone likely to walk in. "What's wrong? And don't tell me this is about the medication error, because I'm not going to buy that."

"It is, and it isn't," Bella mumbled. "I just feel like my life is falling apart. I mess up orders. I'm not doing stellar work at school. It just seems like everywhere I turn I'm messing up with something." She sniffled and flicked a tear away. "I'm sorry I was snippy with you. I'm exhausted and I don't know how much I can take of this." She slumped her head down and stared at the ground as Leona's heart tugged inside her rapidly beating chest. "And now you probably think I just can't handle things like a normal adult."

"That's not what I'm thinking, Bella." Leona reached up and stroked a strand of hair behind Bella's ear, which had fallen from her ponytail. "Bella, look at me."

Bella shook her head and Leona stroked her hand down the length of Bella's arm. "Please look at me."

After a brief hesitation, Bella looked up, her eyes glazed over from tears. "I'll tell you what I see. When I told you my thoughts that you should remain open to other careers, I barely knew you. But I can tell you that I've changed my thinking on whether you should continue to pursue this. Besides, no one should ever try to talk you out of something you want to do. As for the error, things happen. And as for your classes, I'm sure it's not as bad as you think."

"You have no idea," Bella said.

Leona reached up and brushed her thumb against Bella's cheek, making Bella close her eyes. "I know you. I know that you are a strong, caring, and beautiful individual. And whatever you set your mind out to do, you will achieve it. You just have to believe you're worth achieving it. No one can take that light and that drive from you."

Bella bit down on her lower lip and Leona's eyes dropped to her lips. She moved in and claimed her lips against hers, growing breathless. She slid her tongue along Bella's, then opened her eyes. The heat in Bella's stare ignited a fire between Leona's legs. Leona turned and locked the door, then turned back to Bella. She moved in and kissed her hard, pressing her back until she bumped into her desk.

"I want you, Bella," Leona whispered. "But if you tell me no right now, I'll stop."

Bella's eyes lifted to hers and Bella shook her head slightly before grabbing onto her shirt and pulling it up and over her head, revealing her perfectly round breasts, barely hidden under her bra. With one flick of her wrist, Bella's bra fell to the ground.

Leona moved in, latching her teeth onto one nipple and swirling her tongue around the areola. Bella groaned, and Leona knew she was in the right place, at the right time. Nothing was going to end their heated moment together.

CHAPTER SIXTEEN

Bella

Bella handed a chart over to Jacqueline. "It's all yours. We've been relatively quiet all night. Hope it stays the same."

Jacqueline nodded and yawned. She scowled, then rubbed her face. "Are you exhausted?" she asked. "I feel like no matter how much rest I get, it's just never enough."

Another yawn escaped. This time, Jacqueline groaned, her eyes droopy, and her mouth settled into a thin line. "It's all worth it, right?"

"I'm exhausted, no doubt. I keep telling myself that there's a light at the end of the road. Just need to get through a few more bumps."

Bella looked up and saw Leona moving toward them. Instantly, her mind went to their heated encounter in Leona's office. Things couldn't have gotten sexier than that.

"Have a good morning, Dr. Guillano," Jacqueline spoke up, her voice ringing out loudly.

Leona barely acknowledged Jacqueline as she brushed past her and headed straight to the elevator. When Bella turned back to her, Jacqueline had dropped her gaze to the chart in her hands.

"Anyway, enjoy yourself." Bella tossed a wave, then headed toward the elevator to get on with Leona.

As the elevator doors closed them in, Leona turned and grinned at

Bella. "Where were we?" she asked. She pulled Bella to her, catching Bella off guard, but she immediately crashed her lips against Leona's. Leona's tongue slithered into her mouth, making Bella release a moan.

On cue, as the doors opened, they pulled from one another and stepped off onto the main floor. Leona turned to her. "I'm headed this way to get Brad," she said, motioning with her head.

Bella nodded. "So, what was that back there with Jacqueline?"

Leona grimaced. "She's the one who turned me in to the board. Or did I not tell you that?"

Bella winced. "I see." Bella looked past her, then glanced back at Leona. "Guess I'll let you go then."

"Do you have school in the morning?"

Bella shook her head. "Not 'til three o'clock tomorrow."

Leona had a sneaky grin on her lips. She tilted her head at Bella and said, "I'm not sure how you would feel about this, but what would you say about coming back to my place? I could get Brad into bed and then you and I could get into bed." She winked, making Bella smile widely.

The more she considered it, the more she wanted to spend the night with Leona. Just one night of not thinking about her problems or what their future might hold. Was it so wrong to just want some fun, to escape? Eventually, she wouldn't be able to avoid her problems, but for now, she didn't want to think about how everything in her life seemed to be an issue.

"Best idea yet," Bella replied.

Leona nodded, then turned and led the way to the day care. When they got there, the woman working at the desk had her head propped up against her hand and was aimlessly staring at a book. When they opened the door, she looked up, a smile brightening her face.

"Hello, Dr. Guillano," she said.

Leona glanced over at Bella. "This is Marla. She manages the day care during evening hours."

"Hey, Marla, I'm Bella. I'm in the nursing assistant program and I work with Leona. I mean, Dr. Guillano."

Marla didn't seem to notice the uneasiness Bella felt, standing there. The truth was, Bella didn't know how to act to being there with Leona. Would Marla think it odd that she was tagging along? Marla's eyes darted toward Brad, and Bella followed her gaze. He looked so at peace, and Marla clearly wasn't paying Bella any attention. Her fears slipped away.

"After you left, he stayed asleep."

"Glad to hear," Leona said. She walked over and knelt next to him, gently nudging him awake. "Time to go home," she said, her voice an airy whisper.

Bella watched as Brad opened his eyes and rubbed them. Leona helped him to his feet, and he opened his eyes wide enough to see Bella.

"Bella!" he exclaimed.

"Hey, bud." Bella pulled him into her arms. "I wanted to come see you."

"Thank you." He parted from the hug, then turned to Leona. "Mama Lona, are we going home?"

Bella grinned. Leona had the sweetest smile on her lips. "You bet we are," she said. "Say thank you to Marla."

Brad gave Marla his thanks as Leona reached down and picked up the sleeping bag. She started to fold it, but Marla spoke up. "Oh, that's not necessary. That's why I get paid here."

Leona laid the sleeping bag back down and walked over to Brad. She grabbed his hand, and the three of them said goodbye to Marla, then left the day care. "Did you have fun?" Leona asked.

"The best." He then frowned and glanced up at Leona. "I'm sorry I wouldn't go to sleep."

"Brad, you have nothing to apologize for."

Their interaction was cute, and Bella felt that Brad was in the perfect place with Leona. They both seemed to mesh so well together, and the conversation kept going the entire way to the parking lot. Once they reached the lot, Bella turned to Leona. She wasn't sure how they would explain to Brad that they would both be at the house, but Leona didn't even flinch.

"Are you going to follow me?" she asked.

Bella nodded, then turned to her car. She hurried over and got inside so that she wouldn't be left too far behind. She was able to keep up with Leona, and when they turned into the driveway, Bella parked along the street. She hesitated before walking up to meet Brad and Leona.

"Are you guys getting married?" Brad asked, once they got into the house.

Bella felt her cheeks getting excruciatingly hot. She looked over to Leona, but Leona had a smile that spread across her face. "That's a long way off, bud," she said, then giggled. "For now, just think of Bella as a friend who is visiting." She winked at Bella and Bella quickly looked away.

Being called just a friend stung, but she understood why Leona said it. Brad would be too confused about Bella otherwise. Still, Bella couldn't help but think about marriage and a family. Was she ready for that so soon? The plan had always been to have kids when she was thirty.

"Let's get you up to bed," Leona said to Brad.

"Are you coming, Bella?" he asked, turning to face her.

"Um, I, I..."

"Come on, Bella." Leona said, reaching out for her hand. Bella took it, and they headed upstairs to Brad's room. Leona went through a couple of drawers until she found some clothes for Brad. "Get changed and we'll be in to kiss you goodnight."

Leona grabbed Bella's hand again and escorted her out of the room. When the door was closed, Bella glanced over at Leona. "A friend visiting, huh?" she teased.

Leona laughed. "Your face was a tinge red."

"Tinge?" Bella laughed, shaking her head. "I don't think I've ever been more uncomfortable in my life." She leaned back against the wall and stared at Leona.

"What made it more awkward? Him asking the question or you thinking about it?"

Bella shrugged. "Both, I suppose. Do you want marriage? Not with us...I mean, it's too soon. But someday. With someone, or..." She let her words fade, unsure how to salvage her rambling.

Leona reached up and brushed her hand over the side of Bella's face. "Yes. I've always wanted marriage and a family. Is this situation too much? If it is, we can put the brakes on—"

"No," Bella said, maybe a bit too forcefully. "I like whatever this is. It's not too much, only confusing. You know I want marriage and kids, but this isn't at all what I expected or planned for. And I don't want to confuse Brad when I'm still figuring my life out."

Leona brushed her lips against Bella's. "I know. I can't say I'll be happy with things like this forever because both Brad and I need stability, but for now, I'm happy."

"I promise I won't be so undecided forever."

"Good." Before Leona could thoroughly kiss Bella, the door opened. Bella quickly pulled back, and they both turned to look at Brad. "Let's get you in bed," Leona said.

Bella and Leona entered the room and Brad hopped into bed. "Nighty night, buddy."

"Night, Mama Lona." He wrapped his arms around her, and she kissed the top of his head. Bella then moved in and brushed her hand against Brad's forehead. "Night, Bella."

"Night, little guy," she responded, kissing his forehead.

He shifted onto his side and grabbed his teddy bear, holding it tightly to his chest. Bella and Leona stood at the door for a while, and then Leona turned and looked at her. Bella moved in and kissed her softly, going with her emotions, not allowing the feeling to pass.

When they parted, Leona smiled and reached for her hand, pulling her out of the room. They closed the door so that it was just slightly ajar. Leona pulled Bella toward another bedroom and Bella laughed, unable to keep up. Once they were inside Leona's room, Leona closed the door and locked it behind them. She grabbed the bottom of Bella's shirt and slowly pulled it up over her head. She tossed it to the side, and Bella unclasped her bra. When her bra dropped to the floor, she tugged at Leona's jacket and shirt until they were both off.

When they were both undressed from the top up, Leona pushed Bella toward the bed and Bella fell back against it. She looked up, her eyes gazing over Leona's breasts. Leona moved in and kissed her, and Bella tugged at her pants, removing them, then her panties, feeling the warmth in her nether regions. She pulled Leona down on top of her and they eagerly continued to kiss. Bella was no longer exhausted, and it was all because of Leona. The only thing that mattered in this moment was right in front of her.

Leona opened her mouth, just enough to allow Bella's tongue to enter. Bella felt like she no longer needed rest, as long as she was with Leona. She didn't even know what time it was as they continued to make out, the sun barely drifting through the bedroom window.

"I'd better go," Bella whispered. "Brad will be up at any moment, and frankly, I don't know that you're ready to have that conversation with him." She giggled, kissing Leona hard before pulling back.

Leona groaned, the sound echoing through the walls of her bedroom. Bella grabbed her bra and put it on, then noticed that Leona had her eyes directed toward her. "What are you smirking about?" Bella asked, pulling her top down over her.

"You're beautiful."

Bella felt her face get warm as she slipped on her panties and then her pants. Though she had never reacted when Jackson called her that, those words from Leona made her insides melt. "Well, thank you, but I don't quite know how to take your compliments."

Leona laughed loudly, then pushed herself up onto her hands, so that she was on all fours, hovering closer to Bella's lips. "A thank you will suffice." She kissed her softly, then fell back onto the bed and continued to stare at Bella as Bella put her socks and shoes on.

She hesitated, then looked over to Leona. "For the record, you're beautiful yourself."

Leona wiggled her eyebrows, then smiled. "For an older woman?"

Bella shrugged. "For any woman. Age is just a number, after all." She walked over to Leona, as Leona's eyes followed her every move. Bella brushed her hand along Leona's cheek and kissed her. In any relationship, Bella was more the submissive type, scared to take the lead. When it came to Leona, she caught herself in many ways wanting to be the aggressor in the relationship, wanting to open herself to letting go fully. "I'll call you later, after school."

"I look forward to it," Leona said, grinning.

Bella waved goodbye and headed for the door. The moment she opened it, she came face to face with Brad. He had one arm raised, seemingly about to knock on the door. His eyes widened when he looked up and saw her. Bella glanced back toward the bed, where Leona had pulled the covers up tightly under her chin.

"Hey, Brad," Bella said.

"Hey." His wide-eyed expression turned into a smile. "You startled me." He laughed and Bella realized that he wasn't startled by the fact that she was there, but the fact that the door had opened just before he knocked.

"Sorry, bud." She ruffled his hair with her hands, then looked over at Leona, whose eyes were now completely bugged out. Bella turned back to Brad, asking, "Want to grab something to eat in the kitchen?"

"Yeah!" He reached for Bella's hand and practically pulled her down the stairs. Bella laughed as she scuffed down the stairs to get to the kitchen. "Mama Lona has these cinnamon muffins that taste like heaven." He shrugged. "Not that heaven has a taste, but I heard someone say it at the foster home."

Bella smirked. "Well, must be amazing, then. I'd love to taste those."

He pointed to the freezer and Bella made herself at home by taking them out and putting them into the microwave. Before they were done, Leona rushed into the kitchen. Her eyes were no longer filled with embarrassment and her cheeks had turned into a rosy hue.

"What are you both making in here?"

Brad propped himself against the counter. "Those muffins. They were so good." He enthusiastically rubbed his hands together.

When he wasn't paying attention, she looked over to Bella and mouthed, *Thank you.* Bella nodded as the microwave dinged and she pulled the muffins out. "Hmmmm...smells delish," she said. "And breakfast is served."

Despite her hesitancy, she stayed at the house and ate, immediately discovering how easy things were, being there with Brad and Leona. They were like the world's cutest little family, and Bella was finding it hard to leave.

She finally said her goodbyes and left, stopping on the porch. She couldn't remember the last time she had gone so long without checking her phone. Sure enough, the battery flashed red, signaling her phone was about to die. But just below it, she saw the slew of missed calls and texts from Jackson.

Jackson: Bella, I'm at your place. Are you working? Can we talk?

Jackson: Bella. I called the hospital and they said you aren't working tonight. I'm worried. Where are you?

Jackson: BELLA...

Jackson: If I don't hear from you in an hour, I'm calling the cops.

Bella counted a total of twelve missed calls. He had been silent a few days after she had told him she wanted a break, then he had started messaging her more and more. She felt guilty, but why couldn't he give her the space she had told him she needed? Bella groaned and pulled up his phone number. She hit the Call button, but before it started ringing, her phone died.

"Great," she mumbled. She went to her car and dug in her middle console for her charger, but she couldn't find it amid her CDs, business cards, and other trash that crowded the console. She put her key in the ignition and started the car. Since she had some time, she figured she needed to go talk to Jackson in person. Maybe it would help him give her more space and time to consider her options. She still cared for Jackson, but the more time she spent with Leona, the more her heart was with her.

Thirty minutes later, Bella turned down Jackson's road. As she drew closer, she saw his truck parked in the driveway. She was sure she would feel much better the moment she got this off her chest. But when she stood at his door, the nerves came rushing back in. She stepped to the side and looked into the window, where she could see her reflection. Her hair was all frazzled. She hadn't even taken the time to brush it.

Bella sighed and tried to straighten her hair—as if that would relieve her nerves. "He's not going to care what you look like, Bella. By the sound of the texts, he was probably panicking." She cringed, hoping that he hadn't rushed to call the cops.

Getting cold feet, she turned away from the door, her eyes turning to Jackson's truck. She stared at it, trying to build her resolve. "I can't just leave now." There was a hitch in her throat as a lump grew. "You've got this, Bella. He's the person you've always known. Just be honest with him."

Bella turned around and marched back up to his door, knocking before she could change her mind again. *Come on. Answer the door.* After a few more minutes, she rang the doorbell, then knocked again. Ten minutes passed by, and Bella stood there, a bit confused. Again, she knocked. She waited another five minutes before giving up. His car was there, but maybe it was broken down. But if he wasn't home, then there was only one other place to check.

Bella got back in her car and stared at her rearview mirror. She still looked awful. Did she want to rush to the jewelry store when other customers could easily be there? She started the car and backed up. It beat the alternative—running home when she knew that she would find reasons to panic over where Jackson could be. The sooner she talked to him, the better she would be for it.

Several cars were already there when she turned into the store's parking lot. Again, she gave herself a onceover, trying her best to fix herself so that when she walked into the store, she would look at least a little put together. She smoothed her hair again. *Good enough, I guess.*

The bell hanging on the door rang as she entered. Two people stood at a counter, with a clerk hovering over them. When Nelly looked up, she greeted Bella with a grin. "Hey, B, I'll be with you shortly." She always liked to greet people in rhyme, or as much of a rhyme as she could.

Another couple glanced at a case full of bracelets. A third couple stood at a case full of diamonds. Bella looked between the couples and smiled to herself. They all seemed happy. It was already a busy morning, and frankly, Bella considered just ducking out of there and worrying about seeing Jackson later.

The bell sounded again, and she looked over to see a man enter the shop and head straight for the case of rings, like he was a man on a mission. There was a time when Bella dreamed that Jackson would have been that man. But now, she had to admit that she was relieved they hadn't taken their relationship further.

"What can I do for you?" Nelly asked, approaching Bella from the side.

Bella looked around the swamped room. "Are you alone?"

She grimaced and nodded. "Camryn called in sick and couldn't get a replacement. Don't you worry, though. These people have all been waited on."

"Except for that guy," Bella said, nodding toward the man.

She laughed and rolled her eyes. "Mr. Snooty, you mean? He comes in at least three times a week, looks in the case, tosses his nose up, and leaves. Just can't find what he's looking for, I suppose."

"And he keeps coming back? Isn't it clear that maybe this store doesn't have what he wants?"

She laughed. "You would think, huh?" She shook her head. "He just doesn't want to give up hope, I guess. But you didn't come to talk about him, I'm sure. What's up?"

Bella looked around the store. "Just here to see Jackson. He should be out here giving you a hand. Is he hiding in the back somewhere?"

Nelly frowned. "No, he's not here. He's out of town for a few days. Said he needed a vacay or something. Called this morning and left a message. Just assumed you'd know."

Bella frowned, then pretended she had forgotten. "Oh, of course. Silly me." She playfully slapped her forehead. "Work has been crazy, and it slipped my mind."

"Miss? I would like to see this ring please."

Both Bella and Nelly turned to the guy that Nelly had called Mr. Snooty. Nelly's eyes widened, and she threw a side-glance to Bella. "I'll be right with you. Um, I have to go, Bella. See ya." She hurried away, leaving Bella confused.

Bella left the store and thought back to Nelly's words. For one, Jackson's car was definitely in the driveway. Another thing that had her concerned was that in all those texts Jackson had sent her, he had never once mentioned a vacation. She frowned, walking back to the car and finally getting in the driver's seat. What was going on? She only hoped Jackson was okay.

CHAPTER SEVENTEEN

Leona

"Now, are youe sure you want to go to school?" Leona asked, turning to face Brad.

He had a sweet grin on his face, and he quickly nodded. Leona looked up to the school; it seemed so big. Was he ready for kindergarten? She turned back to him and knelt at his level, drawing his eyes back to her. "No one will be upset with you if you've changed your mind."

He released a groan, which made her laugh. "Mama Lona, I want to go. Please." He clasped his hands together. The truth was that sending him to school could be a saving grace for her. If he were at school while she worked, then she wouldn't have to leave him at the day care. With her schedule, she was sure she could work it out to make sure she got him to and from school, even if that meant hiring a nanny who could handle some of the transporting.

She stood up and grabbed his hand. He was ready, but Leona wasn't. It didn't feel like they had been together long enough for her to usher him off to school so suddenly. But, in a way, she understood his need and desire to be with other kids his age. It just felt like a stepping-stone to him getting older already. It really was true what people said about kids growing up so fast.

They entered the building and Leona looked around for the office. There wasn't a huge sign that showed people where to go, even though she thought there should be. She finally found a woman walking down a hallway, headed toward the front door.

"Excuse me," she said, her voice coming out a bit more forceful than she had intended. The woman stopped and arched an eyebrow, then tossed a look down to Brad.

"Yes?" she asked, looking back up and meeting Leona's gaze.

"We're looking for the registration office."

"Just head down this hallway. It's the first door on the right. You'll see a big sign that reads 'office.'"

Leona gave a weak smile. It was exactly the sign she was looking for. She had just thought it would be closer to the front door. "Thank you."

The woman nodded, then disappeared. Leona looked down at Brad, who was ready to pull her down the hallway, but Leona dug her heels into the floor. "I'll give you one more shot to change your mind."

"Mama Lona!" he groaned, tossing her an exasperated look. Leona shrugged. She had to try, at least.

They got to the office and Leona released a breath. Why was she so nervous? It was the same question she had asked herself a million times over, but now that the moment was upon them, her heart was palpitating heavily. It was crazy. It wasn't like he was going off to college or getting married. She couldn't even imagine that happening.

A woman behind the desk greeted them with a bright and easy smile. "Hello, may I help you?"

She caught the woman's name on a desk name tag. "Hi, Melody," Leona began. "I spoke with a Charmaine Allo yesterday afternoon and she's expecting Brad Carver to come into the building today. He's starting kindergarten."

She smiled. "Are you nervous?" the woman asked.

Leona laughed. "How could you tell?"

"I've been around the block a few times. I know several parents who have panic attacks dropping their kids off here. It's cute. I'm not a mother so I wouldn't know the feeling, but you're giving off that vibe. Don't you worry, though. Brad will be well taken care of."

That warmed Leona's heart, and she nodded, her panic slightly dissipating.

Melody continued, "She's waiting for you back in that office. Go ahead and head on in."

"Thank you," Leona said gratefully.

She continued to hold on to Brad's hand as she led him through the doors. A woman looked up and stood up from her desk. "Leona Guillano?" she asked.

"Right. And this is Brad." She presented him, pressing her hand against his back.

"How are you, Brad?" Charmaine held out her hand to him and he shook it with no hesitation. He was excited for this moment, while Leona was doing her best to avoid it. She shook her head, not sure why he was so confident.

"I'm good. Are there lots of kids here?" he asked, hope shining in his eyes.

Leona smiled as Charmaine spoke to him like he was an adult. It eased Leona's mind. After they finished talking, she turned to Leona.

"There are a few papers I need you to sign. We're working with the children's home on getting his papers, birth certificate, etcetera. But we'll get all that sorted on our end."

"Sounds good," Leona replied, swallowing the lump again. Charmaine pushed some papers toward her and Leona saw her hands shaking as she tried to sign her name. Charmaine reached out and touched her hand.

"He's going to be fine," she said reassuringly.

Leona laughed. "He will, but I'm a nervous wreck." She shrugged. "Guess it has to be done." She released a breath and went back to signing the forms. Then it was done, and she was turned away from Brad's grasp. She thought the whole thing would be a longer process, but it had only been a mere twenty minutes before a woman escorted Brad away from Leona. She waved to him until he disappeared around the corner.

Leona looked over to Charmaine, who reached out and touched Leona's arm. "You're not the first person to get emotional in seeing your child go off to his first day of school. He's in good hands, though. And you're doing a great thing in fostering him. Foster kids need great families to be a part of, and I can tell you're one of the best."

"Thank you." Leona backed away from her, still feeling uneasy, but hoping that feeling would dissipate.

"We'll call you if we need anything," Charmaine continued.

Leona nodded, then turned and left the office. She made it to her car before she broke down. Brad looked way too small to be heading off to a place where she couldn't look after him. When she finally regained her composure, she straightened up and pulled out of the parking spot. She was going to have to make it through the day at work. In that moment, she wasn't sure she could. The only thing that brought her comfort was the knowledge that Bella would be there at work.

While they hadn't talked much since Bella had left her house the previous morning, Leona was ready to share some intimate moments locked away in the hospital rooms. It was something that kept a smile on her face.

When she got to the hospital, she took the elevator, hoping that Bella would greet her the moment she stepped onto the floor. That didn't happen, but she continued to look for her until she walked to her office. She was probably tucked in a patient's room. In no time, she would have a real encounter with Bella, and she couldn't wait for that to happen.

LEONA LOOKED UP AND DOWN THE HALLWAYS, TRYING TO FIND Bella. Was Bella intentionally dodging her this morning? It felt like it was a very real possibility. After the night they had spent together, she felt it was only right that they would want to share a few stolen moments. The couple of times they had talked on the phone the previous night, Brad was there to listen to the conversations. Now that she was at work, she wanted that intimate time together. But the only time she was able to see Bella was when they had to work together to take care of a few patients. Not even once did Bella look like she wanted to steal away with Leona.

Jacqueline was sitting at the desk when Leona approached her. She looked up and jumped up from her chair. "Hi, Dr. Guillano." She was always eager to look like she did no wrong, but Leona couldn't let her believe that anytime soon. Even though she wasn't going to confront Jacqueline about what she did, she wasn't going to make things easy on her.

"Have you seen Bella?" Leona asked, keeping the question short and to the point.

Jacqueline lowered herself down into a chair. "She said she was going to stock some shelves. I offered to help, but she said she needed some time alone." She shrugged. "Last I saw her, she was in that stockroom." She pointed toward the room closest to them.

"Thanks," Leona walked over to the room and went to open the door, but it was locked. She jiggled the knob for a moment, then leaned against the door. "Bella, it's Leona. Are you in there?"

The handle turned and then the door pushed open. Leona slipped inside and locked the door behind her. She turned to see Bella sitting on the floor. Bella looked away, but it was too late. Leona saw she had been crying.

"Bella!" she exclaimed. She moved in and sat down next to her. "What's wrong?"

Bella held up her phone, finally looking in her direction. "This is what's wrong. I've tried calling Jackson two dozen times, and he's ignoring my calls. The calls are going straight to voicemail. It makes no sense."

She pushed a button and put the call on speaker. A man's voice came on the phone, asking them to leave a message. She disconnected the call and shook her head. "I know we're on a break, but I can't help worrying. He's been acting strange and a little desperate lately. I worry that I broke his heart and...I don't know. I'm feeling a lot of guilt right now."

"Maybe you should start at the beginning," Leona murmured.

She sighed and looked over to Leona. "Yesterday after I left your house, I saw I had missed calls and texts from him. He seemed concerned, so I decided that we needed to talk in person so I could just be open and honest with him about everything. I feel I owe him that much, so I went to his house."

As Bella continued, Leona listened. She nodded when it seemed right and sighed when it felt like that was what she needed to do.

"I don't know. It makes no sense why he won't answer my calls." Bella slipped her phone into her pocket, sighing. "I can see you looking at me like that. I told him we're on a break and he can do whatever he wants to do. I have this strange feeling though. What if...What if he's had someone on the side for months and I just never knew about it? Part of me is worried he's hurt, and the other part is worried he was cheating."

Leona shook her head. "I'm not looking at you in any way. You guys have a history, so I can understand your concern about him. I get it."

Bella looked up. "Even though I haven't been exactly innocent? We kissed before I went on a break from him."

Leona smiled. "What I've realized through the years of my life is that the heart wants what it wants. You can't curse yourself for that."

"You don't think I'm being crazy?"

Leona shrugged, though there was a part of her that wondered why Bella seemed so upset about it. If she was sure that she had made the right choice, then why would it matter if Jackson had moved on as well? Maybe it was only the thought that he'd been unfaithful while they were still together. "I think you're being exactly how you feel. No one can fault you on what's weighing on your heart."

Bella looked up and Leona reached out and touched her hair, then withdrew her hand. "I know I've been uncertain, but I've been thinking a lot about everything since I left your house. I'm where I want to be," Bella quietly spoke. "I want us to give this a try. I just wish I could talk to Jackson and tell him where my heart is. I hope you understand that."

Leona nodded. "Again, I won't fault you for how you feel, and I'm happy to hear that you're feeling more confident about what you want. I want us to give this a try, too. Maybe this is the absolute wrong time to say this or even suggest it, but I was hoping you would want to go out to dinner tonight. You, me, and Brad. Nothing too fancy. I thought about getting someone to watch him, but I took him to school today and thought it could be a celebration of his first day. If that's stupid, then forget I even said it."

Before Leona could say anything else, Bella moved in and claimed Leona's lips into a heated kiss, giving Leona her answer. Despite how Bella felt in that supply closet, she didn't regret being with Leona, and that was what mattered most. They would continue to see where things could go.

CHAPTER EIGHTEEN

Bella

"Hello, you've reached Jackson. As you can see, I'm not available to take your call. You know what to do. I'll return your call as soon as I can."

"Jackson, it's Bella. Again. I've only tried calling you a million times and you're not picking up. We really need to talk. Call me." Bella disconnected the call as her doorbell rang. She glanced at her reflection and scrunched up her nose. She had an idea of what she wanted to wear but she had torn through her closet, and nothing seemed to suit the mood of the evening.

She went to the front door and opened it. Her eyes looked over the outfit Leona wore, and her face went pale. "Excuse me while I go change," she mumbled.

Leona laughed and grabbed her hand, pulling her toward her. Bella's lips brushed against Leona's. "You look beautiful," Leona said.

Bella grimaced. "I'm underdressed."

Leona stood at her door wearing a floral dress. Bella had never seen her dressed in anything but work attire, so this was all new for her. The way Leona trailed her eyes over her body, she knew she shouldn't be concerned about the blouse and jeans she wore. Still, she felt like a sore thumb next to Leona.

For the first time, Brad cleared his throat and Bella looked down to glance at him. She had forgotten he was even there. He had a sneaky grin and looked up at Bella. "Hey, Brad!" she said, giving him a high-five.

"Hi Bella. I'm with Mama Lona. You look beautiful."

Bella blushed and fought hard not to pick him up in her arms and twirl him around the floor. That was the sweetest thing he could have said to her in that very moment. "Thank you, and you are a sweetheart for saying that. Just for that, you can choose where we go to eat."

"Rocket Place!" he exclaimed.

Leona laughed. "You really shouldn't have let him choose. Now we'll have to sit in those little rocket ships."

Bella grinned. As long as she was with them, she didn't care. "Looking forward to it," she said.

With that, they left her apartment and got into Leona's vehicle. The whole ride to the restaurant, Brad kept up a stream of chatter from the backseat. Bella caught herself looking over at Leona. She had the sweetest smile on her face. When they were nearly at the restaurant, Leona reached out for her hand, and that was how they rode the rest of the way there.

Bella was getting more confident in her choices, more comfortable with letting her life plan pivot. Though they weren't officially a couple, Bella was moving more and more in that direction. She only hoped she wasn't ultimately making the wrong decision, and that things with her and Leona wouldn't fall apart. Jackson had been a sure thing. What she had with Leona still felt rocky for some reason.

Leona turned into the parking lot and Bella's jaw dropped. "Is this place always this busy?" Bella asked.

Leona laughed. "Your guess is as good as mine. I've never been here, but it seems like the place to be on a Thursday night."

"That's Maxine," Brad hollered from the backseat. Bella looked over her shoulder to see him pointing out the window.

"A school classmate?" Bella asked.

He nodded. "She's nice."

Bella grinned and looked over to Leona. "Looks like he's already making friends after just one day. Can't get any better than that."

Leona nodded happily. She looked over her shoulder to Brad. "Are you ready to go?"

He was already hopping out of his booster seat. They all got out of the car and headed up to the front door. When Brad tried to run ahead, Leona quickly grabbed his hand and pulled him back to them. Leona was the motherly type, and it impressed Bella how well she seemed to have jumped into the role, like she was meant to do it her entire life.

Bella grabbed the door and waited for Leona and Brad to step into the building first before she joined them. Brad looked around the restaurant, then he pointed to the corner. "She's sitting over there. Can we go over there?"

"We don't want to bother them, but we'll go grab the ship right next to them." Leona grinned when she looked to Bella. "Words I never thought I'd be saying on a date."

We're on a date, Bella thought gleefully. It calmed her nerves that she didn't have to worry about where the evening could wind up. The three of them headed over to the ship and Brad eagerly waved when Maxine looked in their direction. "Hey, Brad!" Maxine called.

Bella and Leona took one side and Brad slid into the spot across from them. He kept looking over his shoulder to where Maxine sat with her parents. Or, at least Bella assumed they were her parents. She looked over to Leona and gently squeezed her hand. "I think maybe your boy has a crush."

Leona laughed. "Looks that way, doesn't it?" she whispered.

They grabbed their menus and looked through them, waiting for the waitress. Within five minutes they had placed their orders and were sipping on their drinks. "How was your first day at school, Brad?" Bella asked. "What'd you do?"

"Lots of coloring," he said. "They have a board at the front of the class and if you draw a picture the teacher will show...show..." He hesitated. "She said she would do something and used a word. Show something."

"Showcase?" Leona asked.

His eyes lit up and nodded. "Yep. That's what she said."

"You're so smart," Bella teased.

Leona laughed. "The teacher sent home a notebook of things that she does in the class. That was one of the things she mentioned."

Bella reached under the table and took her hand into hers. Leona's grin widened across her face as they held one another's hand and continued their conversation with Brad.

"Mama Lona?" Brad asked.

"Yes, bud?"

"There's going to be a meeting at the school and your presence is required."

Leona snickered. "My presence?"

"That's what the teacher said. Something about seeing everything your kid has accomplished. I'll be bringing papers home about it."

"Just don't forget," Leona said.

He shook his head. "I won't."

Their pizza came, and they took a moment to appreciate the food. A few times, Brad spoke up, and either Leona or Bella would respond, but the conversation soon died to a small murmur as they all focused on their meal.

Bella nodded, taking a bite of the pizza. "This pizza isn't bad. I'll have to remember this place."

"It's hard to miss," Leona teased. That brought a giggle to Bella's lips, and they continued to eat.

"I'm stuffed," Brad moaned.

"Well, you did have three slices and two crazy breads. I'm not surprised. That's a lot of food for such a little guy."

He grinned. "I was hungry, and it was good."

Bella nodded. "Agreed on both parts."

Maxine approached their table, smiling shyly. "Brad? You wanna go play some games?"

Brad sat up in the spaceship and looked over to Leona. "Mama Lona, can I?" he asked.

Bella watched as Leona dug some money out of her purse and handed it over to him. "Enjoy yourself," she said.

"Thank you!" He jumped up and both kids ran off.

Bella laughed and Leona raised an eyebrow. "You're going to have that boy wrapped around your finger. You know that, right?"

Leona snickered. "I wouldn't have it any other way."

Leona beamed with happiness as she watched Brad play with his new friend. Bella was glad that Leona had Brad in her life because everyone deserved something to make their hearts shine, and Leona had found that. More and more, Bella wanted to be another reason Leona's heart shone.

———

BELLA LOOKED OVER TO WHERE BRAD WAS TOSSING SOME basketballs into a hoop. She had moved to the spot where Brad had sat earlier, and she felt Leona's steady gaze on her. Bella looked over and smiled at her. "He's having the time of his life," she said.

"That he is. But what about you?"

Bella smirked. "I can't complain. This is a beautiful place to have our first date."

Leona laughed. "Well, typically I like to shoot for higher standards, but this place does have a cool vibe. Don't you think?"

Bella chuckled. "Very cool." She sipped on her Coke and dropped her eyes to the tray of pizza. They still had enough to make out a second helping for all. The restaurant didn't disappoint with their portions.

"Have you talked to your boyfriend?" Leona suddenly blurted.

Bella looked up, a little startled, and Leona closed her mouth and shook her head. "None of my business. I just saw how upset you were and wondered if things had gotten resolved. You don't have to tell me if you don't want to, though."

Bella leaned back in her booth and waited for her to finish speaking. "Are you done?" she asked, grinning. "If you are, then I can tell you my response. Then again, if you want to ramble for another fifteen minutes, we can discuss it after that."

Leona's eyes widened, then fell. "Just nervous."

"Clearly. Well, truth is, no, I haven't talked to him. It's not because I haven't tried. He's been ignoring my calls."

"Is that usual?"

Bella shook her head. "Could be that he's trying to give me a taste of my own medicine. Who knows? I don't want to think about him tonight, though. I want to think about life beyond Jackson. And there is life beyond him. I know that now." She reached across the table and took Leona's hand in hers. "I didn't realize the happiness I was allowed to have until I started spending time with you."

"Which has only just begun, I hope." Leona winked at her, and Bella felt her cheeks flush.

"Mama Lona," Brad said, coming up to their table. Instinctively, she pulled her hand back from Leona's. She didn't want Brad to feel awkward with them being intimate, but it was only her paranoia. Brad had a grin that didn't quit. "I'm tired."

"You've been playing for a long time," Leona said. "Let's get you home and ready for bed."

Leona reached in her purse to grab her wallet but Bella tossed some bills onto the table. "You're not paying," Leona argued.

"Please." Bella tilted her head. "I want to treat. This was a big day for Brad, and I want to celebrate that. You can get next time."

Leona gave her a soft smile and dropped her wallet back in her purse. That was one win for Bella, but she didn't think there would be many more to come. Leona was the type that usually got her way, being the strong and independent woman she was.

As they drove toward the house, it started to rain slowly, then picked up in speed and intensity. It soon got to the point that Leona was slowing her speed and trying to look around the windshield wipers.

"We can pull off and stop," Bella whispered. "Wait for the rain to stop, if you want."

Leona shook her head. "We're fine. We're almost to the house." Bella glanced over her shoulder at Brad. His eyes were wide as he stared out the window.

"What did you like most about school today?" Bella asked, attempting to take his mind off the rain outside.

"Um...coloring." A loud crack of thunder sounded, shaking the car. "Ahhhh!" he screamed.

"It's fine, Brad. That's just the thunder talking to the lightning. That's what my folks always say, especially my mother."

Brad nodded, seemingly calmed down by those words. A few minutes later, Leona pulled into the driveway.

"Do you have umbrellas?" Bella asked.

"They're somewhere around here. Or we could run..." She looked over her shoulder and Bella glanced behind her. Brad nodded, eager to get inside.

"Get ready," Leona called. Brad unbuckled his seat and then they all grabbed for their doors. "Run!" she hollered.

The three of them opened their doors and ran for their lives to reach the front door. By the time they reached the porch, they were in a fit of giggles and soaked down to their underwear.

"This is the best night of my life," Brad spoke between giggles. He threw his arms around Leona, and they embraced for a moment. It was so heartfelt, Bella felt tears sting at her eyes. How much sweeter could the evening get?

They parted from their embrace and Leona unlocked the doors for them to enter the house. Bella stood back, feeling it was fitting that she allowed the two of them to have this moment together. "I think I'm going to start a fire," she said, moving toward the living room.

Leona looked over and frowned. "Are you sure? You're welcome to come upstairs."

Bella shook her head. "I'm positive. You two enjoy your time together." She entered the living room and went over to the fireplace. Everything was already set out for the fire, so she worked on getting that going.

She would always have time to spend with Leona, but it was time that Leona took the moments she could with Brad and made the best of every minute they had together.

CHAPTER NINETEEN

Leona

W arm water washed over Leona's body. She could still smell Bella's scent on her from the two of them repeatedly exploring one another the previous night, first in front of the fireplace and then in her bed. Time after time after time. A smile broadened across her face. If she could have nights like that forever, she would die a very happy woman.

I need to get home and get changed for class. I'm not doing well in anatomy, or else I would gladly miss the class. Tell Brad I said goodbye.

Those words still rung in her ears. She just wanted to be near Bella every second of every day, but time didn't allow for that. Her phone started ringing, and she groaned and peeked her head out of the shower. It was the hospital, so she quickly turned the water off and answered the phone.

"Hello?"

"Dr. Guillano? This is Tori. I was asked to call you because Dr. Whalen is out sick and there isn't another doctor to cover the shift. They were wondering if you could come in."

Leona looked down at her wet body. The last place she wanted to be was the hospital, when she knew that Jacqueline would most likely be the nurse she would be set to work with. That would make for some awkwardness. But she couldn't imagine leaving the ward not well-staffed.

"I have to get Brad to school and then I can be there. Nine o'clock, maybe?"

"That would be great. Thank you so much. We all appreciate this."

"Not a problem. See you then." Leona disconnected the call and stepped back into the shower to finish up. When she turned the water back on, she couldn't get the hot water to kick in, so she was left with a cold and miserable ending to her shower, but she made do with it.

She got out of the shower and dressed, then brushed her teeth and did her hair. When she got out into the hall and to Brad's room, she saw that he was finishing up getting ready as well.

"How do I look?" he asked.

Leona laughed. Despite having two different shoes on, he didn't look half bad. "You look great. But maybe we should try to match the shoes this time. She reached under his bed and pulled out another Teenage Mutant Ninja Turtle shoe.

He giggled. "There it is."

He grabbed it from her and sat down on the floor, changing out his shoes. "I'm going to run down and make breakfast for us. I just got called into work, so I need to get you to school before heading to the hospital. Does cereal sound okay? Or would you rather have oatmeal?"

"Do you have blueberries in the oatmeal?" he asked.

Leona grinned. "I can make that happen, if that's what you want."

"Yes, please." He continued to change his shoes as she left the room and went to the kitchen to make his oatmeal. As she headed toward the cupboards, she saw a note in the middle of the table. She picked it up and read it, a smile blossoming on her face.

Leona and Brad –

I had a great time last night. Looking forward to doing it again soon!

Bella

Leona held the note to her heart. Bella knew just how to bring a smile to her face. And the fact that she had included Brad only made it that much more special. She heard Brad's feet on the stairs, and she turned to look at him when he entered the kitchen.

"Bella left us a note." She handed the note to him.

"What's it say? I can't read. Not really. But I can make stuff up." He laughed. Leona took the note and read it to him. Brad grinned. "I had a good time, too."

"So did I," Leona admitted. She popped two bowls of oatmeal into the microwave, then grabbed some blueberries from the fridge. When the microwave dinged, she poured some blueberries in and mixed them up fully. "Try that," she said, passing one of the bowls and a spoon to Brad.

"Yummy," he said.

Leona smirked and took a bite of her own. It wasn't bad, but it wasn't some delicious meal she had slaved over the stove to make. Still, it seemed to be enough for Brad. She grabbed some orange juice and poured two glasses.

They finished their breakfast in record time so that Leona could drop Brad off and head to work. Fifteen minutes before he had to be at school, she grabbed her purse. "Are you ready?" she asked.

He jumped down from his booster chair, and they were out the door and into the car. "Mama Lona," he said as they rounded the corner.

"Yes?" She looked in the rearview mirror and stared at him from the backseat.

"I was wondering if I could go in by myself. The other kids don't have an adult with them."

"Are you sure?" she asked, not comfortable with that in any way. Brad eagerly nodded his head.

"I'll be fine." She turned into the parking lot and followed the path of arrows that showed where people could drop off their kids. There were already a few people there, and they followed slowly behind the cars in front of them.

When it was finally their turn, Brad got out of his seat and opened the door. He looked over and waved to her. "Bye, Mama Lona," he called. He grabbed his backpack and headed away from the car. She stared after him, a tear sneaking its way down her cheek. A car honked behind her, and she glanced in the rearview mirror and gave a small wave before pulling away from the curb.

He didn't need her already. How sad was that? Leona had to remind herself that he was bound to be independent eventually. That thought did somehow calm her, if only slightly.

When she turned into the hospital's parking lot, she was no longer thinking negatively about those feelings. She grabbed her phone and pulled up her text messages.

Bella, just wanted to let you know that I was called into work. I know this is a huge ask but would you pick up Brad and bring him to the hospital? It's likely going to be a long day. Dr. Whalen is sick and I'm not sure when coverage will be in. If you can't, then I completely understand. 3:00, though, if you can. Just let me know. PS. That note you wrote us this morning was super sweet.

When she was satisfied with the text, she signed off with a single heart, then slipped her phone back into her purse. Leona got out of the car and headed up to the hospital, humming when she entered the elevator. Everything was working out just perfectly.

She should have assumed that would be the moment when everything was going to fall apart. As she stepped off the elevator, her eyes went straight to the desk. Standing there, a smile on her lips, was Cicily. But why? And what did she want now?

CHAPTER TWENTY

Bella

Bella fell on the couch and closed her eyes, immediately seeing Leona's smiling face playing like a video through her memory. She warmed up every time she was with Leona. When they had sex, she felt like they were one body orgasming together. It was how she always desired lovemaking to be.

Her eyes shot open. *Love?* That was the one word that continuously played through her mind when she thought about and pictured Leona. Slowly, she had fallen in love with Leona, and that startled her because she had spent so much time believing Jackson would be her future spouse.

She jumped up from the couch and went over to her bag of books. If she kept thinking about this, she would be late to class. The last thing she needed was a lecture from Professor Finch on being tardy and the art of making good grades. She still wasn't fully over the embarrassment of messing up by falling asleep in his class.

She grabbed her backpack and tossed it over her shoulder, then went to the door. When she opened it, her jaw dropped. Standing on the porch was Jackson. He had been pacing back and forth in front of the door. Who knew for how long? She gawked at him until he turned and faced her.

"Hey, Bella." This was the first time in what felt like forever that he didn't call her babe.

"Jackson!"

"Got your message. And you're right. We do need to talk. May I come in?"

It was the best time to have things out and speak from her heart, but she couldn't right now. "No," she said. His jaw dropped. "It's not that I don't want you to come in, but I have to get to school. Professor Finch already has it out for me, and I really don't want to give him any more reasons to hate me."

He smiled lightly, his jaw relaxing. "I doubt anyone could hate you."

So he didn't hate her. That was something.

"I want us to talk, Jackson. This isn't me making an excuse, I swear. But..." She adjusted her bag on her shoulder and looked up into his eyes. "If I miss class, I could ruin my chances of graduating. And I think we both know that would not be a good thing."

"No, of course not. I should have figured that you would be rushing off someplace. After all, it's how you've been the past couple of months. So, by all means..." He stepped aside and Bella closed the door behind her. She hesitated and looked back at him. His eyes were sullen and his mouth was in a downward frown.

She walked over to him and wrapped her arm around him, which made him straighten. "It's good to see you, Jackson." She softly kissed his cheek, then turned and left him.

She didn't want him to feel like she was abandoning him. But something had broken them, and it wasn't just because Bella had met Leona. She had never truly loved Jackson, and she had been too focused on her life falling into some perfect plan. She now realized how silly she had been. She had wanted to settle for a life that didn't fill her with passion and excitement, like the way she felt around Leona. How silly of her. Yes, she wanted to prove herself, but she'd carried a chip on her shoulder for too long. She had let her bullies affect her life for too many years. She was different now, and everything about her future was brighter.

It was a future with Leona and Brad, if Leona decided she wanted Bella to be a part of his life in that way. She would be a mom sooner than she expected, but screw the plan. Life was better this way, and she was now open to all of its wonderful possibilities.

She drove to school, trying to put Jackson out of her mind, but the further she got from her apartment, the harder it was to focus on anything but him. She was ready to tell him everything, and she had thought her resolve would make it easier, but Jackson was there, resting in her mind. She pulled into the parking lot, but there was a heaviness in her heart, which nearly caused her to turn around and head straight back to find him, hoping that he was still at her apartment waiting for her.

You have to go to class, Bella. You know this.

Bella forced herself out of the car and walked the long distance to the classroom. When she reached her class, she saw the room had already quickly filled up. Professor Finch stood at the front of the class, his back to the students. If she hurried, she could slip inside and go unnoticed. She hoped.

When she entered the room, though, it was like a loud horn had blared, signaling she had arrived. The professor turned and gazed toward her. "Ms. Strong," he said.

"Good morning, Professor Finch." She tried to move past him, but he wasn't through with her.

"I hope you remembered there would be a pop quiz today, and that you have studied fruitfully."

Bella nodded, her stomach going weak. Had he mentioned a quiz? She didn't recall, but she forced a smile. "Of course. I'm better prepared than I've been for any quiz in my life."

What was the quiz even about? She racked her brain, but nothing came to her.

Professor Finch tilted his head. "Interesting," he said. "There is a quiz, but I hadn't mentioned it to the class. But if you've been studying the whole book, I would say you're well-prepared." He smirked, and Bella's heart sunk.

Was he just out to get her? If that was the case, then why?

"I can assure you I have this down." She turned and stomped up the stairs to her seat.

Nowhere was it mentioned in the school manual that there would be one professor who knew the exact words to say to humiliate their students. But Bella knew she was stuck with Professor Finch, and now she had to worry about one more thing—passing a quiz.

FREEDOM, AT LAST. BELLA GRABBED HER BOOKS AND TOSSED them in her bag, anxious to get out of the classroom and as far away from Professor Finch as possible. His quiz hadn't disappointed. It was as tough as she would have expected to find in a master-level course. She just didn't want to think about how badly she'd bombed it, at least until the next week.

"Ms. Strong," Professor Finch spoke, his voice booming over the sound of shoes hitting the laminate flooring. She looked around, her heart sinking. She had been only two seconds from exiting and not having to look back.

"Yes, Professor Finch," she stated.

He continued to look down at some papers in front of him. "Thought we could finish our conversation from earlier."

"Our conversation?" Bella asked. He looked up and nodded, causing her to fidget from one foot to the other. "I thought we were done." Perhaps that was wishful thinking on her part, but she didn't know what else they possibly had to discuss.

"I was just about to grade your quiz. Would you care to wait?"

Bella dropped her gaze. *Not particularly.* She would have been just fine never to have to see the quiz again. And having him grade it in front of her? She could only imagine the horror of that.

"Well, I have another class to get to," she argued. It was a lie, of course, but what he didn't know wouldn't hurt her. She started to back away, but he looked back down at the pile of papers.

"It won't take much more than a minute." He skimmed over the quiz, and she watched as he took his red pen and marked off a point, then another, then another. She looked down at the floor, not able to stand watching him take more points off. The only thing she was relieved about was that he hadn't chosen to do this in front of the rest of the class. At least he had left her with some dignity.

After a minute ticked by, Professor Finch looked up and handed over her quiz. "Tsk tsk...I don't know what to tell you, Bella, but you had some promise and potential when you first came into the program. Now it just seems like you've gone downhill."

"Sir, I've been under some stress," Bella argued. "You know, with work and everything, it's just been a lot. I will do better. I can promise you that."

"Don't promise *me* anything. You need to make that promise to yourself. If your grades continue in this fashion, you're likely to take the semester over."

Her jaw dropped. "This is my last semester. If I have to take it over, I won't be able to graduate in May with everyone else. Please, don't say that's a possibility."

He shrugged. "That's up to you, but time is running out. I advise you to put everything on hold and focus solely on your classes."

Bella looked down. "I have to work to pay for my bills. That's non-negotiable."

He got up from his stool. "There's not much I can do. Your grade right now could give you a C, at best. You need a B to pass this semester. That means getting an A on every assignment and every quiz and test." Professor Finch heaved a sigh. "You're free to go."

Bella continued to stand there, her mind racing as she thought of various scenarios that could get her through. "Surely you have extra credit I could do. I *will* do whatever it takes to pass this class. I'm a hard worker, Professor Finch. Just give me a chance."

He looked over to her. "Fine, I'll give you an assignment." He walked back over to his podium and rifled through some folders. "Write a five-to-seven-page report on this topic." He handed a sheet of paper over to Bella and she stared at it.

"Artificial hearts?"

He nodded. "If you can get it to me by Monday morning, before the start of my first class at eight o'clock, I will grade it before your class. If I feel it's an A-worthy paper, then you'll have a better shot of passing this class."

"I won't disappoint you," she said, tucking the papers he handed her into her bag.

"I'm sure you won't. Now, good day."

Bella turned and left the classroom, already feeling discouraged, but she had to push herself. Over the weekend, she would get the assignment done and exceed his expectations. It was her best shot to making it through the semester and on to graduation.

CHAPTER TWENTY-ONE

Leona

L eona glanced around the cafeteria until she spotted her. She had thought all morning of why Cicily could be at Capmed, but the more she thought about it, the more anxious she became. Whenever Leona saw her, she immediately had to dismiss her to get to work. Luckily, Cicily didn't make a scene and accepted that they would have to wait until lunchtime.

But now, Leona would have preferred to push this inevitable conversation back another day or two. In fact, if she never had to face Cicily again, she would have been fine with that. She thought she had gotten her point across when she had spoken to her on the phone. Yet, there she was.

Cicily looked up when Leona approached her. "Should we grab our food first?" Leona muttered.

"Oh, sure." They dispersed, Leona heading toward the salads and Cicily toward the sandwiches. Once they both had their food, they paid and headed back to the same table where Cicily had been waiting for Leona.

"This is a nice hospital," Cicily began. "Nice cafeteria. When you think of New York, you'd think they would have all the higher tech and stuff and that Chicago would—"

"Be some Podunk little village?" Leona asked.

Cicily's eyes narrowed, and she looked down at her sandwich, then shook her head. "That's not what I meant or tried to imply." She grabbed her sandwich and took a bite, her eyes still down at the table.

Leona sighed. "I'm sorry. I shouldn't have just assumed that. I guess I'm a little on edge and maybe even a bit nervous. If I get snarky, I'll try to reel myself back in."

Cicily smiled and looked up. "You weren't being snarky. I can see how it would have come across that way, but Capmed is nice. That's all. And you even look happy here."

Leona raised an eyebrow. "You can tell I'm happy despite me being on edge?"

Cicily smiled sadly. "Of course I can tell. We were together long enough, and I can see it on your face. Besides, if you weren't happy, you might have considered coming back to New York."

"Doubtful," Leona mumbled. Leona met Cicily's gaze, seeing tears in her former lover's eyes. "I'm saying all the wrong things, aren't I?"

"You have every right to say what's in your heart." Cicily sniffled and looked away. The table grew quiet, and Leona considered getting up and just leaving. There wasn't anything Cicily could say that would bring Leona comfort. They had said all they needed to say when Leona had left New York, so why was Cicily there? Did she think that she could show up and everything would just magically change between them? Life didn't work like that.

After several minutes of neither of them speaking and only shooting anxious gazes at each other, Leona broke the silence. "I'm not sure why you're here, but I guess I'll start the conversation."

Cicily held up her hand. "No, please. Let me. We left things on an uneasy note in New York. And that's mainly my fault, but I have been trying to pave a way where we could get back in each other's good graces. I miss you, Leona. I miss you as my girlfriend, but most importantly, I miss you as my friend. We used to be able to tell each other everything. When you left, that all changed."

"When you lied to me, that all changed."

Cicily sighed. "You're right. I lied to you. I made you think I wanted to be a mother someday. I knew that would tear us apart, so I misled you. I'm sorry, but at least the truth came out."

"After I got my hopes up," Leona shot back.

Cicily sunk back in her chair. "After you got your hopes up. I apologized then and I'll apologize now. It was awful of me. I'm sorry. Will you ever forgive me?"

"Cicily, I've told you I've forgiven you. And coming to Capmed was on a whim, but I *am* happy here. I've even met someone." Cicily lifted her eyes to Leona. "I'm happy. We're happy. We're slowly getting to a great place. But that's not even the half of it. I have a foster kid."

"You what?" Cicily gawked at Leona, disbelief written all over her face. Leona smiled, thinking about Brad. She quickly pulled out her phone to share a picture.

"He's six and I love the little guy. And so does Bella."

"Bella? The woman you're with?" Leona nodded.

Cicily stared at the picture for a long time. Finally, she smiled. "He's adorable."

"I can picture my life with this woman and with Brad. I can picture us being a family." She pocketed her phone and lifted her gaze. "If you don't want a child, then you should be with someone who shares those same beliefs. I would have never been able to be that person for you. That's why I was frustrated with the lies. I wanted us to start a family, and when the truth came out, I felt betrayed by you. I didn't have any ill feelings for you. I just wished you would have been honest with me before I planned out this perfect life for us."

"You're right. I really should have been. And I'm happy for you, Leona, especially if this all works out."

The two smiled tentatively at each other, and Cicily took a bite of her sandwich while Leona dug more into her salad.

"Tell me about her," Cicily said, breaking the walls completely down. Leona smiled, ready to share everything about Bella and happy that Cicily understood that they were never meant to be.

CHAPTER TWENTY-TWO

Bella

The elevator doors opened, and Bella went down the hall to Leona's office. She wasn't working that day, but she knew Leona was on shift, and she was anxious to see her. After her rough morning with her professor, seeing Leona's beautiful face would surely brighten her mood.

She peeked her head in her office, but Leona wasn't there.

She turned and saw Jacqueline headed out of a room. "Hey, Jacqueline. Do you know where Dr. Guillano is?"

"She's on lunch. She should be done in fifteen minutes or so, but she's down in the cafeteria."

"Thanks!" She waved and then got back into the elevator and took it down to the main floor. The first thing she wanted to do when she saw Leona was plant a passionate kiss on her. She could already imagine the way her body would react.

She stepped into the cafeteria and looked around. There weren't too many people milling around, so it wouldn't have been too difficult to find her in the barely-there crowd, but she scanned her eyes over every table, unable to spot Leona. She frowned and turned around, leaving.

It was possible they could have missed each other from taking the elevator—after all, there were two elevators—but not probable. Bella headed back to the elevator and pressed the button when she spotted Leona in the main lobby.

There you are. She started heading in Leona's way, but then slowed her steps to a complete halt. Leona was with another woman. Bella watched them embrace. It wasn't a friendly hug; there was some intimacy there. When the woman pulled away, she leaned in and gave a peck on Leona's lips.

Bella felt her eyes clouding over with tears. The two of them practically needed to get a room. She looked away, but then forced herself to look back. Leona stood there watching as the woman left through the front door. Bella swallowed the lump in her throat and turned away, then quickly maneuvered her way through the hallways until she reached Margo's office.

She didn't hesitate before she knocked.

"Come in!"

Bella practically burst through the door and Margo looked at her in surprise. "Bella? Did we have an appointment?"

Bella shook her head. "No, and I'm sorry for bursting in like this, but I just came from school. I'm not doing well in my classes and it's possible I could not graduate at the end of the semester if I don't change some things. Unfortunately, I feel it's in my best interest to drop out of the program."

"What?" Margo stood up and gawked at Bella. "Are you sure?"

Bella nodded. "I know it puts everyone in a bind, but I see no other way. If my grades fail, I'm out anyway. I have to do this for me. I hope you understand." She swallowed the lump in her throat. "I hope everyone understands." She grabbed a chair, afraid she was going to fall if she didn't have something to hold on to.

"Of course we understand. You have to do what's in your best interest. We'll all miss you, of course, but we know that you wouldn't do this if there were any other options."

There weren't any other options. Bella couldn't fathom running into Leona, or working with her when she knew that Leona had another woman on the side. Where did she even meet this woman? It didn't even matter. She couldn't let Leona see how much this hurt her. Bella had just opened herself up to life's possibilities with a hopeful heart, and now everything was crumbling.

"I'm sorry," she said again before leaving the room, about to burst into tears. She ran out of the hospital, fearful anyone would see how upset she was. And what was even worse, she didn't know if she was more upset because she had just dropped out of the program, or because of the fact that she had seen Leona making out with another woman. Who was she kidding? She knew exactly what upset her more.

When Bella got to her car and collapsed in her front seat, she couldn't stop the tears from flowing. How had her most promising semester turned into a total nightmare? She took time to dry her tears and then started her car and backed out of the parking spot. She was already emotionally unstable, but she had one more thing to do, and there wasn't any reason to stop herself now.

THE BELL DINGED AT THE JEWELRY STORE AS BELLA ENTERED. It was nearly empty, with only one woman browsing. Bella turned her attention to the desk, where both Jackson and an employee stood, chatting. Jackson looked up as Bella approached and gave a weak smile.

"Excuse me," he whispered to the employee, then walked around the counter and came to Bella. "Hello."

"Hello. Do you have a moment for us to go somewhere and talk?"

He nodded and reached for Bella's hand, walking her outside the store and to a quiet path. They had taken that path many times before, when they wanted to discuss life and the prospects of coming together as a family someday. But now, it felt like the place where they were going to be torn apart, and Bella knew neither one of them was at fault. She just hoped he saw it that way.

"It's a beautiful day today," Jackson said as they settled into a stroll around the block.

"That it is," Bella quietly replied. But they both knew she wasn't there to discuss the weather. And the sooner she got this out, the more at ease she would feel. "I want to start by saying you know how much I care for you, Jackson. Don't you?"

He chuckled. "No great conversation ever starts that way. But, in my heart, I really do."

"Right," she whispered. She just needed to say that. It was how she felt at that moment, and it was something that brought her purpose. "Work and school have rewired my brain. They've left me exhausted and with little time to spend with you. Half the time they made me wonder if I wanted to continue the nursing path, or just go out into the world and get a job in retail. I've been forced to think a lot about my life and what I really want."

Jackson let out a soft chuckle. "Coming from a guy that works retail, I would say that it isn't all that great, either."

"Well, perhaps it wouldn't have pulled me away from you. I curse everything that has kept us apart, because ultimately, it pushed me in another direction. Toward another person."

Bella stopped walking and Jackson slowed until he faced her directly. "Jackson, I didn't go looking to meet someone else. I just wanted to do my job and be happy with that. But I was working long and late hours at the hospital, and there was someone there that I couldn't help but get to know. And I knew that wasn't fair to you, so that's why I asked for the break. I needed time to think everything over."

"I see," he whispered.

"It wasn't something I had ever planned. I thought we would have a great life together, but this person...It was like she knew me better than I knew myself."

"She?" he asked, his jaw dropping.

Bella blushed and looked down at the ground, nodding slowly. Even though Bella realized after seeing Leona kiss another woman that Leona wasn't the woman she could be with, she couldn't deny that Leona had pulled her in a different direction, and she had to tell Jackson.

"Dr. Guillano, the woman I was on rotations with. She made everything exciting. We were constantly together, and it was hard not to find some sort of solace in her arms. And I'm so sorry that I didn't come to you first." She felt the tears stinging her eyes and before she knew it, she had started sobbing. Jackson pulled her into his arms and held her as she wept.

"Shhhhhh, don't cry," he whispered. As he held her, Bella slowly began to relax, then parted from his embrace. His eyes were light and not hollow, which wasn't what she had expected.

"I felt you pulling away, probably even before you were. I was sad that we could never see each other. And the truth is, I turned to someone myself. I didn't cheat on you, I promise. I met her recently, just after you started at Capmed. That's why I kept insisting we see each other. I was confused, too. I guess we were both meant to be with other people in the end."

"Is that who you went on vacation with?" Bella asked. He tilted his head in confusion. "I came here and Nelly said you were out of town or something."

He sighed. "I needed some time away to think. I never did anything with this person, but she was someone I could talk to. I found myself getting too comfortable with her, especially since she's one of my employees. When I saw that it had gotten to that point, I realized the break you asked for was a good thing. Sorry I got a little desperate there and freaked out. That night you didn't answer my calls, I realized I needed to clear my head. I had to give us space to see what I wanted, too. I knew I needed to talk with you and see where your heart was." He shrugged. "And now I know."

"I never wanted to hurt you," Bella began.

"Or I, you." Jackson reached out and touched her arm. "Sometimes people just drift apart. It isn't anyone's fault, but more the fault of the universe. I don't blame you for this. I only want you to be happy."

"I only want you to be happy, too."

He pulled her back into his arms, and in that moment, Bella knew that whatever happened, they would both be okay. But right now, her heart was broken over losing not only Jackson but also Leona.

CHAPTER TWENTY-THREE

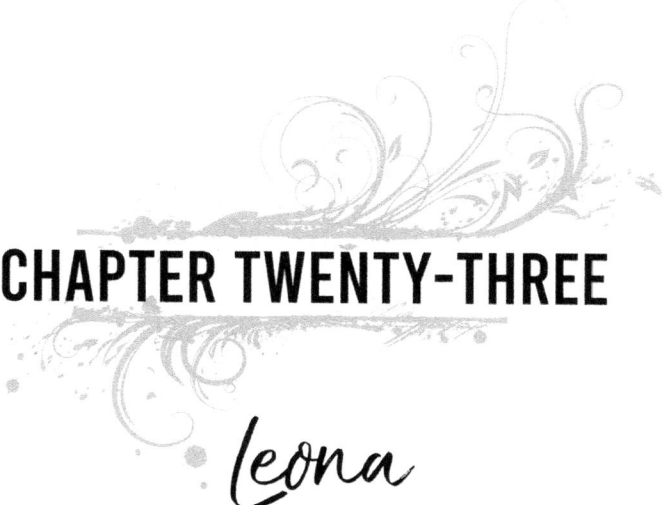

Leona

Leona exited a room and nearly bumped into Jacqueline, who was headed in the opposite direction. "Haley needs her meds," she said.

Jacqueline shook her head. "What'd you say?"

Leona frowned, tilting her head. "Haley Greene needs her meds."

Jacqueline had been known to be a bit flaky when it came to her work, but was acting flightier than usual. Her face was twisted and her eyes were nervously darting around. "Are you okay? You look like you could pass out. Or like you saw a ghost. Do you need to sit down or something?"

"No, I'm fine." She moved closer, closing the gap between them. "I just heard the news. I'm shocked. Like, I'm surprised I'm still standing. If anyone was going to jump ship, I thought it would have been..." She snapped her mouth shut and shrugged. "It's just so confusing, and she was doing well, too, right?"

Leona stepped back. "It would help if I knew what you were talking about."

Leona wasn't the type to get caught up in gossip, which Jacqueline seemed to be full of. She crossed her arms and arched her brow. If she waited any longer for Jacqueline to say something, she'd start tapping her food.

"You haven't heard?" Jacqueline's jaw dropped.

"Maybe I have, but I'm not sure what you're referring to, so it's really hard to know for certain. What is it?"

"Bella," Jacqueline said matter-of-factly. "She dropped from the program."

Leona laughed and shook her head. "Nope. I would know if she had. You're wrong."

She started to turn, but hesitated and looked over to Jacqueline, who was still standing there. "What makes you think that?"

"Just heard from Tori. She asked me to take some of Bella's shifts." She shrugged. "Pretty certain it's for real." She slowly backed away from Leona. "I should get to Haley's meds." She turned on her heel and hurried toward the medicine dispenser.

Leona looked over to the reception desk, where Tori sat, flipping through a folder. If it was true, she needed to get it straight from Tori, but she still hoped that Jacqueline didn't know what she was talking about.

"Tori!"

Tori looked up and gave a weak smile. "I'm doing everything I can to get these spots filled. I'm thinking we might have to shift some people around in the hospital. It could definitely work." She groaned. "Who would have thought, though?"

"So, it's true..." Leona's face fell. Why would Bella run off like this? It seemed to be a bad habit she had. When the going got tough, she got going. But for once, she had felt like they were in a great place. So why now?

"Yeah, I'm sorry. I thought the board told you or something." Tori scrunched up her face. "I didn't expect to be the one. I swore they said they would let you know."

"It's not your fault. But when? Do we know why?"

She shrugged. "Guess it got to be too much. It happened about two hours ago. But don't you worry. I'll do everything I can to make sure these shifts are filled before I leave today. You have my word."

"I have no doubt you will." Leona looked at her watch. "I'll be headed out here in a bit. I have to get Brad from school, but I asked Many in ICU to cover me until I can get back."

"Sounds good. See you then." Tori looked back down at the folder and shook her head as she tried to figure out the new schedules.

If the staff didn't know the whole reason behind why Bella left, then Leona knew what she had to do. She had to get it straight from the woman Bella would have needed to speak with to drop out of the program.

She took the elevator to the main floor and headed straight for Margo's office. Luckily, the door was wide open, and Margo was working at her computer. When Leona knocked, she looked up.

"Guessing you heard," she said in greeting.

"I heard from Tori and Jacqueline, but now I want to hear it from you. Bella was doing well. Do you know why she decided to drop from the program?"

Margo sat back in her chair and sighed tiredly. "Unfortunately, some people just don't make it. I'll be honest. I thought Bella was different, but she said she felt it was too much for her given her coursework, and her grades were dropping. I can respect that. And we can only wish her the best." She leaned forward and grabbed a piece of paper from her desk. "With that being said, I wish she hadn't run out of here in the manner she did."

"She ran out of here?" Leona asked, confused.

She nodded and held up a piece of paper. "And I still need her signature. Without it, her decision to drop from the program can't be abided by. We need the form to be completed for it to be official."

"So, are you saying that if she came back and changed her mind, she would still be in the program?"

"Technically," Margo responded, her eyebrows raised.

"So, she would be welcomed back if she wanted to continue working here?"

Margo stared at Leona. "Do you think you could get her back? I mean, I'm all about second chances. If she just needed a break, a few days off, I could work with that. And until this paper is filled out, she still has a job. If you think you can convince her to change her mind, then good luck."

It was a long shot, but Leona was willing to try. She thanked Margo, then left her office and hurried toward the front door. She only had a little bit of time to get to Brad's school.

She already knew the conversation she would have with Bella once she was able to talk to her, and she knew she was going to speak from her heart.

"WHO ARE YOU HERE TO PICK UP?" THE WOMAN ASKED, looking down at a clipboard as Leona approached the beginning of the line.

"Brad Carver."

The woman looked up and frowned. "He's already been picked up."

"What?" Leona asked, staring at her. "That's not possible? By whom? When?"

The woman glanced around. "Thirty seconds ago. You just missed her. She said that you expected her to, and she was on the list." She turned and looked over her shoulder. "Shana!"

A younger woman hurried up to them. "Yeah?"

"That woman who picked up Brad, what was her name? You checked the list, right?"

She nodded. "Bella Strong or something like that. I can go look." She started to turn away, but Leona put up a hand to stop her.

"No need. In the rush to get here, it completely escaped my mind that I had asked her to get him." Leona smacked her forehead. "Silly me. Thank you, ladies."

She pulled away from the curb and hurried to return to the hospital, hoping she'd be able to catch Bella before she left from dropping Brad off at the day care.

The fact that Bella had still picked up Brad was a sign that Bella hadn't quit on account of Leona. It would have hurt Leona if she was the reason Bella felt she had to leave, especially when they were getting closer. But still, it didn't make sense why Bella didn't think of saying something to her, unless she planned on doing so once they were alone together.

Leona felt like she would never get back to the hospital. She kept imagining Bella getting further and further away from her. Finally, she pulled into the parking lot and made her way to her parking spot. Just a few more steps and she would be there. She rounded the corner of the day care and saw Bella coming out of the room.

Bella looked up and met Leona's gaze. "Hey," Leona said.

"Hey," Bella replied quietly. "I just got Brad settled in there."

"I forgot I had asked you to get him and I showed up at the school. They told me someone had already picked him up, and I about had a heart attack."

"Oh...I'm sorry. But it's all taken care of." Bella started to brush past her, but Leona reached out and touched her arm.

"Are you going to explain why you dropped from the program? You were doing so great."

Bella sighed and looked at her, Leona's hand still grasped on her arm. "Looks can be deceiving, I suppose. Just too much going on, I guess."

"But you didn't even tell me. Guess that hurt a bit."

Bella looked away. "It didn't look like we were sharing everything with each other."

"What's that supposed to mean?"

Bella glared at her. "I saw you, Leona. I saw you with that woman. And maybe I have absolutely no reason to be upset with you. After all, we never defined our relationship. I guess I was just foolish to think that we were exclusive or something."

"What? You've got this all wrong. The woman you saw was Cicily, my ex. I left her in New York when we realized that we weren't meant to be together. She didn't want a family, but she lied to me about it, stringing me along. She showed up here out of the blue. I had lunch with her, and we talked about it. I finally feel closure, and she feels at peace. When she left the hospital, we said our goodbyes, but that was it."

Bella stared at Leona. "Are you serious?"

Leona nodded and reached for Bella's arm, pulling her closer to her. "Is that why you dropped out of the program?"

Bella shifted her gaze to the floor. "Maybe it was part of the reason."

"Bella, you should have talked to me." She reached up and touched Bella's chin, guiding her eyes back to her. "I would have explained everything. And I had every intention of explaining everything once we saw each other."

"I was scared to learn the truth," Bella said softly.

"Well, we need to change that. You can't be scared any longer. Because I love you."

A smile crept on Bella's lips. "I love you, too."

Leona pulled Bella to her, and in the middle of the hall, she kissed her. They could figure out getting Bella back in the program later. For now, she just wanted to focus on Bella, the woman she loved.

Grab the thrilling epilogue here by scanning or clicking on the
QR code below:
[or Type or click here: https://BookHip.com/KWQLLMN]

Happy Reading,
Morgan
P.S: Thanks, www.kindlepreneur.com, for the QR code generator,
and www.booklinker.com for the universal links.

MT CASSEN BOOKS

Available In Paperback, Ebook, And Audio Formats. Click Image:
https://mybook.to/TOOLITTLETOOLATE

Available In Paperback, Ebook, And Audio Formats. Click Image:
https://mybook.to/ATWHATCOST

Available In Paperback, Ebook, And Audio Formats. Click Image:
https://mybook.to/PASSIONWITHOUTTENSION

ABOUT THE AUTHOR

Morgan Cassen

WITH ROXIE

Morgan Cassen writes Lesbian Romance. Her mission is to make the world safer for sapphic stories to be told. Yes, she knows that there are millions of romance writers and billions of romance novels. So, why would she even think of adding to the pile? Well, Morgan has seen enough to know that the truly interesting stories are not what happen between human beings. That gig can seem pretty tame. At least compared to its older, tempestuous sister. Let's bring out Ms. Inner Conflict, the queen of all drama in the human world -- the ruler of the emotional map. Yes, the conflict between everything you've worked for and everything you want. You never imagined that all your hard work would put you so far away from everything you wanted. Also, how about the conflict between the past and the future? Being true to the past would require you to keep the future so far away in the future. But, how long can you postpone the future? What if your whole framing of the past can't stand the scrutiny of thoughtful analysis today even as you resolutely push the future away?

Huh, what do you do with that kind of conflict? The conflict between human beings can look so tame compared to the real thing: conflict between you and you. You are the hero and villain at the same time, but the problem is that the villain thinks she is the hero, while the hero is all caught up in doubt. Which you will you choose? No, nobody else will make that choice for you. You get to make that choice, and your comforting, trusty friend--procrastination--can't seem to do the trick this time. The time has come for you to choose. See, inner conflict is where it's at. Inner conflict is what Morgan writes about in her books. Please join her as she writes the stories of breakup and love that tug at heartstrings.

Morgan is indebted to Sarah Wu (copyeditor) and Dr. Peter Palmieri and Nurse Karen Stockdale (medical advisors) for their extraordinary work and diligence. This book is so much better because of their efforts.

Stalk the author using the link below:

www.mtcassen.com

ABOUT PETER PALMIERI
(MEDICAL ADVISOR)

Peter Palmieri, M.D., M.B.A. is a licensed physician with over 20 years of practice experience in Chicago, Dallas, Houston, and the Rio Grande Valley in Texas. He received his B.A. from the University of California San Diego, with a double major in Animal Physiology and Psychology. He earned his medical degree from Loyola University Stritch School of Medicine and a Healthcare M.B.A. from The George Washington University. He is a regular contributor of original articles to a variety of health and wellness blogs.

ABOUT KAREN STOCKDALE
(MEDICAL ADVISOR)

Karen Stockdale, MBA, BSN, RN is an experienced nurse in the fields of cardiology and medical/surgical nursing. She has also worked as a nurse manager, hospital quality and safety administrator, and quality consultant. She obtained her ASN-RN in 2003 and her BSN in 2012 from Southwest Baptist University. Karen completed an MBA in Healthcare Management in 2017.  She currently writes for several healthcare and tech blogs and whitepapers, as well as developing continuing education courses for nurses.

Karen's websites are:
https://www.linkedin.com/in/karen-stockdale-5aab2584/
and
http://writemedical.net/

ABOUT SARAH WU
(COPYEDITOR)

Sarah was born and raised in the concrete jungle of NYC. She loves traveling, exploring different foods, and giving the occasional tree a big hug. When Sarah isn't polishing up manuscripts, she enjoys spending time with loved ones and lovingly but firmly heckling them to decrease their plastic consumption.

Printed in Great Britain
by Amazon

51084928R00300